IMMORTALS

(Book Two)

Ednah Walters

Firetrail Publishing

Firetrail Publishing
P.O. Box 3444 Logan,
UT 84323

Copyright © 2013 Ednah Walters
All rights reserved.
ISBN: 0983429774
ISBN-13: 978-0-9834297-7-7

ALSO BY EDNAH WALTERS:

The Runes Series:

Runes (book one)

The Guardian Legacy Series:

Awakened (prequel)
Betrayed (book one)
Hunted (book two)

The Fitzgerald Family series (Writing as E. B. Walters)

Slow Burn (book 1)
Mine Until Dawn (book 2)
Kiss Me Crazy (book 3)
Dangerous Love (book 4)
Forever Hers (book 5)

DEDICATION

This book is dedicated to my mother and father.
Thank you for instilling in me the love for books

ACKNOWLEDGMENTS

§

To my editor, Kelly Bradley Hashway, thank you for
Streamlining the story. I am so lucky to have found you. To my
beta-readers and dear friends, Catie Vargas, Jeannette Whitus and
Katrina Whittaker, you ladies are amazing. You lift me up when
I falter and have no problem telling me what needs to be fixed.
This book would not have been completed without you.
Friends like you are a gem!
To my critique partners, Dawn Brown, Teresa Bellew,
Katherine Warwick/Jennifer Laurens and Mercy, thank you.
Mercy, you asked all the right questions, correcting my
Course and inadvertently guiding me when I deviated.
To my family, I wouldn't do this without
your support. Love you, always.

Trademark list:
Google
Nikon
Jeep
Frisbee
Sentra
Harley
Vampire Diary
Supernatural
iPad
iPod
FaceTime
Skype

Glossary:

Aesir: A group of Norse gods
Asgard: Home of the Aesir gods
Odin: The father and ruler of all gods and men. He is an Aesir god. Half of the dead soldiers/warriors/athletes go to live in his hall Valhalla.
Vanir: Another group of Norse gods
Vanaheim: Home of the Vanir gods
Freya: The poetry-loving goddess of love and fertility. She is a Vanir goddess. The other half of the dead warriors/soldiers/athletes go to her hall in Falkvang
Frigg: Odin's wife, the patron of marriage and motherhood
Norns: deities who control destinies of men and gods
Völva: A powerful seeress
Völur: A group of seeresses
Immortals: Humans who stop aging and self-heal because of the magical runes etched on their skin
Valkyries: Immortals who collect fallen warriors/soldiers/fighters/athletes and take them to Valhalla and Falkvang
Bifrost: The rainbow bridge that connects Asgard to Earth
Ragnarok: The end of the world war between the gods and the evil giants
Artavus: Magical knife or dagger used to etch runes
Artavo: Plural of artavus
Stillo: A type of artavus

1. A FRESH START

The east lot across from school was jammed with students trying to find parking. I eased my Sentra beside a four-wheel truck, switched off the engine, and just sat there, staring at the students scurrying past. Any moment, I expected someone to notice me and yell "Witch!"

Being a witch would be preferable to what I was. *What I will become after I complete my training.* A Valkyrie. A soul reaper. Just thinking about it made my skin crawl. Six weeks ago, I was your average student concerned with starting another boring school year and making out with the guy I'd had a crush on, like, forever. My best friend, Eirik Seville.

Then Torin St. James stormed into my life on his black Harley with his wicked smile and brilliant blue eyes. He'd shattered everything I thought I knew about me, life, and love. Made me feel like the most beautiful girl in the world. The focus of his existence.

But before I'd been able to savor the joy of being in love, it all fell apart like a house of cards, destroyed by beings so powerful even the gods quaked in their presence. I shuddered. Two weeks had passed, yet the images from that night still haunted my dreams.

Twelve swimmers from my high school had met their death in the most horrific way. To the rest of the world, they'd been electrocuted by lightning during a swim meet. The media had called it a freak accident. I knew better. Evil Norns had caused the lightning.

Norns, destiny deities from Norse pantheon, were real and as badass as they come. Some blissfully went about guiding disasters, natural or manmade, without caring about the lives they destroyed. The worst part was, I had known about their plan but hadn't stopped them. Couldn't stop them even though I'd tried. Valkyries, or Valkyries-to-be in my case, couldn't prevent deaths. Not without consequences.

Norns, on the other hand, ruled over destinies of gods and Mortals and did as they pleased. My flamboyant, technology-challenged mother might have saved my teammates at one time, but her Norn card got canceled when she fell in love with my father, a Mortal, and chose him over them. She had been training to be a good Norn when she fell; thank goodness. Mom's situation was another tidbit I'd learned two weeks ago. I was still trying to wrap my brain around that one.

Now I had to deal with school, friends I hadn't seen in two weeks, and teammates who'd seen me act like a deranged lunatic during the meet.

I continued to watch the students and tried to muster courage. *You can do this, Raine. Stop whining and get your butt out of the car. You can do this... You can...*

I exhaled sharply and pushed the door open.

The protective runes my mother had painted all over my Sentra to ward off accidents were thankfully gone. I'd insisted. Seeing them would have reminded me of how I'd been spared while my friends had died.

I hoisted my backpack on my shoulder and was reaching for the folder on the passenger seat when the powerful sound of a Harley filled the air. A spasm kicked in my chest, and my heart started to pound.

Torin.

Anticipation and pain flashed through me. Last night when my parents and I had arrived home, his place had been in darkness. I'd worried he was gone again, taken away by sour-loser Norns to punish me for refusing to join them. As if they hadn't done enough by erasing every bit of his memories of us together. I wasn't sure what was worse—having him gone or having him around when he couldn't remember he loved me.

He parked his bike, removed his helmet, and pushed locks of raven hair away from his forehead, baring his chiseled face. The familiar gesture made me smile. He looked exactly the way he had the first day he knocked on my door and took my breath away. Same black jeans, matching shirt and leather jacket. Blue sapphire eyes so brilliant it hurt to look into them.

In the recesses of my thoughts, a fantasy blossomed.

I run to him, wrap my arms around his neck as he circles my waist and pulls me close. I draw a ragged breath, his musky scent filling my lungs, his warmth wrapping deliciously around me. He professes his love, and his voice resonates through me, sending fingers of need through my body. I hear his heart beat fast against my chest, mirroring my own. Then his head dips, and my lips tingle with anticipation. But he doesn't kiss me. He makes me wait. Crave. Bold and cocky, he teases me, his hot breath caressing my lips and igniting a wave of desire as natural as breathing. My body trembles and melts, then we kiss. Souls meld. Two halves become a whole.

Giggles reached my ears and reality crept in like a thief in the night, stealing my fantasy. That was all I had left. Fantasies of what could have been. The two giggling girls almost tripped staring at Torin. Still straddling the bike, he stood. Six-foot-three mass of pure masculine hotness.

I wanted to touch him, kiss him again, claim him like he'd claimed me before the Norns interfered. How could I let them win? Give up on him? On us?

No, they weren't going to win. Not when it came to Torin. If I had to remind him of everything we'd done together, every touch, every kiss we'd shared, I was going to make him remember.

As though he felt my gaze on him, he turned and stared straight at me.

I ducked, the folder slipping from my hand and landing on the wet ground with a dull thud. I squeezed my eyes tight and cringed.

Way to go, Raine. That was the dumbest move *ever.* How was I going to help him remember anything when I couldn't even face him?

Acting cowardly wasn't encoded in my DNA, but what was I supposed to do when I'd thoroughly humiliated myself the last time I saw him? I'd run straight into his arms and kissed him, welcoming him back, thrilled to see him after I thought I'd lost him. I hadn't noticed his initial reaction, the hesitation, the words that should have warned me that he didn't remember me. So he had kissed me back, a stranger, a silly Mortal girl throwing herself at him—a Valkyrie.

Oh, the humiliation.

But that was two weeks ago. Now, I had a fail-proof plan to fix him. Two, to be on the safe side. Dad had taught me to always have a back-up plan. By the time I was through with Torin, he'd either remember we were meant to be together or he'd fall in love with me all over again.

Slowly, I stood and peered over the hood of my car.

Our eyes collided, and I winced. He stood on the other end of my car in the cocky pose I'd come to expect from him, backpack slung over one shoulder, hands in the front pockets of his jeans, brilliant blue eyes studying me with a wicked gleam. A zing shot through me. That gleam still had the power to make me weak in the knees.

"Are you hiding from me again, Lorraine Cooper?" he said in a deep, hypnotic voice, and my entire body flushed in response to the sexy timbre. I wanted to savor the feeling forever.

"No. I dropped my folder. See?" I wiped the wetness off the red leather cover. He flashed a sexy grin, and my traitorous heart leaped. I knew the smile too well. It said he knew I was lying, but chose to ignore it. "How do you know my name?"

"Mrs. Rutledge told me."

I thoroughly disliked that gossipy neighbor, but I forgave her this time. I was still annoyed at her for this morning. She'd crossed herself when she saw me, and then hurried back inside her house as though I was the devil's spawn. I guessed everyone around town knew about the incident at the meet. I hoped they wouldn't start a witch-hunt. Being burned at the stake didn't exactly fit into my future plans.

Then something Torin had said registered. "What do you mean by 'hiding from you *again*'?"

"You disappeared *after* you kissed me."

My cheeks grew warm. Trust him to bring that up. "You think I left because we, uh, kissed?"

"*You* kissed me," he corrected, that charming wicked grin broadening as my face grew hot.

"I went on a cruise with my parents to get away from, uh—"

"Me?"

"Everything." I glared at him. My mother thought we needed a break from Kayville and the endless tragedies, so we'd taken a ten-day Hawaiian cruise. "It had nothing to do with you."

"Yeah. Sure."

Of course he wouldn't believe me. I waited for his next question. *Come on. Ask why I kissed you.* He continued to study me, curiosity replacing smugness, but the question didn't appear.

"Shall we?" he asked, indicating the school entrance.

I loved the formal way he'd worded that, his British accent rearing its head.

"Aren't you going to ask why?" I asked, walking to his side.

"Why what?"

"Why I did it." My face burned, but I couldn't afford to stop. Too much was at stake. "Why I kissed you."

Torin blinked as though surprised by my boldness. He chuckled. "No, I already know why. Women always find an excuse to throw themselves at me. I'm more interested in why you cried. No one cries after kissing me."

Seriously, he could be so arrogant sometimes. "Well, I, uh, I did it 'cause I was angry."

His eyebrows rose until they almost met the locks falling on his forehead. "With me?"

He sounded like that was unheard of. "Yes and no. You forgot about me."

He gave me a slow perusal. "I don't think I'd forget meeting you, Lorraine Cooper. You, on the other hand..."

"Would forget you because Norns erase Mortals' memories after they meet with Valkyries," I said, speaking so fast my tongue tripped. Plan A had better work. I took a deep breath and continued slowly. "They didn't erase my memories, Torin. Instead, they erased yours."

Torin stopped walking, uneasiness crossing his face. "What are you talking about?"

"We met when you and your friends came here a little over a month ago to reap the souls of my teammates. You even saved my life a few times, but that was okay because I wasn't really supposed to die. Three Norns were trying to lure me to their side. When I refused, they decided to punish me. They erased your memories, so you wouldn't remember me."

Torin stared at me as though I had escaped from a psych ward. Then his expression hardened.

"Listen, I've never seen you before two weeks ago. If I had, I would not have forgotten."

"But it's true. How else could I know you are a Valkyrie? We were neighbors. I saw you every day."

He shook his head. "You couldn't have. Someone told you about me." He lifted his head and looked over my shoulder, his eyes narrowing. "I'm going snap his neck and trap him in Hel's Mist for eternity."

I followed his gaze. Andris was getting out of an SUV. "Andris didn't tell me about you. I haven't seen him since he reaped my friends' souls at the swim meet. You were supposed to be with him, but—"

"I had to reap a busload of school kids in Seattle. You're one of his girlfriends, aren't you? After I'd told him to leave Mortals alone, he's back at it again. Did he promise to turn you?"

This wasn't how I expected things to go. "I wouldn't let Andris touch me if you paid me. *You* gave me clues about who you are, and Andris confirmed it." Torin's expression grew thunderous, and I knew I was screwed. "I know about you because *you* told me. You were born during the reign of King Richard. You and your brother James fought during the crusade, and that was where you were turned into an Immortal. When your brother died, you changed your surname from de Clare to St. James to honor him."

Torin stared at me intently, a slow grin lifting the corners of his sculptured lips. The smile didn't reach his sapphire eyes. "Ahh, now I know who you are."

My heart skipped. "You do?"

"You're Lavania's new protégé. It's just like her to do this to me." He started walking.

I stared after him, so frustrated I could scream. Who the heck was Lavania? Surely my trainer wasn't here already. I didn't want to train. Not before I helped Torin remember us. I needed time with him. Alone.

"Did she ask you to kiss me, too?" he asked over his shoulder.

"No, that was my brilliant idea." No matter what I said, he wouldn't believe me. Plan A had bombed. Feeling deflated, I added, "I kiss all new guys in our cul-de-sac."

Torin chuckled.

That was a stupid explanation. Everyone in our cul-de-sac was either old or married. Maybe I could save face with a lie and move on to plan B—make him fall in love with me again. The problem was I had no idea what I'd done to make him fall for me in the first place. I was an average girl, while he was super hot.

Silence hung heavily between us as we crossed Riverside Boulevard, the street running in front of our school. I glanced at him from the corner of my eyes and caught him studying me. I wasn't sure what I saw in his eyes. Pity? I hated to be pitied.

"Actually, I thought you were someone else," the lie rolled off my tongue with such ease I wondered why I hadn't started with it.

Torin stopped walking, forcing me to stop, too. His brow shot up. "You mistook me for someone else?"

The outrage in his voice made me grin. "Yep, my ex."

"Your ex-boyfriend looks like me?" Torin was no longer smiling.

"No, *you* look like *him*. Black hair, blue eyes, even the bike. You could be his doppelganger."

"Doppelganger?" He said it like I'd just called him a troll. His eyes narrowed, and then that sexy grin I loved curled his sculptured lips. "Nice try. No one looks like me, Raine. The world couldn't handle two of me."

His arrogance was rearing its ugly head, but I didn't care. He'd called me by my nickname. Soon, he'd remember he always called me Freckles, a special nickname he'd coined because of the freckles on my nose.

"What's his name?" he asked.

"What's whose name?"

"Your ex-boyfriend."

"Blue Eyes," I said and grinned. I had called him Blue Eyes when we first met. Surely, he'd remember.

Torin snickered. "What kind of a stupid name is that?"

"Hey, no disrespecting the nickname. He had dazzling eyes." Torin frowned while I warmed up to the subject. Maybe I could make him jealous. "They were like blue sapphire. He had gorgeous hair, too—darker than yours, and his smile..." I fanned myself. "Sexiest *evah*. You know what the best part was?"

"Not interested," he grumbled.

Was that annoyance in his voice? "He was completely crazy about me."

"What happened?" he asked, his voice hard to describe.

I glanced at him and caught him scowling. "What do you mean?"

"You keep talking about him in past tense. Did he leave you?"

I stopped. Suddenly, I didn't feel like making him jealous anymore. Instead, anger washed over me, even though I had no idea who I was angry with—the Norns for erasing his memories, him for not even remembering the special name he'd given me, or me for not having a decent plan and feeling helpless. I hated feeling helpless.

"He. Didn't. Leave. Me," I ground out. "He was taken from me," I finished in a shaky whisper then turned and hurried into the school building.

I didn't notice the stares until I was by the lockers. People whispered behind their hands and threw me furtive glances. Others watched me with wide eyes or flashed uneasy smiles when our gazes met. The words "witch" and "crazy" reached me several times. Part of me cringed, wanting to run and hide. Another part had me returning stares. I'd saved lives during that stupid meet. Didn't that count for anything?

Morgan, a girl I knew from my physics class, shuffled backwards as though I was a giant zit. Another girl grabbed her friend's arm and pulled her away, whispering something in her ear. One by one, they created space between us, until I was an island surrounded by gawking students.

"Raine!" Cora pushed through the gathering crowd, hazel eyes filled with mischief. "Look at you. That tan is fantabulous. I hope it rubs off." She brushed her arm against mine.

I laughed, momentarily forgetting the gawkers. I'd missed her crazy humor. "You're silly."

"You should have shared the love and brought home some Hawaiian sun and hot cabana guys." She enveloped me in a big hug. "Smile. Ignore them. They're losers," she whispered in my ear.

Before I'd left, she couldn't look me in the eye. Surprised and happy she wasn't scared of me anymore, I hugged her back.

"Ooh, watch the ribs," she said. I released her, and she leaned back. "When did you get back?"

"Last night."

She glowered. "And you didn't text me?"

"It was late."

"Like that's ever stopped you. Don't they have cell phone reception on these cruises? Don't answer that. You were busy with the cabana boy. I want to hear everything." She threw her things in the locker, removed her folder and some textbooks, and bumped me with her shoulder. "Come on. Start talking."

The crowd parted to let us pass, but the stares and the whispers followed us. In the hallway, students saw us coming and pressed against the walls as though I was a disease-ridden sub-human. Their attitude hurt.

"What cabana boy?" I asked.

"The one I told everyone swept you off your feet whenever they asked if I'd heard from you. *When is Raine coming back? Did she change schools? Is it true she's in a psych ward? Is she a witch?* Gah! People can be such tools. They made up stories, and the longer you were gone the more outrageous they became." Cora glared at a group of girls and asked, "What are you looking at?"

They flinched.

"Everyone knows what happened," I whispered.

"Yeah, I know. We told them your head injuries gave you psychic abilities. Watch this," she said, squeezing my hand. She paused by two girls, one of whom I recognized from my math class. "Want to know your future?"

The girl shook her head so hard I thought it would snap. I was mortified. "Cora—"

"Want to know if your boyfriend is the one?" she asked the second girl and grinned when the girl nodded. Cora was having way too much fun with this.

I grabbed her arm and pulled her away. "Stop it. I don't have the power of premonition. It was a one-time thing."

"You don't know that." She looped her arm around mine. "Okay, so I was totally spooked at first, but I reached a conclusion while you were gone. You are a hero, Raine. If you hadn't jumped into the pool and yelled at everyone to get out, more people would have died." She paused by a group of football players. "Hey, if you want to win on Friday, change the way you've been playing, Jaden."

Jaden Granger grinned. "Is that true, Raine?"

I looked down, wishing the floor would open up and swallow me. This was awful.

"Get behind the new QB, or you're so going to lose," Cora answered with a toss of her glorious blonde hair.

I shook my head. "We have a new quarterback?"

"Oh yeah. He's smoking hot, too, but the guys have been giving him a hard time during practice. Anyway, if you get another premonition, let me know."

I sighed, wishing I could tell her the truth. But where would I begin? Even I hadn't believed Valkyries and Norse deities were real, or that they moved freely between their world and ours, until I met Torin. Nothing had prepared me for the way he'd used runes to heal wounds, acquire superhuman strength, become invisible, or make portals appear and disappear on walls and mirrors. Maybe pretending I had psychic abilities after my accident was the only solution to this nightmare.

"Have you seen Eirik?" I asked.

The smile disappeared from Cora's face. "A few minutes ago. I left him with this group of new exchange students his parents are sponsoring. One of them is the QB. He's pure hotness." Cora fanned her face. "I'm talking about leather jacket, a Harley, sexy eyes. He doesn't say much, but he's a chick magnet. If I wasn't crushing on someone else, I'd go for him in a big, big… Oh, there they are."

I followed the direction of her gaze. Eirik stood at the end of the hallway with Torin, Andris, Ingrid, and a gorgeous dark-haired girl in a trendy dark gray sweater dress, matching tights, and black knee-length boots. From the way her arm was linked with Ingrid and Andris, I'd say she was a Valkyrie. Her hair was held back in a high ponytail like a dancer. When she kissed Andris on the cheek and reached for Torin's arm, I wanted to march over there and yank her arm away.

2. THE GIRLS ARE BACK

"Who's that?" I whispered.

"Lavania something-or-other. A long foreign name," Cora explained. "She's gorgeous, funny, and guys bend over backwards to please her. Makes you want to hate her, but you can't. No one can." Cora sighed.

"Why not?"

"She's super nice and sweet."

So that was my trainer? What was her relationship with Torin? I hated her already. Hated the way she leaned against Torin's arm. Hated that she could touch him while I couldn't. It hurt to see him with someone else.

As though he felt my eyes on him, Torin turned his head, looked over his shoulder, and met my gaze. I held my breath. Waited to see what he'd do. He cocked his brow.

My face warm, I focused on Cora. If she'd noticed the look we shared, she didn't say anything. Thank goodness her memories of the Valkyries were wiped too or she'd remember how Torin often stared at me.

"So, who's your secret crush, Cora Jemison?"

"Uh, there's a reason it's called a secret, nosey. Back to Lavania. She's invites us to their house every time our paths cross, but Eirik always says we have plans. I have a feeling he doesn't like her."

From Cora's voice, she loved it. I wondered if she and Eirik had hooked up while I was gone. I hoped so. They would be great together. We stopped by the door of my math classroom. Torin still watched us. Lavania followed his gaze, smiled, and waved. Cora waved back. Eirik's back was to us, but he, too, turned to see what the others were looking at.

He grinned. I frowned when the girl, Lavania, did something strange. She tilted her head toward Eirik. In a different setting, I'd say she'd just bowed. Or maybe it was my imagination.

"Do you want to meet her?" Cora asked.

Heck no! "No, thanks."

"She's really nice. The superhot guy with black hair is the new QB. His name is Torin St. James."

Torin's presence on the team meant some football player was about to get a one-way ticket to Valhalla. Somehow, I couldn't bring myself to care. I had my own demons to deal with. "What happened to Blaine Chapman?"

"His family suddenly moved. Totally weird." Cora shrugged, her focus shifting to the Torin's group. "The silver-haired guy is Andris. I think he's gay or something because even the hottest cheerleaders don't interest him. The blonde is a cheerleader. Her name is Ingrid."

Andris gay? Very unlikely. He was probably pining for his ex-girlfriend, Maliina, who'd gone rogue and joined evil Norns after she nearly killed me. Good riddance. I didn't hear the rest of Cora's words, my focus shifting to Eirik.

He strolled toward us, intelligent amber eyes twinkling. He looked different, his face more chiseled. It was as though he'd undergone some kind of transformation while I was gone. His usually long dirty blond locks were gone. Shorter hair surprisingly suited him.

Eirik and I went way back to when we were kids and played in our joining backyards. He was my best friend and knew me better than anyone.

"I love your new cut," I said in greeting, reaching up to run my fingers through his hair.

"I love your tan, stranger," he quipped. We hugged. "We thought you'd only be gone for a week."

"Blame my mother." I'd forgotten how comforting his hugs were. Suddenly, I was back to the place I'd been during summer, needing him. Eirik had always been there for me. When my dad's airplane went down and we thought he'd died, Eirik was the first one I'd told. When I started learning about Valkyries and my connection to them, I'd leaned on him to keep sane. Even when Torin disappeared and I thought I'd never seen him again, I'd turned to Eirik for comfort, even though he hadn't known about my feelings for Torin.

"Hey, you're crushing my ribs," he teased.

"I missed you guys." I stepped back and grinned sheepishly.

"Oh, that explains the endless phone calls and texts," he teased. "Don't they have reception on those boats?"

Cora laughed. "I asked her the same thing. Gotta go. See you two later." She hugged me again then briefly squeezed Eirik's hand, their fingers lingering. Eirik noticed my gaze on their hands and flushed, but Cora was already racing back toward the stairs. Maybe I didn't have to play Cupid after all.

"We need to talk," Eirik said, drawing my attention back to him.

"Yes, we do." We never officially ended our attempt at being boyfriend and girlfriend. It was time for me to bow out. He and Cora would be great together. "After school?"

"I'll stop by tonight." He threw me another grin.

I waved, turned and looked toward the end of the hallway where I'd last seen Torin and Lavania, but they were gone. In fact, the hallway was empty. I entered my classroom.

"It's nice to have you back, Ms. Cooper," Mrs. Bates, my math teacher said, eying me with narrowed eyes from above the rim of her glasses. "I'm sure you haven't forgotten I can't stand tardiness in my class."

"I didn't forget, Mrs. Bates," I said.

"Good. We have two new students, so use any empty desk."

Lavania smiled at me from my old position at the front of the class. I gave her a tiny smile. An empty desk was by Torin's. Our eyes met. He studied me as though I was a new species he couldn't figure out.

"Don't keep the class waiting, Ms. Cooper. Please, take your seat."

Exhaling, I made my way to the back of the class. Students turned and stared. The ones near my desk leaned away as though to put as much distance between them and me as humanly possible. My face red, I slid behind my desk and pulled out my textbook. I had no idea how much I had missed, but I was sure it was a lot.

"Oh, see me after class, Ms. Cooper. I have a folder with missed assignments and a breakdown of the concepts we covered while you were gone. If you need help, I'll be available in my office this week after school. When you're ready, I have several quizzes you missed."

No Saturday classes? Yes! I glanced at Torin from the corner of my eye and found him still watching me. How could he not remember being in this class with me?

He pointed at his eyes with two fingers then at the teacher. Face warming up again, I stared ahead.

At the end of the class, I was collecting my things when a soft scent of lavender reached my nose, and I looked up. Lavania stood beside my desk. She was even more beautiful up close, her porcelain skin flawless, her lips lush, and her gray eyes wide like a doe's. How could any guy resist her?

"I'm Lavania Celestina Ravilla, but you can call me Lavania," she said, her voice soft and melodic, her smile genuine and sweet. But I wasn't fooled. She was a Valkyrie, which meant she could move like the wind and flatten a car with a punch.

"Lorraine Cooper, but everyone calls me Raine." I glanced at Torin to see his reaction. His expression was unreadable.

Lavania grinned. "So you are the Mortal everyone is talking about here and there."

"There?" I asked.

"Rain with an E," Torin murmured.

My head whipped toward him, and I, momentarily, forgot about my conversation with Lavania. "You remembered."

His eyebrows shot up. "Remember what?"

"The day we met."

He gave me a look that said he thought I had a few loose screws. "Of course. You ran out of your house when I pulled up and k—"

"Never mind."

"Of course, you two already met," Lavania said and chuckled. "And we're neighbors." She said it as though it explained something.

Torin's face grew red, which was intriguing. He wasn't the blushing type. Still, I hated that they shared a secret, even if it had something to do with my house. "Ah, excuse me. My next class is in the south wing and—"

"So is ours. We'll walk with you." Lavania slipped her arm through mine, effectively stopping me from leaving. Until I knew the nature of her relationship with Torin, she would stay on my hate-list. "Since you're my protégé, we should be friends," she continued. "Stop by the house for a chat this evening. We can get to know each other."

I wasn't ready to be chummy yet. "Maybe some other time. I'm going to be busy catching up on homework this week."

"But I insist." She pouted, as though not used to being refused, and touched Torin's arm. "Tell her how we'd love to have her over. You can help her with her homework." She grinned. "Torin aces everything. Or he would if he paid more attention in class. He's been distracted since we got here though. Do get her packet from the teacher, sweetheart," she added.

I didn't realize she had called Torin sweetheart until he took the folder with my homework from Mrs. Bates. Images of the two of them together flashed through my head, and an ache started in my chest. They were more than friends. I just knew it.

"I have to go." I firmly removed Lavania's arm from mine and took the math packet from Torin. "Thanks."

"Come by later this evening, Raine," Lavania called out.

Needing space between us, I didn't answer her. I shouldn't have bothered running because they were in my next class. Torin carried her books, and they even sat side by side. I told myself I would not look at them, but my eyes kept straying. Each time their eyes would be on me. I understood Torin's fascination. He loved me. He might have forgotten me, but the feelings were there. They had to be. *Please, let him remember our time together before Lavania completely turns his head.* Most of the guys in class couldn't seem to take their eyes off her.

How old was she anyway? Did Valkyries even age? Torin was turned over eight hundred years ago. He'd been nineteen at the time. Looking at him now, he still looked like any teenager. Lavania did too, although she was more confident and sophisticated than any girl around my age.

***

Eirik waved from the doorway when class ended. I collected the folder of homework I'd missed and was headed toward the door when Lavania called my name. I pretended not to hear her.

"What does *she* want?" Eirik asked.

"I don't know."

"I came by after your first period, but you two were busy talking in the back."

He sounded annoyed. I shrugged. "She invited me to their place for a neighborly get-together."

Eirik frowned. "Are you going?"

"Nope. Don't have the time. Every teacher is giving me a folder or packet of missed assignments and reading material. I'm going to be too busy playing catch up to have a social life. Is she always so pushy?"

"And she does it with a smile, which is very annoying."

I took his arm and pretended not to notice the other students treating me like I was a freak show. "You know you don't have to escort me to my classes."

"I don't mind." He glared at a group of students as we walked past them. "Idiots. Cora said they're being total douches."

I bumped him with my shoulder. "So you decided to be my guardian angel?"

"Part-time guardian angel. Cora will take over after third period."

I laughed, but was touched. My friends rocked. "You two are crazy."

"Has anyone said anything to you yet?"

"No. They just gawk. Nothing I can't handle. They'll lose interest in a day or two."

"I hope so, or I'm going to break someone's nose. If anyone does or says anything, tell me." From his expression, he would defend me, which was big. Eirik was the most non-confrontational guy I knew. He had a temper, but tended to withdraw before he snapped and threw things around. I'd seen him vent countless times. It wasn't a pretty sight.

"That's nice, but I can take care of myself. Besides, I don't want you going against your pacifist beliefs."

"Whoever said I was a pacifist is an idiot," he retorted.

"That would be… you." I eased my arm from his hand. "See you at lunch."

He reached down to kiss me. I wasn't sure whether he meant to kiss me on the lips or not, but I turned my head and gave him my cheek just as Torin appeared at the end of the hallway. He stared at us curiously. He'd always hated it when Eirik and I kissed. Would a kiss jog his memories? Even as the thought crossed my head, I knew I couldn't do it. I was done using my friend as a crutch. Besides, kissing Eirik would mess up things between him and Cora.

"Go, I'll be okay." I nudged him and hurried toward my next class.

***

I was wrong. I wasn't okay. I could barely contain my anger in history as we waited for class to start. A group of girls sat behind me and didn't even bother to lower their voices as they talked about me.

"She conjured lightning then stood in the middle of the damn pool, and it didn't hit her once," a girl said, and the memories of that horrifying event came rushing back. I cringed, wishing I could tell them to shut up.

Why didn't anyone remember I'd warned Doc, our coach, and begged him to clear the pool? Where was the gratitude for those I'd saved?

"They said she started talking to herself," another girl whispered.

"No, she was chanting an incantation," the first one who spoke cut in.

I slid lower on my chair, trying hard to tune them out. I never wondered how I must have appeared to everyone when I'd talked to the three Norns or my mother by the pool. They'd been covered in runes and completely invisible to Mortal eyes. No wonder everyone thought I was a witch.

"They said she levitated out of the room then disappeared."

This was worse than I'd thought. Mom must have carried me and taken me through a portal on the wall. Since she'd been invisible, I must have appeared to float. I had to say something in my defense. But what? Would anyone believe me?

I turned to say something, and my eyes met Torin's. He shook his head as though warning me. When did he get here? Was he creating portals through walls again? Maybe stalking me? I hope so. It meant he was intrigued by what I'd said this morning. On the other hand, this was our debate-loving Mr. Finney's history class, and from what I recalled, Torin had enjoyed sparring with him. Having lived through every world event in the last eight centuries, he knew history first-hand.

Ignoring him, I focused on the girls gossiping about me and opened my mouth to blast them, but Mr. Finney spoke. "Lorraine Cooper."

I turned. "Yes?"

"See me after class."

For the rest of the morning, I overheard crazy theories about what I was. To some, I'd gone crazy and had spent the last two weeks in a psych ward. I wasn't sure which one I preferred. A witch, I guess. It came with a fear factor. As for the teachers, they didn't say anything, although I saw curiosity in their eyes.

"She knew her father hadn't died in the plane crash," a girl whispered behind me before last period, bringing back a rush of painful memories from last summer, the endless months of waiting for news from the airline and worrying about Dad.

"But the airline didn't declare him dead," one of her friends said.

"Not officially. They couldn't find his body. I went to their website and read how they stopped searching for survivors after twenty-four hours."

Cora was right. If the students wanted to make me a witch, I might as well be a badass one. I turned, and five pairs of eyes turned to watch me warily.

"Don't you guys know it's rude to talk about a *witch* when she can hear you? I might get angry, and you don't want me angry." I narrowed my eyes. "Bad things happen when I'm angry."

No one spoke. They slid behind their desks.

"Okay, what do you want to know? Hmm, yeah my father. I didn't just know he was alive. I had a vision of his exact location. Before that, I knew his plane was going to go down before it happened, but I couldn't stop it. Just like I couldn't stop the deaths of my team-mates. I tried though."

More silence.

I studied their faces. "What else do you guys want to know? Do I fly on a broom? Use potions?"

They shook their heads. Olivia Dunn, cheerleader and overall annoying bitch, gave me a daring glance. "How far ahead can you see?"

"How far do you want me to go?" I gave her a saucy smile while hoping she wouldn't ask me to foretell her future.

"A year from now."

I closed my eyes, my mind racing. This was the problem with not thinking things through. I lifted my eyelids and said calmly, "What do you want to know?"

"Will I get into my mother's alma mater? Cheer in college? Marry uh…?"

"Jake," one of her friends whispered. Jake Guthrie, two-time sectional wrestling champion, was her boyfriend.

Olivia made a face. "Will I marry a rich, dreamy guy?"

Inspiration hit while they giggled. "Five-hundred dollars. Bring it tomorrow or no deal."

Olivia's jaw dropped. "Five hundred?"

"Not enough? How about eight? Yep, eight is a good number. My head hurts when I search through all the possible futures."

The girls scooted closer.

"What do you mean by possible futures?" one of them asked.

"You know, the choices you make now or tomorrow change the future," I said.

They looked at each other. Olivia studied me as though she could tell I was a fake. Grinning, I turned and found Mr. Quibble, my AP English teacher, studying me with disapproval.

***

Why the Cheshire cat grin?" Cora asked when I joined her at the end of the class.

"I've decided I'm tired of being treated like crap. I'm going to start charging for premonitions."

"No way. How much?"

"Eight hundred bucks," I said.

Cora's jaw dropped. "No one can afford that, Raine."

That was the whole point. "Tough."

"Oh, you're terrible. No, you are awesome. Can I be your accountant?"

We were still laughing when we reached the cafeteria. The salad line was shorter as usual. I got my lunch and headed to our table while Cora still flirted with some band guys in the pizza line. That was Cora. Not above using guys to skip a line.

As soon as I sat, three girls entered the room. A shiver shot up my spine, and it wasn't the good kind. It was cold. Creepy. I recognized the feeling only too well. Norns. Their hairstyles, skin tone, and height might have changed, but they were the same crones in charge of my destiny. Once again, they looked like teenagers.

Was I the only one seeing them again? I glanced around to see if anyone was staring at them. I couldn't tell, but there was no way I would make the same mistake and talk to them in front of people just in case they were invisible.

I recognized Marj first. Just because she looked like some Thai flight attendant didn't fool me one little bit. Her perpetual disapproving expression was the same. Jeanette, now looking like a typical Ginger, red hair and freckles, saw me first and whispered something to Marj. Marj nudged Catie, the peacemaker and nicest of the trio. Catie now had riotous curly hair and walnut-brown skin.

They all turned to look at me and panic rolled through me. Swallowing, I stared right back.

3. HE NEEDS YOU

"I don't understand why the pizza line is always so dang long," Cora said, sliding into the seat across from me with a slice of pizza on her plate.

"Oh, please. You charmed Sim and Rand into letting you jump the line."

She giggled. "It's not my fault guys are so easy. Eew, that looks awful." She pointed at my salad.

"Tastes worse." I poked at the limp lettuce, half listening to her and keeping an eye on Marj and her friends.

"Who's pissed you off?" Cora glanced over her shoulder.

"Nobody." I ignored the three girls and focused on Cora. "How bad were things after I left?"

"Morbid. It was funeral after funeral after funeral. Several on the same day. Half the team quit." She touched her chest. "Yours truly included. Everyone kept saying the team was jinxed or something." She took a bite of her pizza.

I glanced at the entrance. Marj and her girls were now conferring, probably plotting how to further screw up my life. "Did Eirik quit?"

Cora made a face. "He's too stubborn to quit anything. You know him. Besides, he thinks superstitions are lame. Some swimmers returned last week, but the team's not the same. I watch them sometimes. Part of me misses the camaraderie, the dinners, hanging out in Doc's class." She reached for her bottled water and twisted the lid.

"Do you think you'll rejoin the team?" I asked.

"Not if you paid me." Cora's arm jerked suddenly just when she was about to sip her water. Water sloshed and spilled down the front of her shirt and pants.

"GAH! That's cold." She jumped up and slammed the bottle on the table. Hunching her shoulders, she lifted the wet T-shirt from her chest. Across the room, Jeanette grinned, her hand returning to her side. She'd done this. "I'm going to the restroom," Cora added.

"Do you want my help?"

"Do your new powers include drying wet things?" She glanced at the lines of students waiting to get their food. "Besides, Eirik will wonder where we've disappeared."

I watched her go before turning my attention to the Norns. They started for my table, and I sat up straighter. They had better not be coming to talk to me. With the mood I was in, I'd scratch their eyes out.

Even as the thought crossed my mind, I knew I couldn't cause a scene. Being labeled a witch was enough. No need to give the students a reason to believe I was crazy, too. Besides, I still wasn't sure whether anyone else could see them.

"It's nice to have you back, Raine," Catie said, sitting across from me. The others flanked her.

I ignored them, forked a piece of lettuce, and placed it in my mouth. I waved to Eirik. He was now at the front of the pizza line. He stared pointedly at the three Norns. Then he did what he always did. He lifted his camera, aimed it at us, and clicked.

Okay, I wasn't the only one seeing them.

"You care about him, don't you?" Catie asked, glancing at Eirik.

I glared at her. "Leave him alone."

"I'm happy you care about him because he needs you," Catie added, her voice gentle as though she hated to be the bearer of bad news.

"Excuse me?"

She reached out to touch my hand, but I cringed, forcing her to retreat. She was always the nicer and quieter one, but today she appeared to be the trio's chosen spokesperson.

"Eirik needs you more than the Valkyrie does," she said.

"His name is Torin, not *the Valkyrie*," I snapped.

Catie sighed. "I'll remember that. Eirik really needs your help, Raine. You can protect him better as a Norn than as a Mortal."

"Protect him from what?"

The three girls looked at each other.

"I told you she didn't know," Catie said.

"This is no place to discuss these matters," Jeanette said impatiently.

Marj nodded. "I agree, but we don't have time to hang around here and educate her. We have other charges and can't keep playing favorites." She glared at Catie and stood.

"What don't I know?" I asked, getting irritated.

"Who Eirik is," Catie said in a gentle voice. "Ask your mother. Once you know his story, you'll understand why he needs you and why you should be there for him."

"*Must* be there for him," Jeanette corrected.

"Why me?" My eyes swung from face to face.

"Because you owe him," Marj said impatiently.

I cocked my brow. "What?"

"He's the reason we saved your life," Jeanette added.

Catie sighed and glared at her friends. "Girls, couldn't you at least try to be subtle?"

"No, she needs to understand how dire the situation is. We'll need an answer soon, Lorraine." Marj glanced at the others and added, "Let's go."

I stared after them, shock and anger zipping through me. All I wanted was Torin, not another round with these crones. But how could I ignore them when they'd said Eirik needed me? I was still staring at the exit when he sat across from me.

"Who were those three?" he asked, placing his camera and plate on the table.

"They're not important." What did the Norns mean by he was the reason I was alive? And why did he need to be protected? "Are things okay with your parents?"

"Same as usual." Instead of eating, he picked up his camera and fiddled with it. "You're really going to blow me off again?"

His angry tone blindside me, and I blinked. "What?"

He turned his camera and showed me the image displayed on the LCD screen. It was the picture he'd taken of me and the three Norns. Instead of their teenage disguises, the camera had captured their true images. Just like the night I'd seen them at the hospital, their hair was long and stringy, skin wrinkled, eyes piercing and eerie. Beside them, I looked like a helpless lamb, or a puppet.

"Those are the three Norns you've been dealing with."

I stared at Eirik with wide eyes. "You know?"

"Of course I do."

"How... When..." I sputtered.

"My parents told me everything the day *he* appeared." He pointed across the room.

Torin, Andris, and a group of cheerleaders had just entered the cafeteria. One clung to Torin's arm and seemed to be the lead groupie.

Pain, fierce and relentless, stabbed my heart. Was he going to put me through this with Mortals, too? Seeing him with Lavania was already too much.

Torin glanced at our table, and our eyes met. He was the first one to look away. I swallowed the pain, turned my attention to Eirik, and found him studying me with an annoyed expression.

"I know a lot has happened since he got here, so I don't know if you remember that night," he said, frowning.

"I do. You missed swim practice, didn't return my texts or calls, and when you finally came over to my house, you were angry with your parents. They'd come back from one of their many trips and told you about moving back home."

"Except home wasn't Earth." His expression furious, he took a big bite of his pizza.

"What do you mean," I glanced around then leaned forward and whispered, "'home wasn't Earth'? Are you saying *you* are from *there*, too?" I whispered.

He nodded.

I stared. "That's… Wow, that's huge. Mom told me your parents were, but I just assumed you couldn't be. I mean, you were born and raised here."

He shook his head. "Raised, not born. I asked them why, but they wouldn't tell me anything. The more I push for answers the more they clam up. It's all so stupid," he ground out. "I mean, what's the big deal? Why the secrecy?"

"The Norns said you were in danger."

A snicker escaped him. "From what?"

"They didn't say."

"Screw them. They're messing with your head again, Raine." He twisted the lid off his water bottle and chugged. "I wish they'd spoken to me. I would've told them to eff off." He put his water on the table, his grip tightening around the plastic bottle.

Wishing I could reach out and touch him, maybe reassure him, I studied his angry expression and chewed on a piece of limp lettuce. "What's happening to us, Eirik?"

He scowled. "What do you mean?"

"We never used to keep secrets from each other. Why didn't you tell me what your parents said that night?"

"They said I couldn't because, you know, you're Mortal and I'm...
whatever I am." He took another bite as though the pizza was his
enemy and chewed, his eyes staring into space though he was having an
internal argument with himself.

"Did they at least tell you who your real parents are?"

"No." He glowered. "But Mom said I'm *special*. Yeah, whatever
that means. I told her I wasn't going anywhere until I got some
answers. Guess what? It's been six weeks since we talked and I'm still
here." He demolished the rest of the slice in two bites, guzzled his
drink, and started on his second slice. "I should not have listened to
them. If I'd told you everything, you would've told me about the Norns
when they first appeared. They almost killed you."

I shook my head. "You can't blame yourself. And these three
Norns weren't the ones who hurt me. They have their own agenda.
Evil Norns caused the lightning."

"These Norns are good? They looked mean."

"They can be. Could we promise not to keep secrets from each
other anymore?"

He grinned and gave me a thumbs up. Then the smile disappeared
from his face. "Why didn't *he* protect you?"

I winced at his tone and followed the direction of his gaze to
Torin, who was now seated at a table with his entourage. "He tried.
Norns are too powerful. It was hopeless."

He wore a skeptical look. "Then what's his problem?"

"What do you mean?"

"He couldn't leave you alone while we were dating, and now he's
treating you like a stranger."

"It's not Torin's fault. The Norns erased his memories."

Eirik scowled. "Why? Norns only scramble Mortals' memories."

"They did it to punish me."

"What? Why?" Cora entered the cafeteria, and his eyes zeroed in
on her. She'd changed her T-shirt and pants for a dress that looked
really great on her. She must have had it in her car because there was
no way she'd driven to her house and back that fast. Eirik dragged his
eyes from Cora. "Never mind. We'll talk later," he added just as Cora
slid beside him.

"Talk about what?" Cora asked, her eyes volleying between us.
"What did I miss?"

"I was telling Eirik about my psychic business and my rates."

Cora laughed.

Eirik wore a bewildered expression since he had no idea what I was talking about, but he caught on fast. "Yeah, brilliant idea."

"I'm going to be the accountant." She bumped him with her shoulder. "You can be the muscle."

Eirik flushed.

***

For the rest of the afternoon, all I thought about was Eirik—his identity and why I was supposed to protect him. He might have dismissed the Norns' warning, but I couldn't.

During last period, a student aid came to my class with a note from Mrs. Underwood, my counselor. Somehow, I knew she'd want to see me.

I collected my books and headed toward the front office. We had three counselors and several students were already waiting. The only empty place left to sit was between two guys, one listening to his iPod while hitting imaginary drums and the other looking like he hadn't bathed in decades.

Choosing the wall by the door, I let my backpack drop by my feet, placed the oboe case beside it, and pulled out my cell phone. I barely put in the earbuds when Mrs. Underwood's door opened and a boy stepped out.

"Lorraine," she said, opening the door wider.

I grabbed my things and followed her. I sat and hugged my backpack. The last time she and I had spoken, we met with the principal in his office. They'd been worried that my father's accident had left me unhinged. I hadn't blamed them or felt insulted. The school security officer had spotted me talking to an invisible Torin and assumed I was talking to myself.

Torin. I'd completely pushed his problem aside. What was I going to do about him? I had to help him remember me. I didn't care what the Norns had said. He needed me just as much as Eirik did because he and I were meant to be together.

"Did you hear what I said, Lorraine?" Mrs. Underwood asked, leaning forward on her desk.

I blinked and stared at her. "I'm sorry. What?"

"How are you feeling?"

I shrugged. "Okay."

"No effects from your surgery?"

I shook my head and wondered if she would ask me about the meet and how I'd known the students were in danger.

"I know today was your first day back since we lost your teammates, and it couldn't have been easy. I want you to know that my door is always open if you need to talk."

"Thanks, Mrs. Underwood." I started to get up.

"Please, don't leave yet. I want you to come see me every day after school for the rest of the week."

I groaned.

She smiled. "Just for a few minutes to catch up. How did things go today?"

"Good."

"Did anyone give you a hard time?"

"Not really."

She studied me intently as though she knew I'd just lied, but then she nodded. "Okay. You can go now." She got up and walked me to the door. "See you tomorrow."

She meant well, but there was really nothing she could do for me. Students still loitered around the school's front entrance and silence fell when I walked past them. Like this morning, whispers followed and people moved aside to clear a path for me. This time I didn't cringe. I expected it.

Outside, some of the buses were still at the curb while others had pulled away. A group of students gathered somewhere to my right were laughing and pointing at someone or something in the east parking lot. Hopefully, it wasn't some poor student. People were such idiots. Shaking my head, I started across Riverside Boulevard.

"Raine!" someone called.

I looked left. Lavania and Ingrid stood beside the SUV I'd seen Andris drive this morning. Lavania waved me over. I wanted to ignore her, but she was my trainer. If I wasn't in love with Torin, I'd tell her right now I didn't want to be a Valkyrie. But the thought of spending the rest of my life as a human, aging, while Torin stayed young for goddess knows how long didn't appeal to me.

Sighing, I walked toward them.

As I got closer, I noticed Andris behind the steering wheel staring at me with an unreadable expression. Had his memories been erased, too? Why wasn't Torin with them? His bike was still parked at the curb.

"We're going to get something to drink at the Creperie before heading home. Why don't you join us?" She indicated the car, and Ingrid hurried to open the back passenger door.

I shook my head. "Sorry, I can't. I'm meeting my dad at the shop."

"Your dad can wait."

Who died and made her my guardian? "No, he can't."

Lavania stepped forward, her eyes boring into mine. "Listen, I've been sent down here to train and help you with your transition. I think—"

"Yeah, about that," I interrupted her. "I haven't really made up my mind whether I want to be a Valkyrie or not. Could I have more time to decide? A week or two?" Maybe forever.

She chuckled, but her eyes grew cold. "No, you can't. I've already wasted two weeks of my life hanging around while you were gone. You see, my naïve novice, it's been six hundred years since I've had to deal with Mortals or even pretend to be one. Until two weeks ago, I had a life I enjoyed, friends my age, whom I loved chatting with, and an important position in Goddess Freya's hall. Then she called me to her quarters and told me of a special Mortal that needed my guidance. A Mortal who can see Norns. A Mortal who can *stop* Norns from doing their job. That might seem like nothing to you, but up there, it is huge." She moved closer, her eyes narrowing. "If the goddess is mistaken and you're not that Mortal, tell me right now so I can stop wasting my time."

Shocked by her attitude, I gawked. "But I didn't stop the Norns. Twelve of my friends died."

"There were supposed to be more," she said. "At least five..." she glanced at Andris.

"Seven," he said.

Lavania smiled. "Thanks, sweetheart. See, you saved seven people, including Eirik and your blonde friend. Did you know that you pushed Eirik so hard he flew across the pool deck, slammed against the wall, and lost consciousness? Have you asked yourself how you, a mere Mortal, managed that?"

I shrugged. I'd wondered how Eirik had ended up unconscious on the dry end of the pool deck. Had I protected him without even knowing it? How had I done it? Only Valkyries had that kind of strength. Did the Norns do more than mark me when I was a baby? I really had to talk to my mother.

"I gotta go," I said. "I've tons of homework, and my father is expecting me. I, uh, can join you when I finish with him."

Lavania shook her head. "Not good enough. You must come with us now."

Was this how she planned to teach me? Do things her way or the highway? "Fine. I'll follow you in my car."

"No. We'll bring you back to pick it up."

I glanced at Ingrid. She looked worried. Andris was amused. He shrugged. "Never argue with her. She always wins."

I sighed. "Fine. I'll leave my backpack and oboe in my car." I turned to leave, but she grabbed my arm. I winced as her nails dug into my skin.

"We have enough space in the SUV, Raine," she said. "Now be a dear and enter the car."

What was her problem? "Then let me collect my wallet. I left it in my car."

"The drinks will be my treat." She tugged my arm.

A bad feeling washed over me. She didn't want me to go to my car. Why? I glanced over at where I had parked. Eirik and Torin appeared to be doing something to my car. Somehow I hadn't realized that the crowd I'd seen earlier had been near my car.

Lavania's grip tightened. "Okay, some students trashed your car, and Torin is taking care of it," she said, her voice gentler.

I yanked my arm from her hand and ran across the nearly empty parking lot, my heart pounding. Torin and Eirik knelt by the back tire. Torin was sketching runes on the tire, which had a huge tear and was deflated. More runes covered the windows of my car.

"What did they write on the windows?"

"It doesn't matter," Torin said. He glanced at Eirik. "Get her out of here."

I raised a finger when Eirik stood. "No, I'm not going anywhere. What did they write on my car, Eirik?"

"Die, witch, d—"

"Shut up, Seville." Torin's eyes narrowed on my face. "We'll find whoever did this, Freckles, and make them pay."

4. MISUNDERSTOOD

"You called me Freckles," I whispered, staring at Torin.

A bewildered expression crossed his face. "What?"

"Freckles, my nickname." I touched my nose. He looked more confused, which told me he must be remembering things on a subliminal level without understanding what they meant. I sighed. I was in for a very long and very painful recovery phase. I should've been happy his subconscious was spitting out information, right? It meant his memories were there, just suppressed. Somehow, I couldn't bring myself to celebrate yet. "Never mind."

I caught Eirik's eyes. He was staring at us and scowling. His gaze shifted to someone behind me and I turned. Lavania and Ingrid had followed me. Andris hadn't left the SUV.

"You were supposed to keep her away," Torin snapped.

Lavania's eyes narrowed. She obviously didn't like his tone. She glanced at me. "You have a week." Then she whipped around and nodded at Ingrid. "Let's go."

I watched her leave, hating her attitude, wishing I could tell her I didn't want to train period, even though it wasn't true. I wanted to, but at the same time, it seemed like a huge step to take. So permanent. When I'd thought I'd be with Torin, it had seemed like the right thing to do. Now, not so much. Then there was Eirik's situation to consider.

When I turned around, Torin was working on the next tire. He didn't seem to care that someone might see him. Eirik offered him cover, but it still wasn't safe even though the parking lot had only a few cars left. The staff parking lot had more cars, but it was on the west side of the school compound and too far for them to notice anything. I opened the front passenger door and put my backpack and the oboe inside the car before joining Torin and Eirik.

I studied the runes Torin had just sketched. Air filled the deflated tire, then the slashes sealed. I tried to catch his eyes, but he moved to the last tire. I followed, loving the fact that I could be this close to him. I wanted more. To touch him. Kiss him. Force him to look at me again. Really look.

I cleared my throat. "What runes are you using? Air-flow-into-the-tire runes or fix-a-flat runes?"

The corners of his lips lifted into a half-smile. "More like they'd-bloody-well-stay-inflated-forever-or-else runes."

I laughed. His British accent became stronger when he was pissed. "Do I need to take the car to the shop after this?" I asked.

"Nah. This will hold until the treads wear thin and need changing. The next person who tries to slice your tires is in for a surprise."

I frowned. "Do you think that's a good idea?"

"Oh yeah." He still didn't glance at me.

Short of grabbing his head and yanking it toward me, I had to wait. I hated the way he was acting. The old Torin had openly sought me out and got a kick out of shocking me. "They've already labeled me a witch. A tire that can't deflate will only confirm it."

"I don't care what they think," he snarled. "Your safety is more important."

At least his instinct to protect me was still there. "I can't afford to think like that, Torin. I want all this," I indicated the car with a brief wave, "to go away."

"It will. Mortals don't mess with what they fear. They'll leave you alone for a while, which is not bad."

"Spoken like a loner."

He grinned. "True. You should also charge more for your psychic readings for those brave enough to ask. A thousand bucks perhaps?"

"Oh, you sneaky... You eavesdropped on me?"

"I couldn't help it. You had them believing everything you said and..." His voice trailed off as our eyes finally met. The moment stretched. The grin disappeared from his lips, and blue flames leapt in the depth of his sapphire eyes. We were so close I could count his eyelashes.

How could he forget moments like this when we'd looked at each other and gotten lost in our little world? His eyes shifted to my lips, and I stopped breathing. It was as though he'd reached out and touched them. My lips tingled, then parted slightly in an invitation. All we had to do was move a few inches toward each other and we'd kiss.

He must have thought it, too, because he inched closer, his eyes burning.

A sound came from above me, and my head whipped up. Eirik. I'd completely forgotten his presence. From his annoyed expression, he knew it, too, and didn't like it. My cheeks warmed.

"I've swim practice, so see ya," Eirik said through clenched teeth and took off.

Torin ignored Eirik and continued to study me with a conflicted expression as though he wasn't sure whether to grab me and kiss me or run. I wanted more time with him, but it wasn't going to be now.

Sighing, I jumped up.

"Eirik, wait up." He kept walking. I didn't catch up with him until he stopped by his Jeep. "Eirik—"

"Freckles? How close did you and Torin get before the Norns scrambled his memories?" he practically snarled.

This wasn't how I'd wanted him to find out about Torin and me. "We talked a bit."

"A bit? He has a nickname for you, Raine. One you hated when we were kids. Were you seeing him behind my back?"

Heat seared my face. "Not really. We were neighbors, Eirik, so we talked, and he gave me a ride to school once."

His eyes narrowed, and I wondered if he was remembering the few times Torin came to my rescue when he wasn't around. "Did you kiss him?"

"Eirik," I said and sighed.

"I guess that means yes." His glance shot past me to Torin. "Bastard."

"Don't. You don't understand."

He yanked open the door of the Jeep and paused before getting inside. He studied me and smiled, but it was a sad smile. "Actually, I understand perfectly. He took advantage of you. You're seventeen while he's older and more experienced. He healed you when he wasn't supposed to, and I bet he told you he was a Valkyrie. They are not supposed to tell Mortals such things."

"He didn't take advantage of me," I insisted. I glanced over my shoulder to find Torin watching us from my car. I hoped he couldn't hear our conversation. "He didn't tell me he was a Valkyrie. Andris did. On the night of Homecoming Dance. By then Torin had already disappeared."

Eirik frowned as though mentally taking a step back. "So, what are you saying?"

"I'm saying things are a lot more complicated than they seem." I wish I could just tell him the truth about Torin and me, all of it. I hated keeping secrets from him. Until I knew what the Norns meant by he needed my help more than Torin did, I had to play it safe. Unlike Eirik, I didn't doubt the Norns. There had to be a reason why he was raised on Earth. "We'll talk tonight. I'll explain everything."

His eyes moved back and forth between Torin and me. For a second, I thought he'd say no. I sighed with relief when he nodded curtly. "Okay. Tonight."

Eirik was changing, and I hated it. Hearing him use the word 'Mortals' several times as though he and I hadn't grown up as neighbors, fought over stupid things like sand shovels and buckets in our backyards, shared everything including the same bedroom during naptime and sleepovers bugged me. I wanted the old Eirik back. He'd been sweeter, cocky but lovable.

I waited until he drove away before walking back to my car. Torin watched me with an unreadable expression, fingers shoved into his front pants pocket except for the thumbs.

"What's his problem?" he asked.

You, I wanted to say. "He's worried about me. That's all. Thanks for fixing my car."

"No problem. Is he your boyfriend?"

I stared at Torin. Maybe the stress finally got to me, but the question hurt. *You are my boyfriend*, I wanted to yell even though I knew it wasn't his fault he couldn't remember. Needing distance between us, I shook my head, turned without answering him, and pulled open the car door with more force than necessary. He gripped the door before I could slam it shut.

"Raine," he whispered softly.

"Don't. I'm trying really hard to be understanding, but it's hard." Tears welled in my eyes. *No, I'm not going to cry. No, no, no!* I was better than this. Crying over a guy was something I'd never done until I met Torin. I looked away from him and blinked hard to stop the tears from falling.

"Look at me."

"No, go away." I pushed the key into the ignition.

"Please." He took my chin, lifted it, and turned my face toward him. A spasm crossed his face as though seeing the misery in my eyes—there for the entire world to see—was too much for him. He caressed my cheek. "I'm sorry I always make you cry or angry."

"I'm not crying," I ground out and blinked harder. "And I'm not angry."

He pressed his thumb on my lips to stop me from talking, and the effect on me was instant. My lips tingled, his touch searing. A storm of longing burst deep in my soul, and I shuddered. I was completely helpless against the effect he had on me.

He pulled his hand back as though scalded and scowled, blue eyes dimming. For a moment, we stared at each other. He looked shocked by his response. I wasn't.

"I am," he said, frowning.

"You're what?"

"Angry, but I don't know why. It's obvious that Lavania and Andris didn't tell you about me, yet you know details about my personal life only the two of them know."

"That's because—"

"Please, let me finish. I was here when Andris and a bunch of Valkyries came to collect the souls of your swim team members."

"You were one of them," I cut in. "You lived here then left just before the meet."

"You must be mistaken." He sighed. "I don't remember living here, but it's familiar, so I must have visited them. I was in Washington to reap some college kids while the others were here. We hadn't yet decided to make Kayville our base."

I shook my head. "The Norns gave you false memories, Torin. We were neighbors."

"Norns don't mess with the memories of Valkyries. There's no reason to."

"But—"

"Look, I don't want to argue with you. You tell me things you insist I did and said, yet I have no memories of ever saying or doing them. I thought Ingrid or Maliina might have told you, but Andris swore he never told them anything about my past. Maybe Maliina overheard stuff and shared them with you before she went rogue. I don't know. All I know is I never met you until two weeks ago when you kissed me. I've spent the last two weeks thinking about you, and I think I now know what might have happened."

His voice came to me as though from afar, hope slowly dying with each word from his mouth, until a giant gaping hole remained. I wanted to say something, but my tongue stayed glued to my mouth, which had gone dry. So I waited, heart pounding.

"Our paths must have crossed and you misunderstood," he said gently.

"Misunderstood?" I whispered.

"The nature of our relationship." He let go of the car door and shoved his hands in his front pants pockets again. "I make a point of not getting emotionally involved with Mortals. It is counterproductive. So if I did something to mislead you in any way, I'm sorry. It was not my intention."

He paused, his jaw tense, his gaze steady. I wanted to look away, but I couldn't, the finality of his previous words echoing in my head like my worst nightmare.

"I'll not always be a Mortal," I whispered. "I plan to start training as soon as possible."

His eyebrows shot up. "Why?"

My mind went blank. Then jumbled thoughts slammed into my psyche. Just because he couldn't remember didn't give him the right to write us off. Anger slowly crept in and mingled with the pain. Misunderstood the nature of our relationship? Emotional involvement with me was counterproductive? He wasn't willing to find out the truth or give me the benefit of the doubt. He just assumed he couldn't have gotten involved with me, a Mortal.

"Why? What kind of question is that?" I asked through clenched teeth.

His brow shot up. "One you should be asking yourself."

Hating that I had to look up at him, I stood. He didn't even have the decency to step back. The heat from his body leaped and wrapped around me, messing with my head. Usually, I welcomed the effect he had on me. Now, it just pissed me off.

"I've asked it a gazillion times, and I keep coming back to me, my mother, my entire existence. *My mother* is a Valkyrie. Norns marked me when I was a child for their diabolical reason, so Valkyrie and Norn magic flows in my veins."

He smirked. "So? That doesn't mean you have to become one."

"The Norns are after me, Torin. Just because you don't remember things doesn't mean I don't. Dealing with them was horrible. I have to be prepared this time."

He cocked his eyebrows. "I heard you stood up to them and accomplished something. Do it again. Show them you are one Mortal they can't bully. Being a Valkyrie is a lonely, crappy existence. Being a Norn is even worse."

His attitude stank, even though I knew about his loneliness. I was meant to take it away, complete him. The thought fueled my anger. Before I realized my intention, I poked him in the chest. "It's only crappy because you are too pig-headed to change. You choose to be alone when you don't have to be. You had a chance to make me immortal, and you took the moral high ground."

He grabbed my finger. "I'd never knowingly sentence a Mortal to this life, not even one as lovely as you."

That hurt. I yanked my finger from his grip. "I wouldn't want you to if you got down on your knees and begged."

Blue flames leapt in his eyes, which moved to my lips before locking with mine. "I don't beg, Freckles."

"You lost the right to call me that, *Valkyrie*. And FYI, if I wanted to, I could make you beg."

He leaned closer, making me catch my breath. He smirked at my reaction. "I could turn the tables on you like that, *Freckles*." He snapped his fingers.

I cocked my head. "Oh, is that supposed to scare me?"

"It should. In fact, get your lovely ass back in your car and drive as far away from me as possible."

I swallowed, feeling reckless. "I'm not afraid of you, Torin St. James."

He leaned even closer, his breath fanning my face. Memories of our kisses mocked me. I wanted to reach up, grab his face, and force him to remember, make him tremble and breathless.

"Just because I don't like emotional nightmares with snarky little Mortal girls doesn't mean I can't take what I want when I want it and move on without losing sleep over it."

Thoughts of kissing him disappeared from my head. Snarky little Mortal girls? I wanted to smack him. "You're a jackass."

He laughed. "Now we're getting somewhere."

"I loathe you."

"That's even better. Don't forget it when you come to my house for lessons," he added and flashed that smile I'd once thought was sexy, but now made me want to kick him. "I'll try to make myself scarce, but I'm not promising anything. So try to keep the snarky comments to a minimum. As for the girlish crush you think you have on me, it will pass. They always do."

"It already did at 'misunderstood'," I shot back, getting behind the wheel and slamming the car door. He was the most annoying, shits-for-brains guy I'd ever met. Girlish crush? That was the last straw.

He stared at me through the window, then turned and strolled to his Harley. Each step that took him away felt like a spike through my heart. If I thought he'd hurt me before, this was ten times worse.

I wasn't sure how long I sat in my car seething, nursing my pain, trying to think of ways to erase every trace of feelings I had for him from my heart. I should have kicked him. Bet I would have sent him flying across the parking lot. Or hurt myself. He was a Valkyrie, after all, and had superhuman strength. I wonder where mine came from. Probably from the three Norns healing me when I was a baby. What else had they done to me?

***

Within minutes, I pulled up behind Mirage, my family's store. The back door made its usual annoying ding as I entered, and Jared looked up. He smiled and waved. He was my parents' only employee. Now that Dad was back, the temp Mom had hired was gone. I glanced around the display room.

"Where is everyone?" I asked.

"Your mom just left. Your pops is in the office," Jared explained.

"He's not with a customer, is he?"

"No. Go on in." I walked between displayed mirrors and picture frames. Most of the merchandise was kept in the back, so there was enough aisle space for browsing. Even though we custom-framed print pictures for a furniture store and a few works of art for museums in Portland, majority of the work done at the store was for the Valkyries. One had to look closely to see the runes etched on the frames of the larger mirrors, which Valkyries used as portals. We shipped them all over the world.

"Yes?" Dad's deep voice said when I knocked.

I stuck my head in the office. He was on his laptop. "Are you busy, Dad?"

"Not too busy for you." He waved me inside and stood.

"I thought I'd pop by and see how things are going." The urge to cry rolled over me. I closed the gap between us and hugged him. When he tried to step back, my arms tightened.

"Pumpkin?"

"I'm okay, Dad. I just need a longer hug today. That's all," I mumbled. He was still thin from being sick and almost dying after his plane crashed into the Pacific Ocean. The tan from the cruise made him look less starved, but he was far from his old self.

He pressed a kiss on my head. "Was it that bad?"

"Gruesome." Especially my last encounter with a certain stubborn Valkyrie. I let go of Dad and gave him a sheepish smile then walked around the desk and dropped onto the chair opposite his. "I have tons of catching up to do. Piles and piles of reading material, packets of assignments, pre-tests... Grr." I slouched on my seat. Dad watched me with an indulgent expression. "I know I should be happy my teachers care, and I will, once my grades are no longer pitiful. But right now, I just want to scream."

He chuckled. "Go ahead. No one will hear you but me, and I don't mind. I've missed your vents."

I rolled my eyes. He was such an enabler. I inclined my head to indicate the computer. "What are you working on?"

"Accounts. Boring stuff."

"I thought Mom already did them."

"She did." He flipped through the pages of a ledger. "She does an amazing job, but it doesn't hurt to have several copies in different formats."

"Where's Mom?" Her coat was missing from the pegs by the door.

"She went home to get the rest of the ledgers. She should be back any moment." He got up and reached for his coat. "Come on. I'll buy us coffee from down the street."

"Yay!" I hopped up. "I thought you'd never ask."

He laughed. "I thought you came to see me."

"I did, because I know you never mess with tradition." As long as I could remember, we'd walk down to Café Nikos for hot chocolate and pastries whenever I stopped by the store after school. Decaf lattes replaced hot chocolate when I turned fifteen.

I hugged his arm as we left the store. It was cold and wet, and very few people walked along the storefront. Café Nikos had its regulars, most of them local artists and students. Some, hunched over their laptops, were online using the free wi-fi Nikolaus provided. Others were busy having heated discussion at their tables.

"Tristan, nice to have you back," Nikolaus, said, hugging Dad.

"It's nice to be back, my friend," Dad said.

"That must have been a horrifying experience. It's good to hear the airlines never gave up," Nikolaus added. He and Dad were locals and had known each other since high school.

Dad chuckled. "I wish I could give them the credit, Niko. That honor goes to Svana. She never gave up."

Salivating over the pastries, I only partly listened to my father's miraculous rescue story. Dad had told me the same story before we left for the cruise and all of it was half-truth. Mom never hired a private security firm to search for him, and their investigators hadn't found him two weeks ago at a remote hospital in a little town in El Salvador and flown him home. The reason Mom never gave up was because she'd contacted her Valkyrie sisters, who'd reassured her that Dad's soul hadn't been reaped. Every time I'd caught her talking to the mirror, she'd been using it as a portal to communicate with them. They'd even tried to locate Dad's whereabouts, but Torin was the one who had found my father and brought him home. He'd probably used a portal.

We bought half a dozen pastries and sipped our drinks on our way back. The sound of a motorcycle filled the air and my heart danced, but I didn't turn to look. Torin and I were done. I refused to allow him to mess with my head again.

***

Mom still was not yet back when I left the store, but her car was in our driveway when I entered our cul-de-sac. As I drove past Torin's, my gaze automatically went to the garage to see if his bike was there. The door was closed. I berated myself for looking, for wondering if he was home. It was going to take a while to get over him and completely erase him from my heart and my head.

"Mom?" I called out when I entered the house.

No response.

I checked Dad's office then headed upstairs. She wasn't in her bedroom or mine. I placed my bulky backpack on the desk and my oboe by the door. Just as I was about to turn and leave the room, the telltale prickly feeling on my nape told me I was being watched. I glanced out the window, and my eyes connected with Torin's.

My heart trembled. *Stupid heart.*

He smiled and gave me a mock salute. I flipped him off. He laughed and turned, and I saw that he wasn't alone in his bedroom. Lavania walked to his side and touched his arm. She'd changed out of the gray outfit she'd worn to school and now wore a violet silk dress. It looked like lingerie. Sexy lingerie.

She saw me and waved.

Feeling a little sick, I turned and left my bedroom. It was official. My tutor, trainer, or whatever they call Valkyries like Lavania, was my boyfriend's new girlfriend. No, my *ex*-boyfriend's girlfriend. The worst part was our houses were so close I could see inside his room, which meant I might actually see them making out. Imagining them together hurt, just like watching him with Jess had months ago. He wasn't supposed to be with anyone but me.

Refusing to let it get to me, I headed downstairs for something to eat.

"Ah, there you are," Mom said.

I jumped. "Where did you come from?" I noticed the portal in the living room shimmer and remold itself until it was once again a wall mirror. "Did you just use *that?*"

She grinned. "It's so convenient, isn't it? I was next door talking to Lavania, and two seconds later, I'm here. I'm so happy I can do that freely without worrying about you seeing me."

"What if Dad saw you?"

She dismissed my concerns with a flicker of her wrist, charms jiggling on her bracelet. "Sweetie, he's a Mortal and can't really *see* portals. Come here." She enveloped me in a hug and perfumes that defied description, then leaned back and studied me. "You look terrible."

I made a face. "Thanks. How come I couldn't see portals even after I could see runes?"

She cupped my cheeks and planted a kiss on my forehead. "That's because the veil lifts slowly and gives a person time to adjust. If it happens fast, which is rare, a person can become overwhelmed and think they are hallucinating. Imagine seeing invisible Valkyries with their glowing skin, souls of the dead, portals appearing and disappearing. You'd go crazy." A scowl settled on her face. "You're not seeing souls yet, are you?"

I shuddered. "No."

"That ability will happen with time. So, Lavania told me what happened at school. I plan to call your principal first thing tomorrow morning. Name calling is bad enough, but slashing your tires? Spray-painting your car? I will not have you bullied by anyone."

"Don't, Mom. I can handle this on my own. Please."

She shook head head. "No, I can't do that. Your father... Oh, he's not going to be happy when he hears about this."

"Please, don't tell him. Just let it go. Torin fixed the tires, so no one can slash them again, and I really don't want to draw more attention to myself."

Mom's lips pinched as she mulled over what I'd just said. She shook her head. "I don't know."

"Please, Mom. Just don't do anything. If we make a big deal out of it, the students will only become more hateful."

She sighed and pressed a kiss on my forehead. "Okay. But if they do it again, I will make them pay."

I sighed with relief. "Sure." Then I remembered that a Valkyrie's idea of "pay" might be very different from humans. "Pay how?"

"Oh, sweetie, the things we can do with basic runes. Clean magic." She took my arm and led me toward the kitchen. "I could have their hair fall off, warts grow between their toes, give them diarrhea for a week, pig ears, snouts..."

"Okay. Let's not go Morgana on anyone." I tugged my arm from her hand and picked up an apple. "I have enough to deal with without worrying about you turning people into pigs."

She pinched my nose. "I was just kidding. Your dad already made dinner, so go finish your homework and don't worry about a thing. Oh, how was your first day with Torin?"

I didn't want to discuss Torin. "Like I expected. He doesn't remember me."

"Give him time. He will. If he doesn't, he'll fall in love with you again."

I wasn't holding my breath. First, he had to want to. That wasn't going to happen if he thought I had a crush on him. Second, I had to spend time with him for anything to happen. He had offered to disappear every time I went to their house. Jerk.

Mom reached for the keys she'd left on the counter, and I realized she was about to leave. "Do you have a minute, Mom?"

She glanced at her watch. "Your father is waiting, but what's a minute more. What is it?"

"Can we sit down, please?" I indicated the breakfast nook in the kitchen. Eying me curiously, she pulled out a chair and sat. I sat across from her and played with the apple while rearranging my thoughts.

"You're beginning to worry me, sweetheart. Just say whatever is on your mind."

"Who is Eirik?"

She blinked. "Why do you ask?"

"He cannot be a Mortal. You told me his parents had special duties here, and he knows everything that happened to me, which means the Norns didn't erase his memories. So, who is he?"

Mom sighed. "Oh, hun. This is one of those questions your trainer will answer."

"But I need to know now. The Norns came to see me at school and said things." Color drained from her face. She opened her mouth to speak, but I gripped her hand. "Let me finish, please."

She pressed her lips tight, green eyes flashing.

"They said Eirik needed me and in order to protect him I had to join them. They also said that once you tell me his story, I'll understand why he needs me."

"The sneaky, conniving hags. If I talk I break my oath, which buys me a one-way ticket to Hel's Mist. They have no authority to lift the sanctions the High Council placed on me. I cannot believe how low they're willing to sink to manipulate you. Stay here." Mom patted my hand then stood. "Lavania will explain everything. For once Goddess Freya's got one on the Norns."

I followed her to the living room. "What do you mean?"

"She sent Lavania to train you now instead of next year when you turn eighteen. The Norns will not think of searching for her right now. The bitter crones think they have us at their mercy." Mom stopped in front of the mirror portal in the living room and placed her hand on the surface. "Since Lavania was a teenager when she became immortal, she can blend in easily with the kids at your school." Runes appeared on her hand, and the mirror responded, shifting and ebbing until a portal appeared.

I inched closer, curious to see where it led. The short hallway had a cloudy floor and walls like it was made of swirling smoke. The other side was a bedroom done in violet, white, and purple.

Lavania appeared. She still wore the sexy lingerie.

"Svana? Did you forget something? Oh hi, Raine," she added with a broad grin when she saw me.

I gave her a half-wave, hating her and fascinated by her at the same time. How old was she? And why did she have to be so damn beautiful?

"My daughter has a few questions about young Eirik. Could you join us, please?"

"Of course." Lavania disappeared out of sight and returned with a floral robe with large violet flowers, which she shrugged on. We stepped back to let her in.

She entered our home and looked around.

I wondered what she thought of Mom's décor, which was like her fashion sense—earthy tones mixed with colorful cushions, paintings, knick-knacks from various cultures, flowers, and candles. Mom loved candles. Dad's cherry wet bar in the corner was the only contemporary area in the room. He'd built it with Eirik's help and was proud of it. Every time Mom put a candle or a carving on the counter, Dad moved it. It was like a game they played.

"What a beautiful room, Svana." She sounded genuine. "It's warm and cozy, like a real home."

Mom chuckled. "It is a real home, and thank you. Please, sit." Mom waved toward the living room sofa. "Do you want something to drink?"

"Water is fine," Lavania said.

While Mom went behind the bar counter to retrieve bottled water from the fridge, I studied our guest on the sly. She sat with her back straight, hands on her lap, and legs crossed at the ankle and tucked to the side. I found myself sitting straighter. After a few seconds, I went back to slouching. Copying her wouldn't make me feel better or bring Torin back. It was over, and the sooner I accepted it the better off I'd be.

"Here you go." Mom placed the water on the side table then gripped Lavania's shoulder. "Be nice to my daughter, Lavinia. Don't frighten her with too much information at once."

"Don't worry. She's safe with me." Lavania patted Mom's hand.

"You're leaving?" I asked, my voice rising. I wasn't ready for one-on-one with this particular Valkyrie.

"Your father is waiting, sweetheart. In fact, I came home to get our account ledgers when Lavania distracted me with news about your car." Her green eyes flashed, and I knew she was about to start berating the students.

"That explains why he kept checking his watch. I went by the store, and we swung by Café Nikos."

"You two and those pastries." She chuckled and turned to Lavania. "Norns visited Raine at school today. Be careful. If they discover your presence..."

"They'll be onto us. I know. Don't worry. I'll be careful."

"You still think attending her school while here is the right thing to do?" Mom asked.

Lavania nodded. "It is the perfect camouflage. Your neighbors won't suspect anything and incessant chitchat from the students will conceal our presence." She glanced at me and added, "Norns tend to eavesdrop on their charges when not weaving the destinies of newborns."

"I'll see you later, sweetie." Mom dropped a kiss on my forehead and left.

Blowing out a breath, I glanced at Lavania and found her watching me with a weird smile. "What can Norns do if they learn you are here?"

"Plenty. They're unpredictable, but I'm more concerned with what they might do to you and how your mother might react. She sacrificed a lot to be with your father." Lavania sounded amazed.

I bristled. "Why is that surprising?"

"Not many people are willing to give up immortality for love."

"Are you saying my mother is no longer immortal?"

She nodded. "No. She's aging, just slower than your average Mortal because of the runes. Since she returned her runic blades, she cannot add more and when you don't add more, their effects wane."

I frowned, finding it hard to imagine Mom older.

"It's one thing to hear about her and quite another to actually meet her." Lavania leaned back against the sofa. "She is quite the legend back at home."

"Why?"

"Norns rarely fall from grace. Even Norns-in-training like her, yet she did for your father. She was also Goddess Freya's favorite, powerful like most Valkyries from your bloodline, and a ferocious fighter."

My mother a fighter? With her boho-chic style and outgoing personality, I could see her prancing around with floral lei promoting peace. "Fighting who?"

"Warriors. We train the warriors we reap. But I'm digressing. When she was chosen to join the Norns, Goddess Freya was very disappointed, yet when she fell in love with your father and Norns wanted her banished to Hel's Hall, the goddess intervened on her behalf. Freya went before the High Council and fought for your parents to stay together."

That made sense. Freya was the goddess of love and female sexuality, and the leader of the Valkyries. I wanted to meet her someday. "Why did she let them strip Mom of her Valkyrie rights and forbid her to talk about you guys or go back to Asgard?"

Lavania chuckled. "Because those are the rules, sweetie. Valkyries fall from grace all the time and choose to remain on Earth with their mates. Your mother is very lucky she was powerful enough to retain some knowledge of runes to protect you. Most fallen Valkyries are not that lucky." She took a sip of water and wrapped her hands around the glass. "So, my young protégée, what do you want to know about Eirik?"

"I don't mind learning about Mom. How old is she? Are her parents alive? Do I have grandparents, aunts, uncles, cousins?"

She laughed. "What happened to being undecided, needing more time?"

I winced. "I do need time to think about things and finish my homework, but—"

She raised her hand. "Okay, okay, I was only teasing."

"I'm not always this flaky. I really want to learn." My heart pounded with a mixture of excitement and dread. It was now or never. *Torin and his know-it-all attitude can take a hike.* "I would like to start my lessons right away."

Lavania frowned. "Are you sure? Your mother said not to push or—"

"Yes. I'm sure."

She smiled, reached forward, and gripped my arms. "Good girl."

I exhaled, feeling lightheaded. This was what I wanted. I blew out a breath again.

Lavania smiled. "Okay. What are your plans for tomorrow?"

"I have an appointment with my doctor at three twenty. I should be home by four."

"Then let's start at five."

I nodded.

"Now about your mother. I don't know anything personal about her, except she's older than I and I'm old. Don't ask how old because I will pull rank on you. One day she'll be allowed to tell you everything. For now, be patient and focus on being the best student I've ever had." She sipped her water and leaned back. "Now, what did you want to learn about our young deity?"

I blinked. "Diety?"

Lavania's eyes lit up. "Yes. Eirik is Odin's grandson. I took one look at him when I arrived here two weeks ago and I knew he was the one. He looks exactly like his father."

I couldn't wrap my brain around the fact that my best friend since we could crawl, the goofball who loved pizza and licked his fingers when he ate chicken wings, was actually the grandson of a Norse god.

"Then why is he being raised here as a human orphan?"

5. WHO IS EIRIK?

The smile disappeared from Lavania's lips. "He's being raised here for his safety."

My mouth went dry. The Norns were right. How I'd hoped they were up to their nasty tricks. "What's after him?"

"Let me start from the beginning. Odin and his wife, Frigg, had a son named Baldur. He was one of many, but the most beautiful of all the gods. He was wise like his father, fair in his judgments like his brother, and very gracious like his mother. His golden beauty rivaled the sun, so they made him god of the summer sun. Everyone loved him, but not as much as his parents. One night, he and his mother had the same prophetic vision of his death. Odin went to see a seeress and confirmed it. Baldur was going to die. To prevent his death, Baldur's mother went to all the realms and made all the people and elements—earth, air, water, and fire—take a vow not to hurt her son. And it worked. They said the young gods and goddesses would use Baldur for target practice for fun. They'd take turns throwing spears, arrows, knives, and daggers at him only to watch them bounce off him without leaving a scratch." Lavania chuckled.

"You saw this happen?"

She shook her head. "No. We, the Valkyries, are often too busy with the warriors to attend most court events, but his story is chronicled and placed on the walls of Valhalla for all to see and to remember who was responsible for his death."

She paused to sip her water. I sat on the edge of my seat, fascinated even though at the back of my mind was concern for Eirik. Something or someone was after him.

"Who killed him?" I asked impatiently.

"Loki. Loki found out that there was one thing Baldur's mother overlooked in her quest to keep Baldur safe. She forgot to get a vow from mistletoe. Mistletoe doesn't grow on or under the earth like most plants. It is considered a lowly plant because it grows on oak and apple trees like a parasite. Loki created an arrow from the mistletoe and gave it to Baldur's twin brother, who was as blind as a bat. While the gods and goddesses were playing one of their target games, Baldur's blind brother threw the arrow and killed Baldur. In his grief, Odin had Baldur's twin brother killed."

And they said humans fought over nothing. These gods were petty, ruthless, and unforgiving. Was one of them after Eirik because of his father? Maybe one of his uncle's kids. "I hope Loki was punished."

Lavania shook her head. "No. Everyone suspected that he directed the arrow. After all, how good is the aim of a blind man, even if he is a god? But no one could prove Loki did it. Do you know anything about Hel?"

I nodded. "She's Loki's daughter and the ruler of the Land of Mist, where those who die of old age and illness go."

Lavania nodded with approval. "You've been reading. Very good. I don't normally use books when I train my charges, but if you prefer them—"

"No, that's okay. I don't. I rather learn through practice. Why did you ask about Hel?"

"Baldur didn't die in a battle, so his soul went to her, to Hel's Hall. I've never been there, but they say it's huge with many mansions and high walls, and it's very damp. His mother, desperate to have her son back, sent messenger after messenger to Hel, begging her to release Baldur. Hel promised to send Baldur back if everyone, alive and dead, mourned his death. We all did, except a giantess who refused to shed a tear. So Hel kept Baldur. At least that's what we thought. In the meantime, Odin discovered that the giantess who didn't weep was actually Loki in disguise."

"Oh, please tell him he was punished this time."

Lavania grinned. "Yes. He's bound to a rock in a pit. Above the pit is a serpent dripping venom on him, a just punishment for killing a beloved god. Unfortunately, evil is stirring, and it's only a matter of time before he escapes. He has many followers doing his bidding, including his children." She drained the water and put the glass aside. "Now, you're probably wondering what the story of Baldur has to do with Eirik."

I nodded.

"A little over seventeen years ago, three Norns stopped by Valhalla with a baby boy. They claimed he was Baldur's son. *How is that possible?* everyone asked. Did he escape? Did Hel set him free? Is he living in one of the realms? The Norns didn't say, but Odin and Frigg took one look at the baby and knew he was Baldur's, their grandson. The blond hair, the fair skin, the beautiful features, and eyes like drops of the sun."

She'd just described Eirik down to his amber eyes.

"*Völur* came from far and wide, and they all confirmed he was the one."

"*Völur?*"

"Seeresses. We have very few of them left, but when they talk, the gods listen. The *Völur* had visions of our young deity as an adult reunited with his father. But a dark shadow followed the boy. They all said it couldn't be stopped. The three Norns knew something, but no one dared ask them."

"Why not?"

"Norns tend to want something in return, and it's always what your heart desires the most. It doesn't matter what you're willing to give up. They always know what to go for. Not even the gods make deals with the Norns. I knew this Valkyrie…"

Those lying, sneaky crones. They hadn't just erased Torin's memories to make me suffer. They'd taken away his heart's most desire. Me. The deal Torin had made was for my life to be spared in exchange for eternal servitude to Hel or evil Norns. Instead of servitude, they'd taken his memories away. Yet they'd known I wasn't meant to die. It was all a lie. *Just wait until I see them again.*

"Raine?"

"Oh, sorry." I gave her an apologetic smile. "Can you repeat what you just said?"

Something flashed in her eyes. Annoyance or disappointment, I couldn't tell. "Is something wrong?"

"No. Every time someone mentions Norns, I remember my interactions with them. Not my happiest memories."

She squeezed my arm. "I understand. I might not know the details of what you went through, but I know how Norns work. Maybe one day you'll share your experience with me."

I doubted it. "Sure."

"Okay, back to Eirik's story. To protect him, the Norns suggested he should be sent to Earth to be raised as a Mortal, his location kept a secret from everyone, including his grandparents. The Norns promised he'd be showered with love, never want for anything."

I laughed. "Have you met his parents? They're cold and..." I remembered who I was talking to and winced. "Sorry, I interrupted."

The smile disappeared from Lavania's face. "Don't be. I like that you speak your mind, Raine. Your mother told me you and Eirik are very close."

I smiled. "Yes. My parents treat him like a son. He probably spends more time here than at his house."

"Then the Norns were right. He got all the love and caring from your family and the material things came from his Immortal guardians."

If that was her polite way of saying we were richer in love and poorer in material things, she'd nailed it. Eirik's parents were loaded. Their new house at the top of the hill was huge. Even their old house was bigger than most of the houses in our cul-de-sac.

"Anyway," Lavania leaned back and smiled, "that's the story of how our young deity came here."

It explained the way Eirik and I were practically raised together and Mom's friendship with his aloof parents. What I still didn't understand was what the Norns had meant by he was the reason they'd saved my life.

"Do Torin and the others know who Eirik is?"

"Of course not. I recognized him because I knew his father."

Maliina, Andris' ex-girlfriend, had suspected something. It was the only explanation for the way she'd behaved the first time she'd seen Eirik. She'd asked him all sorts of personal questions about his background, almost like she'd known he wasn't human. At the time I thought she was trying to hurt him to get back at me.

"Who is Eirik's mother?"

Lavania shook her head. "Sadly, no one knows."

"I do," a familiar voice said, and I looked up. Eirik stepped into the room, using the mirror as a portal. How much had he heard? I couldn't tell from his expression.

"What are you doing here?" I asked, getting up. "I thought you had swim practice."

"I didn't go." His gaze shifted to Lavania. "So that's the big secret? I'm Odin's grandson? Or is it the scary boogeyman after me?"

Lavania moved away from the sofa and toward him. She looked worried. "If your guardians didn't tell you the truth, it's because they were following orders, Eirik."

Something else occurred to me. "Are you going to get in trouble for telling us, Lavania?"

She cocked her eyebrows. "Are you going to tell that I told you?"

"No." I shook my head.

"Then the secret stays with us. Do you have any questions for me, Eirik?" she asked.

"Nope." He headed toward the kitchen. I noticed he only wore socks.

"I can train you and Raine if you'd like," Lavania added.

"No thanks." He disappeared behind the fridge door as he searched for something to eat.

"Don't mind him," I said apologetically. "Once he processes everything, he'll have plenty of questions and won't mind joining us."

Lavania looked skeptical. "I hope so." She glanced toward Eirik, who stepped away from the fridge with a bowl of leftovers from last night. He opened the lid and grinned. As we watched, he opened a drawer, retrieved a spoon, and scooped cold chili. Yuck.

"This really is his second home," Lavania said softly.

"Yes, it is." It was surreal watching him, the son of a Norse god eating cold chili in my kitchen. Then I noticed Lavania in front of the mirror waiting for the portal to form. I wanted to tell her to use the door. Mom thought nothing of using portals, but Dad could get spooked by people appearing or disappearing suddenly. Mrs. Rutledge from across the street also had more time on her hands than any of the housewives in the cul-de-sac. She liked nothing better than to watch people and gossip. She'd notice if someone was at our house one second and the next at Torin's without crossing our yards.

Lavania waved and disappeared through the portal. I waited until the mirror was whole again before joining Eirik.

"So, do I bow in humility," I bowed, "curtsey out of respect," I curtsied, "or grovel every time I see you?" I grabbed his hand and rained kisses on his knuckles.

"Shut up." He yanked his hand from mine, but he was smiling.

"You really should warm that." I pointed at the chili.

He stopped eating and glanced at me. "This, uh, wasn't your dinner, was it?"

"No." I plopped on a stool, leaned against the counter, and watched him shovel spoonful after spoonful of the mixture into his mouth. "So the Norns were right."

"About?" he asked between scoops.

"Your life is in danger from this, uh, dark shadow."

He shrugged. "Whatever."

"Don't say that. Maybe you should listen to them, Eirik. Keep an eye out for this *thing* after you."

He laughed. "I'm not going to look over my shoulder because of something those three crones said. If the shadow, or whatever it is, wants a piece of me, let it come."

That meant I'd have to do the watching and the worrying. "Do you really know who your mother is?"

He nodded. "Yep. I have Sari Seville. She might be standoffish and strict, but she has moments when she does something very, uh... What's the word?"

"Mom-ish?"

He grinned. "Yeah, Mom-ish. Do you remember J.P and Kyle?"

"Fourth grade bullies. I hated them. I wonder what happened to them."

"They probably ended up in juvee. They ganged up on me one summer. The next day, they both apologized and never bothered me again. Apparently, Mom paid their families a visit. Either she runed them or she put the fear of Hel in them. When you were in the hospital after the accident, she sat with your mother and got all of us drinks and sandwiches while we kept vigil. I'm talking about everyone who went to Torin's party and came to the hospital with us." He pointed his spoon at me. "That deserves the Mom-of-the-Year award."

"Yes, it does."

"And 'mom number two' is your mother. Hope you don't mind sharing."

I grinned. "I don't."

"Good." He licked the spoon and got up to put the empty bowl in the sink. "She fills in for mine most of the time, so I'm good mom-wise." He turned on the water and soaked the bowl.

He was so sweet. I gave my mother credit for that. His parents often traveled, leaving him with nannies when he was little and housekeepers when he became a teenager. My parents practically raised him.

He turned, leaned against the sink, and crossed his arms and legs. "So, why were you and *the Valkyrie* discussing me?"

He made it sound like Valkyrie was something vile. I guessed he was still ticked off at Torin for "stealing me" from him. "I saw her bow to you at school, so I got curious."

He rolled his eyes. "Okay, start talking. I want to know everything."

Leaving out the personal stuff, I told him everything that had happened from the day I saw runes on Andris to the attack during the meet. When I finished, Eirik stared at me with an unreadable expression.

"Say something," I whispered.

He shook his head. "Torin is one lucky bastard."

Was a lucky bastard. Now he was lower than a slug. Eirik sounded sad. I approached him, wishing I could ease his pain. "I'm sorry."

"For what?"

"Hurting you. I didn't mean to."

He moved away from the counter and pushed his hands in the back pockets of his pants. Cloudy amber eyes studied me intently. "I thought we had something special, Raine."

"We did. We do. Our friendship *is* special. It always will be."

"But it's nothing like what you and Torin have. I mean, he was willing to be a slave to evil Norns and Hel for you. How…" He blew out air and scowled. "How can I possibly compete with that?"

I sighed, my heart aching for him. If I could spare him I would. No matter how often I told myself it was over between Torin and me, I knew it was a lie. I was pissed at him, but my heart still belonged to him.

"I don't want you to complete with him. I love both of you, just differently."

Silence followed, his scowl deepening. When he pulled his hands from his pockets, reached up, tucked my hair away behind my ears, and cupped my face, I barely stopped myself from pulling back. Torin loved to do that.

"Are you absolutely sure about your feelings for him? I mean, if I were to kiss you right now, you wouldn't be tempted to rip my clothes off and have your way with me?"

I stiffened then I saw through his cockiness. His pride was hurt, but he was doing his best to cover it up with half jokes. "My heartbeat would probably shoot off course because of a boost in oxytocin and dopamine."

"In plain English, please," he said, a smile tugging the corner of his lips.

"My eyes would dilate, my heart would beat harder, and I'd start panting like a cocker spaniel after chasing its tail." He laughed. I went for the kill. "You're an amazing kisser, and I'm only human."

He grinned. "Am I really a good kisser?"

Now he was fishing for compliments. On a different day, I'd blow him off, but he was too emotionally fragile for me to play games. "Yes, you are, and there's a girl out there—"

"No." He stepped away from me. "I'm done dating."

His feelings for Cora were strong. I'd seen it in his eyes. He just wasn't ready to admit them. "Don't say that."

"I still have to figure out who I am, who my biological parents are. A ghost for a father and a nameless mother doesn't exactly sound like something you want to share with a girlfriend." He shook his head. "Besides, the first thing my mother told me after they'd finished explaining about Asgard and Valkyries was not to get involved with a Mortal."

Sounded like something his mother would say. I did the math. The night after they'd talked to him, he'd kissed me. "So what were you doing with me?"

He rolled his eyes. "Like I was going to listen to them? I'd wanted to kiss you since the day I caught you changing. Unfortunately, my mother saw me watching you and one thing led to another."

A few weeks later, they'd moved. I guessed that had been his mother's way of making sure he didn't become involved with me. It hadn't stopped him. Hopefully, his need for answers about his parents wouldn't interfere with his growing feelings for Cora or I'd have to play Cupid.

"I'm happy we talked," I said.

He made a face. "I don't know. I think you should make it up to me."

"Anything. Just say it."

"Make-out with me." His expression changed, until he wore a lost puppy look. The corner of his mouth twitched. "It will mend my broken heart."

He was such a goofball and a sucky liar. "Very funny. You need to go."

"No making out?"

"In your dreams."

He pretended to think about it. "Okay. I can work with that. So, what's your plan to help Torin remember you?"

This was one subject I didn't want to discuss with him. "I don't have a plan."

"Yeah, right. You always have a plan."

"Not this time." After the painful encounter in the parking lot and seeing Lavania in his bedroom, I was a bit bruised.

"Do you want me to talk to him?" Eirik asked.

"No." If anyone was going to rub Torin's nose in what he was missing, it was going to be me. "So, are you going to train with me?"

He shuddered. "No way. I have things covered." He walked toward the mirror in the living room.

"At least you've learned enough to open portals."

"Yeah, lucky me." He didn't meet my gaze. Instead, he looked at the mirror and cursed.

"What?"

"I can't open the portal again."

"Why not? I thought you had things covered."

He grimaced. "I, uh, forgot my *stillo*."

"Your what?"

"The rune knife for writing on solid surfaces. I must have put it on my dresser." He gave me a sheepish look. "Do you think you can give me a ride home?"

"Sure, your royal godliness."

He shot me a mean look. "You keep that up and I'll kiss you in front of Torin. See how you like it."

Torin wouldn't care. "Mrs. Rutledge is going to go crazy trying to figure out how she missed seeing you arrive, which reminds me. No more using this particular mirror." I pointed at the living room mirror. "Or someone will give my father a heart attack."

"What if I want to talk to you? Our tree is gone, so I can't sneak up to your bedroom."

"Use your cell phone."

He rolled his eyes and pointed at his face then mine. "Face to face."

"Skype or FaceTime? Fine," I added when he made a face. "Use the mirror in my room."

He grinned, his eyes twinkling.

"Text me first, you perv," I added.

***

I tried not to glance at Torin's place when we drove past, but bad habits were hard to break. Lights were on upstairs and downstairs, and music filtered through the open windows.

Eirik's place was two minutes away, so I was back in no time. Andris' presence drew my attention as I entered the cul-de-sac. He sat on the porch rail, a clear drink in a glass in his hand. His eyes followed me. He was one Valkyrie I'd been hoping to avoid. His girlfriend had joined evil Norns because of me, and I knew he didn't particularly like me.

By the time I stepped out of the car, he was sauntering across my lawn. "What in Hel's Mist are you doing?"

His combative tone didn't surprise me. Was he wasted? He tended to be brutal when drunk. He was the one who'd told me the truth about Torin, that he was Valkyrie. He hadn't been nice about it. His silver hair looked disheveled like he'd run his fingers through it several times, but his dark-brown eyes weren't glazed.

"What do you want, Andris?"

He placed his hands on the car, neatly boxing me in. He leaned in, further invading my personal space. "You and Torin should be in his room with the door locked, making up for lost time. Why in Hel's Mist are you with your Mortal boyfriend while Torin is over there," he waved toward their place, "eating his heart out."

That answered the question about his memories. They were intact. "Eating his heart out?"

"Skulking around. Morose. Whatever you want to call it. When he's not hiding in his room, he snaps at everyone. I thought now that you're back things would change. So I'll ask again." He peered at me. "Why are you with golden boy?"

If only he knew about Eirik. So Torin was miserable. Good. I hope it only got worse. "Do you mind moving aside?"

"I do," he retorted.

I slipped under his arm. He could have easily stopped me. Valkyries moved faster than humans once they engaged the runes on their bodies.

"Talk to me, Raine. What happened? Is it because the Norns scrambled his memories?"

I blinked. "You know?"

"Of course I know. I live with the guy. I had to give him directions to the house and school. Have you talked to him about the two of you, your past?"

A delicious shiver shot up my spine. Only one thing had that effect on me. Torin. I glanced over my shoulder at his window. I couldn't see him, but I knew he was watching us. Could he hear us? Even if he couldn't, there was no way I would confide in Andris about my problems with Torin. We weren't close like that.

I shrugged. "It doesn't matter."

"Let me guess. While you were away, you lost interest in him, fell out of love, and decided to go back to that insipid Mortal," Andris said.

His attitude hurt. "No."

"Then what is it? It's obvious Torin is still into you."

"We agreed that the past..." my voice broke. I swallowed and lifted my chin. "The past doesn't matter. I've moved on."

Andris sneered. "You should be trying to help him remember, especially after everything he did for you. Even now, he's still taking chances and sacrificing so much for you, and you, as usual, have no clue."

Panic coursed through me. "What do you mean?"

"Why do you care? You've moved on." He shook his head. "You're an idiot. Torin is ten times the man Seville will ever be." He stepped back then walked to the porch, picked up his empty glass, and threw me a glance full of loathing before disappearing inside their house.

I blew out air. Once again, I glanced up at Torin's bedroom window. I still couldn't see him even though I felt his presence. What did Andris mean? I hated riddles.

Sighing, I went inside my house and headed straight upstairs to change into comfortable clothes and start on my homework. Before I drew the curtains, I glanced across at Torin's. This time I could see him.

He sat on his window, his nose buried in a book, the lock of hair falling across his forehead. "What things are you doing or sacrificing for me?" I asked.

He glanced up and cocked his eyebrows. Funny how he could convey so much with just a look. Right now, his expression said I was bugging him.

"Are you talking to me?" he asked.

"Yes."

He smirked. "Can't keep away from me, can you?"

My cheeks grew warm. "I'm not stalking you if that's what you're thinking."

"Looks like it from here. I'm sitting here, minding my own business and you—"

"Please, just answer the stupid question and I'll leave you alone."

He laughed. "I'm not sacrificing anything for you, Freckles. Andris is mistaken."

So he'd overheard our conversation. Why would Andris imply something if it weren't true? I'd hate for Torin to put his life in danger again without me knowing about it. He went back to his book, completely ignoring my presence.

I studied him, his chiseled cheekbones and the slope of his strong jaw. My heart squeezed. I missed looking into his teasing sapphire eyes, the wicked grin he'd switch on and off on a whim. I didn't want to walk away from him. From us.

"You're staring," he said without looking up.

I wanted to ignore him, move away from the window, go downstairs, and lick my wounds, but my mouth tended to move faster than my brain.

"You wish." He glanced up and smirked. "I'm sitting in my favorite place, and you just happen to be in my line of vision," I added.

He cocked his eyebrows. "From that look in your eyes, you are plotting something. My untimely death perhaps?"

His previous words echoed in my head. ...*the girlish crush you think you have on me, it will pass.*

"I'd have to care to contemplate hurting you, bonehead. You're nothing to me."

"You know what they say about people who protest too much." The smile on his face broadened. "Just in case you were wondering, the only way to kill me, or any Valkyrie, is by decapitation, or, if you're strong enough, reach inside my chest and yank out my heart."

Then stomp on it. "Thanks for the information. Now go away."

"No. You go away. I was here first." He gave me a slow, wicked smile.

This was my favorite spot, and he knew it. "You're such a jerk."

"You'll have to do better than that to get a rise out of me, Freckles. Bye." He blew me a kiss and wiggled his fingers.

If he wanted me to hate him, he was going to get his wish. I closed the curtains, but the book in his hand reminded me of another. One that meant a lot to him. *Please, let it be there, so I can hurl it at his head.*

I hurried across the room to my chest of drawers. Under my panties in the back of the top drawer, my hand closed on the envelope, and I sighed with relief. I opened it, reached inside, and removed the ancient book of runes Torin had given me weeks ago.

Instead of walking back to the window and throwing it at Torin, I brought it to my nose and inhaled. It smelled of leather and his intoxicating scent. For a brief moment, I clutched the book to my chest as though the simple gesture would bring him closer. Maybe if I returned it, he'd start believing me.

No, he just said I needed to come up with something better to get a rise out of him. I needed a better plan. The kind that would make him wish he never threw that girlish crush crap at me.

6. PEOPLE ARE SUCH TOOLS

"Where are you going, young lady?" Dad called out when I started out of the kitchen.

"Upstairs." He opened his mouth, but I quickly added, "I know I'm not supposed to eat upstairs, but I have tons of homework. Please, Dad."

"Okay, tomorrow…" he cocked his brow.

"I'll eat downstairs. Promise. Love you." I gave him a toothy grin and raced upstairs before he could detain me further.

In my room, I placed my plate on the side, picked up garlic toast, and nibbled on it as I continued with the math packet. I enjoyed math most of the time and didn't mind learning new concepts when the teacher explained them, but trying to understand them on my own was a nightmare. I was tackling the second problem set when a knock resounded on my door.

"Can I come in, pumpkin?"

"Door's open." I didn't look up when he entered.

"You need to take a break," Dad said.

"I know. I'm almost done."

He sat on the edge of my desk and crossed his arms. "Your food is cold, your drink untouched, and the oil from your garlic toast is leaving a nice stain on your otherwise nicely written report."

My eyes flew to the papers on my left. Oh crap! I grabbed the toast, threw it in the garbage can, and shook the crumbs off the top paper. The translucent stain had spread to the other pages under it. "Damn!"

"Watch your language," Dad said firmly.

"Sorry. I'm out of printer paper, and I wanted to turn this in tomorrow." I pulled out the paper tray to confirm it. There was only one piece of paper.

"Get some from downstairs *after* dinner."

"I used it all. I meant to buy some, but…" I checked my watch. It was after nine. "Do you think Kinko's or Staples is still open?"

"We'll discuss what to do about your paper problem *after* you eat. Come on." He picked up the plate of cold meatloaf, mashed potatoes, and peas. It looked good, but then again, he was an amazing cook. My stomach growled, and he laughed.

I guzzled half the glass of the orange juice, got up, and followed him. "I'm starving."

He snorted. "It's just like when you were little. You'd forget to eat because you couldn't stop reading. It's good to feed your mind, but you must also feed your body. A healthy mind—"

"Needs a healthy body," I finished. "That's not necessarily true."

"Is that a rebuttal?" Dad asked, easing back into a debate-like banter the two of us used to have before his plane crash.

"No, Dad. This is the rebuttal. One name. Stephen Hawking. Bam. Debate over." I gave him a triumphant grin.

Dad chuckled. "You can't win a discussion without an explanation. Who is this Stephen Hawking? What has he done?"

As if he didn't know. I rolled my eyes. "You made me watch the documentary they did on him. He is *the* Stephen Hawking. No explanation necessary."

"Be specific with his contributions, so I can have a counter argument," Dad said, tongue-in-cheek.

"I give up." I suppressed a giggle when he stopped at the foot of the stairs and arched his eyebrows. "I'm afraid I'm not particularly crazy about physics. Most of his theories are impossible to understand, let alone explain."

"Then you lose, my little debater. You don't swim a lap by doing a length." Dad waited for me to join him, draped his arm around my shoulders, and dropped a kiss on my temple. He didn't have to say he'd missed our heated discussions. I saw it in the twinkle in his eyes. The indulgent look on Mom's face as she watched us from the kitchen counter said she'd missed it, too.

Dad placed my cold dinner in the microwave, covered it with a paper towel, and punched the buttons. I plopped on a chair at the breakfast nook and waited.

"Did you get a lot of work done?" Mom asked, wiping down the counter.

"I finished today's math homework and started on the ones I missed. I wrote several reports, but, unfortunately, I ran out of printer paper."

"Your father keeps some in his home office."

"Not anymore." Dad placed the steaming plate in front of me, and I picked up the fork. "I thought I'd drive to the nearest store and pick up some. Most of these megastores sell printer paper, right?"

"You're not driving anywhere this late at night," Mom said firmly.

Dad got up. "I'll get some, honey."

"No, Tristan. I'm not letting either of you drive anywhere this late." Mom pulled on his arm until he sat on a chair. "I'll get Raine paper from next door."

Dad frowned. "Next door?"

"Remember, I told you we have four teenagers living next door who go to Raine's school. I was at their house earlier and noticed they had a printer and a fresh box of paper."

I shook my head, not wanting to be beholden to Lavania or Torin for anything. "Mom, don't. I can buy some tomorrow."

"I'm sure Lavania won't mind. Besides, I meant to invite her and the others over for dinner this weekend and forgot to mention it to her. I want your father to meet them. You two can go back to your debate while I'm gone." She kissed Dad and squeezed my shoulder.

"I think our accidents really spooked her," I said. "She's become clingy."

Dad chuckled. "Clingy is not a word I'd ever associate with your mother, pumpkin. She's loving and caring, and extremely fastidious. Have you met these new neighbors?"

I nodded, placing a big chunk of meatloaf into my mouth so I didn't have to discuss the Valkyries, but I forgot he'd just heated it up. My mouth burning, I jumped up to get water. By the time I sat again, Dad was behind the newspaper. He read while I ate.

"This is good. Is it a new recipe?"

He lowered the paper. "No, same old recipe."

"I guess I missed your cooking. I tried some of your recipes, but the results were pitiful."

"Then I'm happy I'm home to cook for you." Dad folded the newspaper and put it away. His eyes followed me as I rinsed my plate, glass, and utensils, and placed them in the dishwasher. When our gazes connected, I gave him a tiny smile. He didn't return it.

"I think I'll go back upstairs."

"Sit with me for a minute." He indicated the chair I'd vacated and waited until I sat before adding, "We haven't discussed what happened to your friends two weeks ago."

My stomach dropped. That was one subject we'd avoided during the cruise, and I'd hoped it would be history by the time we returned. "I, uh, I'll probably stop by the cemetery and pay my respects next weekend."

"That's very sweet of you, but I don't think anyone expects you to do that. You already did enough."

He knew. "I'd still love to. I'd known some of them since elementary school when we started swimming for the Dolphins."

"Do you want me to come with you?"

"Oh, no. I'll be fine. I'll probably go with Eirik or Cora."

"Okay." When he continued to study me, I knew someone must have told him what had happened. Mom and I hadn't come up with an explanation, and my dad wasn't someone you bullshitted. I hated lying to him, but I couldn't tell him about Valkyries and Norns. It wasn't my job to do that. Mom should have told him eons ago, since she was one of them.

"I have to finish math, Dad."

"You're sure you don't want to talk about what happened at the meet?"

"I can't. It's still very fresh and haunting, and talking about it will be like reliving it. Maybe later." I hurried back up the stairs, but I couldn't escape my guilt or the hurt expression on his face. I'd never kept a secret from him. He was the one I'd run to when I had problems.

I tried to finish the math problem set, but my heart wasn't in it. I kept seeing my father's face. Why hadn't Mom told him the truth about who she was? Or maybe I was jumping to conclusions. I angled my head and listened for sounds from downstairs, but there was silence, which meant Mom was still at our neighbors. What was taking her so long? I checked out the window.

Lights were on downstairs at Torin's. Upstairs was in darkness. I wondered if he was already in bed. Memories of how he'd held me until I fell asleep came back to haunt me. I wish I could talk to him. He'd understand my wish to keep the secret of his world from my father. His own parents had believed he'd died during the crusade when he was actually alive. Had he felt guilty lying to his parents? How had he dealt with it?

Voices drifted from downstairs. When they rose, I realized my parents were having an argument. I'd never heard them fight. Careful not to make any noise, I opened my door and crept along the hallway. I caught the tail end of Dad's question.

"...happened?" His voice was sharp with frustration.

"It was chaotic when I got there, and everyone was panicking. She was in the water being so brave." Mom spoke soothingly as though trying to calm him down.

"They're calling her names, Svana. I wanted to punch those bastards. What if Raine was with me when they came to the store?" He added something I didn't catch.

"What did Nikolaus say?" Mom asked.

"He gave me a long speech about how we've been his customers since Raine was a child, how he's watched her grow into a polite young lady and nothing will change his position. If those people want to boycott his café because of us, so be it. But what if they approach her when we aren't there? She'll be defenseless."

"Our daughter is a strong, intelligent young lady, Tristan. She can take care of herself. Besides, she never goes anywhere alone. She's always with Cora and Eirik."

I tiptoed back into my room and gently closed the door. Keeping secrets sucked. It led to nothing but conflict and unhappiness. Dad had sounded devastated and frustrated. He would feel ten times worse once he learned the truth. Poor Nikolaus. Would people really boycott his café because of me?

When Mom knocked on the door, I had reached a conclusion. "You must tell Dad the truth about this whole Valkyrie thing, Mom," I said as soon as she closed the door.

She was already shaking her head before I finish speaking. "I'll speak to your father when the time is right."

"When will that be?"

"Leave this alone, sweetie. Here." She gave me an unopened ream of printer paper.

I took the pack, but my mind was on Dad. "I hate keeping secrets from him."

Mom sighed and sat down. "This is not easy for me either. Before this, I'd never kept a secret from your father."

I blinked as realization hit me. "He knows about you?"

She nodded. "Of course. I told you Norns put us through a lot before letting us go. I had to explain to him what was happening. It took him weeks to come to terms with it. Weeks of questions, asking me to demonstrate my abilities, reading up on Norse pantheon, and more questions. He finally accepted who and what I am. He knows I come from a line of spiritually gifted women. He knew you'd follow in my footsteps and see past the rune veil. What he doesn't know is that you've managed to do so at seventeen and not eighteen like I'd told him. I need a perfect moment to tell him what happened. He's not going to like it."

"Are you worried he'll not approve of my training under Lavania?"

Mom hesitated then sighed. "Yes. But I will talk to him before you start your lessons."

"I'm starting lessons tomorrow."

Mom groaned. "Then tonight it is."

"Have you ever thought of turning him and making him immortal? I mean, he's growing old while you look the same?"

She laughed. "Yet I'm older than him by thousands of years. If I could turn him, I would have a long time ago, but the stipulations make that impossible. Luckily, I'd already told him about me before the High Council came down hard on us. Besides, at forty-five, your father has more vigor than he had when I met him."

I made a face. "Eew. Too much information, Mom."

She chuckled, got up, and dropped a kiss on my forehead. "Goodnight, sweetie. Don't stay up late. Oh, it was nice seeing Torin again," she added. "He doesn't remember me, of course, but he looks…" She sighed.

I tensed. "What's wrong with him?"

"Honestly? He looks miserable."

I sighed. No matter how much he pissed me off, I didn't want him to be miserable. "You didn't, like, try to remind him of the past, did you?"

Mom chuckled. "No. After what your father went through, I wouldn't mess with a man's head when Norns are through with him. Did you?"

I cringed and nodded.

"Oh, sweetie." Mom gripped my shoulders and shook her head. "We should have talked about this before the cruise, but you were hurting so much. Then the two weeks away was our time for healing as a family, so I put off bringing up Torin's name."

Mom always avoided unpleasantness, but there were some things you just couldn't ignore. "So what did you do to help Dad?"

"I waited for him to find his way back to me. I knew he would, and he did."

"How long did that take?"

"A couple of years. He started by going to places we'd visited, searching for me even though he had no idea what he was searching for. I was forbidden to see him or do business with him, but we were bound to meet again. The day we did, he took one look at me and knew I was the woman for him."

"Did he ever remember your previous time together?"

She nodded. "Yes. The memories trickled in slowly over the years after he fell in love with me again. They might have made him forget here," she tapped her head, "but he never forgot here," she touched her chest above her heart. "The heart always remembers."

I didn't want to wait years for Torin. A plan was already forming in my head. "Thanks, Mom."

***

"Can I get a ride to school?" I texted Eirik the next morning. "Sure."

His reaction would tell me whether I had succeeded in getting ready for one, pig-headed Valkyrie. I caught movements in his room, but he didn't come to his window. He must still be home because I didn't hear the Harley leave. When Eirik's Jeep entered our cul-de-sac, I grabbed my backpack and headed for the door.

"Wow," Eirik mouthed when he saw me, his eyes widening. When he gave me a once over and swallowed, I grinned. Nailed the look I was going for.

"Stop right here." He reached inside his Jeep for his faithful Nikon and lifted it to his face. I posed as he clicked. He lowered his camera and grinned. "You look…"

"Amazing?" The skinny jeans hugged my hips, and the push-up bra gave the already flattering green top an extra oomph. Green anything, top, dress, or eye shadow tended to bring out that particular color in my hazel eyes. My hair and makeup, the mirror had shown me, were both perfect. Knee-high boots finished my new look.

"That's a given. I meant you look like you are out to make someone suffer. When did you grow big boobs?"

"Shut up." I sashayed past him. He turned, and I could see his reflection on the Jeep's window. "And quit staring at my butt."

"What did you say about not having a plan?" He glanced over at Torin's and added softly, "Poor bastard."

"Hey, the outfit and makeup is for the people who called me a witch," I fibbed.

"Yeah, right." He slid behind the wheel and put his camera in the tray between our seats. "Looking like that, no guy will care if you're flying around on a broom, cackling. The girls will only hate you more."

I didn't care. I was only interested in the reaction of one guy. Torin's garage door lifted and my heart picked up tempo, but it was Andris backing out their SUV. He looked at us as though we were stinky aliens invading his personal planet. He wasn't going to spoil my good mood. I grinned and waved. His expression didn't change.

"What's his problem?" Eirik asked.

"Don't mind him. He thinks you and I are dating again."

"Why is it any of his business who you date?"

"Last night he asked me why I'm not with Torin. I told him we decided to go our separate ways. He thinks I gave up on Torin too easily."

Eirik chuckled. "I guess he hasn't seen your outfit. I assume the plan is to make Torin drool and follow you around like a besotted idiot."

Eirik got it right. I want Torin to notice me. Not take his eyes off me. Think about me. Maybe even fall in love with me again. He wasn't the drooling type, but a girl could hope. I sighed.

"What's wrong?" Eirik asked.

There was no way I'd share my thoughts, so I repeated what Mom had told me about her experience with Dad and his erased memories. "Reminding Torin of our past will only screw with his head. Can you imagine people telling you about things you did together but you can't remember? I'd go nuts trying to remember."

"I wouldn't. I like to be hit right, left, and center with the truth."

"Yeah, I tried that, but it got me nowhere." Eirik went silent as though thinking about what I'd just said, and then he grinned.

"Whatever you're planning, don't do it," I said.

"He stole you from me."

"He did not."

"From where I'm standing, he's a girlfriend stealing a-hole who deserves everything that comes to him."

I sighed, not sure whether he really meant it or was only kidding. I studied his profile. "Just leave him alone, Eirik. Okay? For me. Please."

He elbowed me and laughed. "Gotcha! I still haven't lost my touch."

I elbowed him back. "Jerk."

"Seriously, he's off the hook for now, but if he hurts you, I will rearrange his face."

Torin already hurt me, but it was up to me to deal with him. "Anywhere but his face."

Eirik looked at me with disgust. "Change of topic. Do not tell Cora about me."

I hadn't planned to, but I couldn't help giving him a hard time. "Why not? She'll absolutely want to make out with you once she learns you're a deity."

"Don't." His hands tightened around the steering wheel.

"I was only teasing."

"It pisses me off every time I think about them. What kind of grandparents listen to crones and dump their grandchild in another realm? I might have cousins I've never seen. Uncles and aunts. Missed out on family gatherings." He glared ahead and only stopped when I rubbed his shoulder. "You know what? Screw them. My family is here. People who've been there for me since..."

He ranted against his absent family for the rest of the drive. He kept going back and forth, so I wasn't sure whether he wanted to meet them or not. Anger and a sense of betrayal laced his words, just like yesterday. His angst wasn't lessening. Usually he was so easygoing.

When we entered Riverside Boulevard, he stopped, sighed, and added, "Remember, ease up on the D word."

"Aye, aye, ex-boyfriend-now-officially-my-big-brother."

He snorted. "That sounded awful. There she is." He pulled into the parking lot and sure enough, Cora was standing by her car waiting for us. She waved. "Not a word," Eirik reminded me.

I pretended to zip my mouth.

"Is it true...? Whoa," Cora squealed. "What did you do with my best friend? You know the one who never wears makeup to school." She touched my hair. "I'm so loving your hair like this, and your makeup is flawless." She pressed the side of my breasts and shamelessly sized them. "God bless PUBS," she added, using her abbreviation for push-up bras.

"What are PUBS?" Eirik asked.

She laughed and threw him a naughty grin over her shoulder. "Women's most guarded secret." She faced me, her smile dimming. "Is it true someone vandalized your car?"

"Yes." I retrieved my backpack from the backseat. "They wrote *Die, Witch, Die*. Who told you?"

"Kicker. Argh, people can be such tools. You need to get even, Raine. Get mean. This," she waved to indicate my makeover, "is great, but it will only work on guys."

"What do you suggest I do?"

Cora shrugged. "I don't know. Something that will scare the beegeebees out of everyone. Where's your car now?"

"At home."

"See? You didn't drive because of them. You're giving them too much power. And you," she leveled Eirik with a look, "why weren't you at swimming yesterday?"

"Ooh, you missed me?" He wiggled his eyebrows.

She threw me a quick glance, her cheeks growing pink. "No, but Doc asked about you. Where were you?"

"At Raine's."

Light dimmed in Cora's eyes, and I wanted to kick Eirik. How could he be so blind? He should have realized by now Cora only attended swim practice to watch him. We walked in silence, but it was strained. Eirik appeared oblivious. Cora kept glancing at him from the corner of her eyes.

"Why didn't you tell me you guys were hanging out?" she finally asked, hurt in her voice.

"We weren't," I answered quickly before Eirik could open his mouth and make things worse. "Eirik stopped by for just a few minutes, raided my fridge, and left. Actually, I was talking to Lavania, who'd stopped by for a visit, when he interrupted us. He was so rude to her."

Eirik snorted. "That was me being polite."

"I don't understand why you don't like her," Cora said, sounding chipper. "Oh, I asked Doc if I can rejoin the team."

"That's great," Eirik said. "What did he say?"

"I'm in, but I can't compete at the upcoming meet. Kicker also rejoined, and she convinced Lexi…"

Completely lost in their little world, I gave them space and lagged behind. They looked so cute together. The sound of Torin's Harley reached me before I entered the building, but I refused to look back. It wasn't easy.

Inside, students stood in groups, chatting. One by one, they nudged or whispered to their friends, and a wave of silence swept across the hall. Stares followed us. I didn't make eye contact, but the vibes were different from yesterday. Eirik and Cora noticed, slowed down, and flanked me, Cora to my left and Eirik to my right.

He paused, bowed, and waved. "Thank you. No photographs or comments. You guys are too kind. You don't have to, but thanks."

Cora giggled. Even I fought a smile. He was such a goofball. Once we left the hall, he disappeared toward his locker while Cora and I headed to ours. We both stopped when our lockers came into view.

Someone had scribbled in red lipstick, *Witches! Burn! Burn! Burn!* This time, the ugliness touched Cora.

"I'm so sorry," I whispered.

"It's not your fault." She turned and glared at the students watching us. "Who is the loser behind this? Show your face, you coward."

I gripped Cora's hand. "Don't. This is about me, not you." I turned and studied the faces of the students watching us. Some looked down. Others stared back with uneasy smiles. "I'm not explaining myself to anybody. You want to burn me? Come and get me. But don't you dare hurt someone who's done nothing but stand by my side. That's what friendship is about, something most of you wouldn't understand. You mess with her," I pointed at Cora, "and I'm coming after you with everything I've got."

The students scrambled to get as far away from me as humanly possible. Grimacing, I turned to face my locker, and my eyes met with Torin's. The grin died from my lips. How long had he been standing there? Cora threw her arms around me.

"I love you, Lorraine Cooper," she said in a trembling voice.

I chuckled. Her tear glands were connected to her emotions. "Love you too, Cora Jemison."

She squeezed me hard. At the other side of the hallway, Torin watched us. I ignored him. Cora finally let me go, stepped back, and wiped her wet cheeks. We turned and studied our defaced lockers.

"I have a box of tissue for cleaning up," she said, punching in her locker combination.

"No. Let's show them exactly how we feel."

"Yes, let's." Then she made a face and added, "How do we feel?"

"We don't care what they think." We put our backpacks away and collected our folders and books. After we agreed to meet during lunch, I took off toward the math floor while she headed to the English building.

"Wait up, Raine," Eirik called from behind me. I pressed against the wall and waited for him to catch up. He made sure he placed himself between me and the students rushing past us.

"Shouldn't you be going in the opposite direction?" I asked.

"Why?"

"A certain perky blonde would love to be escorted to her class." He blinked. "Cora?"

I chuckled. "Why would you think I'm talking about her?"

His cheeks grew pink. "Lucky guess."

"Admit it. You like her."

He snorted. "She's snarky and gets bored with guys too easily. I wouldn't want to be her next victim. Besides, I have a new motto. No Mortals."

"Of course. Too bad. I think she likes you, too." I started upstairs. After a few steps, I realized he hadn't moved. I glanced back and grinned at his stupefied expression. "Coming?"

"You're screwing with my head," he said, hurrying to catch up.

I'd just planted the seed. "Nope. Thanks for the escort."

"My class is on this floor," he reminded me, but he wore a preoccupied expression. "How do you know?"

"How do I know what?" I said, faking ignorance.

"That she likes me."

"I just do. Call it a woman's intuition. Later." I watched him walk away and grinned when a group of girls tried to attract his attention and he walked right past them without noticing. Playing Cupid was fun.

The first person I noticed when I entered the class was Torin talking to two jocks—Drew Cavanaugh and Keith Paulson. One sat on my chair, the other on my desk. They were laughing and high-fiving each other.

Torin glanced up as though he felt my presence. My chin shot up, and I tucked my hair behind my ear, my fingers grazing the titanium screws under my scalp. I started to tug my hair to hide the patch then remembered I had cleverly hidden the shorter strands when I'd curled my hair this morning.

Half of the students were already seated, but their stares didn't bother me. I was too conscious of Torin's. He had this weird ability to completely grab my attention, making everyone and everything else insignificant. As though his friends realized they no longer had his undivided attention, they followed his gaze and found me.

My heart pounded harder the closer I got to them. Keith said something to Torin, but he didn't respond. Drew did. I didn't care what they were saying. The admiration in their eyes was all I needed to see. Cora was right. Men were easy. Glam up a little bit and you had them.

"Hey. Um, you are sitting in my chair, Keith."

"I am? Sorry." He scrambled to his feet, wiped the chair as though he'd dirtied it, and stood back. "It's Raine, right?"

"Right." I sat and put the books and folder on my lap.

"I've seen you during home games," he added. "You play in the band."

"Yes, I do." Drew still hadn't moved from my desk, which gave him a very nice angle to ogle my chest. On a normal day I would have cringed. Today, I was celebrating my curves and hoped a certain Valkyrie notice them. "Can I have my desk back, Drew?"

His grin broadened. "You know my name."

I giggled, which was something I loathed. *The things I do for you, Torin St. James.* "Like Keith said, I play in the band, and you guys are stars on the field." They grinned and puffed their chests. Seriously, guys were beyond easy. I didn't dare look at Torin yet. He hadn't spoken, though I felt his eyes on me. "So when is the next game?"

"Friday night in Portland," Keith said.

"Will you be there?" Drew asked.

I wasn't too crazy about football, but they didn't need to know that. I gave them a playful smile. "Will you guys win?"

They both nodded.

"Then I might consider it."

"Guys," Torin cut in and pointed at the door. "Go."

The two jocks protested, but something in Torin's eyes had them moving. Still, they kept whispering and glancing back and almost bumped into two girls in the doorway.

"Idiots," Torin mumbled, but I pretended not to hear him. I could feel his eyes on me. After a few minutes, I had to know, so I turned.

"What?" I asked with feigned annoyance.

Something flashed in his eyes, but he didn't speak.

"Uh, you do know it's considered rude to stare," I added, starting to feel hot.

He shrugged. "So?"

"So, do you mind?"

His eyebrows shot up. "I'm trying to figure you out, Raine Copper. Do you always go around threatening the entire school to protect your friend?"

I pretended to think about it. "At least once before the first bell."

He laughed, and Lavania, who'd been talking to some guys, turned and looked at us with narrowed eyes. I pretended not to notice. Instead, I stared into Torin's blue eyes and pretended our relationship wasn't over, that he wasn't a jerk, my silly heart pounding hard like the hooves of a racing horse.

"Whoever wrote on your locker will not stop just because you refused to clean it."

I shrugged. "Why should we clean them? We didn't put them there."

"They don't bother you?"

Big time. "No. Everyone deserves to be notorious once in their lifetime. This is my moment."

He snorted. "Liar."

I hated that he could read me so well. "Not. You can't force people to act the way you want them to, so why bother?"

He stopped smiling, and I'd bet he assumed I was talking about him. Poor guy. He had no idea he was the exception to the rule. I planned to force him to see things my way.

7. FIRST LESSONS

Nervous energy twisted my stomach into a knot as I made my way to my first lesson that evening. What if Torin was right and I didn't need to become a Valkyrie to stop the Norns from coming after me? I hated that he'd planted the seed of doubt in my head. Training was the right thing to do. I had to get the Norns off my back, find out why Eirik was in danger, and help him. Then there was Torin. I refused to give up on him no matter what he'd said.

Lavania, dressed in a caftan-like white dress, opened the door with a broad smile. "Come in. This is exciting, isn't it?"

Yeah, like a visit to the dentist.

"What did the doctor say?" she asked.

For a moment I drew a blank. Then I remembered I'd told her about my appointment with my doctor. "He sent me to see a physical therapist, but my head's healed."

I glanced around curiously. Except for the night he'd thrown a party, Torin hadn't tried to furnish the living room. One brown leather sofa and a coffee table had been it. The night of party, he'd gone all out. Large TV screen like you see at clubs, audio system with sick output, and couches galore. Now, the room was done conservatively in white and grays with framed nature pictures on the wall. An attention-grabbing aquarium took up an entire wall. Myriad fake coral in the tank added splashes of color to the stark room. The house was quiet, the music I'd heard earlier turned off.

"Where is everyone?" I asked.

"Torin is at football practice, and Andris and Ingrid are reaping."

"How does that work? I mean they're at school most of the time and people are dying."

She chuckled. "They do their share of reaping, and there are thousands of Valkyries around the world. Don't forget healthy people die at a much lower rate than those dying of illness or old age. Hel's reapers tend to be busier than our Valkyries. Come on."

She lifted the hem of her dress and kicked off her sandals. Instead of sitting on a chair, she curled up on the plush white rug and pointed at the other end of the table. "Sit, please."

I toed off my shoes, left my socks on, slipped my cell phone into my back pocket, and joined her. On the table was a pitcher of water and two glasses. There were no books, no writing materials, nothing. The coils in my stomach tightened a bit. I gave Lavania a tiny smile.

"You're nervous," she said.

"A little."

Lavania frowned. "Why?"

I couldn't tell her the truth. That Torin had tried to talk me out of training and it was messing with my head.

She reached for my hand and sandwiched it with hers. "It's okay to be scared. This is a big moment."

I nodded. "Can I be honest?"

"Always." She let go of my hand, leaned back against the couch behind her, and wrapped her arms around one bent knee.

"What if I'm not supposed to be a Valkyrie?"

She frowned. "Who's making you doubt your destiny? Your mom? Your dad?"

"No." I poured water in a glass and guzzled some of it. "I'm just concerned. What if it's not my destiny?"

She smiled. "Maybe it is, maybe it's not. That's for you to decide. Being chosen to become such a powerful being can be overwhelming, and it's normal to have doubts. Back in Valhalla, we often discuss our first encounter." She paused to pour water into a glass and took a sip. "It didn't matter what our trainers called themselves—high priestess, shaman, medicine woman, diviner, spirit-medium, oracle, sibyl, or more ethnic terms like *machi, sangoma, eem, babaylan,* and *mae de santo*—learning who we would become, the power we would wield was scary. Do you know why all Valkyries were women for millennia before men joined us?"

"Men went to war, so the gods needed women to collect their souls and lead them to Valhalla and Falkvang. You only started recruiting men when women became warriors."

Lavania laughed. "Which one of my boys told you that?"

My boys? "Torin."

She chuckled. "I'm afraid that's my fault. I had to tell them something when I chose them."

"When you chose... You trained Torin?"

She smiled. "Yes and countless other girls and boys after him, including Andris."

"You were the angel in the field during the crusade?"

Her smile disappeared. "When did you and Torin discuss how I turned him?"

Warmth spread to my cheeks. "I, uh, overheard him talking to Andris and Ingrid about their first encounters," I lied and hoped my face wasn't as red as it felt.

Lavania smiled, a far away look entering her eyes. "For weeks I watched him fight, interact with the wounded, his fellow warriors, his brother. He had an essence I couldn't ignore, and I had to have him. It wasn't easy telling him, or others after him, that he was spiritual and more in tune with nature and the cosmos than any young man I'd ever met. Women have always been more spiritual than men, more accepting of their gifts, and that's why most Valkyries were women for a long time. Occasionally, we get lucky and find a man."

"Andris is spiritual?"

She chuckled. "Don't underestimate my youngest. He might be impulsive, but he feels things a lot deeper. He just covers it with smirks and shenanigans. If I'd had more time, I would have guided him more. He definitely needed it. Most of the mistakes he's made could have been avoided. Torin, on the other hand, always does the right thing." A thoughtful expression crossed her face. "Sometimes I wish he didn't."

Even though he'd refused to make me immortal, he had tried to fight his feelings for me and failed. So he'd bent a few rules. Sometimes I wished he was more like Andris. No, that wasn't true. I loved that he'd bent the rules just for me.

Lavania was still talking. It was surreal hearing her talk about Torin and Andris as a mother would when she looked around our age. How could she have an affair with Torin if he was like a son to her?

She smiled and sipped her water. "In my day, one started out as a healer, learning herbology and divination. When the high priestess saw that you had talent, she chose you to be her protégé. After more private training, you became a priestess and finally a high priestess like her. Only a select few were chosen to become Immortal. It was a higher calling, an honor."

"When does one become a Valkyrie?"

"Once you can convince a soul to leave with you."

I blinked. "What?"

"You think you just stand there and they get up and join you? People don't like being dead, especially young, healthy ones. They will insist they have unfinished business, beg for more time, try to bargain with you. When that fails, they get angry and run. Where do you think ghosts come from? Silly souls who don't want to leave with Valkyries. It is a lot easier to reap the sick and the elderly than people in their prime."

"What about children?"

"Their souls are recycled, taken to a special hall run by Norns. It's their job to find new bodies for them, which is why they're always visiting hospitals. Ask Torin about it. Of all my children, he's the only one with the patience to reap children. I tried it once and hated it. They reminded me too much of my brothers and sisters and how I felt leaving them."

"Where did you grow up?"

"Rome. I was a Vestal Virgin."

"Vestal what?"

"Oh, honey, you have a lot to learn. Unlike other cultures and civilizations, where male high priests hoarded power and locked out women, high priestesses in the Roman Empire were revered. We had temples in every major city of the empire. They called us Vestals or Vestal Virgins because we served Vesta, the goddess of hearth, home, and family. But Vesta has been called by many names in different cultures. She's the Greeks' Hestia, the Celtics' Brighid, ancient Egyptians' Isis, the Ashanti's *Asasa Ya*, the Yoruba's *Yemaya*, Babylonians' Ishtar, Mayans' *Ixchel*, and so on. In Valhalla, she's Frigg, Odin's wife. My best friend is Celtic. She told me that her people also openly celebrated the power of their high priestesses. The Druids, as their priests and priestesses were called, were just as powerful as the Vestals. Still, the transition to Immortals and finally Valkyrie was a well-kept secret throughout the world, no matter how advanced the civilization." She smiled.

I was caught in her narration and got impatient when she paused to pour more water into her glass. My cell phone buzzed. I pulled it out impatiently, saw that the text came from Cora, and turned the power off without responding.

"I find that instrument amazing," she said, staring at my cell phone. "The advances Mortals have made..."

Was she seriously discussing something mundane like modern technology now? I needed to hear more. I waited impatiently for her to stop gushing over my smart phone. "Why are there no more high priests and high priestesses?"

She sighed. "They are, but newer religions have emerged, and anyone following the gods is considered a pagan. Premonitions, spells, and charms are now considered ridiculous and the practice demonized. It started with "witch trials" and burning high priestesses across Europe, the destruction of the Wu in Mandarin, stumping out the Women's Mysteries in Rome, and so on. Yes, we've gone underground, but we're still recruiting."

We were still talking when Torin arrived home. My heart started its crazy rickety dance, and my mouth went dry. His hair was wet, probably from showering at the gym after practice. I wanted to run my fingers through it. Play with the wet strands. He also had a shadow on his chin, which made him look sexier than usual. Our eyes met, and my breath caught. His eyes had darkened to the color of stormy ocean water. What was he thinking? Did he miss me even a tiny bit?

"How was practice?" Lavania asked in an upbeat voice.

He dragged his eyes from mine, mumbled something unintelligible, and continued across the room into the kitchen. I stared after him, my heart aching.

Lavania shook her head. "I apologize for his rudeness. I don't know what's gotten into him lately. He's been such a grouch since I got here, and he's only getting worse."

I hoped I was the one who'd gotten into him, despite the crap he'd spewed yesterday. In the kitchen, Torin opened the fridge and got bottled water. Suddenly he looked up, snaring my gaze. I expected him to smile or give me a mock salute. Instead, he twisted the lid off the bottle and chugged.

How could he make something as simple and mundane as drinking water look so sexy? Maybe it was the way he tilted his head. He wiped his lips with the back of his hand and disappeared inside the fridge again. Lavania's voice reached me as though from afar and forced me to focus on what she was saying.

"We'll try to cover backgrounds on Immortals, Valkyries, and the major deities this week. Next week, we'll start on runes. Since the Norns are back already, I'll see what I can do to speed up your education."

I heard her, but my gaze kept drifting to the gorgeous hunk in the kitchen. He placed bread, peanut butter, and jelly on the counter. His movement fast and efficient, he made a couple of sandwiches, grabbed a stool, sat, and starting munching, his eyes returning to me, completely distracting me and screwing with my lesson. I bet it was deliberate, too.

"...stop now," I heard Lavania say. "You're too distracted."

Heat warmed my cheeks. "I, uh, yes. I promised my parents I'd be home by seven." I glanced at my watch. It was a quarter past.

"We can continue tomorrow at the same time."

In the other room, Torin smirked, looking pleased with himself and confirming what I'd suspected all along. He'd deliberately distracted me. "Could we start earlier tomorrow?"

Lavania's eyes narrowed. "How early?"

"Four o'clock, so we can be done earlier."

"Okay." Lavania escorted me to the door. I stole a glance at Torin behind her back and caught him scowling. He knew exactly what the time change meant. I'd be done by six, way before he came home from practice.

I threw him a triumphant grin. His eyes narrowed, his expression annoyed.

Score!

Smiling, I crossed the lawn to our house.

***

The next day, Drew and Keith were by my math class door talking to some girls. By the time I reached them, the girls were gone. A quick glance inside the classroom told me Torin wasn't at his desk.

"I'm throwing a Halloween party next week. Want to come?" Drew asked.

"Maybe." Cora, Eirik, and I had a weird Halloween tradition. We went treat-or-treating together then poured all our candy on the bed and traded pieces. Trading was the fun part. "Can my friends come, too?"

"If one of them is Cora, then yes," Drew said and smirked.

Before I could respond, a telltale shiver rushed under my skin. Torin.

"What are you three plotting," he asked from behind me. He was so close I could feel the heat from his body. Did he have to stand that close? I'd bet it was deliberate.

I took a deep breath before glancing at him, which was a mistake on so many levels. His scent, earthy and masculine, filled my nostrils, and my traitorous body responded. I wanted to wrap myself around him like a pretzel, bury my face in his neck and just soak him in. He looked so good in a dark-blue shirt under his leather jacket, which made his eyes pop. He hadn't shaved again, but I wasn't complaining. The shadow on his chin made him look even yummier.

"Cat got your tongue?" he teased.

"No. It's still here." I stuck out my tongue.

His eyes drifted to my lips. My mount went dry, my heart picking up tempo. When our gazes met, I blinked. How could he claim he didn't want me yet look at me with such heat? I wanted to kick him or yell at him then kiss him senseless.

"We're discussing my Halloween party," Drew said.

"You're coming, St. James, right?" Keith said.

Torin didn't even look at them, his hot gaze on my face. "Are you going?"

His voice was velvet soft, making me want to purr. I had to swallow before answering. "Yes. Are you?"

"Aren't you too busy to be partying?" he asked sharply, disapproval on his face.

Just like that, he destroyed my romantic thoughts. I shot him a mean smile.

"For Drew and Keith," I hugged the two jocks' arms. "I'll make time. So are you going?"

"I don't do Halloween." He smirked and sauntered past me.

"Chicken," I retorted.

He stopped and turned. The glint that entered his eyes should have warned me he was about to do something I wouldn't like. He took a step that brought him closer. My first instinct was to walk away. Run. Say something. But the terrier in me was wagging its tail. His hand slipped around my waist and nudged me closer. My breath hitched. He grinned, liking my response. I stopped breathing altogether when our bodies touched. He felt so good, all muscles, heat, and pure temptation.

"Chicken? Me?" he mocked, his head dipping slowly, eyes daring me to, I don't know, repeat what I'd said, stop him?

I wanted to say something snarky, but my mouth was too dry. When his nose gently brushed mine, I moaned. He was going to kiss me. Yes! My lips parted in anticipation.

"You don't want to play games with me, Freckles. I always win. Always." Cold air rushed in to replace him as he moved away. He slapped Drew on the back. "Have fun, guys."

I glared at his retreating back, my sense still humming, my heart pounding and lips tingling. Oh, he was so... so Torin. Bold. Sexy. Irresistible. The worst part was he knew it. He glanced back and winked.

"What's up with you two?" Keith asked, his eyes on Torin.

I shrugged, feeling deflated. I was supposed to be yanking *his* buttons, not the other way round. "Nothing."

But I didn't fool Drew and Keith. The two of them and a friend sat at our table during lunch. Cora didn't seem to care. She was buddies with most of the football players because of her vlog. Eirik wasn't too pleased, especially when Drew started flirting with Cora. Across the cafeteria, Torin didn't miss a thing that happened at our table. Keith was the first to notice the way Torin kept staring at me during lunch.

"Nothing?" he teased. I just shrugged.

For the rest of week, Torin kept his distance. He became a distracting presence at the back of my math and history classes. The way he watched me didn't indicate he was miserable. No, he was plotting something. I saw it in his eyes and in the slow smiles he gave me whenever our eyes met.

Things were definitely not going according to plan. He was supposed to be consumed by jealousy. Instead, I was the one who wanted to gouge out the eyes of the cheerleaders flocking around him like pampered exotic birds. My senses were tuned in to his presence, his voice, his scent. A storm of desire brewed in my soul whenever he was around. When he spoke, his voice resonated through me, sending shivers up my spine, reminding me of what we once had. No matter how hard I tried to harden my heart, it still skipped for him. No matter how often I told myself I didn't care about the cheerleaders, it still hurt. And no matter how often I caught him watching me, it didn't ease my frustration. I wished he wasn't under my skin, in my heart, imbedded deep in my soul. Ignoring him or pretending he didn't matter was like saying I didn't need air.

At home, I divided my time between lessons with Lavania and working on my homework packets. When Torin had said he'd stay out of my way when I went to his house, he hadn't been kidding. He came home after seven even though my lessons ended at six. He no longer came to his window and looked at my house.

And I hated it.

***

Eirik and Cora were by his Jeep when I pulled up outside school on Friday. They looked cute together. Or maybe not. They stood close to each other, but weren't holding hands or talking. Tension hung thick in the air. Things weren't going as well between them as I'd hoped.

I hugged Cora then Eirik. He had shadows under his eyes.

"You look like crap," I said.

"Gee, thanks. Can we go now?" he added in an annoyed voice and started for the school building. Cora and I looked at each other and followed.

Cora sighed. "Ask him what's wrong. He won't talk to me."

The two of them went to swim practice together and no longer butted heads, so I'd just assumed everything was great between them. "You guys have a two-day meet coming up, right?"

"You think he's worried about that?"

I shrugged. I'd noticed how tired he looked lately. Even in the mornings. "Maybe or maybe it's something else. He can be stubborn, so just keep pushing until you wear him down."

"I've tried. Short of dancing naked with a big sign that says 'Talk to me, Eirik,' he'll just ignore me."

"You know I can hear you," Eirik mumbled.

"Yeah, we know," Cora said. "Maybe I'll vlog about it and see what my followers come up with. I'll bump Torin to next week after the game."

Eirik stopped and glared. "You vlog about me and I'll... I'll..."

"What? Stop talking to me? You haven't said a word to me in three days. In fact, you've made a point of not talking to me or returning my texts. At least Raine has an excuse for not wanting to hang out. She has to finish her homework packets."

Eirik gripped the strap of his backpack and glowered. "I'm busy, too."

"Doing what?" she asked. Eirik made a face. "I guess that means you're not going to the game tonight."

"You got that right," Eirik retorted.

He was being a total douche. I wondered what happened. I didn't dare ask around Cora in case it was deity/Norn related.

"Come with us, Raine. A bunch of us from the swim team are going together, and they won't mind if you join us," Cora said.

Yeah, right. None of the swim team members had talked to me since I returned, which meant I was still a *persona non-grata*. I made a sad face. "I'd love to, but I still have a pile of homework to finish." I glanced at Eirik. "You should go, Eirik. Think of all the pictures you'll take for the newspaper."

"It's the new QB's first game, and we're all dying to see how he performs," Cora added. "I've watched him during practice. He's amazing."

"Of course you'd think that." Eirik took off toward the school's entrance.

Cora watched him go with a frustrated expression. "What did I say?"

Was I ever this clueless about guys? I took Cora's arm. "You mentioned Torin."

"So?"

"So you've always…" Then I remembered Cora couldn't remember how she'd gushed over Torin's looks.

"I've always what?" she asked.

"Openly drooled over hot guys."

She made a face. "No crime in that. What's your point?"

I sighed. She was hopeless. "It bugs Eirik when you do that."

Her grin broadened. "It does?"

"Oh, you two are so annoying. Did he tell you he and I are officially no longer dating?"

Cora stopped. "No."

"With everything that went down and my trip, we've sort of drifted apart. We discussed it on Monday night. That's why he was at my place. We agreed we're better off as friends, honorary sister and brother."

Cora frowned. "He hasn't said anything."

"You know how he clams up sometimes. Now you can go for it."

Cora glanced at me in confusion. "Go for what?"

"Eirik. Why do you think he took off in a huff just now? You were talking about Torin, and he was jealous."

"Yeah, right," she retorted.

"For someone who claims to know guys, you sure are clueless about him."

A we entered the school, she became quiet and chewed on her lower lip. "I don't think it's cool to hook up with your best friend's ex."

I rolled my eyes. "Cora, we kissed. We never even made it to second base."

She made a face. "Spare me the details." Then she threw me a glance from the corner of her eyes. "Never made it to second base?"

"Nope." She shot me a skeptical look. "Don't think I didn't want to. I wanted plenty, but something always stopped *him*. I guess he wasn't feeling me as much as I was feeling him." *Oh, the lies we weave.* But the relief in Cora's eyes said I'd used the magic words.

"You really don't mind."

I shook my head. "Nope. Besides, I've always suspected he was into you."

Cora became quiet as we crossed the hall. I met wary glances from the other students in the hall. They no longer gawked, though I still got uneasy smiles whenever I came too close. I made a decision to not let them bother me. Even whoever had defaced our lockers had stopped.

We walked past Lavania, Andris, and Ingrid. Lavania waved and smiled. Ingrid ignored me as usual. Whenever I went to their house for lessons, she stayed in her room. Andris, on the other hand, still gave me looks like I was a slug.

"I can't stand that guy," Cora said, staring pointedly at Andris.

"Why?"

"He's so stuck up and so is his sister."

I laughed. "Ingrid and Andris are not related. Ingrid is kind of lost because she misses her sister, and Andris is… Andris."

Cora frowned. "How do you know so much about them?"

Oops, I'd completely forgotten that to Cora, I'd only known the Valkyries for a week. "We're neighbors, duh."

"So what can you tell me about Torin?" she asked, her eyes narrowing. Something in her expression sent heat up my face.

"Nothing. He's one of them."

"So how come he stares at you a lot?"

My face grew hotter. "He doesn't."

"Even his harem noticed."

"His harem?"

"The cheerbitches who… Oh my. Look."

I thought she was talking about Torin at first, until I turned and saw that she meant our lockers. Someone had used a plastic jump rope to create two nooses and looped them around the locks on my locker and Cora's. I was so looking forward to mastering the powers of runes just so I could trap whoever was doing this.

Students scurried past us pretending not to see the nooses. Others gave us side-glances as though waiting to see what we'd do. I yanked them and threw them down.

"I thought the loser doing this stopped," Cora said sighing.

"The security around here sucks," I muttered. "They should have cameras monitoring the halls twenty-four-seven."

I didn't notice Eirik had joined us until he picked up the rope from the floor. He lifted it and cocked his brow at someone behind me. When he made a face and shook his head, I followed his gaze to see who he was eye-talking to. Torin stood at the end of the hallway. As soon as he realized they had my attention, he turned and walked away.

"What's going on?" I asked, my eyes studying Eirik's face for signs of lying.

"Later," he mouthed and inclined his head toward Cora, who was still venting. Since Eirik couldn't talk, that left Torin. I opened my locker, put away my backpack and oboe, selected my books, and took off after him.

"Torin, wait up."

He kept walking.

"Torin St. James," I called out.

He continued to ignore me.

Getting ticked off, I got creative. "Mean ol' Valkyrie."

His feet faltered, but he didn't stop.

"Anyone want to meet a real live soul reaper?" Students stared at me like I'd lost my marbles, nothing new there, but he stopped and turned to study me with a long-suffering expression. I grinned.

"Was that really necessary?" he asked.

"You stopped, didn't you? What was that about?"

He cocked his eyebrows. "What was what about?"

"You and Eirik. When did you make a love connection?"

He smirked. "I don't do guys. I'm purely into chicks."

I narrowed my eyes. "You know what I mean. What's going on? What are you two hatching?"

"Do you know your eyes change color when you're angry?"

Sidetracked, I stared at him, remembering the first time he'd said those words to me. He'd wrapped me in a sensual haze, and we would have kissed if it hadn't been for our neighbor. My eyes went to his lips, and I caught his grin.

Argh, when did I become so easy. He'd deliberately distracted me. Again.

"Stop messing with my head, Torin. I want to know what's going on."

Before he could answer, several jocks, including Drew and Keith, joined us. The game in Portland was later that evening, and they were hyped.

"Guys, you know Raine, right?" Drew said, dropping an arm around my shoulders.

"The smoking hot witch," Jaden Granger said and leered. "Feel free to bewitch me anytime."

I never liked Jaden. He was the kiss-and-tell kind of guy, and he had greasy hair. Sadly, some girls found him irresistible.

"Can you use your witchy powers," he wiggled his fingers, "to see if we're going to win tonight?"

Annoyance zipped through me. "No, I can't predict something like that, but if he," I pointed at Torin, "comes through, you will win or die, uh, trying."

Torin shot me an annoyed look. "Excuse us." He grabbed my hand and tugged. "Come with me."

"But I was enjoying their company," I protested half-heartedly.

"No, you are acting like a brat."

Ouch. That stung. "Thanks for the compliment, knucklehead."

He chuckled.

"I've been meaning to ask you something. Who are you escorting to Valhalla among the players? Keith? Drew? Both of them?" He's been spending a lot of time with the two players, just like he'd done with Jessie and her friends, and they all had died.

"None of them is going to Valhalla." He opened a door and pulled me inside.

It was dark, but not for long. He flipped a switch, and I looked around. We were in a broom closet. Not just any broom closet. It was *the* make-out broom closet students often used because it was roomy and Officer Randolph rarely checked it for some reason. I grinned, remembering the last time Torin and I had been in here.

"What?" he asked, eyes narrowed.

"This brings back memories. You do know that by lunchtime, everyone will know you and I were in the make-out closet."

He frowned. "You've made out with some guy in this closet."

He sounded annoyed. I gave him a toothy grin. The only time I'd ever used the closet was with him. "We didn't make out. We closed a deal."

He made a face like he'd swallowed a rotten egg and opened the door, almost bumping into his friends, who had either been eavesdropping on us or keeping a lookout.

"Do you guys mind?" Torin snapped, and the jocks walked away laughing. He started for class, but I was right behind him.

"You never answered my question about you and Eirik," I said.

"I will during lunch. I also have a solution to your witch problem."

That threw me off. "You do?"

"Meet me in the hall at lunchtime. We'll go somewhere and discuss it."

Too shocked, I could only stare at him. For most of the week he'd played cat and mouse with me and now he wanted to do lunch? "No, I'll pass."

"No, you won't. If you need my help, you eat lunch with me. I hate eating—"

"Alone," I finished, forgetting I'd decided to stop bringing up the past. Instead of a frown, he grinned and sauntered into the classroom. I stared after him, wishing I could figure him out. He was so unpredictable.

8. EVERYONE NEEDS LOVE

Torin was waiting when I reached the front hall during lunch. "You really have a solution?"

"Yep." He led the way to his Harley. "You're not going to ask where we're going?"

"Should I? You're not kidnapping me, are you?"

He chuckled. "If I wanted to kidnap you, you'd be in my bedroom in a matter of seconds."

Kidnap me already, I wanted to say.

"Look around. If you haven't noticed, we're being watched."

I turned and sure enough, students watched us through the glass windows. The ones hurrying to their cars also turned and stared. "Is this your grand plan to make me less witchy? Being seen with the new QB?"

He waved at someone. "Brilliant, isn't it?"

I rolled my eyes. "Sure, except you haven't won a game yet."

"We will tonight." He said it like it was a done deal and stepped closer with the helmet. I stepped back and stuck out my hand. He stared at my hand then my face. "I was just going to help you with it."

"I know, but I'd rather you didn't." I took the helmet, put it on, and snapped the strap while he scowled and studied me as though something bothered him. "What?"

"You're a prickly little thing, aren't you?"

"Quit with calling me little. I'm five-seven. And being cautious doesn't make me… prickly," I finished weakly when he reached out and tucked a stray hair out of the way, catching me by surprise. His eyes not leaving mine, his hand lingered on my nape. I shivered, and I allowed myself to forget how horrible the last few days have been. I welcomed his touch and got lost in his gorgeous, blue eyes.

He touched my nose. "I love your freckles."

Reality returned and I stepped back. "Don't do that."

"Do what?"

"Everything. No tucking my hair. No compliments. And absolutely no looking at me like you just did."

"Like what?"

"Like you did a few seconds ago." A wicked grin curled his lips. "And you're not allowed to smile at me like that either. Let's go before I change my mind."

He shook his head then slipped on his wraparound sunglasses. "You're the most contrary girl I've ever met."

I gave him a beaming smile. "Thank you."

"It wasn't a compliment. Replace contrary with annoying."

"That's a compliment in my book." I straddled the bike and wrapped my arms around his waist. At last. Holding him felt wonderful, like coming home. I lay my head against his back and inhaled. I'd missed this. The feel of him. His scent. His warmth. He took off at normal speed, which told me we weren't going far. The ride was over too soon.

"Are you asleep back there, Freckles?"

"No. I love riding with you. It feels like fly—" My face warming, I let him go, got up, and stepped away from the bike. "Let's go. I'm starving."

Torin removed his sunglasses and studied me with narrowed eyes. "You love riding with me?"

"You, my ex... I told you my ex had a bike too, right?" I didn't dare look at his face to confirm if he'd bought my lame explanation. I focused on the restaurant instead. "Noodles & Company?"

"I love their pasta, but if you want to go somewhere else just say the word."

"No, it's okay. I love their salads." He held the door for me and followed me inside.

The restaurant was packed with businessmen and women sprinkled with a few stay-at-home mothers and their children. He ordered beef stroganoff while I went for Mediterranean salad. We got our drinks from the fountain and found a corner table by the window. He sipped his coke and studied me with the same expression he'd worn the last few days.

"What are you plotting?" I asked.

He chuckled. "What makes you think I'm plotting something?"

"The look in your eyes says so. It's calculating. Smug. Like you can't wait to unleash a fiendish plan. So what's cooking between you and Eirik?" He didn't answer right away, his expression thoughtful. "He doesn't hide things from me, so you might as well tell me."

"You're stubborn."

"Tenacious."

"Same thing." I just cocked my brow and waited. He sighed. "Fine. We've been removing graffiti from your locker and Cora's the last few days, including today. The bastards responsible must have hung the nooses after I left."

I leaned forward. "Why didn't you guys tell me? What did they say?"

"It doesn't matter now. If they continue next week, I'll have a little surprise waiting for the bastard behind this."

"Like what?"

"It's a surprise," he said firmly.

"You're going to use runes to trap the person, aren't you?"

He made a face. "You have a diabolical mind. Have you seen the Norns since you came back?"

"Yeah, on Monday. Marj was her usual bitchy self. I wish they'd never healed me when I was a child, then I wouldn't have this special connection with them."

Torin's frown deepened. "Marj?"

"The annoying, sanctimonious leader of the three Norns that keep hounding me."

Amusement flashed in his eyes. "You think you can see them because they marked you as a child?"

I shrugged. "What other reason is there?"

"There's something special about you, and they know it. No one has ever defied them. Seven people survived because of you, Raine. You, a Mortal girl, stopped them from doing their job."

Then why didn't I feel like a hero? No matter what Torin and even Lavania said, I was a tool. A means to an end. Someone the Norns were willing to use to reach their objective, namely protecting Eirik. I wish I knew why or what was after him.

"Can we focus on stopping the witch hunt instead? I can't stand talking about the crones."

Torin grimaced. "Then you're going to hate my suggestion."

"What suggestion?"

"Summon the Norns, and order them to fix this witch mess."

I choked on my drink and started coughing. Torin reached over to pat my back. I wiped my lips and shot him an annoyed look. "Who says I can summon them, let alone order them to do anything?"

"They will listen to you because something about you scares them."

I snorted. "When I saw them in the cafeteria on Monday, they didn't look scared. They were still barking orders and giving me ultimatums. I hate them."

Torin frowned. "What did they want?"

"The usual. Join them to protect Eirik."

His eyes narrowed. "Protect Eirik? From what?"

I chewed on my lip, undecided whether to tell him or not.

"Raine, what is it?"

This was the guy I loved, someone I trusted implicitly even though he didn't know it. "Whatever I tell you stays between us. You tell Andris or Lavania, and I'll knee you so hard..." My face warmed when he cocked his eyebrows. "You don't tell anyone."

"You have my word." He glanced over my shoulder. "Hold on to that thought. Our food's ready. No, don't move," he added, getting up. "I'll get it."

I sipped my drink and turned to watch him walk away, admiring the way his jeans fit. Seriously, the guy had the sexiest walk ever.

"Raine Cooper?" a man said hesitantly. I turned to face him, and he thrust what appeared to be a digital voice recorder under my nose. "My name is Gerry Ferguson. I'm a reporter with the Kayville Daily News. We've tried to contact you for an interview, but your parents refused to return our calls and we're not allowed inside the school. Is it true you developed psychic abilities after a near-death accident? Was that how you knew the swimmers were about to die?"

"Hey!" Torin yelled. "Leave her alone." The next second he'd dropped the tray with our lunch on the table behind me and reached ours. "I told you if I saw you again, you'd be sorry."

"Come on, man. I just want an exclusive," the reporter protested.

"I'll give you an exclusive," Torin snarled and grabbed the guy by the collar of his shirt.

People in the restaurant stared, their eyes volleying between Torin, the reporter, and me. I slid a little lower in my seat, but the booth walls weren't high enough to hide.

"Are you a psychic, Lorraine Cooper?" the reporter yelled before Torin hauled him outside. There was no way we could eat lunch in the restaurant now. People were staring and whispering.

I got up, grabbed our tray and hurried to the counter. The two women stepped back, their expressions wary. "Pack these to go."

They hesitated, neither one of them willing to make the first move. This was ridiculous.

"Now," I added through clenched teeth.

The one to my left snatched the tray and moved away. I turned to check on Torin, but he was done. The reporter appeared to be walking away unscathed, which meant Torin put a whammy on him with his runes.

Torin entered the restaurant and silence filled the room. He turned his head slowly and looked around, his eyes cold, daring anyone to say or do something. People developed interest in their food. His eyes locked with mine, and I shivered. I'd never seen him this angry. His eyes fierce, his face was tight like he'd tear the room apart if anyone looked at me wrong.

"You okay?" he asked in a low, intense voice when he reached my side.

I nodded.

He took my arm. "Let's get out of here."

"Our lunch…"

He gave me a look that said I was crazy to be thinking about food now.

"I'm hungry, and we've already paid for it," I said stubbornly.

His eyes narrowed. Then he signaled the women behind the counter. The one with our food gave him the plastic bag using the tip of her fingers. We headed for the door.

"Has he been following me?" I asked as soon as the door closed behind us.

"He wasn't the only one." Torin glanced around and put his sunglasses on. "I etched runes on the trees around our cul-de-sac and the school to stop them from snooping or getting too close. So far the runes have worked." A growl rumbled through his chest. "What was I thinking bringing you here?"

I slipped my hand through his and squeezed. "It's okay. He blindsided me, but you were here and you stopped him. That's what matters. Thank you."

Torin stared at our hands, his grip tightening when I could have let him go. "Your safety is important to me."

"Oh? Why?"

He let go of my hand, a frown on his handsome face, eyes shadowed. "I don't know. It just is. Like a lot of things about you." He pushed the lock of hair from his forehead and rubbed his nape. His feelings for me were definitely resurfacing, but he was overanalyzing them.

"You should have told me about the reporters and the lockers. I can't protect myself by being ignorant."

"I don't mind protecting you."

Cute, but very old-fashioned. "You can't be with me twenty-four-seven, so I'll have to do my part."

His eyes narrowed stubbornly; then he sighed. "I'll remember that. In the meantime, summon the Norns and order them to fix this mess. They created it."

"You really think they'll listen to me?"

"Absolutely."

His confidence in me was daunting. "I've threatened them with exposure before, and they didn't like it. Maybe it might work again."

"It doesn't hurt to try." He glanced around again. "Let's go." He placed our lunches in the Harley's saddlebag while I snapped on the helmet.

I checked my watch. We had seven minutes before lunchtime was over. "Do you think you can get us to school in under a minute?"

"Sure." He shot me a weird glance.

I had put my foot in my mouth again. "I was told Valkyries can travel fast when they engage certain runes."

Despite my explanation, he was still frowning when we took off.

***

We made it back to school in thirty seconds. I noticed the school bus parked at the curb and the football players storing their gym bags.

"Oh, you have to leave," I said, disappointment rolling through me.

"Not for half an hour. You want to eat on the bus?"

"Will Drew and Keith be there?"

His eyes flashed. "You do know that Keith is gay and Drew is still in love with his ex."

He was jealous. How sweet. "That's okay. I'm presently into emotionally unavailable guys."

He laughed, eyes twinkling. I loved it when I made him laugh. "You say the craziest things."

"It's the truth." Actually, I was convinced he planned to reap Drew and Keith's souls. They were such nice guys. "Let's eat in my car. It's closer and beats hurrying inside to find a table in the cafeteria." I gave Torin his helmet, led the way to my car, and unlocked the doors.

He slid in the front passenger seat, making the inside of my car seem small with his vibrant presence. We never used my car when we first met. We always rode his bike. I studied him from the corner of my eyes as we ate.

"Are you nervous about your first game?" I asked.

He laughed. "No. We'll crush the Titans."

"You do know they're ranked number-eight in the state, while we are—"

"Catching up," he finished. "You should cancel your lessons with Lavania and come watch us."

"I can't. I'm getting my rune daggers today." I could barely contain my excitement, but then I remembered he wasn't crazy about me training. "Anyway, I'll watch you in two weeks during playoffs."

He flashed a wicked grin.

"What?"

"You said you'd watch *me*."

I rolled my eyes. "The team."

"I am the team."

"Boy, that ego of yours is going to get crushed if you lose."

He chuckled, the sexy sound rippling through me. "Not going to happen. Why do you need to protect Eirik?"

The clock on the dashboard said my time was up. "Let's talk about that later. I have to go, and the bus is waiting."

"They can't leave without me." He threw his empty carton back in the plastic bag.

"But Mr. Q. *will* start teaching without me." I opened the door and shifted to leave the car, but Torin grabbed my wrist. Blue flames leaped in his eyes, and I swallowed, my heartbeat shooting up.

"Don't do this, Torin," I whispered. *Unless you mean it.*

He didn't let go of my hand. Instead, he ran his thumb across my knuckles, moved to my palm, and stroked it. Shivers ran up my arm, but I didn't protest again. Couldn't protest was more like it. I'd missed his touch. I savored it.

"What is it about you that makes me...?"

"What?"

He sighed. "Feel so much. Want. Need. I know I should leave you alone, but..."

My chest tightened, trapping air in my lungs. "But?"

Instead of answering, he released my hand and flashed a smile that was both mocking and challenging. "Go, Freckles."

I stared at him, wanting to demand answers. Close the narrow space separating us and kiss some sense into him. He was driving me crazy. "I'll, uh, see you later?"

"Yeah, I want to hear about Eirik. If it involves Norns, it can't be good."

I nodded and took off, and didn't look back until I crossed the street. He still stood by my car, his eyes on me. He didn't look happy. Yeah, he was definitely very confused about his feelings for me, and I couldn't be happier.

***

"Ms. Cooper," Mr. Q., my AP English teacher, called out and waved a piece of paper as I hurried past his desk.

"Thanks." I read the note. Coach Fletcher wanted to see me in his geography classroom at the end of the day. I frowned. What did he want? I hoped it wasn't about the swim team. I didn't really feel like rejoining. Between schoolwork and training with Lavania, I doubted I'd have time. Or maybe he wanted to talk about what had happened during the meet.

Thinking about the meeting bugged me for the rest of the afternoon. I left my last class and made my way to my locker. Excitement hung in the air, students racing along the hallway and talking on top of their lungs. Most planned to carpool to Portland for the football game. I'd only ever seen this kind of excitement during home games.

"Go Trojans!" two guys yelled, jumping and bumping chests.

I sidestepped them, almost being hit by another student walking backwards while talking to his friends about the game. I wasn't sure whether Torin, the new quarterback, was the cause or the fact that we were playing one of our archrivals.

Cora grabbed me from behind. "I wish you were coming with us, Raine."

"Me, too." Once again, I faked sadness. "Promise to text me every ten minutes. I want to know how the new QB performs."

"So does every girl in the school," Cora said. Two girls walking past high-fived her.

I laughed. "You guys are so bad."

"You have no idea. Over here, Eirik. I got your text." She waved, but instead of waiting for him to come to us, she ran and hugged him. His right arm looped around her waist. "You're the best."

I was surprised she didn't kiss him in her exuberance. Eirik rolled his eyes when I gave him thumbs-up. I hoisted my backpack onto my shoulder, grabbed my oboe, and gave both of them a hug. "Have fun, guys. Text me."

Some students had already painted their faces with the Trojan colors—gold, black, and crimson. A few diehards had painted their chests and ran down the hall shirtless. For the first time since I'd come back, no one seemed to notice me. I loved it.

I turned the corner and saw Andris lounging by the entrance to the counselors' offices. His eyes followed me even though he was talking to a guy I recognized from a school play.

"Going to the counselor's again?" Andris asked as I got closer.

Surprised by his lack of animosity, I nodded. "Yeah. How do you know?"

"You're a creature of habit, Raine Cooper. Like clockwork, you stop by her office every day after school and leave ten minutes later. What do you two discuss?"

"None of your business." I disappeared inside the counselors' offices.

"Are you going to Portland to watch the game?" Mrs. Underwood asked me as soon as I sat.

"No. I still have a lot of homework to finish."

"That doesn't mean you can't take a break, Lorraine. Put everything that's happened behind you and move on. Get involved in afterschool activities again."

I nodded. "Coach Fletcher wants to see me upstairs after this."

"Good. Go back to swimming and doing things with your friends." The counselor stood. "You don't have to come see me anymore unless you want to."

"Thanks, Mrs. Underwood. I know I acted like I didn't want to see you on Monday, but our talks have helped me cope." I made a face. "I, uh, even looked forward to them."

She smiled. "That's why I'm here, dear. Just remember, my door is always open." She closed her hand on the knob and paused before opening the door. "I'm sorry we haven't caught the students vandalizing your locker. Officer Randolph has tried everything, including hiding in a closet and watching the hallway, yet someone somehow made it to your locker and vandalized it without him seeing anything. It's a puzzler. Mr. Elliot has been informed, and he plans to talk to the students on Monday about it."

My stomach had started churning at "someone somehow." Someone who could move fast or become invisible was deliberately reminding the students of what happened during that meet. Could Norns be doing this to nudge me to their side? I always knew when they were around, and I hadn't felt them since Monday. That left our resident Valkyries.

Andris disliked me and was crazy enough to do it just for laughs, or because Maliina had joined evil Norns and he blamed me. Ingrid always acted like a total pushover, but she was Maliina's sister. Could she be angry enough to want to hurt or humiliate me? Lavania was my trainer, so I couldn't see what she'd gain from my misery. On the other hand, she and Torin were close. I hadn't seen hints of anything more between them, but you just never know. Then there was Torin. He would never hurt me, but he didn't want me to become an Immortal. Even when I first met him, he'd refused to use healing runes on me after that first time. But wanting me to stay human and seeing me suffer were two different things.

Andris was still chatting with the same guy when I reappeared. I frowned when the guy reached up and touched Andris' hair. He'd chopped his silver hair and spiked it at the top. Their body language was almost lovers-like. Could Cora be right? Was Andris dating guys now? Knowing him, he was probably toying with the poor guy.

"Wait up, Raine."

I ignored him and kept going toward the north wing.

"Quit ignoring me, Mortal."

I glanced back. The guy he'd been talking to stared at us with open curiosity. "What mischief are you up to now, Andris?"

"Me? I'm an open book. You, on the other hand, are a complex girl. Why did you lie to me?"

"Lied about what?"

"Your love triangle situation."

I sighed. "What do you want, Andris?"

"What do you think? Big brother asked me to babysit you while he's gone playing ball, which means I have to follow you around when I could be doing fun stuff with Roger." He glanced back to his boy toy and indicated "call me" with his fingers. "Isn't he beautiful?"

"Since when are you into guys?"

"Since always. Whatever catches my fancy is my latest craze, and he caught mine. He's sweet, adorable, and very loving, and I need some TLC. So where are we going?"

"Nowhere. I don't need a sitter."

"Tough. Why did you lie to me? Why didn't you tell me you tried to help Torin remember the past?"

I shrugged. "I don't know. It seemed pointless."

"So you led me to believe you'd ditched him, let me get away with calling you names and treating you like crap rather than tell me the truth?"

I studied his face. "You are feeling guilty."

He grimaced. "Nah."

"Oh yes you are, and you don't like it." I laughed then felt bad. "Don't worry about it. They were just words, Andris. Half the time you say things just to get a reaction."

He grinned. "I knew you got me."

Did I? He could be the one messing with my locker. I stopped outside Coach Fletcher's classroom. The door was partially opened.

"I have to go," I whispered.

"I'm coming in with you. Don't shake your head," he added. "My orders are to stay glued to your side."

I narrowed my eyes. "The orders have been rescinded. By me, so wait here."

"Why? Who's in there?" His eyes grew suspicious, and he wiggled his brow. "A new boyfriend?"

"You have a one-track mind. I'm meeting my swim coach, and there's no other exit except this one, so wait here. I'll be out in a minute." Turning, I walked to the door and peeked inside the room. "Doc?"

Coach Fletcher gave me a broad grin, jumped down from where he'd been seated on his desk, and walked toward me. Behind him were three students. "Come inside, Raine. Sit. You know Jake, Sondra, and Caleb." The students waved and gave me forced smiles. "They're the new captains of the swim team."

Jake and Sondra were seniors while Caleb was a junior. Jessie and the other captains hadn't made it. I sat next to Sondra, put my backpack by my feet, and placed the oboe case on my lap. I had no idea what was going on. Doc sat on his desk, his legs crossed at the ankles. Watching him cross and uncross his arms only made me more uneasy.

"Raine, the team needs you," he started. "As the fourth captain, you should be at the front—"

"Whoa, Doc. I don't think I'm ready to come back to swimming."

"Allow me to finish, Slinky. Of course, you must pass your physical again before you can rejoin the team."

"That's not what I'm talking about." The way he used my swimming nickname kind of bugged me. He was buttering me up. "Right now, the whole school thinks I'm a witch." A rumor probably started by members of the swim team. "I highly doubt anyone on the team wants me back."

"We do," Sondra said and glanced at the others, who nodded. "We talked to everyone on the team, and we agreed unanimously that you can come back."

"Some people are curious about how you knew, but that's all," Caleb added.

"No one really thinks you're a witch either," Jake added. "I mean, witches don't exist."

If that were true, they would have given me some support over the last five days. The swimmers had acted like the rest of the students. Maybe I was taking out my frustration and worries about the identity of the person vandalizing my locker on my coach and the captains, but I hadn't seen the solidarity I often associated with the swim team. Their words also sounded so rehearsed.

"There are a few things I'd like to say," Coach Fletcher said. "I want to thank you for what you did during the meet. You saved many lives that night. If we'd listened... if *I* had listened to you, more lives would have been saved. That's my burden to carry." He paused and sighed before continuing. "Like Caleb and Luke, your teammates are curious about how you knew, but no one thinks you're a witch.

However, we all agree on one thing. You were a hero that night." He glanced at the captains, who nodded. "I also just heard about the vandalism to your car and locker. The principal and I had a meeting this afternoon, and he's assured me the culprits will be caught."

Not if he or she was a Valkyrie. I hadn't really thought about rejoining the team. Between taking lessons from Lavania and my regular schoolwork, I didn't have time for anything else.

"How soon can you come back?" Doc asked as though my return was a given.

"We need you," Jake said.

"You, Cora, Sally Peters, and I will be the relay dream team," Sondra added.

Cora had been a backup despite making the state time the last two years. She would be thrilled, but I refused to go back just for her.

"Can I give you my decision later? I have to talk to my parents first." Doc nodded. I got up and gave them a brief wave. I had no intention of going back to the team.

Outside, I found Andris waiting, his expression annoyed.

"Un-freakin'-believable." He pushed against the opposite wall and walked toward me. He took my backpack before I realized his intention. "Don't tell me you're thinking of going back. Not after the way they've treated you."

"Shh. They'll hear you."

"Where have they been since you came back? What did they do to stop people from treating you like a worm? You should have told them to stick their offer up their—"

I covered his mouth and practically pushed him away.

He removed my hand from his mouth. "That's the problem with you, Raine. You're too nice. When dealing with Mortals, you have to be tough. You'll learn once you've transformed." He turned his head and yelled, "She's not coming back. Do you hear me, you self-serving pricks?"

"Shut up, Andris."

He grinned. "Are you seriously considering rejoining the team?"

"Maybe." We exited the school building. The parking lot was deserted, except for my car and Torin's Harley. "Are you taking the bike?"

"Yeah. Do you want to come for a ride?"

My feet faltered at his words. Torin used to ask me the same question but in a husky voice and with a wicked twinkle in his eyes, making the request sound naughty. "No, I have to stop by the store before heading home."

"Oh come on," he protested. "You're supposed to go home, where it's safe and warm, and not so wet. I hate this weather. Why couldn't we make our base in Florida or Malibu, where it's warm and fun, and co-eds frolic half-naked at the beach?"

I laughed. "I told you I don't need a sitter." I unlocked my car, put my oboe case on the seat, and turned to take my heavy backpack, but he'd already thrown it in the backseat.

"Sorry. You're stuck with me." He glanced up at the gray sky and grimaced. It was drizzling. "Damn Oregon weather."

Somehow, I doubted Andris was the person vandalizing my locker. He was blunt about most things. He'd probably brag about it and tell me in excruciating detail why he was doing it. "Follow me. And FYI, Oregon weather is perfect."

9. ARTAVO

Andris followed me downtown, parked beside my parents' car, and was right behind me when I entered the Mirage. "Browse, but don't break anything."

He gave me the finger using both hands. Rolling my eyes, I turned and froze. Dad watched us from the customer desk, his expression unreadable. Had he seen Andris' rude gesture? Jared usually manned the store, and from the looks of things, he wasn't around. There were no customers inside the store either.

"Hi, Dad," I said. "Did you get my text?"

"Yes." He moved closer. "Hi there, young man."

Andris turned from examining the frame of a mirror and offered Dad his hand. "Mr. Cooper, nice to finally meet you."

Dad frowned, glancing at me before shaking Andris' hand. "Finally?"

"I'm one of your new neighbors. Your wife…" Andris glanced at me and grinned, "Raine's mother invited us over to dinner tomorrow night."

A spasm shot across Dad's face. "Oh, yes. She told me."

Did he know our neighbors were Valkyries? Mom had said she'd talk to him last night about my training, so he must know. "Where's Mom?"

"She went grocery shopping for tomorrow," he answered, but his eyes were still on Andris, who was busy running his finger along the runes on the frames.

"Jared?" I asked.

"He's getting us coffee. I thought it might be nice not to walk in the rain."

I sighed. "I know about Nikos and how his customers feel about me, Dad. It's okay. We don't ever have to go there."

Anger flashed in his hazel eyes. "Wait for me in the office."

"Who's Nikos?" Andris asked, his eyes volleying between me and my father.

"A café down the street," I said, starting for the office. "You should try it. They sell tasty pastries."

"Why do his customers have a problem with Raine, Mr. Cooper?"
I heard Andris ask.

"That's a private matter, young man," Dad said in a firm voice.

I grinned. My father calling Andris "young man" was funny.
Despite looking like a teenager, he was probably ten times my father's
age.

"Sir, anything that affects one of us affects all of us."

"My daughter is *not* one of you," Dad snapped, confirming that he
knew Andris was a Valkyrie.

I stopped walking and turned. Dad pinned Andris with a glare.
Andris stared right back. This wasn't good. "Dad?"

"What's your name?" Dad asked.

"Andris."

"Where are you from, Andris?"

Andris made a face. "We don't really have a home, sir. We divide
our time between Asgard and a temporary home of our choosing here
on Earth. From the looks of things, Kayville is going to be home for a
couple of years. It's not exactly my cup of tea, but I didn't get to decide
this time."

Dad's lips tightened. "I meant your country of original... what
century..."

"Constantinople before the Ottoman captured the city," he said,
which made him at least five hundred years old.

Interest flared in Dad's eyes. He loved history, but all he said was,
"It's nice to meet you, *young man*. Now if you don't mind, I'd like to talk
to my daughter. Alone." He turned toward me.

"About Nikos, sir—"

"Let it go, Andris," I said, getting exasperated by his persistence.
Dad put his hand on my shoulder and started to lead me into his office.

"If someone is bothering Raine, Mr. Cooper, we can deal with
him a lot faster than you."

"Really?" Dad turned, and I groaned. "Where were you when the
Norns tried to take her? She ended up in the hospital and almost died
because of you people. I will not have you use magic to fool people
around my town. *I* will protect my daughter."

I swallowed, my heart pounding with dread. I wanted to tell them
to stop, but Andris didn't know the meaning of the word and Dad's
protective instinct often went into overdrive where I was concerned.
He looked like he might attempt to rip Andris apart if he said another

word, which would be a big mistake. No human could take out a Valkyrie.

"Dad, please."

"With all due respect, Mr. Cooper," Andris said at the same time. "You have no idea what we're dealing with. Norns could level this town without losing sleep, and Mortals would just call it a phenomenon and spend decades trying to understand it. We don't have time to pacify a few disgruntled people—"

Dad cut him off by raising his hand. The doorbell dinged, and Jared walked into the store, carrying two cups of coffee in a holder and a box of pastries.

"Leave," I mouthed to Andris.

He shook his head. I was so going to kill him after this.

Dad took the coffee and pastries from Jared, thanked him, and glanced over at Andris. "Feel free to look around, Andris. If you see anything that interests you, I'll be in the office. Jared, he's a special customer."

"What does special customer mean?" I asked, following Dad into his office.

He waited until I closed the door before he said, "Valkyries, but Jared only knows them as the people who order floor-to-ceiling mirrors with special designs on the frames."

I sat, rested my elbows on his desk, and warmed my hands on the paper cup as Dad studied me with a thoughtful expression. He sipped his drink. "Is he your boyfriend?"

"Nooo. He's just, uh, a friend." Calling Andris a friend felt weird, but I guessed he was. Everything he'd done since my talk with the counselor said he couldn't be the one vandalizing my locker. Or maybe I was being too trustful. "So Mom told you everything?"

Dad nodded.

"And you're angry."

He leaned back and shook his head. "Not with you."

"With Mom?"

"Of course not. I knew you were special before you were born. That one day you would follow in her footsteps. I thought we had more time to prepare, time for you to lead a normal life as a..."

"Mortal?"

He shook his head. "No, as a typical teenager. Boys, prom, graduation without runic magic, portals, and dead souls."

My heart squeezed, hating to see him in the dumps. "If you don't want me to train until I graduate from high school, I can wait."

"You could be twenty or thirty, pumpkin, I'd still have a problem with this immortality thing, but your mother said it was better this way. Both Valkyries and Norns want you, and from the sound of things, being a Valkyrie is a better option." He made a face like he'd swallowed a bitter pill.

I sighed. "You don't like them?"

"Other than your mother, the ones I've met are pompous, condescending, and have little regard for humans."

He just described Andris. Torin wasn't like that. "You always tell me not to discriminate against a group of people because of a few rotten apples."

Dad chuckled. "That's true. I guess when it comes to you the rules go out the window." He put his coffee aside, leaned forward, and gripped my hands, his expression becoming sober. "Is this what you want, pumpkin? Immortality? Reaping souls for eternity?"

When I thought I had Torin, I hadn't cared. But I didn't have him, and I might never have him. This was about preparing myself to deal with the Norns. As a Mortal, I was too vulnerable. They might snap my little neck like a twig and send me straight to Hel's Mist, and there was nothing I could do about it. As an Immortal I had a fighting chance.

"Raine?"

"Yes, Daddy. I want to do this."

His eyes bored into mine. "Will you promise me one thing?"

I nodded.

He leaned forward. "If you have any doubts at all, promise to come talk to me. Okay?"

"Okay, Dad."

"Good." He got up, walked around the desk, and gave me a hug. "Now get out of here and take *him* with you." He inclined his head to indicate the main floor of the store.

He grows on you, I wanted to tell him, but I was sure he wasn't in the mood to hear anything nice about Valkyries. "I love you, Dad."

"Love you too, kiddo."

Andris was signing a piece of paper when we left the office. "I'll make arrangements to have it picked up tomorrow," he said.

"Yes, sir," Jared said with a grin.

"What did you buy?" I asked.

Grinning, he pointed at the largest mirror in the room. "A couple of those. We have one, but could use a few more."

Dad didn't make a comment about Andris' purchase and waved as we hurried outside. The drizzle had stopped.

"Has anyone ever told you that your father is one scary dude?" Andris said.

"Nope. He's just worried about me."

"How can he hate Valkyries when he's married to one?"

"He doesn't hate anyone." I opened my car door and got behind the wheel. This dinner thing hadn't seemed like a good idea when I first heard about it, and it was even less appealing now.

"I wonder if I can skip dinner tomorrow," Andris said and made a face. "I mean, he might decide to poisons us."

I glared at him. "That's ludicrous and insulting. My father is not that diabolical. Besides, aren't you immune to things that make people sick?"

"Yes, but cramps are a bitch, even if they last seconds."

I couldn't think up a response, so I just closed the door and started the engine. Andris knocked on the window of my car, and I rolled it down.

"What is it now?" I asked with as much exasperation as I could muster.

"Watch it with the 'tude, missy."

I rolled my eyes. "I don't have an attitude."

"What time is your lesson with Lavania?"

"Five."

"Okay, let's agree on one thing. Once you get home, you stay put. You don't go anywhere without swinging by my place first. Got it?"

Was he kidding? "Yeah, sure."

His eyes narrowed. "Remember, I'm not Torin."

"Meaning?"

"I'll have no problem runing your door and windows, confining you to your room."

I laughed. "You and whose army?"

"Try me." Smirking, he turned and swaggered back to the Harley.

Grinding my teeth, I took off. Torin was so dead. Andris stayed behind me all the way home. After parking the bike, he stood in the driveway and waited until I entered my house.

Upstairs, my eyes fell on the brown manila envelope on my side table. Torin's rune book. I picked up the envelope and sighed. Somehow, I couldn't bring myself to part with it. Soon. Turning, I walked to my closet, opened a drawer, and hid it in the back.

***

"Come in. We have the house to ourselves today." Lavania waved me inside before closing the door. She was always courteous. Today she wore a sleeveless light-blue gown with dark-blue jewels along the hem and neckline, and a broad bedazzled belt with runes circled her waist. A matching headband held her hair back, and armlets adorned her upper arms.

"You look pretty," I said.

"Thank you. I have a date tonight. A celebration."

With who? Torin? "Andris is gone?"

"With Ingrid. They left when you were crossing the lawn. He almost came to get you." She chuckled. "He's always been impatient."

"They used a portal?"

Lavania chuckled. "What other way is there to travel? Come on, we're going to use the kitchen."

I hadn't been in their kitchen since I was last there with Andris and Ingrid. At the time, there were huge moving boxes filled with Torin's things. I looked around with interest and smiled. Someone in their house loved to cook. There were a lot of modern cooking gadgets on the counters. Across from the kitchen was the family room with a sectional couch and a high-def flat screen TV on the wall. The party Torin had held here, before everything went to Hel and back, flashed through my head.

"Over here," Lavania called and waved toward a stool. "Sit."

She sat on the other side of the kitchen island counter. In front of her was a neatly folded brown leather cloth. She waited until I sat before she carefully unfolded it.

It wasn't exactly a cloth. It was some kind of leather knife belt with six pouches. One by one, she pulled out the instruments from their sheaths. All were the size of a pencil, but varied in color, the shape of the blade, handle, and the guard. Half of them had black, shiny blades, while the others were white. Runes ran from handle to blade. One blade was shaped like a sickle, another like a stag knife, and the rest were of various thicknesses.

"These are called *artavo*, meaning ritual knives. One is called *artavus*. Some high priestesses called them artanus, artany, or arthame. A more corrupted version used by the present magical world is athame." She picked up a black artavus with a pointed blade and a guard. I had seen Maliina (or was it Ingrid?) use one just like it. "This is called a stillo. Try it for size."

I closed my hand around the ridged handle. My fingers fitted the ridges as though it were made for me. The blade extended about three inches from my fist.

"It's light." I touched the blade and gasped when pain radiated up my arm and blood pooled at the tip of my finger. Wooziness swept over me. I hated the sight of blood, especially mine. I stuck my finger into my mouth and carefully put the artavus down like it was a poisonous snake.

Lavania chuckled. "You're as white as a ghost." She reached down and came up with her own rune blade. "Give me your hand. I'll take care of the cut with healing runes."

I shook my head. I so wasn't ready to be runed yet.

"The sting doesn't last and that cut is deep, if you hadn't noticed."

The pain radiating from my finger told me it was. Slowly, I removed my finger from my mouth and moaned when blood rushed to the wound. This was bad.

"Come on," Lavania urged impatiently.

Cringing, I offered her my hand and closed my eyes. When she chuckled again, I opened one eye and fought the urge to snatch my hand away. My finger was bleeding profusely, the blood dripping onto the counter.

"Try to relax, Raine."

"This *is* me relaxed," I retorted through clenched teeth. "I hate blood, and it hurts."

Moving so fast her hands were blurry, she etched runes on the back of my hand. She was right. The sting was brief, and the cuts weren't really cuts. They were more like burns.

I forgot about my churning stomach when pink burn marks criss-crossed my skin. They darkened to beautiful sketches like the ones I'd seen on Lavania's hand, the ends forming whorls and tendrils. I stared at my hand with morbid fascination, but the beautiful runes ebbed away. A tingle started at the tip of my finger, and I turned my hand. The dip cut closed, too, and the temporary pink skin lost its color until my finger was normal again.

When Torin healed me the first time, I had been flat out unconscious. The second time the remnants of his runes sealed my knife wound, so I hadn't actually seen it happen. Watching my skin close like someone was zipping it up was surreal.

"That wasn't bad," Lavania said, wiping the blood from the counter. I snapped back to reality.

"No, it wasn't. Thank you." I got up to wash the blood off my finger.

"You'll have to overcome your aversion to pain, you know," Lavania said. "I can start you off by etching the healing runes with my artavus, but eventually you'll have to etch your own and create a bond between you and yours. Since your movements are not as fast, the sting will last longer."

"Gee, thanks." I felt woozy just thinking about it.

She waited until I sat before saying, "You'll be fine. Maybe Torin will help."

"No." I didn't want him to see me acting like a baby. "I can do it on my own. You know, once you etch the first ones."

She grinned. "That's the attitude. Now, where were we?"

"You asked me to hold the stillo," I reminded her.

"Oh yes. After you've bonded with them, no one else can ever use them, but you. That's the mistake young Valkyries make when they try to turn Mortals on their own. They don't realize they cannot use their stash of artavo. Eventually, the person you turn must have their own rune daggers to bond with and complete their transformation."

No wonder Torin always warned Andris to stop turning Mortals. Had Maliina gone a little crazy because Andris had screwed up? I hoped not. It might mean Ingrid was in trouble, too, because Andris had turned both of them.

I touched one of the white blades. "What are the blades made of?"

"The black ones are made of special onyx found in Asgard. The white stone is made from selenite found from Goddess Freya's realm. Do you remember where that is?"

"Vanaheim," I said.

"Good. The runes etched on their surface help channel the magical energy. That one," she indicated the black one I'd nipped myself on, "is used to sketch the first runes. It is powerful and, when not used properly, can make a transformation go wrong. But you don't have to worry about that. I'm here to guide you. See the runes on the handle and the blade?"

I recognized the prominent one. "That is Goddess Freya's symbol."

"That's right. She is your protector, so all your artavo will have her symbol. This one is called *bolino*." She picked up one that looked like a cylindrical block with a nail at the tip. She gripped the handle and pressed it on the counter. When she opened her palm, the bladeless handle looked like a wooden block a kid could play with. "It has retractable blade and is used on surfaces to create portals. You can carry it anywhere and no one would consider it a weapon. As soon as you engage the runes on your arm, the blade slides out."

"Can you show me?"

"This is yours, so it won't respond to me." She gave me the harmless-looking wood, then reached under her belt and pulled out hers. Her handle was darker and ridged for better grip. Runes appeared on her hand, their tendrils coiling between her fingers and up her wrist as though an invisible artist was painting a masterpiece on her skin. They looked like henna decorations. The blade shot out from the base with a sharp whoosh, and I gasped. She chuckled.

"It's a bit rusty from lack of use. Don't worry. Yours will come out smooth and easy, hardly making a sound." The runes disappeared from her hand, and the blade retracted.

"The blade self-retracts?" I asked.

"Once you can control your runes, you can control anything. The artavo, the portals, the ability to move fast, become invisible." She put her blade away and reached for another that looked like the one that had nipped me, except the blade was white. "This is a portal stillo. When you first learn to create portals, you want to use this one. It is a bit forgiving when you make mistakes with your sketches."

"How do the runes know where you want to go when there are so many portals around the world?"

Lavania chuckled. "The runes respond to your thoughts. We'll cover all that in the coming weeks. Today, let's just focus on the artavo."

***

It seemed like forever before she stopped, stood, and stretched. "Oh, I'm starving. Will you stay and join me for dinner? With the guys and Ingrid gone, I have to eat alone, and I hate that. We can discuss anything you want. Schoolwork, boys, girlfriends…"

Her expression was expectant, and I hated the idea of going home to work on more homework packets. I guessed we could discuss school. Boys were out of the question because I was only interested in one and I refused to discuss Torin with her.

"Raine?"

I looked at my watch. It was almost seven. My parents would be home soon. "I'll call Mom first."

"Good. I'll start on dinner."

"You cook?"

She chuckled. "Yes. Cooking relaxes me."

A model look-a-like who cooks? Could she be any more perfect?

I pulled out my cell phone from my back pocket, turned it on, and speed-dialed Mom's number, leaving the kitchen for the privacy of the living room. Dad picked up after several rings. "Hey, Dad."

"How is it going?"

I heard the worry in his voice. "Good. Is Mom there?"

"She went to pick up dinner. We should be home soon."

"I'm going to have dinner with Lavania, my trainer. The others are in Portland for the game, and she's alone. Is that okay?"

There was silence, then, "Okay. I'll tell your mother."

He didn't sound too thrilled about it, but there was nothing I could do about that. I had several text messages from both Cora and Eirik. We were winning. I quickly responded then followed the sounds to the kitchen.

Lavania already had two fresh salads on the kitchen counter. She moved around the kitchen at an accelerated speed. I could see right through her hands to the dough she was kneading and rolling. Lined before her were several containers of cheese, meats, and vegetables.

I sat on a stool and watched her. Did her brain work as fast as her hands? If I moved like that, I could be done with all my homework in one day. She put the tray in the oven, rinsed her hands, and faced me.

"Do you like calzones?" she asked.

I grinned. "Oh yeah."

"Then you're in for a treat. Wine or juice?"

Wine? "Juice."

We started with the salad. The calzones, when she removed them from the oven, were golden and tasty. Inside they had cheese, different meats, vegetables, including mushrooms, and fresh herbs. She placed sauces on the side for dipping. I hated mushrooms.

The conversation somehow drifted to my childhood, and soon we were laughing over escapades Eirik and I had gotten into. Before I knew it, we were discussing my dealings with the Norns. I found myself telling her everything that had happened, including how I got my head injuries. She didn't pass judgment on Maliina or Andris, who had obviously turned her when he shouldn't have. Discussing my relationship with Torin was out of the question, but she blindsided me.

"What's going on between you and Torin?"

I choked on my juice, cleared my throat, and fought a blush. "Nothing."

Lavania chuckled. "I'm not blind, Raine. I've never seen two people try so hard not to look at each other, yet steal glances when the other's not looking. He hasn't brought a girl home since I got here, even though they trip over themselves to flirt with him wherever we go. I've even seen waitresses scribble their phone numbers on receipts. It's quite hilarious."

Jealousy rippled through me. "It's not funny," I said before I could stop myself. Heat crawled up my face when she cocked her eyebrows. "I mean, uh, don't you find it annoying?"

She shook her head. "No, but what bothers me is why he's not calling them. Why night after night he's in his room with the lights off. Why he's become such a grouch." She grew silent and studied me intently. "I've seen the way he looks at you."

"Really, there's nothing between us," I insisted.

"And I've also seen the way *you* look at him, Raine."

My face on fire, I became defensive. "Why do you want him to call girls back? Aren't you two, uh, together?"

"What?" She chuckled and was soon laughing so hard I felt like an idiot.

"Never mind. I should be going home anyway." I stood, but she gripped my wrist.

"I'm sorry I laughed. Please, don't go."

Slowly, I sat.

"Raine, I could never be involved with one of my boys. He's beautiful and can be charming, but..." She shook her head. "He's like my son. Besides, I have a mate. Whatever gave you the idea about me and Torin?"

I felt even stupider, so I shook my head. As though she knew I didn't want to discuss Torin, she switched to Eirik. "I would love to train both of you. Try to see if you can convince him to join us. There's so much I can help him with that his parents can't."

"I'll try."

She looked ready to say more, but changed her mind, reaching for her glass of wine and sipping. "Since you insist you have no interest in Torin, have you ever thought of dating Eirik?"

I laughed. Been there and done that.

"Why do you laugh? He's the grandson of a god and an extremely attractive young man. We don't interact with the gods much, so you should take this opportunity to be his first consort."

"Consort, as in his wife?"

"Wife, mate, partner, whatever you want to call it. The gods take many consorts, but the first one stays by their side until the end of the world."

I shook my head. "I love Eirik, but I'll never be his, uh, consort. We did date, but we decided we were better off as friends. Besides, he likes someone else."

Lavania's eyes narrowed. "The Mortal blonde?"

"Yes. Her name is Cora Jemison."

"She's not right for him."

I frowned. "You don't know that. Cora is nice and funny and loving. They're perfect together."

"She's a Mortal, Raine. She'll never be good enough for him," Lavania said calmly without derision or anger. "Surely, you see that. You cannot allow this relationship to continue and must find a way to stop them."

"Why? My parents married despite the odds. Who are we to decide who Eirik dates or loves?"

Her eyes flashed. "Eirik's not just any deity. He's Odin's grandson. His family would never allow him to associate with someone like her."

"You don't like her because she's human?"

"No, this is beyond the fact that she's a Mortal. There's something about her that bothers me." She leaned forward, her eyes acquiring a weird glow. "Please, convince him to come here for lessons. I can help him."

By making sure he didn't hook up with Cora? Why did Lavania care so much about Eirik anyway? "Okay, I'll talk to him, but I can't make any promises."

Sounds came from upstairs, and we glanced up. Footsteps and raised voices followed.

"They'd better not track mud on my bedroom floor," Lavania mumbled, standing. She walked to the foot of the stairs. Her frown cleared, and she smiled. "How did it go?"

"As expected," Andris said, his feet appearing first and then the rest of him. "Torin owned the field. She thinks he cheated." He jabbed his thumb to indicate Ingrid, who was right behind him. "I've seen Torin play all sorts of sports, and he's a natural. The Titans didn't stand a chance." He turned and saw me. "Still here?"

"Don't be rude," Lavania said, smacking the back of his head as he walked past her. "Did you have fun, Ingrid?"

"Yes." Ingrid smirked and threw Andris a mocking look. "Torin cheated."

"Torin would never cheat," I jumped in. "He's honorable, hard-working, and noble. He'd rather lose than take shortcuts." Silence followed my outburst. Three sets of eyes studied me with varied expressions. Lavania's was thoughtful, but Andris smirked with amusement while Ingrid's could only be described as mocking. Once again, heat crawled up my face. I stood. "I gotta go."

"Not after such a heartfelt speech. Don't you want to know how your man did?" Andris asked, stopping by the counter and throwing me a teasing smile.

I cringed. "Uh, we won, and that's all that counts."

"So true," Lavania said. "I'm out of here, children. I'll be back tomorrow night. Don't mess up the house while I'm gone. You throw a party, you clean up. Andris, remind your brother to get a portal and put it in this room or you will start using the bathroom mirror or walls."

"Already bought two," Andris said with a proud grin. "I'll pick them up tonight."

Lavania blinked. "That's great. Thank you."

"Told you I'd remember."

"So you did." She patted his cheek. "I'm proud of you."

Andris grinned. "Say hi to old man Belmar."

"My mate is not old, but I'll tell him you said hi. Be good. Tell your brother I'm proud of him, too. Ingrid," she pinned the girl with a censoring glare. "My boys don't cheat."

Ingrid swallowed. "I didn't mean it. I was just, you know, messing with Andris. Tell her we were just goofing around." She threw Andris a pleading glance. He smirked, but didn't come to her defense.

"Then all is forgiven, Ingrid, even though I think the joke was in poor taste." Lavania glanced at me and added, "I'll see you tomorrow, but we will start early on Monday. I'll let you know when." She didn't wait for my response. As she disappeared upstairs, I started for the door.

"Whoa, where are you going, Raine? Stay with Ingrid until Torin gets back." Andris glanced at his watch. "Or until I get back."

I didn't want to stay with the Valkyrie. She didn't like me.

"I don't need a sitter," Ingrid snapped.

"*She* does." He pointed at me. "Torin's orders. I have a hot date I can't afford to miss, so see ya. Don't do anything I wouldn't do." He chuckled and disappeared toward the garage, but I saw the pain in Ingrid's eyes. She liked him. Maliina had bragged how she'd asked Andris to turn her sister into an Immortal just because he had once shown an interest in her. How had she put it? You always keep your enemies closer than your friends. She'd seen her own sister as an enemy because Andris had shown interest in her. Some sister.

"Where are you going?" Ingrid asked when I started for the door.

"Home. Goodnight."

"But you heard Andris."

"I sure did, but that doesn't mean I have to do as he says." I reached for the doorknob.

She moved so fast she was by the door before I opened it. "You're going to get me in trouble. When Torin gives an order, we follow it to the letter. You can watch TV or read something. I've plenty of books on my Kindle."

"You know something? Torin is not my keeper or whatever, so I don't have to listen or agree with everything he says." Annoyance flashed in her eyes, and I felt bad for putting her on the spot. "Why don't you come over to my place instead?" I heard myself say.

Ingrid's brow rose. "What?"

"Come and hang out at my house. I have homework packets I'm still working on, but I can take a break. We can get to know each other."

Her eyes narrowed. "Why would I want to do that?"

For one brief moment, something in her eyes reminded me of Maliina. She definitely hated me. Could she be the one vandalizing my locker? "I'm leaving. You can either follow me or stay here. That's up to you. The invite is open."

"Not interested. Oh, and Raine," she added, stepping away from the door. "Just because you have everyone around here panting to turn you doesn't mean it's the right thing to do. You're too emotional and juvenile to make a good Valkyrie. Maybe you should just do everyone a favor and tell them you're not ready."

Please, who did she think she was talking to?

She glared as though my face reflected my thoughts. "Don't leave the cul-de-sac without telling me first."

I waved and left. After her smug speech, I couldn't wait to become an Immortal just to rub her nose in it.

10. UNEXPECTED RAGE

Hours later, light flashed on and off outside my window. That had been our signal when Eirik lived next door, but Torin had used it once, too. I ran to the window and sighed with disappointment when I realized it came from Eirik's Jeep, not Torin's window. I crawled out of the window to the balcony and peered down. Cora and Eirik waved.

"Keep it down, guys."

"Then get your butt down here," Cora yelled. "We won."

"Come on," Eirik added. "We're going out to celebrate."

I missed my tree and the way they'd just climb up. Across the street, Mrs. Rutledge pushed aside the curtain and peered outside. Any more yelling and she'd slap me with a noise ordinance. She hated me. Always had.

I checked my watch. It was almost ten. Crawling back into my room, I pulled on a pair of jeans and a shirt. Lights were still on under my parents' bedroom door. I knocked, heard Dad's deep voice respond, and opened the door. He was doing something on his laptop and had headphones on. Mom snored slightly on the other side of the bed.

"Can I go hang out with Cora and Eirik?" I whispered. "They just came back from Portland, and we won."

He smiled. "I heard." He checked at his watch. "Isn't it a little late to be going out?"

"It's only ten."

He went silent, and I was convinced he'd say no. "Be back by midnight."

"Thanks, Dad." I hurried beside him and kissed his cheek. "Goodnight. Love you." I raced for the door.

"Uh, Raine," he said before I closed the door, and I turned. He studied me intently, a gentle smile on his narrow face. "Do you want to go for a run tomorrow morning? I plan to leave around nine."

Somehow, I had a feeling he'd meant to ask about my time with Lavania. Was he ready to start running? He'd been in a coma for months and still looked, I don't know, sickly. "Okay. Be ready to eat my dust."

He chuckled. "We'll see. Have fun, and be careful."

I closed the door and frowned. He was taking this Valkyrie business hard. Running with him might bring some normalcy back into his life. Dad was a triathlete and had done several triathlons the last couple of years. Before the plane crash, he'd been training for his first Ironman competition. Even when I used to swim, he and I would run on weekends. We often entered local 5K and 10K races together.

Makeup done and hair brushed, I grabbed my ID, debit card, and a jacket. Downstairs, Cora met me in the driveway with a hug.

"You should have been there, Raine. Torin was amazing."

I glanced over at his house. The lights were on. Was he home? "Where are we going?"

"Cliff House," Cora said.

Cliff House was on 14th North and had arcade games, bowling, and rock walls, which was the biggest attraction for most teens. I slipped in the back while Cora took the front passenger seat.

Funny how everything was reversed now. I often sat in front with Eirik even before we'd started dating. Cora always took the backseat. Sitting in the back felt weird. I stared at Torin's house as we drove past and wished he was with me. I hated being a third wheel.

***

We parked behind the tall L-shaped, two-storied building and piled out of the Jeep. The taller part was in the back, the climbing walls with their color coded rocks visible through the glass walls. The entrance was located on the center of the lower rectangular building. Visible through the walls were the Jump Zone's huge, colorful air-filled slides, hoops, trampolines, and a karaoke stage. In the middle, separating Jump Zone from the rock walls, were the video games, bowling lanes, and the rollerblade track. Cliff House was a giant money-sucking den of badassness, and I'd blown away part of my allowance in this place countless weekends.

Eirik slung his Nikon around his neck. He worked on Kayville High's newspaper and never missed a chance to photograph students. The parking lot was crowded, which meant inside was packed.

Sounds from video games, music, and children screaming greeted us when we pushed open the door at the front entrance. People milled from machine to machine, some paired while others hung out in groups. I didn't see anyone from the football team, which meant Torin wasn't here. Disappointment rolled through me.

"Are we rollerblading, bowling, rock climbing, or just blowing our money on video games?" Cora asked, waving to someone she knew.

"Rock climbing." Eirik glanced at me and cocked his brow. I shrugged. I didn't care what we did. It was nice to be around people who didn't recognize me and treat me like stale leftovers.

We paid the climbing fee, got our wristbands, and headed toward the arc leading to the high-ceilinged rock climbing room. Most parents preferred to keep their kids jumping, tumbling, and playing dodge ball in the Jump Zone, so there were very few under-ten kids around machines. The walls were popular with people of all ages. I'd seen kids half my age race up the walls like giant spiders.

Boisterous laughter welcomed us when we entered the rock climbing room, and I saw why. The football players, their girlfriends, and fans filled most of the tables and chairs, eating pizza and recapping today's win.

My eyes found Torin, and something inside me wilted. He was getting the star treatment, two cheerleaders by his side and two more seated behind him. He looked up, and our eyes met. He cocked his brow, as though surprised to see me.

Yeah, right back at you, pal.

Despite my mental bravado, it hurt to see him with other girls. Drew and Keith saw us and waved.

"Maybe we should start with the games," Eirik suggested, and I knew he was trying to spare my feelings.

"No. Let's do this." We found an empty table, left our jackets, then headed to the counter and showed the guy behind the counter our wristbands. We had passes to try all four levels.

Cliff House color-coded their levels. Orange was for beginners and corresponded to levels v-zero to v-two according to the outdoor rock climbing grading system. Green was for intermediate climbers on v-two to four, yellow for advanced climbers on v-five to seven, and red markers were for seasoned climbers like my parents. They'd passed v-seven eons ago. During our last climb, I'd made it to v-five. I sucked at rock climbing. Even Cora had passed me a while back. Eirik often climbed with Dad and was a monkey in human form. But then again, he'd had plenty of practice climbing the tree outside my window.

"Can we have a contest?" Cora said, coming to stand beside me.

"That's a no-brainer. He'll win." I jabbed my thumb to indicate Eirik.

"No, he won't," Cora retorted. "I've been practicing."

"Since when?" Eirik asked.

"Since our last contest. Just so I can beat you." She went on her toes and pushed her face closer to his. "So bring your a-game, hotshot."

"How about a dare?" he said so softly I barely heard him.

Cora nodded. "Okay."

"If I win, you go a whole day doing everything I ask without being mouthy."

Cora's eyes narrowed. "If I win, you're mine for a day, too."

I loved the way she'd worded it and grinned when uncertainty flickered in Eirik's eyes. Poor guy. He had no chance against Cora. My eyes went to the ballplayers. Torin was gone. Where did he go? I started to search the room, but the vibes from Eirik and Cora drew my attention.

They were both still, their faces inches apart. The next second, they stepped away from each other, both of them blushing. A near-kiss and they didn't even glance at me? Progress.

"We'll start on green," I told the guy behind the counter.

He checked the computer scene, tapped a key, and signaled his coworker. Soon we were strapping on the harnesses. I was halfway up the first wall when I felt like I was being watched. I looked over my shoulder to find Torin's eyes on me. If he continued watching me, his harem would notice. For the rest of the climb and the next one, Cora and Eirik were lost in their little world. I was happy for them, but at the same time, envious.

"You'll have to wait," the harness guy said. "There're only two open."

"I don't mind sitting this out." I glanced at Eirik then Cora. "You guys go ahead."

Cora shook her head. "No, I need a break and a drink. Eirik?"

"I'll get us some."

She already had him trained. Nice. "I'll head to our table," I said.

Cora watched Eirik walk away, a tiny smile on her lips.

"Drooling much?" I teased.

"Can't help it. He's so hot." She glanced around and whispered, "See you at our table. I have to talk to someone." Cora walked toward the ballplayers and was soon high-fiving them and bumping fists.

"What does a guy have to do to be on your vlog, Cora?" Trenton, a wide receiver asked.

"If Rita says it's okay."

Everyone guffawed. Even Rita, Trenton's girlfriend, laughed. Cora tended to give personal stats on the guys she featured on her vlog after talking to their girlfriends and ex-girlfriends. The people who didn't know her assumed she'd dated every guy she featured. Eirik hated her vlog.

Jaden Granger grabbed her and pulled her onto his lap. She pushed his head and stood. Immediately, she looked toward the food counter, where Eirik was still ordering our drinks, his back to us, which meant he hadn't seen her. She continued to make her rounds. Sometimes I forgot how popular she was, another thing Eirik hated.

As soon as I sat at our table, someone slid beside me. A shiver of pleasure raced under my skin. Torin. His scent was as familiar as the freckles on my nose and so intoxicating. The heat from his body swirled around me, filling me with a need so strong it hurt to breathe.

My heart pounding, I turned and looked into his brilliant blue eyes. I tried to force my heart to behave. Unfortunately, when he was this close, my body and my mind were never in sync. I tingled. My insides turned into jelly. My heart... Oh, my heart recognized and beat just for him, the craving for him shooting off the chart.

"What are you doing here?" he asked in that spellbinding voice.

For a moment, I let it wash over my senses and soaked it in. When he cocked his eyebrows, sanity returned. I faked indifference and arched my brow. "Right now? Waiting for Eirik to get our drinks and Cora to finish flirting. We have two more climbs. Then we might go shoot hoops at the Jump Zone. What are *you* doing here?"

A tiny smile tugged the corner of his lips. "Celebrating with the guys. We won."

"I heard." I glanced over his shoulder. His teammates were watching us, his harem of cheer bitches glowering. "But I meant, what are you doing here at *my* table when you should be at yours being worshipped by your adoring fans?"

He shook his head. "They are not important. Where's Andris?"

"I ditched him."

His eyebrows arched. Why?"

"Because he was being a tool. You won't believe what he did. He followed me all over the school like some Doberman guard dog, insulted my swim teacher, came to our store and pissed off my father, and then he had the nerve to tell me that *you* asked him to do it. You know, to keep an eye on me like I'm some helpless dimwit that can't take care of herself. You'd never ask him to do something that demeaning to me, would you?"

"No." He shook his head and flashed a wicked grin. "Never."

"Good, because if you had, I would have made your life miserable."

He laughed. "And I'd absolutely deserve it."

"Dang, you're good."

"I know."

I snorted. "I meant you're good at lying."

"It's called self-preservation." His eyes heated up. It took an effort to look away, but a lock of his hair had fallen on his forehead and I was dying to reach up and push it back. Fighting the temptation, I glanced at the girls at his table. They still glowered.

"So which one of the airheads are you dating?" *So I can plot her slow and painful death.*

He glanced over his shoulder. "None."

"Why not?"

"Something is missing." He smiled at Nancy Carpenter, the girl who usually clung to his arm. "Take Nancy for instance, her voice—"

"Is whiny and annoying," I finished.

He shuddered. "Half the time I want to tell her to shut up. Gina giggles incessantly, and Wendy is a total pushover."

I grinned. "Meredith is perfect, like a Barbie doll."

"I'm not into blondes or women who look like dolls." His eyes not leaving mine, he added, "I love spunky brunettes with curves."

And I love you too, Torin St. James. Before I could stop myself, I pushed the lock of hair from his forehead, my hand lingering on his warm, smooth skin. He went still, blue flames leaping in the depth of his eyes. I pulled back, balled my hand, and brought it down to my lap, my face burning.

Torin exhaled sharply as though he'd held his breath for too long. "Do that again."

His voice had dropped an octave, gone all husky and sexy. I shivered. "No."

"Touch me, Raine," he whispered achingly.

I wanted to touch him. Kiss him. Rip his shirt off and feast on every stretch of his hot body. I stared at his hands, my heart pounding with excitement and anticipation. One rested on the table, balled into a fist as though he was struggling for control. The other rested on the bench between us. He's shed his varsity jacket and only wore a short-sleeved black polo shirt that hugged his masculine arms and hinted at the hard chest and abs underneath.

"Please," he begged.

He'd sworn he would never beg me, I wanted to remind him, but this was not a time for snarky comments. He sounded like he was in pain.

I reached out and ran an unsteady finger along his knuckles. His breath hitched, but I didn't dare look up. Getting bolder, I ran my palm up his wrist, loving the way his muscles trembled and clenched. I stopped when I reached his elbow and let my hand drop.

"Let's get out of here," he ground out.

Once again, his husky voice sent a shiver of pleasure through me. "But—"

"No, buts." He got up, practically lifting me off the seat. My eyes met with Eirik, who already had our drinks. He was scowling. Where was Cora? I turned to search for her, but Torin took my wrist and tugged me toward the door. He took long strides, and I had to jog to keep with him.

"Wait. I have to explain to Eirik."

"His hands are full with Cora. Later, guys," he called out to his teammates.

The guys whistled, others caterwauled and made obscene gestures. I fought a blush. Cora stared at me in shock. She was still flirting with the players and Jaden pulled her onto his lap again, but since she was busy gawking at me I doubted she even noticed. I was going to have some explaining to do later, but I didn't care. The shocked expression on the other girls' faces was priceless.

Yeah, he's mine.

Cold air skidded on my skin when we left the building, and I shivered. I'd left my jacket behind. "Where are we going?" I asked.

Torin stopped and smothered a curse, an angry snarl rumbling through his chest.

"I forgot I hitched a ride from the bus," he ground out, the molten fire in his eyes churning as he stared down at me. He cupped my face, caressing my cheeks with the pads of his thumb. "Forget privacy. I can't wait."

He lowered his head, his warm breath chasing the cool air off my skin. My lips tingled. In my fantasy he'd made me wait, teasing me and making me crave his touch. This was real, and I didn't want to wait. I reached up, gripping his wrist, went on my toes, and met him halfway.

The taste of him sent every thought from my head. Every breath I took was filled with his scent. My hands moved to his chest and curled up, bunching the fabric of his shirt. His slipped through my hair and gripped the back of my head, the other moved lower, wrapping around my waist and bringing my body flush with his as he deepened the kiss. With each caress of his tongue, the hole inside my chest shrunk. This was what I'd been craving, this connection, the blending of our souls. Sensation after sensation rocked through me, and a moan escaped me. He echoed it then tore his lips away and pressed his forehead against mine, his breath ragged, his eyes closed.

"I needed that," he whispered, his voice tight.

Me too. I buried my face on his chest, my arms wrapping round him.

"When I stepped off the field today, I kissed Nancy."

I stiffened, but his arm tightened around me. He buried his head in my hair.

"Then Gina."

The hole inside me returned, tears rushing to my eyes. Why was he tormenting me with images of other girls in his arms?

"Wendy and Meredith were next, but something was missing. I didn't feel anything. I needed you, Freckles. Waiting for me." Air rushed out of my lungs, and my body relaxed. He leaned back, and his face tightened. "I'm sorry I made you cry again."

I shook my head, too choked up to talk. He was coming back to me. I wrapped my arms around his neck as we kissed again. The air was cool, yet my skin burned hot. His lips left mine and trailed along my jaw. He nipped my skin, and I gasped. He soothed it with his tongue, making me shudder. He chuckled, the sound heaving through me. It didn't matter what he did; my body responded, soaking it all in. I was hungry for him and greedy, and he knew it.

"Will you be at the field during playoffs?" he asked, his breath hot on my skin.

"Try and stop me."

Chuckling, he lifted me up, and I wrapped my legs around him. Through the glass wall, mothers glared at us. Another grabbed her daughter and dragged her away. Her little girl was still pointing at us. I giggled. I'd had no idea we were by the Jump Zone.

"We're disgraceful."

His arms tightened around me. "No. I might not understand this helpless pull you have over me, but I'd never call kissing you disgraceful."

I turned his head. "I meant to them."

He winked at the women glaring at us and chuckled when one harrumphed and gave us her back. But I saw the smile tugging her lips and the appreciative gleam in her eyes. No woman could resist Torin.

"Do you want to go back inside?" he asked, his voice smooth and low, reluctant.

"No." Now that I had him, I didn't want to share him.

"Did you come in Eirik's Jeep?"

"Yes. We parked west of the entrance by the trees." A weird, slightly familiar shiver washed over me, but I ignored it. Nothing was going to intrude on my time with Torin. Not even the Norns. "We can get the key from Eirik."

"We don't need a key." He gave me brief kiss and started down the sidewalk, his arms tight around me. Mine tightened around his neck and my legs around his waist.

The weird feeling grew stronger, sending a shiver down my spine. It was different from the kind I often felt whenever the three Norns were around. "Something is here."

Torin stopped and looked around. "What? Norns?"

"I don't know." I wiggled, forcing him to lower me down. I looked around, but nothing moved in the parking lot. Through the glass windows, I could see mothers grabbing their children's hands, jackets, and shoes. They seemed to be hurrying toward the exit.

We started back. What were we dealing with now? Or maybe my heightened senses from kissing him were messing with my Norn radar. Two girls burst from the exit and raced toward us. I recognized the cheerleaders before they stopped.

"They're killing each other, Torin," one said, her eyes wide. "It doesn't make sense. One minute they were okay; the next, they started punching each other."

I ran ahead before she finished talking. Torin stayed behind me even though I knew he could engage his runes and move faster and through anything. We almost bumped into mothers and their children racing toward the doors. A crowd gathered near the entryway and the wall of the rock climbing room.

Thuds and yells filled the air as we pushed through the crowd. The evil vibes I'd felt outside hit me hard, like an Arctic blast, and I winced.

"What in Hel's name?" Torin murmured.

Chaos was everywhere. The football players pummeled each other like mortal enemies, when a few minutes ago they'd been bonding over their victory. Their girls were at it too, yanking hair and screaming obscenities. Some climbers tried to kick and knock each other off the rock surface while others dangled in the air, their arms and legs locked. The ones who made it to the floor didn't bother to remove the harnesses before barreling into each other. Even the employees were fighting. I searched for Cora and Eirik, but I couldn't see them. Maybe they were on the other side of the wall.

I started forward, but Torin grabbed my arm. "No, stay with me."

"I have to find Eirik and Cora."

"You're not leaving my side. Whatever is causing this will have to go through me first to get to you."

I shivered, my eyes darting around. I couldn't see any strange women among the fighters, but I knew something was in the building. I felt its presence. "They're not Marj and her friends. This thing is pure evil."

I finally found Eirik. Why was he taking pictures at a time like this? He was also grinning as though the chaos was funny. I waved to attract his attention. "Eirik!"

He continued to take pictures, the smile on his face creepy.

"What's wrong with him?" Torin asked.

"I don't know, but that smile could rival the Joker's." I started toward him.

"Be careful, and stay where I can see you," Torin warned. He went toward his buddies, yanked them apart by the collars of their shirts, and snarled something. It didn't seem to work. As soon as he pulled them apart and moved to the next fighters, they lunged at each other again.

The violence was escalating. The evil sensations also seemed to grow more intense. I reached Eirik and grabbed his arm. "What are you doing? Where's Cora?"

"Who?" he asked as though he'd never heard of her and continued to press the button on his Nikon.

"Damn it, Eirik. What's wrong with you?" I yanked at the strap of his camera, forcing him to look at me. "Enough with the pictures."

He stared at me with unfocused eyes. Then something strange happened. His amber eyes acquired an eerie glow. I blinked.

"Eirik, your eyes." I touched his cheek.

The glow faded, and a confused expression settled on his face. "Raine? What are you doing here? I thought you left."

"I'm here now."

He looked behind me. "What the Hel is going on?" Before I could answer, he rushed past me.

I followed him. He reached down, pulling Cora out from under a table and into his arms. Her blonde tresses were riotous mess, and she had scratches on her face.

Still trying to understand what I'd seen in Eirik's eye, I stared at them. Then something else registered. Everyone had stopped fighting. It was as though someone had switched an off button. Groans and moans filled the room as people peeled themselves from the tables, the floor, and off whomever they'd pinned down. They all wore bewildered expressions as though they'd been under a spell or some weird power trip that made them act without thinking.

I closed my eyes and angled my head. The vibes I'd felt earlier were gone. Whatever had caused this mayhem was no longer in the building.

"That was weird," Torin said from behind me. Once again, I hadn't seen him move to my side.

"More than weird." I glanced at Eirik again, remembering the glow in his eyes. Whatever had been here had affected him differently than the others. Everyone had experienced unexpected rage, maybe loss of control. Eirik had slipped into some sort of trance. Laughing and taking pictures of people hurting each other was so not him. What if he'd been the target? What if the evil had waited until I left the room before striking?

Torin cupped my face. "What is it? You look stricken."

"I was supposed to protect him, but I left."

Torin's face grew tight. "You're talking about Seville?"

"Yes." Eirik and Cora joined the customers helping the employees put the chairs back and fix up the room. He seemed okay. Normal. I picked up a chair and turned it over the table, keeping my eye on Eirik. "Whatever it was waited until I left him alone then attacked. I should not have left."

Torin cursed, and my eyes swung to his. His eyes were narrowed, his jaw tense. "Do not blame yourself. You can't watch him twenty-four-seven."

"I have to." As a Norn, I could. I studied Torin's face. How could I be with him when Eirik needed me? "I must protect him."

Torin gripped my face and stared into my eyes. "I want to know everything the Norns told you. Everything."

I nodded. Cora and Eirik were walking toward us. "Tonight. When we are alone. Right now I need to get him out of here."

11. NIGHT TERRORS

There was mass exodus from Cliff House, most people spotting bruised chins, jaws, or knuckles. I walked silently beside Eirik and Cora, listening to conversations of students hurrying to their cars.

"That was jacked up, man," someone said behind us. "One second I was talking to Hollinger, the next I remembered the horse-collar tackle he pulled on me during practice a few days ago. Punching him just made sense."

"At least you have a reason. I don't know why I hit Granger. I mean, he's a douche, but that never bothered me before," another one said. "I just wanted him to shut up."

"Sorry, man. I saw you smiling at my girl and I lost it," another student said to our right as they crossed the street to their cars.

We piled inside the Jeep, and Cora immediately turned on the overhead car light and flipped down the visor.

"I can't believe that bitch Colleen attacked me." She studied her right cheek. Two welts ran from the corner of her mouth to her ear. One was puffy and red. "I'm going to be scarred forever."

She was so melodramatic. The wounds were superficial.

"No, you won't," Eirik said, cupping and gently stroking her face. "Two days and you'll be good as new."

"You sure?" Cora asked.

"Absolutely." He continued to stroke her jaw.

I hated to interrupt their moment, but I had to know one thing. "What happened back there, Cora?"

"I was talking to Jaden—"

"Flirting," Eirik corrected.

"I was not. We were discussing how I choose guys for my vlog when—"

"He pulled you onto his lap," Eirik finished again, not masking his annoyance. "I saw you through the mirror behind the food counter."

"Was I really flirting with anyone tonight, Raine?" Cora asked in a trembling voice, turning to glance at me.

Cora loved to flirt. Even though she thought it was harmless, Eirik always hated it and often gave her a hard time. "I, uh…"

Eirik snorted and started the engine. "I'll drop you off first, Raine."

Surprised he didn't offer to drop off Cora first, I sat back. The silence during the drive was thick with tension. My thoughts turned to Torin, and I smiled. Maybe things would work out between us after all. I felt a little guilty for being happy when my friends weren't even talking to each other. Maybe they'd have a chance to talk once they dropped me off.

Eirik pulled up outside my place, and I glanced over at Torin's. It was in total darkness. He wasn't home yet.

"Talk to you later, Raine," Cora said.

I nodded and waved.

"Later," Eirik added, but his expression said we needed to talk. He was smart enough to know that the incident at Cliff House was supernatural, which meant his people were involved.

I started toward my house as they took off. Muted light was visible through the living room window, and I wondered if Dad was asleep. He tended to leave the stair lights on when I hung out with my friends late at night. An SUV pulled up into Torin's driveway, and I stopped. He jumped down and hurried toward me.

"I was just going inside," I said.

"Not yet." The SUV took off, the driver hitting his horn. Torin waved and took my hand. "We need to talk."

I checked my watch. It was a little past eleven, so I had time. "I have to be home by midnight."

"I'll make sure you are tucked in bed."

I smiled at the visual. I'd pull him under the covers and not allow him to leave. He picked up a bag he must have dropped when he left the SUV, and we walked to his place. Inside, we headed to the family room. Ingrid didn't come out of her bedroom, but she must have cleaned up because there was no evidence of our earlier meal. While Torin went to the fridge for drinks, I shrugged off my jacket and put it on the counter, watching him.

"Soda or juice?" he asked.

"It doesn't matter."

He grabbed two bottles of apple juice, sauntered to where I stood, took my hand, and tucked it under his. "Come with me."

"Where are we going?"

"Upstairs to my room. It's private."

My heart started a crazy staccato beat, excitement washing over me. I didn't protest his assumption that I wouldn't mind going to his bedroom. I loved his take-charge attitude. Besides, I wanted to be with him, fall asleep in his arms again, and not because I just had a craniotomy.

"I need to know everything the Norns said about Seville, so I know what I'm up against."

I liked having him in my corner, though his words didn't match the look I'd seen in his eyes or the vibes I got from him. "Don't you mean what *we* are up against?"

"It doesn't matter how you phrase it, Freckles. I'm not letting Norns screw with your head again or force you to join them just to protect Seville."

Norns were maidens with zero interest in men or love. I wasn't that noble. Not now that Torin was back in my life. "I have no intention of becoming a Norn."

"Good because I wouldn't let you."

"Let me? Who died and gave you the key to my future?"

He stopped, his eyes roaming my face. I swallowed at the heat in his eyes. He let go of my hand, reached up, and pushed the hair away from my face.

"You did when you ran across your yard and fell into my arms like it was where you belonged. When you look at me with a mixture of innocent wonder, seductive charm, and enough defiance to make a lesser man back off." He lifted my chin, running his thumb across my lower lip. My breath caught. He gave me a slow, sexy smirk. "When I touch you and your breath catches." Slowly, his eyes not leaving mine, he lowered his head. "When you forget to breathe because I'm about to kiss you."

Just like that, thoughts of Eirik and Norns became insignificant. Anticipation rolled through me. I reached up and placed my hands on his chest, the thin material of his polo offering no barrier against the heat from his body.

"Do you know how hard this week has been for me?"

I swallowed, shaking my head, wishing he would stop talking and kiss me already.

"Wanting you, telling myself I shouldn't. Watching you flirt with those idiots Drew and Keith. Wanting to protect you from the morons at school and always coming short." He rubbed his cheek against mine, the contact sending heat coursing through me. "You have no idea how close I came to going from class to class at super speed and marking everyone with forgetful runes."

"It's okay." My hands fisted, bunching his shirt. The anticipating was killing me. "You protected me against the reporters."

"It's not enough. I plan to do more." He dropped kisses along my cheekbone, the corner of my eye, my temple. Slowly, he came down along my other cheek. My insides went all mushy at his tenderness, my heart pounding. Our breath mingled as he rubbed his nose against mine, and I trembled.

Getting impatient, I gripped his jaw. "Stop teasing me."

He chuckled, the sound rippling through me. "Funny, you tease me all the time. With a smile. A look. Walking into a room."

He rubbed his lips across mine, kissing my upper lip then my lower. I pressed against him, needing to get lost in him. The taste of him exploded in my senses until I was consumed with one thought: Torin. He became the reason I was breathing, all my senses tuned into him. If it were possible to be fused to another person, we would be one.

He lifted me up, one arm looping behind my knees, the other cradling me close, our lips locked. He kicked something, his door I presumed, and entered his bedroom. Lights came on and the door closed behind us. Gently, he laid me on his bed. He didn't give me a moment to look around. Not that I needed to. This used to be Eirik's room. I knew it was spacious and as big as the one across the hallway. My focus stayed on Torin's face. I heard the bottles of juice he'd carried knock as he put them on the table, then he lowered himself beside me, one leg trapping mine.

The feel of his body against mine took my breath away. He rained kisses on my face and my neck, taking little nips that had me gasping. I pressed against him, needing more. A low growl escaped him, and he was back to kissing my mouth, sucking me down into a whirlpool of emotions and sensations. I could stay with him like this for hours. Forever.

His knuckles moved up and down my bare arm before stopping at my waist, where my shirt and jeans met. He slipped his hand under my shirt, and I stopped breathing. The feel of his skin against mine was nothing like I'd ever imagined. I shivered. Was it possible to die from too much sensation? Maybe from not breathing.

I sucked in air, bunched his shirt, pulled, and imitated him, touching him intimately. He shuddered then went still. Sure I had done something wrong, I froze, too. My eyes flew to his. His eyes burned, his face tight with tension.

"Don't stop," he said in a voice an octave lower. Then he sat up and yanked off his shirt.

I was like a kid in a candy store. My eyes feasted on his broad chest. Golden skin. Rippling muscles. Taut abs. It was one thing to ogle him from afar and quite another to have him this close. At my mercy. Blood roaring past my ears, my pounding heart threatened to explode, I drooled.

He leaned against the pillow, hands behind his chest. "Go ahead."

I did. His skin was hot, smooth, his muscles flexing under my palm. A few times he held his breath, telling me without words what pleased him. I grew bolder, loving the feel of him.

He caught my wrist when I reached his belly button. "That's enough."

"But—"

"Come here," he whispered, studying me from under his lashes.

I crawled up his hot bod, draped myself over him like I'd always fantasized, and stared into his eyes. The fire in them had dimmed for some reason.

He pushed my hair back and cupped my head, his expression serious. "Tell me what the Norns said about Seville."

I blinked. "Now?"

He chuckled. "Yes, now. I have to tuck you into bed by midnight, and we have..." he checked his watch, "twenty minutes."

I pouted. I'd rather make out than talk about Norns, but from his expression, that wasn't going to happen. I sighed. "First, Eirik is not human. He is Baldur's son."

Torin tensed. "Odin's son Baldur?"

"Yes."

Torin cursed softly and sat up, forcing me to leave my comfortable position on his chest. He dropped a kiss on my lips then hopped off the bed and started to pace. The way the muscles shifted on his chest and stomach had me mesmerized. He had such a beautiful body. Lean. Hard. Masculine without being overpowering.

"This explains everything," he muttered. "Lavania's behavior, why he'd looked familiar when I first saw him, the crap that happened tonight. A force so dark and scary is after him they had to hide him down here." He sat, his blue eyes piercing. "Tell me word for word what the Norns said."

By the time I finished, Torin was pacing again.

"Say something," I said.

He continued to pace.

"You're seriously beginning to scare me."

He stopped, his eyes narrowed on me. "The Norns were right. He will need protection until we catch this thing after him. I don't know what happened tonight or if whatever affected the others was this, uh, shadow. He acted strange, almost like he was enjoying the carnage."

"Which is very strange for someone who hates violence. I think he was possessed."

Torin came to sit beside me, his eyebrows cocked. "What are you talking about?"

"When I went to talk to him, he didn't recognize me. I asked him about Cora, and he had no idea who she was either. Then his eyes glowed strangely. When they cleared, he seemed surprised by the chaos. The person we saw smirking and taking pictures wasn't the Eirik I know. Do Norns possess people?"

"Not that I'm aware of, but they never sleep, which makes them perfect watch dogs."

My stomach dropped. "Are you saying I have to be one of them to protect Eirik?"

"Hel's Mist no." He gripped my arms, his eyes flashing. "Never. I'm saying we have to find a way to protect him. You can't take on this responsible on your own, and the Norns had no business asking you. We will protect him together."

I liked it. The weight on my shoulders lifted, and I sighed. "You and I?"

"Andris, too. But first, we have to get Eirik out of his house and bring him here."

"His parents will want to know why."

"Leave them to me." He got up and offered me his hand.

"Are you sure about him living here? You have four bedrooms, and they're all taken." I glanced around. When Eirik lived here, there was a large-screen TV, gaming consoles, and a table with cameras and packs of photographs. Right now it held a large chair, a table with magazines about motorcycles, and a shelf with sports trophies. The wall that used to have pictures Eirik had taken over the years now had posters of different models of motorcyles. Some were modern, like his Harley, while others looked like they were straight from a steampunk novel. On the opposite wall were schematics of motorcycle engines. His love affair with motorcycles must have started hundreds of years ago.

"Or he could share your bedroom. It used to be his," I added

Torin pulled me up and into his arms, a wicked grin tugging his lips. "I don't share anything that belongs to me, Freckles. And I don't let anyone under my protection down. He will room with Andris."

"He's a god," I reminded him, wrapping my arms around him.

He snorted. "Yeah, some god who needs a slip of a Mortal girl to protect him."

I stuck out my tongue. "I'm not a slip of a Mortal girl, and I'll soon be Immortal."

He sighed. "I still don't understand why. You're perfect the way you are."

My insides turned into jelly, but I couldn't help wondering if my training was really an issue. "You're just saying that because you don't get emotionally involved with *little* Mortal girls."

He flashed a super wicked grin. "No, I don't. I use their bodies and move on, but I could be persuaded to seek more."

"Don't look at me. I'm still waiting for someone to persuade me to stop chasing emotionally unavailable guys."

He chuckled and leaned down to kiss me, but a loud noise from somewhere in the house interrupted him. We both froze.

"Stay here," he said and moved toward the door.

***

I was right behind him when he opened the door. More bangs and curses came from across the hallway. No, they came from behind Lavania's closed bedroom door.

"Do you think she's back?" I asked.

Torin glared at me over his shoulder. "I told you to stay back."

"You didn't say please. You think she and her husband are making out?"

He laughed.

"Shh." I gripped his arm. "They might hear... Yikes, let's go." The doorknob turned, and the door swung open. The edge of something wrapped up with brown paper appeared. Andris followed, gripping the sides of a large package. Black runes were on his face and arms, and he didn't seem to be straining. The edge of his package hit the opposite wall and left a dent.

"A little help here, bro," he said. "The damn thing keeps knocking things over."

Torin was still laughing when he went to help him. "What's this?"

"Portal. I just picked it up from Raine's family's store."

"Where's mine?" Torin asked.

"Do I look like a delivery man to you?" Andris retorted. "It's back in there."

"Remind me again why I'm holding one end of yours?"

"Because you're trying to impress your girlfriend." He winked at me as they walked past. They continued downstairs, still trading barbs.

Shaking my head, I peered inside Lavania's bedroom. The floor-to-ceiling mirror in the room was now a portal leading to Mirage. I could see a familiar aisle. What would Jared think when he found the mirrors gone? Dad would probably tell him Andris had picked them up after Jared had gone home. I was sure they had a system that shielded him from the Valkyrie world.

I touched the wall of the portal. It was solid though it looked like a swirling, white cloud. I tested the floor.

"Go ahead and try it," Torin said from behind me. He was alone. "It's solid."

"What happened to Andris?"

"He's being an ass."

"Thanks," Andris said, stepping off the stairs.

I followed them into the store. Both men engaged their runes, which glowed and lit up the dark room. Through the window, I could see the deserted street. I checked my watch. It was time to head home. I didn't want to leave, but my father would go ballistic if I wasn't home by midnight.

"I should head home," I said, watching Torin and Andris lug the mirror to his room.

"Wait for me," Torin said.

"I'll be downstairs." I went to the kitchen to get my jacket and shrugged it on. Torin was there when I turned around. He'd put on his shirt. He lifted the hair from under my collar, followed through and gripped my nape as though he couldn't stop himself, and kissed me again.

"I don't want you to leave," he whispered.

"I have to. My dad—"

"I know." He kissed my nose then reached down and gripped my hand. We started for the entrance just as Andris entered the living room. He chuckled.

"Look at you two love birds. I guess I haven't lost my touch." Andris grinned and pulled off biker's gloves. "I should fly around with an arrow and a sling."

I frowned. "What are you talking about?"

"Ignore him," Torin said, opening the door.

"You owe me, big bro."

"Whatever you want," Torin threw over his shoulder.

"Your Harley," Andris said, following us outside.

"Take it," Torin said without hesitation.

I looked over my shoulder to see Andris punch the air. "Are you really going to give him your bike?"

"He's earned it, but he won't keep it. As usual, he was trying to prove a point."

"Which is what?"

"What is more important to me. It's a no brainer." We started down the driveway, then down the sidewalk. It was cold and wet, and the skies overcast. Cold sipped through my thin jacket, and I shivered. Torin's arms tightened around me. "You're cold. Next time, we'll use the portal and go straight to your room."

I loved the idea. "I have a thing about portals, you know."

"What?"

"I don't like using them unless absolutely necessary."

"That's too bad. I was planning on sneaking into your room sometime and holding you until you fell asleep."

My stomach dipped, but in a good way. I would love that. We stopped outside the door. "Maybe I'll change my mind about portals."

"Maybe I'll do it for you." And he did with a long, toe-curling, make-me-want-to-rip-his-clothes-off kiss. He stopped too soon and pressed his forehead against mine. "Do you have plans for tomorrow?"

My mind was too scrambled after the kiss to understand anything. I couldn't think, let alone string together a sentence.

Torin grinned. "Take deep breaths, until your head clears. If that fails, I'll take a step back and give you space. You know, stop messing with your head."

Reality returned at his teasing. I playfully punched him in the gut. "Shut up."

He doubled over, laughing. "Okay, about tomorrow. Do you want to hang out?"

"Oh, yes. I'm jogging with Dad in the morning, and after lunch I was planning on visiting a few graves." Dad might have been right about that one.

Torin shuddered. "Why?"

"Some of my friends died during the meet. I left before the funerals and uh... Anyway, I thought I'd place flowers on their graves." His eyes grew intense as he studied me. Heat crawled up my face. "I know it sounds morbid. Even Dad said I'd done, uh, enough. Will you stop staring at me like that?"

"You're amazing." He pressed a kiss on my temple. "No, it's not morbid, but I'm starting to learn it's the kind of thing you, Lorraine Cooper, do. Better go inside before your father comes to the door with a shotgun."

"Dad doesn't believe in guns," I said. "Goodnight."

"Really?"

I reached up and kissed him, taking my time. "Better?"

He chuckled. "For now. See you tomorrow."

He waited until I was inside.

***

Upstairs, I changed into flannel pajamas, brushed my teeth, and glanced out the window, but Torin's room was in total darkness. Tomorrow couldn't come soon enough. I slipped under the covers and relived the evening. I was almost falling asleep when my cell phone buzzed.

I dived for it. Eirik. Disappointment rolled over me. Of course Torin wouldn't text me. He shunned modern technology.

"I'm coming over," Eirik's text said.

"Now?" I texted back.

"Yeah. We need to talk."

"Tomorrow."

A warm draft swept across my room, and I sat up, my eyes flying to the mirror. It rippled like water. Sighing, I scooted to the edge of my bed. By the time I turned on the bedside lamp, my mirror had become a churning whirlpool of cloudy mass. I seriously needed to rethink having the mirror in my room. It didn't even have stupid runes on its frame. The cloudy mass formed a vortex as it peeled back and formed a doorway.

Eirik entered my room.

"It's after midnight, Eirik. Did you read my last text?"

"Yes, but tomorrow is not good enough for me. I can't sleep. I haven't been able to sleep for weeks."

Something in his voice killed my protest. I patted my bed. "Sit. Why?"

He sat, leaned forward and rested his elbows on his knees. He scrubbed his face.

"What is it?" I asked, moving closer to rub his arm. He was trembling. "Eirik."

He blew out air and sat up. "I don't know what's happening to me, but after the incident at Cliff House, I had to talk to you. Every night, I go to sleep, and the next thing I know, my parents are holding me down, trying to calm me. I wake up sweating, breathing hard like I sprinted, and my heart pounding, Raine. My parents said I bolt upright screaming."

"Are they nightmares?"

"No. Mom said they are night terrors. I wake up scared out of my head. Can I, uh, sleep here?"

"Sure."

He got up, pulled out the rollout bed, and grabbed extra pillows from my bed. He knew where everything was because he often slept over. He plopped on his back, hands crossed behind his head. Torin had pulled that move earlier, baring his body for me to explore. Thinking about him made me ache. I swallowed and pushed the image aside, forcing myself to focus on Eirik, who needed me.

I lay on my stomach and studied him. He looked like crap. I'd noticed the shadows under his eyes this morning, and he'd lost weight, which now made sense.

"When did these night terrors start, and how often do you get them?"

"They started right after the meet. They happen every few days, but they're getting worse. I think I hurt my mother last night." He paused and scowled. "She seemed afraid of me."

"What's causing them? I mean, do you remember anything when you wake up?"

He shook his head. "Nope. Tonight, I felt the same intense panic before I blacked out. I blacked out at Cliff House, didn't I?"

I nodded. "You looked confused, didn't recognize me or Cora when I asked you where she was. Did you see any strangers before that happened?"

His scowl deepened. "You think the Norns are doing this to me?"

"I wouldn't put it past them."

He shook his head. "No, I didn't see anyone. One second I was watching Cora flirt with some stupid jock, the next you were yanking my camera and telling me to snap out of it. I have no idea what went down. When did you go back inside? The last time I saw you, you couldn't wait to disappear with St. James."

There was just a slight bite in his voice, which told me Torin was still a sensitive subject. "We were outside when I felt a presence so powerful I couldn't ignore it. At first I thought the Norns were back, but there was something different about the vibes. It's kind of hard to explain." I told him everything—what we'd seen, including him smirking and taking pictures of the people fighting, then his reaction when I'd approached him, the shadow in his eyes. "It was as though you were, uh, not you."

He closed his eyes and pinched the bridge of his nose. "Maybe I'm *not* me anymore. First the night terrors, now blackouts, and you know what? I bet it has something to do with *their* world." He pulled the blanket to his waist and covered his face with his arm. "Can you turn off the lights? I don't want to talk about this anymore."

My heart ached for him. I reached down and tugged at his arm. "Hey." He resisted before lowering his arm. "We'll figure this out and stop whoever it is. I promise."

He snorted. "You can't help me, Raine. Let's go to sleep."

"No, you don't understand. It is my job to protect you. The Norns told me when I saw them at the cafeteria."

He sat up, resting his weight on his elbows, amber eyes narrowed. "What?"

"I couldn't say anything before because I, uh, kind of didn't believe them. I thought they were just trying to manipulate me. That's why I asked Lavania about you." He frowned, and I knew I was doing a crappy job of explaining. I started from the beginning, telling him what Marj and her friends had told me without bringing Torin into it. "I wasn't sure how to bring it up because there was really no reason to, until now."

He shook his head. "What did they mean by you're alive because of me?"

"I don't know. Maybe they saved me because they knew one day I'd stop this monster from coming after you."

He plopped on his back. "You're crazy, so are the Norns. You're just a girl, a Mortal. How can you possibly stop some supernatural monster you can't even see?"

Maybe I had to become a Norn to see it, and the first step to being one was becoming an Immortal. The thought made my stomach hurt.

12. PLAYING CUPID

It was eight when I woke up. Sprawled on his stomach across the rollout bed, Eirik snored softly. He had removed his T-shirt during the night.

I slipped from my covers, left my bedroom, and carefully closed the door so as not to wake up Eirik. Downstairs, Mom was finishing her breakfast. The presence of a plate in the sink and a folded newspaper on the table said Dad had already eaten. The smell of coffee chased sleep from my eyes.

"Hey, sweetie," Mom said.

"Hey," I mumbled.

"Rough night?"

"Late night." On the stove was a covered pan. I lifted the lid and grinned. Eggs and bacon. Enough for two. I snatched a piece of bacon, poured myself a cup of coffee, and added creamer. Mom's eyes followed me the entire time. I sat on a chair across from her, sipped my drink and rested my head on my arm.

"Did you go out last night?" she asked.

"Yeah. We went to Cliff House. I asked Dad, and he said it was okay."

"Who did you go with?"

"Cora and Eirik." I got up and served myself, leaving enough for Eirik. "Are you going to the store soon?"

She checked the clock on the microwave. "Jared is opening, but I'll be leaving around ten. Why? Did you want to come with me?"

"No. I'm running with Dad in," I glanced at my watch, "fifty minutes."

"No wonder he was so chipper this morning." She sipped her drink. In the middle of the table were a box of chamomile tea and a bottle of honey. Mom was a serious tea-drinker. "How's Eirik?"

She had an uncanny way of knowing things. Must be her Valkyrie abilities. She'd known the moment Torin moved next door. How had she put it? She had enough runic magic left to tell if a Valkyrie was nearby. Did her radar pick up deities or a grandson of deities like Eirik? It might explain how she always knew whenever he was in my room. Another thought occurred to me. According to Lavania, Mom was famous in their realm. Had Torin known she was a Valkyrie before he healed me? It might explain why he'd talked to me about magic and hadn't been bothered by the runes on my car.

"Raine?"

I focused on Mom. "Eirik is okay."

"Are he and Cora dating?"

"I don't know. I mean, it's not official or anything but they do stuff together."

Mom's eyes narrowed. "Like what?"

I rolled my eyes. "Boyfriend and girlfriend stuff. When did you say you're going to the shop again?"

"Why do I have a feeling you're trying to get rid of me?" Her eyes shifted to a spot behind me, and she smiled. I turned, expecting to see Eirik.

Dad, in black running pants with matching shirt and a red and black jacket, walked toward us. In his hands were a fuel band with four empty water bottles, several packets of energy gels, and a bottle of electrolyte tablets. He planned to turn our morning run into a training session. Go figure. The tablets were for replenishing the salts he was sure to lose sweating, and the gels were energy boost packs. On his wrist was a band, which contained his ID and emergency contacts. He covered all bases when he ran or biked long distance. I still thought he wasn't ready for serious training.

"Want some?" he asked, dangling the electrolyte bottle.

"No, thanks. I plan to be back in an hour."

He chuckled, putting everything down. "You're going to desert me?"

"Oh yeah. Thirty minutes out, thirty back. I'm not training for the Ironman." I went back to my breakfast while he kissed Mom. She got up to help him fill the water bottles, which he put back into the pouches on the fuel belt. He slipped a few power gel packets in the narrower pouches. When they kissed again, I rolled my eyes.

"I'm eating you know," I reminded them.

"Then don't watch," Dad said.

I left them kissing and went back upstairs to change. Eirik was still out. I put my hair into a ponytail and checked my iPod. It was fully charged. I still had time to spare, so I powered up my laptop to read up on night terrors.

There was so much information on the subject. Words popped out at me, confirming what Eirik had told me. Bolting upright. Screams. Excessive sweating. Harsh breathing. Pounding heart. Eyes wide with terror. Punching. Swinging. Kicking. Acting like you are fleeing, which could translate into sleepwalking. People with night terror could seriously hurt themselves. When awoken, they experienced confusion, inability to be consoled, and they were unresponsive and unable to recognize anyone. Most often they lashed out at the person waking them, physically hurting them. Worse, they didn't remember the incident. No wonder Eirik thought he'd hurt his mother.

I saw the time and winced. Grabbing my iPod from the recharger, headphones, and a baseball cap, I ran around to the pullout bed and tried to wake up Eirik. He mumbled something and turned. Dang it. I scribbled him a note, taped it on the mirror since I knew he'd use the portal, and hurried out of the room. Mom was still in the kitchen, cleaning.

"Where's Dad?"

"Garage."

"Bye, Mom." I slipped on the baseball cap.

"Do you want me to wake up Eirik before I leave?"

Damn her Valkyrie antenna. Grimacing, I turned. "Will I be all-knowing once I become a Valkyrie?"

She grinned. "Maybe. How's the training?"

"Great. I got my artavo and next week, we'll start on runes."

"Wow, you're on a fast track. Okay, go. I'll wake up Eirik before I leave and make sure he eats breakfast."

I ran back and gave her a kiss. "You're the best."

"No, I'm not. I plan to show him the pull out couch in the den and remind him of what I told him weeks ago. I don't mind him sleeping here, but he cannot do so in your room."

"It's okay, Mom. I don't mind." I ran toward the garage door.

"I wasn't asking," I heard her retort before I closed the door.

Dad was adjusting something on his bike. "You're not planning on biking today, too"

He glanced up. "Maybe tomorrow if the weather behaves. Come on."

I studied him as we started down the driveway. Maybe I was worried about him for nothing. He seemed to be in a happy mood. Mrs. Rutledge peered at us from behind her curtain. Dad didn't seem to notice because his attention was on Torin's house even though no one was outside. I waved to Mrs. Rutledge, and the curtain fell back in place. Grinning, I adjusted the strap of my iPod around my arm.

"You're going to listen to that?"

"Yes, once I leave you behind." I grinned.

He laughed. I shoved the headphones in my pocket because I knew he liked to talk. It was warmer than usual, though the sky was overcast, and we weren't the only ones taking advantage of the weather. Kayville had numerous walking and running trails. Some looped around the parks scattered around town, while others led to the nature trails east of town and the surrounding mountain range. We headed toward the closest park, Willow Community Park. It had a 1-K trail.

Dad avoided talking about Valkyries or my training as we walked first then jogged. Instead, he focused on upcoming local events. He planned to participate in 5K and 10K races. After two loops, we stopped and drank some water. He munched on an energy bar after chewing on an electrolyte gel. I liked the gels because they tasted like gummy bears.

"I'm going down to Baker Creek Road, then loop back on Fox Ridge."

"That's a long stretch," I said, not sure whether to worry.

"Three hours." He rotated his head and flexed his shoulders.

Even with the electrolyte and engine bars, marathon runners' legs tended to cramp if they pushed themselves too much. Mom had picked up Dad a few times after he cramped.

"Do you have your cell phone?" I asked.

He chuckled. "Yes. I'll be fine. Go."

I took off, glanced back a few times, and found him watching me while jogging in place. Soon I took a corner and couldn't see him anymore.

I hadn't gone for ten minutes when Torin suddenly appeared beside me. I slowed down to a walk, surprised, and not in a good way. I looked like a walking ad for sweat. I pressed stop on the iPod and removed my earbuds.

"What are you doing here?"

"Jogging. Don't stop on my account," Torin said, turning to jog backwards.

He looked sinfully hot in running shorts and a sleeveless shirt that bared his arms and clung to his sculptured chest. There was sheen of sweat on his arms and face, and an appreciative gleam in his eyes as he studied me. How could he possibly find me attractive now? I was a serious sweater, and this morning was no different. I had removed my jacket to cool off and tied it around my waist, leaving me with my fitted tank top.

"You didn't see me earlier?" he asked.

"No. Was I supposed to?" I tugged at the visor of my cap and wiped the sweat off my forehead.

A sexy smirk curled his lips. "I was behind you and your dad. The best view I've ever had during my morning runs."

Heat flooded my cheeks. "I'll tell Dad he has an admirer."

Torin laughed. "Come on. Let's go."

I put the headphones in the pocket of my jacket and started jogging again.

"You want to have lunch with me?" he asked, falling beside me.

"Today?"

"Yes, and tomorrow, and the day after tomorrow, and the day after..."

"If you catch me before we reach the entrance of the park, then I'm yours."

He flashed another wicked grin. "A dare. I'm game."

"No cheating with runes." I took off. I could hear him behind me. I glanced over my shoulder and shook my head. He wasn't even trying. Instead, he winked at me, clearly patronizing me. I faced forward and sprinted toward the entrance. Next second, I was airborne.

I screamed and grabbed his neck. "What are you doing?"

"Catching you. Claiming you. You're now mine." He stopped jogging and kissed me. He didn't seem to care that I was sweaty. Oh, he tasted great and salty and naughty. He lifted his head. "Lunch?"

"Yes."

He put me down and took my hand. We walked all the way home.

***

The house was silent when I entered, but I still called out, "Mom?"

No response.

"Eirik?"

Again, silence greeted me.

There was no message from Mom, so I assumed she had left for the store. Upstairs, Eirik had pushed back the rollout bed and put away the beddings and pillows. My note was gone from the mirror, but he'd sent me a text to call him when I got home from my run.

I showered first, blow-dried my hair, and curled the tips. I was really loving my hair curled. Carefully, I applied make-up. The skinny jeans I chose hugged my hips, and the green cowl-necked top was sexy without being too much. I added boots and texted Eirik as I headed downstairs. Dad still wasn't back. I tried his cell phone, but he didn't pick up. I hoped he was okay.

Outside, I took a deep breath and started toward the driveway. Anticipation rolled through me, and my heartbeat kicked up a notch at the thought of seeing Torin again. I noticed a movement at their patio, but it was Andris. Dressed in his trademark black—silver hair disheveled—he lounged on a patio swing chair for two, coffee mug cradled between his hands. The chair was new. He watched me intently, until I stepped on their porch and he stopped rocking the chair.

"Nice. The outfit says available without screaming desperate," he said.

"I'm sure there's a compliment in there somewhere."

He chuckled and patted the seat beside him. "Sit and visit with me, sweetheart."

I glanced toward their door.

"He's in the shower, unless you're planning on joining him." He wiggled his brow.

Heat crawled up my face. Instead of sitting beside him, I leaned against the patio rail and studied him. "Are you having lunch with us?"

"Nah, I have plans."

Last night he'd had a date with the cute guy from school. "So how was your date?"

"Beautiful. I think I might be in love. Or in lust. I can never tell the difference. So what do I get for making this happy reunion happen?"

I cocked my brow. "What?"

He leaned forward and rested his elbows on his knees, causing the swing to rock. "You think big brother woke up on Friday and decided to come after what he wants? Nope." He pointed at me. "I beat some sense into him on Thursday night."

Yeah, right. I'd seen the destruction they caused when they fought. "What did you tell him?"

"Everything from the moment I saw you and thought you were available to your selfless willingness to save your friends at the meet."

I wasn't sure how to take his confession. I'd tried to tell Torin the truth, but he hadn't believed me. "Why?"

"Why what?"

"Why did you tell him?"

"His moping around was beginning to drive everyone nuts. Was he happy hearing about your shared past? Nope, but he couldn't tell me to shut up with Lavania around." He chuckled. "That's one thing about Torin. If you want him to behave, you wait until she's around."

My conversation with their maker flashed through my head. "Are you saying she was there while you talked to Torin?"

"She was in the kitchen cooking, but I'm sure she overheard us. So what do I get for playing Cupid?"

"Um, a thank you?"

He scowled. "Is that what he's worth to you?"

Last night's conversation between him and Torin made sense now. Torin had given him his Harley for bringing us back together. How romantic. My insides softened. "Anything you want."

The smile left his eyes. "Answers about Maliina."

His ex? "What do you want to know?"

"Everything she did to you while I was off escorting souls home. It might give me a clue to what I did wrong, so it never happens again. Torin, with his jacked up memories, can't help me and, uh," he scratched his temple, "I don't want to ask Ingrid. She's still sensitive about Maliina's disappearance."

My phone buzzed. It was Eirik again. I ignored it, and focused on Andris. "Okay. What do you want to know?"

"We'll talk later." He leaned back against the chair and gently swayed. "Go on in. Maybe you might catch him changing and never leave his bedroom."

I reached a conclusion as I listened to him. "You're definitely not the one vandalizing our lockers at school."

He snorted. "You suspected me? That hurts." His mock outrage didn't last. "Why?"

"I didn't suspect just you. I suspected all Valkyries. My counselor said Officer Randolph staked out the lockers, yet someone slipped by him and wrote on it. That means the person responsible—"

"Moved so fast the human eye couldn't see him or her," he finished.

I nodded. "Don't worry. You're off the list now."

He glared at me. "Oh gee, thanks."

I grinned. "You're welcome. Of course, Torin wouldn't do anything to hurt me."

"Yeah, he's whipped. That leaves Ingrid." Andris jumped to his feet and marched to the door.

"And Lavania," I added, following him.

"She is above reproach."

"Spoken like a loyal son," I mumbled.

"I heard that, smarty mouth. She wouldn't harm a Mortal, or would-be Immortal." He opened the door and yelled, "INGRID! Get your lovely ass out here."

"You're going to ask her now?"

"Of course. Don't give me that look," he added. "I'll be subtle." His eyebrows shot up when Ingrid appeared wearing a lacy, see-through blue camisole and matching panties. "Nice, but inappropriate, young lady. Get dressed. I'm taking you out to lunch."

Ingrid grinned.

"Wipe that grin off your face. It's not a date," he added rudely. "We're leaving the house to give Torin and Raine some privacy."

Ingrid pouted then turned and walked toward her bedroom, the sway of her hips exaggerated. Andris watched her with a transfixed expression. As if she knew he was watching, she stopped and threw him a glance over her shoulder before disappearing into the hallway. He blew out air and scrubbed his nape.

"You like her," I said, grinning.

He glared.

"Andris and Ingrid sitting in a tree," I sang and danced. "K-I-S-S-I-N-G."

He made a face. "She's off limits."

"Why?"

"Because I say so," he said in a firm voice, sounding so serious and grownup all of a sudden. "You'll get your answer when we come back from lunch. Personally, I don't think she's the one. She's incapable of doing anything mean."

He really liked her. "That leaves no one."

"No, that leaves the Norns. Think about it. The more you are ostracized the more you'll do what they want. Norns wipe out memories. The first thing they'll teach you is how to make everyone forget what happened at that meet."

"No, they won't," Torin said, stepping into the living room. "Raine will never become a Norn." He looked gorgeous in a blue shirt that made his eyes even more brilliant. He didn't stop until he was in front of me.

As usual, having him this close sent a flurry of activities in my stomach. He reached up and tucked my hair behind my ear, then lowered his head ever so slowly, making me wait and anticipate his kiss. I hated it when he did that and loved it when he made up for it.

I closed my eyes, but all he did was brush his lips against mine then lean back. My eyes flew open. He smirked, the tease, then said, "You should have left five minutes ago, Andris."

"Damn straight," Andris said. "I don't want to hang around like a third wheel while you make googly eyes at each other."

"Ignore him," he said, gripping my hand. "He's just jealous." He led me to the kitchen. "You sit here," he directed me to a stool. "I'll take your order. Salad or sandwich." There was a head of lettuce, tomatoes, red onions, bread, different cold cuts, and slices of cheese. He planned to make everything fresh.

I grinned. "Salad."

"Ah, I thought you might say that." He reached for the cutting board and pulled out a knife from a knife-holder. He started slicing tomatoes like a pro, his movements fast and efficient. The slices were evenly cut.

"Where did you learn to do that?"

"Here and there. One thing we Valkyries have is time. When not pretending to be in high school or college waiting for some poor guy to die or escorting souls to the halls, we keep busy learning things. I can cook better than most chefs," he bragged, "repair any engine blind-folded, name every city in every country and speak all languages known to man, including extinct ones." He picked up a red onion and cut it in half from the stem tip to the root end. He chopped the first half without shedding a tear.

"Okay, you have to show me how you did that."

"Come here." I got up and walked to his side. He guided me to stand between him and the counter with my back to his front. Resting his chin on my shoulder, his cheek against my ear, he gave me the knife and guided my hand.

It wasn't easing concentrating when his breath brushed my cheek or when I knew I could easily turn my head and kiss him, and slice my fingers off. He rubbed his cheek against mine and I sighed.

"Focus," he warned.

"Then stop messing with my head," I muttered.

He chuckled, the sound sexy and rich, and I found myself grinning back. Somehow, he managed to show me how to hold the onion with my knuckles bent so I wouldn't cut myself and slice pieces horizontally without my eyes watering. "Good job."

I turned my head and whispered in his ear, "Thank you."

He groaned and kissed me.

"Score," I said.

He leaned back and cocked his eyebrow. "You want to play?"

"No." I shook my head.

"Oh, yes. Let's see who can tempt the other more."

We spent an hour preparing what should have taken us ten-fifteen minutes, and I lost by a mile. He showed me how to wash a head of lettuce and make a mouthwatering sandwich without making the bread soggy. It was probably the most fun I'd ever had preparing a meal.

"Tell me how we met," he said after we finished eating.

"But Andris—"

"Gave me his version, which was embellished to make me look like a jackass. I'm sorry I didn't believe you before, Freckles. Will you forgive me?"

I nodded, laughing and trying hard to fight tears. I would forgive him anything if it meant he'd remember what we had. Not leaving anything out, I told him how we first met to when he disappeared. His eyes became shadowed and his jaws clenched when I explained how devastated I'd felt when he'd disappeared, how I'd searched for him during the dance and made a deal with the Norns to bring him back. I wasn't done talking when he pulled me into his arms.

"Enough," he whispered harshly. "I'm so sorry I caused you such pain."

I wasn't sure who was more shaken, me from reliving that horrifying week or him from hearing it. "No, it's not your fault. The Norns did this to us."

"But I let it happen. I should have healed you when I had a chance and faced the consequences." He leaned back and ran his knuckles under my eyes, and I realized I was crying. He caressed the side of my face, touched the tip of my nose. "I promise you here and now, I will never make you go through such pain again."

I nodded.

His eyes searched my face. "I want to remember everything. Will you help me?"

"Okay, but my mom said Norns are thorough when they scramble people's memories. My dad never remembered their time together when the Norns were through with him."

"Your father is a Mortal. I'm a Valkyrie. I will remember." His arrogance reared its ugly head, but I didn't care. "I want to remember seeing you for the first time, how I felt when we first touched, our first kiss. I want to remember holding you while you slept after your surgery. I want to know the pain of almost losing you, so I can appreciate having you—"

I kissed him this time, shutting him up. "It's the same every time we kiss, Torin. Every time you touch me or look at me. We can create more memories."

"I still want our memories back," he insisted stubbornly, and I knew hearing about what happened wasn't the same as having those memories back. He stroked the right side of my head where I'd had the craniotomy. "May I?"

Feeling a little self-conscious, I nodded. He parted my hair and ran his fingers along my lumpy scalp, searching for the titanium screws holding the piece of bone the surgeons had cut out and fused with a titanium plate.

"Does it hurt or feel uncomfortable?" he asked in a low voice as though he was imagining my pain.

"No. I don't think about it except when I shampoo my hair," I lied. The area no long hurt, but it was lumpy, which was uncomfortable, and a few times I thought I felt a loose screw. "I saw a physical therapist a few days ago, and he massaged the scar. He encouraged me to do it often to make my scar and scalp more flexible."

"So that's why you were at the hospital," Torin said.

That explained the sound of a Harley engine I'd heard. "You've been stalking me."

"Keeping an eye. Not the same thing." He massaged the scar, his movements light and tender. It felt nice. "How about I take you in next time? That way I don't have to stalk you."

I glared. "You're not going to start treating me like a breakable doll."

He wrapped his arms around me, lowered his head, and buried his face in my hair. I was seated between his thighs on the family room couch with my back to his chest. "Why not? You're a delicate Mortal, and I never want you to feel any pain again. Besides, you got hurt because of me."

"Hmm, let me think about that." I scrunched up my face. "One, I won't be Mortal for long, and that's something you must accept. Second, it was definitely *not* your fault. Third, you're not going to the hospital with me. My PT finally got enough guts to mention what happened at the meet. I have a feeling next time he'll ask me outright how I'd known the swimmers would get hurt, and I don't want you scaring him and making him think the worst. I plan to give him a reasonable answer in a calm voice."

Torin had gone still as soon as I'd mentioned the meet. "Okay."

I leaned sideways and studied his face. "That was too easy."

"I'm easy."

"Yeah, right." I slid from between his legs and turned to kneel in front of him. "I want to show you something."

He looked at me expectantly.

"Come to the cemetery with me."

Torin shuddered. "Why? I hate cemeteries."

He was such a baby about some things. "And hospitals, too, I know. Yet you spent a week with me after my surgery."

"There's a big difference between staying in a hospital with the girl I'm crazy about and willingly visiting a graveyard where souls float around because they're too stupid to realize there's nothing left for them here."

He was crazy about me? I loved it. "If you're too chicken to go with me, you don't have to," I teased and almost laughed when his eyes narrowed menacingly. I got off the couch. "You can wait by the church, which is why I want you come anyway. It might help trigger some of your memories."

He jumped up as though I'd said the magic word. "Did you just call me chicken?"

13. IT IS OFFICIAL

"I can't believe he took my ride," Torin complained as he parked the SUV outside a local dollar store that afternoon. It was the tenth time he'd mentioned it, and I couldn't help rolling my eyes. "After modifying and tweaking the engine to perfection, there'll never be another Rod."

Did he say ride or Rod? "Then buy him another one," I suggested.

"I can't. He deserves this one." He switched off the engine and threw me a glance. "We've been through a lot, you know."

"You and Andris?"

He snorted. "No. I'm talking about Rod."

I giggled. "You named your bike?"

"Of course, doesn't everyone?"

I shook my head. "Not that I know of."

"Not even your ex who happened to look just like me and rode a Harley?"

I grinned, remembering the lie I'd thrown at him to save face. "Oh yeah, him. He never told me, but he would never part with his."

"He just did. Don't move." He hopped down, walked around, opened the passenger door, and offered me his hand. "Careful," he warned. He looked at the front of the store and grimaced. "Why are we at a *dollar store*?"

He made it sound like the store was a cesspool of everything disgusting. Worse, his voice carried and people turned to stare. He just glared at them, not apologetic in the least.

"I don't think they sell fresh flowers here," he added.

"I'm not looking for fresh flowers." I pulled him inside and down an aisle to the shelves with silk flowers. When I selected several yellow roses and turned, he stared at me in disbelief. "This is the best place to buy cheap silk flowers. We'll grab a pair of scissors and a reel of ribbon to make timeless bouquets. I wish Cora was with us. She makes the best bouquets ever."

Torin rubbed his chin, his eyes volleying between me and the flowers in my hand. "You know, I, uh, can afford to pay for real flowers for your friends' graves, right?"

"I know." After hundreds of years, he, like most earth-based Valkyries, was loaded. "But the local cemeteries have a policy about what flowers you can put on graves in different seasons. Only silk flowers between the months of October and April."

He got a cart and insisted on paying for the flowers. We left with several bulky bags and headed north. Grandview Baptist Church on was on 10 North and Fulton Street. The church had a graveyard, but it was smaller than Northridge Cemetery, where most of the swimmers were buried.

Outside the church, Torin looked around curiously. "You and I came to this church?"

"Yes. Remember Kate, the swimmer I told you died after the accident at the club?" I waited until he nodded before adding, "She was buried in Northridge Cemetery, but the service was held here. The swim team came."

He looked toward the church. "Did I go inside?"

I nodded. "I was halfway through a badly rehearsed eulogy when you appeared. Things got a bit crazy after that, and you had to take me home." Torin's eyes narrowed as though he wanted to ask a question, but I didn't give him a chance. I grabbed his hand and pulled him toward the entrance. "Come on. It's always open."

I was happy when he didn't ask why he had to take me home. Thinking about my complete meltdown in front of everyone, including him, still made me cringe. I also felt a little guilty at how I'd envied Kate's family for finding closure. At the time, my father had been missing for months and we hadn't known whether he was alive or dead. My personal grief had intruded during my speech.

"You stood right here while I was over there." I left him by the door and went to the podium. I pretended to talk and made goofy face. He rolled his eyes. He'd stood at that very spot, arms crossed, and encouraged me with a smile whenever I'd faltered. That was before the meltdown. I think that was the moment I knew he had my heart.

I left the podium and rejoined Torin, but there was a shift in his mood. Even though he slipped his arm around my shoulders, he was quiet as we left the church.

"Did you, uh, remember anything?"

He shook his head. I started to worry when we sat in the car and he helped me make bouquets without saying a word. It was as though his mind was elsewhere. When we finished, he insisted on coming with me to the graveyard behind the church, which was totally sweet.

"Are you sure?" I asked.

He shot me a tiny smile. "Someone has to protect you from wandering souls."

My feet faltered, cold fingers crawling up my back. I couldn't tell from his expression whether he was serious or joking. He could be messing with my head again.

"Are you saying there could really be ghosts in the graveyard?"

"Lost souls. I'll let you know when I see one or two. Or three. Or—"

"Quit scaring me." Swallowing, I moved closer to him, and his arm tightened around my shoulder. "Let's finish and get out of here."

Grandview graveyard wasn't spooky like some cemeteries I'd seen around the state. It had trees on the outskirts, well-tended grass between tombstones and colorful silk blooms in the built-in vases. I pulled out the piece of paper with the locations of six graves circled in red. Cora had given it to me a few days ago, though she wasn't exactly sure about the exact location of some of them.

"There's one," Torin said. I jumped and looked around frantically. "The child's tombstone to our right with daisies. Don't look right now. She's studying us as though she knows."

"Knows what?" I managed to squeak, my heart pounding.

"That we're Valkyries."

"I'm not one yet," I protested.

"But they can sense your connection to us," Torin whispered in my ear, laughter in his voice. When I looked at him, he was trying hard not to laugh.

"That wasn't funny." I jabbed him with my elbow.

"You should have seen your face."

"I can't believe you'd joke about something so," I shivered, "creepy. I've walked across cemeteries and never worried about ghosts until now." I tried to elbow him again, but he jumped out of the way laughing.

We moved from plot to plot. Even though Torin was relaxed, I knew we weren't alone. Call it sixth sense or whatever, I just did. A few times, cold air rushed past us and I looked at him to see his reaction, but he just grinned.

"How many were there?" I asked when we went back to the SUV.

"Five. Four men and a woman."

I shuddered. "What were they doing?"

"The woman was near the grave with the daisies. The men just floated around looking lost. One looked angry. He was younger than the other three."

Poor lost souls. I didn't say anything until we left the cemetery and headed toward the city center. "Why can't you just reap them?"

Torin shrugged. "They are not my responsibility. They had their chance to leave but chose to stay. Idiots."

His indifference surprised me, but I guessed he'd grown numb after centuries of reaping souls. "So they just wander around forever?"

"No. The Grimnirs will collect them."

"Grimnirs?"

"Hel's soul collectors. Skeleton faces, black robes, huge artavo or as humans call them, scythes."

"Grim reapers?" I asked.

"Yep, cold and unfeeling bastards. Working with them is a nightmare. Whenever a Valkyrie is punished, they're sent to Hel to help the Grimnirs."

He and Andris once worked for Hel, I'd overheard him say. I never got a chance to ask him about it, and I probably never would. From her pictures, Hel looked scary. One half of her face was human-like while the other half was blackened skeleton. "I'll never look at cemeteries the same again."

"You think cemeteries are eerie? Try hospitals. They—"

I covered my ears with my hands. "La-la-la-la-la-la. I'm not listening to you anymore. You're ruining things for me." He was still laughing when he parked outside the Creperie. "What are we doing here?"

"Getting lattes. We need something hot after tramping through cemeteries."

The Creperie, a favorite hangout for students, was only a block from our school. The four major groups—the jocks, the nerds, the rebels, and the preppies—each had their corners, so I wasn't surprised to see Andris and Ingrid with a bunch of preppies at a table.

"Great game, St. James," someone called out as soon as we stepped inside the restaurant. Everyone's attention shifted to us.

"Hail the new QB," a jock shouted from their corner, and his friends pounded the table with their fists and yelled, "OOH! HA! HA!"

"Football is life," the same jock yelled.

"Get in the game," his friends finished the slogan.

"Hustle and heart…" another one yelled.

"Set us apart," echoed around the room.

"Winning isn't everything."

"It is the ONLY thing," they hollered and drummed on the tables. Torin bumped fists with those near us.

Stares and whispers followed us to the counter, where we placed our order. I caught sight of bold girls with raised cell phones taking pictures. Did Torin bring me here to get people talking about us? Brilliant as it might be, I was sure not all were impressed. I was still Kayville High's wicked witch.

"Not joining us?" Andris asked when we stopped by their table.

I didn't mind staying, but Torin gave me an intimate grin. "Nah, we have other plans." He didn't bother to lower his voice, giving the people listening something more to text about. Next, we stopped at the jocks' table.

"Raine, meet the gang. Everyone, Raine Cooper, *my girlfriend.*"

Nods, smiles, and nice-to-meet-yous came from the guys. I didn't care that the girls' smiles were stiff and their expressions resentful. I'd known most of them since elementary school, but they acted like we didn't breathe the same air because they were popular. Having Torin claim me was the perfect ending to our crazy date, especially when he smiled down at me and slid a possessive arm around my waist.

My cell phone buzzed as we left the restaurant. It was a text from Cora.

"Is it true about you and Torin? Is it official?" she wrote.

I laughed and texted her back. I guess it was official. I was Torin St. James' girlfriend. It felt right. "It's Cora," I explained when Torin cocked his eyebrow. "Word travels fast."

"About?"

As if he didn't know. I reached up and kissed him. "How you're an amazing boyfriend."

"Oh, so I'm *your* boyfriend?" His eyebrow shot up again and met the lock of hair on his forehead.

I reached up and swept the bangs aside. "You claimed me back there, so I have no choice but to take pity on you and claim you, too."

"I think I'm going to like being claimed by you, Lorraine Cooper." Grinning, he took my drink, placed it on top of the SUV with his, then rested his hands on my waist. Slowly, he pulled me closer until our bodies touched, a wicked grin dancing on his beautiful lips. Then he proceeded to claim me in front of the customers of the Creperie, who could see us through the glass windows.

***

Eirik's Jeep was parked at the curb when we entered our cul-de-sac. Torin pulled into his garage, hopped down, and came around to open my door. Not that I was complaining, but I wasn't sure whether he was just being a gentleman or if he feared I'd trip and hurt myself again. I wasn't accident prone or anything like that, but I'd noticed how gentle he was whenever his hand came anywhere near my cranial scar. It was sweet, but so unnecessary.

Eirik stepped out of his Jeep, but he didn't come toward us. Instead, he leaned against it and crossed his arms. That usually meant he wanted me to go to him.

"Give me a minute," I told Torin and headed down the driveway. Torin crossed to their patio and lounged on the swing chair Andris had used earlier. Aware of his eyes on me, I hugged Eirik. He was tense. I stepped back and studied his face. He looked a lot better than yesterday. "You okay?"

He nodded, his eyes darting to where Torin sat before shifting back to me. "I didn't, uh, wake up or anything last night, did I?"

I shook my head. "No. You were dead to the world when I left this morning."

"Yeah, that was the first time I slept through the night without, uh, you know." He glanced at Torin again. "Does he know?"

"Of course not."

"Good." He shoved his hands in the pockets of his hoodie. "The fewer people who know the better."

"I was hoping you'd tell him."

Eirik scowled. "Why?"

"Because I'll have to explain why you sleep in my room. I'm assuming you plan on coming back."

He grinned. "If we can fool your mother. She wasn't too happy this morning and gave me a long lecture about proper behavior now that we're older. What did you tell her?"

"That it was okay for you to stay over. She wasn't happy with me either. Why didn't you just tell her the truth?"

He shrugged. "I will when I'm ready." His glance shifted to Torin again, but this time he nodded and said, "Hey."

I glanced over my shoulder and smiled. Torin was coming toward us. He slipped his arms around my waist and pulled me against him. I liked that he couldn't keep away from me. Or maybe he was jealous. I leaned against him and forced myself to focus on Eirik. "You want to hang out with us or are you going to Cora's?"

"Cora and I are done." He pushed against the Jeep and straightened his body. "See you two around."

"What do you mean done?" I asked, my voice rising in shock.

"Nothing is going on between us." He walked around the hood of his car and slipped behind the wheel.

"I'll be right back." I wiggled out of Torin's arms, yanked open the passenger door, and slid inside.

Torin didn't look happy. As I watched him walk away, I reached a decision. He was my boyfriend and shouldn't come second to Eirik. He might not remember the past, but I'd put him through the same crap before, always putting Eirik's feelings before his. I refused to do it again.

I waited until he was inside the house before I turned and faced Eirik. "Start talking."

"Can we do it inside?" He indicated my house with a nod. "I need something to eat."

"We can go to my place *after* we talk. Why are you pushing Cora away? She's crazy about you, and you're crazy about her."

He threw me an unreadable glance. "Crazy is not how I would describe it."

"Crazy, nuts... It doesn't matter what you call it. You like her, and I'm not going to enable you."

He snorted. "Enable me?"

"Yes, enable you. As long as you have me to hang out with, you don't need to have someone special in your life. We did that for sixteen years, Eirik. We are best friends, and we'll probably be..." I had no idea how long Valkyries and gods lived. "Forever."

"But?"

"But I have Torin now, and he means a lot to me, too."

A lost puppy expression settled on Eirik's face. "Does that mean we're not going to hang out anymore?"

He wasn't being fair. "We will, just not all the time. I hurt Torin a lot when you and I were dating because I knew how he felt about me, but I was determined to make things work with you."

A thoughtful expression entered his eyes. "You were?"

"Of course. I can't put him through that again by hanging out with you all the time and keeping secrets from him. Not being honest with him will destroy our relationship just as it will destroy whatever you and Cora have."

He was silent for a long time then he sighed. "I don't want whatever is after me to hurt her."

Oh, that was sweet. It also confirmed what I'd suspected all along. He was totally into her. "That makes sense, but you won't let anything hurt her just like I won't let anything hurt you and Torin won't let anything happen to me. We are all connected whether we like it or not. We're all in this together. If anything affects one of us, it affects all of us."

Silence followed.

"Okay. I'll take care of it," he said. "I don't like it, but I don't see any way out."

"Good. I hope she doesn't freak out."

"You think I'm going to tell Cora the truth about me?" He snorted, opened his door, and jumped down. "I'm going to talk to your boyfriend. And thanks for telling me you fought for us."

He'd never stood a chance the moment I met Torin. I left the Jeep and followed Eirik as he strolled toward Torin's front door. By the time I reached the steps leading to the porch, Torin stood the doorway. His eyes swung from Eirik to me, then to back to Eirik.

"What's going on?" he asked.

"She said no more secrets because she won't enable me and she doesn't want you hurt like before." When Torin looked at me and lifted his eyebrows in question, Eirik added, "She explains it better. The bottom line is we need to talk."

Torin stepped aside to let Eirik enter. They both turned as though to make sure I was following. I shook my head. "You two talk. I'm going to call Cora and have a little girl talk, so I'll be at my house."

I turned and hurried away before either of them could protest.

***

I texted Cora several times, but she didn't return my texts. I still couldn't believe Eirik had pushed her away. He could be so stubborn sometimes. I glanced outside, but there was no movement at Torin's. Sighing, I sat at my desk and started on one of the homework packets the teachers had given me.

When I heard Eirik's voice, I rushed to the window. He was crossing the lawn alone and talking to someone in my driveway. My parents were home already? I checked my watch. It was almost five. I tried to attract Eirik's attention, but he didn't look up.

The door opened downstairs, and Dad's voice drifted upstairs, mingling with Eirik's. Dad must be home early to start on dinner. I'd noticed the leg of lamb and chicken breasts he'd left in the fridge. Once again, I checked Torin's bedroom window. He wasn't there. I wished he could embrace modern technology and just buy a cell phone.

Sighing, I left my bedroom and started downstairs.

"You know our rules, son. In this house, if you want to eat, you cook. So grab an apron," I heard Dad say and grinned. Eirik had just been roped into helping Dad cook. It wasn't the first time either.

Dad had taught him everything, from shaving to changing a tire, making a mean burger to mixing a dirty martini. Whatever that meant. Did he know about Eirik's true identity? Somehow I doubted that it would matter. Eirik was like a son to my father.

I watched them from the bottom of the stairs, where I had a clear view of the kitchen. Dad had a barbecue apron with "Super Dad" written across the chest. Below it was "Tristan, King of the Grill." It was last year's Father's Day gift from me. I'd bought it at an online site, where you personalized apparel. Eirik's said "Real Men Grill."

Hoping they didn't hear me, I retraced my footsteps and checked my phone again when I reached my room. There was still no message from Cora. I grabbed my keys and went back downstairs, making as much noise as I could.

"Where are you going?" Dad called out.

"To Cora's." I joined them in the kitchen. Eirik was washing baby red potatoes while Dad shoved garlic into the leg of lamb. "She's not answering my calls, and I'm kind of worried about her." I shot Eirik a mean look.

He made a face and dangled an apron my way.

"You're not going to help us cook?" Dad asked.

"Uh, I wasn't planning to. I'll only be in your way."

"Okay, go. Dinner is at seven, so be back to set the table."

"Thanks, Dad." I stuck my tongue out at Eirik and ran out the door. I was backing out of our driveway when Torin stepped outside and waved me over. I slowed down and turned into their driveway. I pushed down my window. "How did it go with Eirik?"

"Good. We'll need to come up with a plan to stop whatever is messing with his head." He reached inside the car and tucked my hair behind my ear. "Where are you going?"

"To see Cora. I'm worried about her."

"You know you can't force two people to be together unless they both want to."

I snorted. "Watch me."

He chuckled. "You're stubborn."

"No, I'm right. The two of them belong together."

"Is this a guilt thing? Because we're together and Eirik has no one?"

"Eirik has me, you, Andris, my parents, and his parents. I'm not sure about Ingrid cause she hates me, and Lavania is an unknown entity. I told him that if one of us is not okay, we're all not okay. Just as we will all work together to stop the shadow from hurting him, we will get him and Cora back together."

Torin shook his head and rubbed his finger across my lower lip. "You should come with a warning label, Freckles."

My lip tingled, and I found myself licking it. "And what label is that?"

"Snarky, bossy, pain-in-the-butt." He stepped back. "See you at seven. Oh, Ingrid doesn't hate you. She just happens to be in love with someone who's in love with someone else, too."

Too? Did he believe Eirik was in love with me? Not wanting to argue with him, I ignored his statement. "Could you buy a cell phone?"

He cocked his eyebrows. "Why?"

"I want to be able to text or call you instead of always looking out the window to see if you're in your room."

He grinned. "We don't need modern technology to communicate, Freckles. If you need me, I'll know it."

Nice. "Really? How?"

He touched his chest. "Right here. Your essence knows mine, just like mine knows yours. We can still communicate when all our other senses fail. I can hear you if you don't speak. Sense your presence without seeing you. Feel you without touching you." He winked and sauntered away.

14. THE DARKNESS INSIDE

With Torin's words ringing in my ears, I grinned like an idiot until I turned into the narrow road leading to Cora's home. Her family lived ten minutes outside town on a farm that once belonged to her paternal grandparents. Her parents, both retired elementary school teachers, had home-schooled her until her grandmother was diagnosed with cancer. When Cora and I met in junior high, she'd just started public school.

The patio door opened before I parked, and Cora's mother stepped out. She wore her standard farm outfit, dungarees and galoshes. I'd never seen her in anything but dungarees, even at Farmers' Market where she sold the organic produce they grew, including different types of apples. Like Cora, she had blonde hair, except hers was sprinkled with gray.

"Hey, Mrs. Jemison," I said.

"Hello, dear." We hugged. Her clothed smelled of spices. She baked apple desserts, which she supplied to some stores in Kayville. "We haven't seen you around lately."

"I was away for a few weeks, and when I came back, I had to catch up on schoolwork." There was an awkward pause as she studied me intently like she expected me to say more. "I know I should have called first, but, uh, is Cora home?"

"She's in her room. She was helping Jeff with his research earlier, but she's probably updating her video blog right now." She chuckled. "Go on inside. I'm sure she'd love company."

Cora was a serious vlogger, although her subjects were usually guys from school. I entered their house, expecting to see her father in the alcove off their living room, tapping away on his keyboard. The chair was empty. He was a novelist and kept weird hours.

I headed upstairs.

Cora's laughter filtered into the hallway. She sounded way too chipper for someone broken up about a guy.

"I'm in the middle of something, Mom," she yelled when I knocked.

I opened the door anyway and popped my head inside her room. She was painting her toenails while talking on the phone. She must have just left the shower because she wore a robe and a towel wrapped around her head. Seeing it was me, and not her mother, she grinned and waved me over.

"Okay, six thirty," she said into the phone then rolled her eyes. "Fine. Tell him it's a date." She dropped her phone on the bed and scooted to the edge. "Hey, Ms. Popular. I love your hair. If you go back to wearing it in a ponytail, I'll so disown you."

I snickered. She spent way too much time on her hair. I only did mine for Torin. "Ms. Popular?"

"You're trending among our friends on every social network right now, Raine. I was just about to call you." She stood, hobbled to where I stood because of the toe-spacers, and hugged me. "Phew, Kicker can sure talk a girl's ear off. She kept me on the phone for, like, forever wanting to know about you and Torin. When did you meet? Was this your first date? Blah blah this and blah blah that. FYI," she added, pointing at me, "I'm milking your fame for my vblog."

Somehow I'd expected her to be heartbroken. You know, wearing the standard wrinkled sweatpants and matching shirt, hair unwashed. Instead she was making a date. A date! That bugged me. No, it more than bugged me. I was outraged on Eirik's behalf.

"Trending?" I asked.

"See my laptop." She waved toward her desk. "Torin has already been voted the best kisser and loving boyfriend *evah*. Everyone who posted a picture of the two of you tagged me. Your fame is already rubbing off on me," she added, grinning.

Yeah, right. She'd always been popular because of her vlog. Besides, guys found her hot. I walked to her desk and touched the screen of her laptop. She had logged in at a popular social network site, but her page had pictures of Torin and me walking hand-in-hand inside the Creperie. The two of us talking to Andris. Several even captured the wicked gleam in Torin's eyes as he'd glanced at me before telling everyone who could hear that we had plans for the evening. I scrolled down. Majority of the photographs were of us kissing. One even had the caption "Hot! Hot! Hot!" The comments under it sent blood rushing to my cheeks.

"People need to get a life," I mumbled.

"Why, when we are living vicariously through you? You just moved from being the most hated girl at school to the most envied." Cora pointed at her laptop. "You and Torin are officially the hottest couple now. If you click on the second tab, you'll see how many comments I've received since posting on my vlog, uh," she looked at her watch, "an hour ago."

I didn't bother to check. Her gushiness was over the top. Was focusing on us her way of dealing with her failing relationship with Eirik?

"Cora, I wanted to talk about Eirik," I said.

"Funny, I don't want to." She snapped shut her laptop, determination gleaming in her eyes. She thrust her right hand toward me. "Can you repair my pinky?"

The bright red nail polish was pretty, but it made her skin look even paler. Cora often wore dark colors when she was in the dumps. The red was too bright. I took the nail polish remover and cotton balls, sat on her bed, and removed the damage she'd done.

"So what plans do you and Torin have tonight?" she asked.

"We're having dinner."

"At home or somewhere romantic."

I didn't want to discuss my relationship. "At home. Eirik told me what he did."

Cora glared. "Stop talking about him already, sheesh."

"I can't."

"Argh, I hate you. We tried. It bombed. End of story. I've moved on." She glowered defiantly as though daring me to say anything. I opened my mouth to argue, but then I noticed her chin tremble. She was taking this harder than she let on.

"Oh, Cora," I said and sighed.

"What do you think of my nails?" she asked. Her eyes were overly bright.

"It is a pretty color," I said, focusing on repairing her nail.

"It matches the top I plan to wear tonight. I have a hot date."

"Who with?"

"Jaden Granger. It's a double date with Kicker and her boyfriend."

Jaden Granger? Gross. What was wrong with her? She hated Jaden. On the other hand, she'd flirted with him last night. Eirik was going to lose it when he found out. *Serves him right.* He deserved a kick in the rear. Cora was not the kind of girl you messed with. She made you pay. Hanging out with them was going to be a nightmare.

"I wish you wouldn't give up on Eirik so fast," I said.

"I didn't give up on him, Raine, because I never had him to begin with," she said calmly, too calmly, then reached down and touched her toes. "These are dry."

"What makes you think you never had him?"

She closed her eyes. "I swear you're like a dog with a bone. Why do I think I never had him? Because Eirik is still into you. He's never gotten over you. He was a mess the two weeks you were gone. I tried to be there for him, but I wasn't enough. Seeing you with Torin must be killing him because he's gotten worse. Now if you don't mind, I need to blow-dry my hair and fix this," she indicated her face and crossed her eyes dramatically, "before I leave for my date." She disappeared into her bathroom.

Her pinky nail was going to get smudged again. Shaking my head, I went through her stash of nail polish until I found an emerald-green one that matched the top I planned to wear tonight. If I didn't know about Eirik's night terrors, I would have believed everything she'd said about his feelings for me.

Cora was still blow-drying her hair when I finished doing my nails, so I plotted my next move. When she walked back into her bedroom, I had a plan. Her hair looked amazing. It fell in gentle waves around her shoulders. I'd never seen her use a curling iron. She often preferred using her home salon, which was at the corner of her room. It had a professional hooded dryer and a chair.

"I thought you left," she said.

"Why?" I blew on my nails.

"Because of what I said."

I chuckled. "Please. If Eirik were in love with me, which he wasn't even when we dated, he wouldn't be so chummy with Torin now. Didn't you ever wonder why Eirik never liked any of the guys you dated? Or how he'd be mean to you whenever you gushed over some guy? The constant bickering between the two of you? And even though you'll deny it, you were hurt when he and I started dating." Cora made a face, but I just ignored her. "The signs were there, but I was too dense to figure it out. Things clicked during the meet when I saw the way he looked at you while you were flirting with some guy by the pool. Eirik likes you, Cora. A lot. I think something is bothering him."

She grew still, her eyes fixed on my face. "What?"

"I don't know," I lied smoothly. "Until he confides in us… in you, date whoever you like and make him see what he's missing. You have my total support."

She scowled.

"In fact, I'll make sure I tell him you're on a date tonight," I laid it on thick. "Where are you guys going?"

"Dinner somewhere then the movies. We haven't decided which movie yet."

"Text me when you know for sure. Maybe Torin and I can join you guys."

"Okay," she mumbled with less enthusiasm, and I knew my plan was already working. If she was into Eirik, as I suspected, she wouldn't want to see him suffer.

Pretending not to notice her reaction, I blew on my nails. She pulled on jeggings, dropped her robe, and added a red dress top that hugged her chest and flared around her hips. By the time she finished with her makeup, she looked stunning.

"Jaden is not going to take his eyes off you," I said.

"That's the idea." Once again, her smile seemed forced.

Smiling, I gave her a hug and headed downstairs. Her mother wasn't in the house though the scent of freshly baked pies filled the air. She usually supplied local stores with baked apple desserts.

***

Eirik's Jeep was gone from the curb. Dad sat at the kitchen table alone, his feet up and a drink in his hand. He hadn't changed out of his cooking clothes. From his position, he had a clear view of Torin's house, including the driveway. Had he seen Torin and me earlier? Probably.

"Something smells good," I said, peeking inside the oven. The roast sat on a bed of crisp-looking vegetables. Beside it was a large oval bowl of scalloped potatoes, my favorite, while a tray of baby red potatoes was on the bottom rack. "*And* looks good."

"Try the soup and tell me what you think," he said.

I got a spoon from a drawer, lifted the lid off the pan on the stovetop, and scooped some of his famous onion soup—another one of my favorites. I gave him two thumbs up and went to the fridge to get bottled water. A tray of deviled eggs covered with plastic wrap was in the middle rack. Wow, he had gone all out.

"Set the table for ten and call us when our guests start to arrive," he said, slowly getting up. He stretched and groaned.

"Ten?"

"Your mother paid Eirik's parents a visit earlier today. They will be joining us."

Dinner just lost its appeal. I must have made a face because Dad chuckled, but he didn't say anything. I hated dinners with Eirik's parents even though having them over was now something of a family tradition. At least tonight, Torin would be here.

I set the table and hurried upstairs to change. Mom often insisted we dress up for dinner. The emerald top was flattering, and I loved that it matched my nail polish. I traded my jeans for black tights and a black skirt, then added ankle-length, heeled boots. Mascara and plum lip-gloss and I was ready. My hair was still perfect from earlier.

Downstairs, Eirik arrived just as I cleared the stairs. He was dressed for the occasion and looked good. If Cora could see him now...

"You look amazing," he said, giving me a hug.

"So do you. Where are your parents?"

"They'll be here. You know how they are. When you say seven, they'll arrive at seven on the dot, not a second early or late." He tugged the collar of his shirt. "Why do we still have to dress up for these stupid dinners?"

"Tradition." When we were young, we'd eat quickly then sneak away while our parents lingered at the table. "Maybe we could tell them we're going to the movies after dinner and make a quick getaway."

"I don't feel like watching anything," he muttered and wandered aimlessly around the formal dining room we rarely used except for these occasions. "How was Cora?"

Oh, the perfect opening. "Good. She was getting ready for a date when I saw her."

Eirik froze.

"She looked amazing," I added.

His hand clenched. "Who's she going out with?"

"Jaden Granger."

Eirik made a face like he'd swallowed a fly.

I continued his torture. "She's supposed to text me the movie they're planning to watch, so we can join them." The doorbell rang, and I left to answer it. Eirik stayed in the dining room, probably plotting mayhem. I felt a little guilty. Maybe I should have waited until after dinner before saying anything about Cora's date.

I opened the door to find our neighbors, led by Lavania, who looked breathtakingly beautiful as usual. My eyes went straight to Torin. He looked gorgeous in a navy-blue dinner jacket over a white shirt. He didn't wear a tie and the top buttons of his shirt were undone. He winked at me. Blushing, my eyes reluctantly moved back to Lavania, who carried a covered crystal bowl.

"You're back," I said.

"Just for dinner." She placed the bowl in my hands. "This is dessert. It must stay frozen until it is time to eat it."

"I'll put it in the freezer. Come in, please." I stepped back and turned to call my parents, but they were already walking down the stairs.

Mom wore one of her free-flowing dresses that reached her ankles. A headband sat on her head like an ancient Egyptian princess' crown, her black hair cascading down her back. She looked amazing. Like Dad loved to say, these dinners were for her. She loved to entertain. Dad looked handsome in a V-neck black sweater over a light-blue shirt. His curly brown hair, which I'd inherited, minus the curls, had grown and almost brushed his collar. I wondered if he'd dislike Torin.

Dad studied Lavania intently after they were introduced and surprised me when he said, "I hope my daughter is being a good student."

"Yes, Mr. Cooper," she answered politely.

"Call me Tristan." He smiled at Ingrid before acknowledging the guys. "Andris, nice to see you again." Really? I wondered. "St. James, nice to meet you."

That answered the question of whether Dad had been conscious when Torin rescued him from the hospital in Costa Rica.

Mom led the way into the living room before going to get appetizers—deviled eggs, and goat cheese with pepper and almonds. Eirik's parents arrived just as we started serving drinks. It was seven on the dot. Eirik, our designated bartender, stationed himself behind the wet bar, while I waitressed. Once again, I was reminded that even though Torin and his Valkyrie buddies might look around our age, they were much, much older and could consume alcohol. Eirik and I were the only ones having soft drinks. Eirik shook and mixed concoctions like an expert and grinned, but the smile didn't reach his eyes. Once again, I wished I hadn't told him about Cora's date.

Dad played host. His standard opening line was "Where are you originally from?" He had asked Andris the same question the first time they'd met.

Ingrid was really from Norway and was about two hundred years old. I noticed the way Andris' eyes kept drifting to her as she talked about her town. She looked beautiful in a simple black dress, her makeup flawless.

Torin's fingers lingered on mine when I handed him his drink, his eyes telling me I looked beautiful. My cheeks warmed. I had taken extra care tonight with my makeup, and I knew the emerald top was flattering. I hoped my eyes spoke for me, too. He looked so dashing tonight I wanted to stay right there and drool. He often wore jeans and T-shirts under his leather jacket, so this was the first time I'd seen him in anything formal-ish. I hoped we sat next to each other during dinner. Having him as my boyfriend was slowly sinking in, and I wanted to savor it.

Andris, seated on the other side of the couch and flanking Lavania, cleared his throat, and I realized I was taking too long giving Torin his drink. Andris winked at me and said, "I'll have a martini."

I turned to find Dad's eyes on us. He was probably still trying to understand the dynamics of my relationship with these Valkyries.

"What part of England were you from, Torin?" I heard him ask as I went to get Andris' drink.

As soon as Torin mentioned the crusade, the conversation shifted to history of that period, King Richard I, and his accomplishments.

"He was a generous man and a brilliant military strategist," Torin said, explaining how King Richard got his first taste of battle at age seventeen.

"Could he speak the English language?" Dad asked. "There's no record that he could."

Torin chuckled. "Fluently, but he couldn't write it as well as he did the language spoken in northern and southern France."

"How tall was he?" Dad asked. "Some books say he was about his brother's height, while others insist he was a giant of a man."

The Q and A continued until Mom motioned me to join her in the kitchen. Reluctantly, I got up and followed her.

"This was a wonderful idea, wasn't it?" Mom whispered. "Look how much your Dad is enjoying himself."

We had a clear view of the living room from our position. Dad laughed when Andris called King Richard III a douche. Even Eirik's parents appeared more relaxed. While they continued to discuss the British monarchy, we put the food on the table.

"Now for the seating arrangement. Your father and I will sit at our usual places at the ends of the table. I'll have Sari and Johan on either side of me, and you and Torin on either side of your father."

"Can Torin sit beside me?"

Mom pursed her lips then smiled. "How are things between you two?"

"Better. We went to the cemetery together yesterday."

Mom smiled. "Okay, you can sit beside him, but you two had better behave. Your father needs a little time to adjust to your training without learning you're dating a Valkyrie as well. Across from you two, I'll have Eirik and Lavania."

I shook my head. "No. Eirik and Ingrid."

She frowned. "Why not Lavania?"

"He doesn't like her."

"What? Why?"

I shrugged. "I don't know."

Mom sighed and gave me the seating cards. "Go ahead and place the seating cards." She didn't let go of the cards when I reached for them. "Look at me. I had a long talk with Sari and Johan and learned a few disturbing things. How long have you known about Eirik's night terrors?"

"Uh-mm, since yesterday."

"Oh. Did he have them last night?"

I shook my head. "No."

"Hmm." A pensive look settled on Mom's face. "Okay, he can sleep on the pullout bed, but be careful when he gets an episode."

"Okay, Mom." Eirik would never knowingly hurt me, but what if he did? I didn't have runic magic to heal me like his mother. On the other hand, telling him he couldn't spend the night in my rollout bed might reinforce his belief that things were different between us. Sighing, I pushed the matter aside.

My seating arrangement was perfect, alternating the men and the women with Eirik and me on either side of Dad. Andris sat beside Ingrid, which seemed to make her happy. The men held the chairs for the women, waiting until we sat before taking their seats. I didn't pay attention to the conversation once we started to eat. Torin's left hand reached for mine under the table. The way Dad's eyes kept straying to us, I wondered if he knew.

We were having Lavania's mud-pie dessert when a familiar chill crawled up my spine. I frowned, recognizing the feeling too well. No, they wouldn't dare come to my house. Even as the thought crossed my mind, the doorbell rang. Oh, that was bold.

"I'll get it," I said, my heart pounding. Torin's eyes narrowed on my face, a question lurking in their depth. I shook my head. "Excuse me."

My mouth went dry as I hurried across the living room and yanked the door open. My eyes locked with Marj. Behind her stood Jeanette and Catie. So angry I wanted to scream, I stepped outside and closed the door behind me.

"What are you doing here?" I said through clenched teeth.

Marj's eyes narrowed. "Looking for Eirik. Where is he?"

I indicated my house with my thumb. "Inside. You can't come to my house."

"We can do whatever we want," Marj retorted.

"We didn't mean to intrude," Catie said at the same time. "But when we didn't feel young Eirik's essence, we were concerned. Is he okay?"

"Yes. What do you mean you didn't feel his essence?"

"It's the way we monitor our charges," Catie explained. "We focus on their essence. Something is shadowing Eirik's. Are you sure he's okay?"

My eyes volleyed between Marj's foreboding expression and Catie's concerned one. Jeannette had turned and now looked away from the house as though on sentry duty, so I couldn't see her face. "He's been, uh, having night terrors, and last night he blanked out."

They looked at each other.

"The transformation is happening already," Marj said.

"The darkness is too powerful," Jeanette added and shuddered.

"No, it's not," Catie protested. "Something is wrong. Seventeen years of love and nurturing cannot crumble this fast. Someone is doing this to him."

"What were you talking about?" I asked.

Marj pinned Catie with a glare. "No one is doing this to him. The darkness is taking over because she," Marj pointed at me, "failed him."

"It's not her fault," Catie protested.

"She fell in love with a Valkyrie and forgot him," Jeanette added.

"I never forgot Eirik," I protested. "I love him, and he knows it. I'd do anything for him."

"Then why is the darkness consuming his soul?" Marj asked.

"It is moving too fast," Catie said. "Someone is helping it."

"No, the boy is just weak," Jeannette piped in.

"Eirik is not weak," I snapped.

"You know what that means." Marj looked at Catie with a challenging expression. "She'll have to use the dagger to stop him."

"Whoa! No one is daggering anyone." I tried to understand their banter. "So what you're saying is Eirik is possessed by this, uh, darkness?"

Marj looked at me as though I had lost my mind. "Of course not. Didn't your mother explain anything to you?"

"Kind of." Marj opened her mouth, but I lifted my hand, my attention going to the window on my left. A shadow shifted behind the curtain, which meant that someone just entered the living room. Probably Mom looking for me. "Listen, I know who Eirik is and why he was raised on earth. I also know that you knew about the shadow or darkness following him, but you refused to explain to anyone what it is, just like you didn't explain to me what you meant by I was alive because of him. I know you are powerful and invincible, but you," my eyes swept their faces, "suck at explaining things. If Eirik is really in danger, I need to know from who or what. If you're playing mind games and something happens to him, I will hold you three accountable. But if this is a concocted plan to lure me to your side, I will become a Norn just so I can break every rule you hold sacred. So, I'll ask again. What is this darkness after Eirik?"

"The darkness is not after him. The darkness is *within* him," Marj said.

I stared at her. "What?"

"She's coming," Jeannette warned. Lights from a car swept the cul-de-sac.

"Come with us, Lorraine, and we'll explain," Catie said.

I hesitated. Even though I wanted to help Eirik, I still didn't trust these three. This could all be another one of their tricks to get me to leave with them. "No, I can't leave right now, but I can meet you somewhere in, say, an hour."

Marj snorted. "We don't have time—"

"We'll make time," Catie said. "Meet us at The Hub in thirty minutes."

Thirty minutes would be pushing it, but...

"We have to go. She's almost here," Jeanette warned.

They moved toward the driveway and blended with the darkness. The tap-tap of heels on pavement reached me. Then Cora appeared from the same direction, a puzzled expression on her face.

"I thought I heard voices. Were you talking to someone a few seconds ago?" she asked.

"No, just talking to myself." I glanced behind her, but the three Norns were gone.

"So what are you doing outside? No, let me guess," she added, not giving me a chance to answer. "You just came back from your date."

I gnawed on my lip, still mulling over what the Norns had told me. *The darkness is inside him.* Everyone had a light and a dark side, so that couldn't be bad.

"Raine! Snap out of it. Did you have a fight with Torin?"

"No. I saw your car and came outside to meet you." That sounded lame. From the grimace on Cora's face, she thought so, too. "Aren't you supposed to be on a date?"

She shuddered. "Worst. Date. Evah. What a douche Jaden turned out to be. Anyway, I texted you, but you didn't return my messages, so I took a chance and drove over. Are you done with your private dinner with the gorgeous QB? I mean, can you hang out?"

"Maybe later. We're having dinner right now. Mom decided to have one of her dinners and invited Torin and his friends over."

The door opened behind me just as I finished explaining. "Raine, what's taking you...?" Mom's voice trailed off when she saw Cora. "What on earth are you two doing outside? Let her inside, Raine." She rubbed her arms. "It's too cold to be talking out here."

"I just stopped by to see if Raine wanted to go to the movies, Mrs. C."

"You can ask her inside. Come on." She stepped back to let us enter the house. "Have you eaten?"

"No. I kind of walked out before they served dinner." Cora and I traded smiles.

Mom glared with disapproval. "You had a fight with your parents and walked out?"

"No, Mrs. C. My parents and I are okay. I had a bad date."

Mom chuckled. "Never consider them bad dates, dear. They're growing pains. One day you'll find *the one* and all your pains will disappear." Mom closed the door and patted Cora's cheek. "Oh, you poor child. You're frozen. Raine, take her to the dining room. I'll fix her a plate."

"I'm not really hungry, Mrs. C."

"But you must eat something. Tristan made the most mouth-watering lamb roast and scalloped potatoes."

"Really, I'm not hungry."

"Then have some dessert," she insisted. "I'll get you some."

"Quit while you're ahead," I whispered to Cora. "Just agree to dessert so we can get out of here. I have to be somewhere in thirty minutes."

I doubted Cora even heard me. She froze when she saw the number of people in the dining room. Then she found Eirik, and her gaze locked with his. Her cheeks grew pink. He got to his feet along with the other men, his eyes not leaving her.

Erik stepped away from the table and gripped the back of his chair. "Have my seat, Cora."

"No, son," Dad said. "She can take mine. We're heading to the living room." He led the others out of the room, leaving Torin, Eirik, Cora, and me behind.

"One slice of mud-pie coming up," Mom said, entering the dining room with a dessert bowl. She placed it in front of Cora. "Eat up, sweetheart."

"Mom, can we go to the movies?" I asked her before she left the room.

She paused, turned, and studied us. "Sure. After Cora's done eating."

As soon as she left the room, Eirik asked Cora what she wanted to drink, and he left to get it. Her eyes followed him and so did mine, but for a different reason. Marj's words kept ringing in my head. *The darkness is inside him.*

I needed answers. A quick glance at my watch said I had twenty-five minutes to come up with an excuse and leave.

15. MY BROTHER'S KEEPER

"What's wrong?" Torin whispered in my ear, the warmth of his breath on my ear sending a shiver through me. I smiled, amazed at how well he could read me.

"The Norns were here," I whispered back. "They're the ones who rang the doorbell."

Torin's eyes narrowed. "What did they want?"

"I'll explain later. I need to get out of the house."

"When?"

"Next ten minutes. I'm meeting them in twenty."

"Where?"

"The Hub."

Eirik's voice intruded in our conversation with, "I heard you had a date tonight, Cora."

"Yeah, a bad idea on so many levels," Cora said, scooping some of her dessert. "Jaden was a total douche."

"But you knew about his reputation," Eirik ground out through clenched teeth.

Cora glared at him. "Your point is?"

"Why do it unless you wanted him to treat you the way he treats the other girls?"

Her eyes narrowed. "Yeah, I guess I wanted to see how it felt to have a guy grope me under the table during dinner. You should try it sometime, Eirik. You might even score." She got up with her half-eaten mud-pie and headed toward the kitchen.

I glared at Eirik. "Did you have to bring that up?" He shrugged. "Go after her," I added.

He shook his head and leaned against his chair. I groaned in frustration. He was so stubborn. I pushed back my chair, got up, and started out of the room. I nearly bumped into Cora in the doorway connecting the dining room and the kitchen.

"Are we going out or what?" she asked. "The movie starts soon."

"Dying to see Jaden again?" Eirik threw in the dig.

Cora gave Eirik a sweet smile. "Since you and I are done, it's none of your business who I date." She turned to me. "Let's go."

Even though Mom hadn't said it, Eirik and I often cleared the table after dinner. From the way he was glaring at Cora, Eirik wasn't going to be much help tonight.

"Give me a moment to clear the table," I said. Torin jumped up to help. "Don't. You're a guest."

"I don't mind." We left Cora and Eirik still glaring at each other in the dining room. "Are they always like that?" Torin asked.

"They've gotten worse." It was sweet of him to help clear the table, but he went beyond the duties of a boyfriend when he helped me load the dishwasher.

"Very domesticated," Andris mocked, entering the kitchen. He sat on a stool and leaned against the counter. "You do know her old man is watching your every move and imagining several ways to disembowel you."

I glanced toward the living room, but Dad's back was to us. Mom, on the other hand, could see us. She lifted her glass and grinned, which caused Dad to turn to see what caught her attention. He frowned. I waved. Once again, I was sure he was trying to figure out my relationship with these two Valkyries.

"Go away, Andris," Torin said.

I elbowed Torin. "Don't be rude. We need to finish here and head downtown, Andris."

"He doesn't need to know everything," Torin retorted.

I nodded. "I know."

"What's going on downtown?" Andris handed his glass to Torin, who snatched it and faked a move as though to clock him on the head. Andris ducked and smirked. Then he reached for an apple from the apple bowl, rubbed it against his sweater, and took a bite. He wore a black and gray V-neck sweater with buttons halfway up and gray slacks. Very J-Crew.

"We're going to the movies," I said. "Want to come?"

"Sure. Do I bring a date?"

I nodded. "Ingrid. Or you can't come."

Torin laughed. Andris flipped him off with both fingers and sauntered back to the living room.

I checked my watch. "We have to leave."

"I'll get the car." Torin glanced over his shoulder at my father then lifted his hand and ran his knuckles down my cheek. "You look amazing tonight. But then again, you always do." His hand came down to grip mine before letting go. I watched him walk away.

"Quit drooling," Cora said from the other side of the counter. I hadn't seen her enter the kitchen.

"Shut up."

"Just sayin'. Ready to leave?"

"Yep." She said something, but I didn't hear it. I was busy watching Torin say his goodbyes. I wasn't sure what he said, but Dad stood and shook his hand. Mom got up and gave him a hug. As though he felt my eyes on him, he glanced toward the kitchen and smirked.

"Still drooling," Cora said when I turned.

"Yeah, shoot me. I hope you don't mind if we go in his SUV."

"That's okay. I'll pick up my car later." She headed back into the dining room to get her purse, totally ignored Eirik, and walked out of the room. Eirik watched her every movement, his jaw tense.

I sighed. This could end up being a very long night. "Are you coming?"

He jumped to his feet. "I'll take my Jeep and follow you guys. I'm not letting Jaden anywhere near her again."

I wanted to shake him. "Don't tell *me* that. Tell her." I pointed in the direction Cora had gone.

"Why, so she can throw it in my face? She's impossible to have a conversation with."

They were both impossible. I gave Dad a kiss, hugged Mom, and said bye to Eirik's parents. Andris, Ingrid, and Lavania must have left with Torin. Outside, Torin pulled up to the entrance of my driveway and opened the front passenger door. He'd also gotten rid of his shirt and dinner jacket and replaced it with a T-shirt and his leather jacket.

Eirik hopped into his Jeep, which was parked in our driveway. He'd been the first one to arrive. I got in the car. Behind me, Cora stared at Eirik through the window. I could tell she was frustrated. She was in the middle seat, while Ingrid and Andris sat in the back.

"He's going to follow us," I reassured Cora.

She harrumphed. "Why?"

"You'll have to ask him."

Andris leaned forward and rested his arms along the back of Cora's seat as Torin looped the cul-de-sac and took off. "So you and golden boy are together?"

"No, we're not," Cora snapped.

"Ooh, the lady doth protest too much, methinks," he said, quoting Shakespeare's Hamlet. He leaned back against his seat and smirked. "I guess Cupid must intervene again."

That wasn't a bad idea.

"No, he can't," Torin said. "Stay out of their relationship, Andris."

"Hey, I'm good. If I fixed them, I could ask for anything. Maybe a few centuries in Asga—"

"Shut up, Andris!" Torin warned in a voice I'd never heard him use before, and it stopped Andris. Cora wore a bewildered expression. She had no idea what Andris almost gave away.

"You told him?" I asked Torin.

"No, I didn't. Probably Lavania. I'll talk to him about keeping a lid on things."

Torin pulled up outside The Hub. By the time he walked to the passenger side of the car, Eirik had parked beside us. The Hub was a video store, but it also sold books, comics, and manga, and had a café. From the number of vehicles in parking lot, it was packed.

"Drop them off and come back for me," I said. "I should be done in fifteen-twenty minutes."

"I'm not leaving you alone with them," Torin whispered in an uncompromising tone.

"I'll be fine."

"I don't trust them."

"Me neither, but they're too worried about," I indicated Eirik with a nod, "to try to pull something."

Torin's eyes narrowed stubbornly. "No. I'll give you space to talk to them, but I'm coming inside."

The back passenger door opened, and Andris stared at us. "What's the hold up?"

Torin dangled the car keys. "You go ahead and get us tickets. We'll join you in a few minutes."

"Why?" Cora protested, peering at us from behind Andris.

"I need to buy something," I said. "It's a surprise for my, uh, Dad. We'll be there before the movie starts, Cora. I promise." Her eyes narrowed suspiciously, but she nodded.

How we were going to get to the theater was going to be a problem now that Torin insisted on coming with me. Pig-headed man. Andris stepped out of the car, closed the door, and crossed his arms. He was no longer smiling.

"Okay, you two. The truth or I'm not driving anyone anywhere."

Torin's eyes narrowed. "Stop being an ass."

Andris smirked. "Still not going."

I closed my eyes in annoyance. Andris was like a child sometimes, and Torin only egged him on. "Fine. The Norns came to my house, and I'm supposed to meet them," I whispered, looked at my watch, and added, "Like right now."

Andris shuddered. "Ooh, nasty hags. Good luck with that." He ran around to the driver's side and took off.

Torin laughed.

"Did you say Norns?" Eirik asked, stepping out of his Jeep instead of following Andris.

"Yes. I've got to go." I started for The Hub.

"Wait," Eirik called. "I want to ask them a few things."

I turned. "No, Eirik. Don't. Stay away from them."

He shot me a look that said he was coming whether I liked it or not, but Torin gripped his arm and cut him off. "She talks to them first, Seville. We'll make sure they're not up to their old tricks, but you don't join them until Raine's done."

Eirik yanked his arm from Torin's grip and snarled, "Who do you think you're talking to, St. James?"

"Ease up, man."

Convinced Torin would stop Eirik, I raced across the parking lot and entered the video store, almost bumping into a couple standing too close to the door.

"Excuse me," I mumbled and hurried past them. Not sure where to start searching for Marj and her girls, I looked around. Two lines of customers waited to check out. Directly ahead, a mother was losing a battle against her daughter over cotton candy. Beside them, a couple of girls giggled over the CD cover of their latest idols.

"There you are," Marj said, appearing beside me.

She was alone. I hated talking to her. I would much rather deal with Catie. "Where's Catie?"

"Waiting for young Eirik to enter the building. You shouldn't have brought him with you. Come on. Follow me." She led me toward the back of the store, where picture books were displayed. It was empty this time of the night. She reached inside her jacket, pulled out a leather sheath, and offered it to me. "Take it."

My eyes volleyed between the sheath and her face. "What is that?"

"The special artavus we talked about. You will need it."

I took a step back, anger slamming through me. "I want to talk to Catie."

"Take the dagger, Lorraine," Marj insisted. "Young Eirik has darkness inside him that will infect everyone around him and start something no one can control. Mortals will feel whatever he feels magnified. If he's angry, everyone will be filled with rage. If he's envious, everyone around him will experience murderous jealousy. His darkness will consume this town."

I stared at her with round eyes. No wonder the people at Cliff House had gone ballistic. He had infected everyone with rage. Was it because I'd left with Torin or was it because Cora had flirted with the jocks?

"He cannot be allowed to live if the darkness takes over."

"NO!" I shouted, and a few people peered at us from behind the shelves. I ignored them and leaned toward Marj. "I will never willingly hurt Eirik. I don't care if he becomes a murderous monster or the devil incarnate. Never. I'll find a way to help him."

"Raine! You okay?"

I looked behind me. Torin stood a few feet away, runes glowing on his face and hands, eyes flashing. I nodded, too pissed to answer him.

He extended his hand. "If you want to leave now, we'll leave."

"Stay out of this, Valkyrie," Marj snarled.

Torin's jaw clenched, but his eyes didn't shift from me. "Raine?"

"I'm fine. She's just testing me."

Torin continued to study me. "Fine, but I'll be by the CDs if you need me."

The CDs racks were at the end of aisle and visible from where I stood. Having him that close was reassuring. Marj glared at him as he strolled away. He stopped by the first rack, leaned against the wall, and crossed his arms. His stance said he wasn't going anywhere.

"Foolish, Valkyrie. He didn't learn anything when we erased his memories. I should have sent him to Hel's Hall. Maybe I will if he continues to defy me."

Panic rolled through me, but I refused to show it to this petty and vindictive hag. "I'm sure he knows just how powerful you are, but he's more concerned about my safety right now."

Marj's head whipped toward me. Her eyes narrowed as though she was trying to see if I was being disrespectful. Cold crawled under my skin, and I shivered.

"This isn't a test, Lorraine," Marj said. "Eirik cannot be saved. When the time is right, you will have to kill him."

"Never," I said.

Her eyes glowed eerily. "You're an insolent child. Saving your life was the worst mistake we ever made. A total waste of time and runes."

That hurt. "So why did you?"

"We thought you'd save the boy, but from the looks of things, you've failed." She shoved the artavus at me again. "Take it."

I ignored the knife. "How was I supposed to save him? Maybe I can still do it."

She snorted, and for a moment, I was sure she'd refuse to answer. "It's too late, but I'll explain. Eirik comes from a powerful family."

"I know. He's Odin's grandson."

"Not just *that* side of the family. I'm talking about his mother's side."

"Who is she?"

Her eyes hardened. "It doesn't matter who she is. Do not interrupt me again," she snapped. "His mother comes from a dark family, and that darkness runs through Eirik. We saw the future, where he leads the enemies of the gods in the destruction of Asgard and the inhabitant of other realms, including Earth."

"Ragnarok, the war between the giants and the gods," I said before I could stop myself.

Her eyes glowed, but she didn't snap at me this time. "Yes. In our vision, we saw a war started, not by Baldr's death, but by his child. A boy born to hatred, nursed on anger, and raised in darkness. A boy with a heart so cold even the Norns trembled in his presence."

No wonder they haven't tried to take Eirik away. They were scared of him. She looked over my shoulder and grimaced. I turned to see what held her attention. Torin had moved closer, his eyes not leaving us. I wondered how much he'd heard.

Marj continued to glare at Torin, who stared right back. Her eyes acquired that chilling spooky light. "We chose a different path for the boy when we took him from his mother and brought him to Earth to be raised among humans. Instead of darkness, we wanted him surrounded by light. Instead of hate and anger, we wanted him to experience love, find joy and happiness. Warmth was supposed to replace the coldness in his heart. It hasn't."

"That's not true," I said, my heart pounding with dread. "Eirik is the most loving, giving, and warm person I know."

"Yet his essence has dimmed since we first made contact with you."

Maybe it was their fault Eirik was changing. Even as the thought flashed through my head, I knew it wasn't true. Last year, we'd studied *Tempest* by William Shakespeare in English lit and discussed what shaped a person's behavior and character. Heredity and the environment all played a part. Maybe the darkness inside Eirik had been waiting all these years to crawl out. "How can I help him?"

"Catie thinks you can." She said it as though it was unlikely.

"Catie also thinks someone is helping the darkness."

"She is wrong. Just like she's wrong about you. I don't think you have it in you to help the boy. Both you and your mother have failed the boy."

I bristled. "My mother?"

"Despite your mother's tendency to ignore rules, she's a very giving woman. Your father has proven himself to be a noble man, too. The plan was to have them be Eirik's guardians. No one would have thought of looking for him at the home of a fallen Valkyrie. But by the time we arrived, your mother was pregnant and desperate to have you. Losing you would have devastated them, changed them, and maybe even made it impossible for them to want or love another child. So we helped your mother through the rest of her pregnancy and made sure you both survived. We placed the boy with an Immortal couple and made sure they understood he was to be raised as close to your family as possible. The love from your parents to you was supposed to naturally flow to young Eirik."

Everything made sense now. Eirik living next door to us. My parents' relationship with his. His parents probably "traveled" a lot so Eirik could spend most of his childhood at our house. I'd just assumed they were cold and indifferent. "It did."

"So you say," Marj said.

"You don't know him the way I do," I insisted. "He's going through something right now. That's all. Once everything is sorted out, he'll be fine. If something is drawing this, uh, darkness out, I'll be there to help him."

"Don't believe everything Catie tells you. There's nothing messing with the boy. The darkness is coming out of him like a web out of a spider. But if you want to help…"

"Yes?"

"Prove it," Marj said.

I blinked at her. "How?"

"You have a few weeks, maybe a month before the darkness consumes him. If you fail, show that you care by giving him a quick death." She gripped my hand, pulled out the wrapped blade from inside her jacket, and placed it in my hand. "This is a special weapon known to destroy his kind. Use it."

His kind? I tried to pull my hand from hers, but her hold was firm. Torin! I glanced over my shoulder, but he was already moving toward us.

"Stay back, Valkyrie," Marj snarled, but her eyes didn't leave me. "Are you confident you can help him?"

"Yes."

"Then why are you afraid to take the artavus?" She leaned closer. "Your fear proves you're not as confident as you claim. That you know you will fail and you'll have to use the knife. That means you don't believe he's good."

"He. Is. Good."

"Then take it," Marj snapped, her eyes glowing.

"Stop pressuring her," Torin snarled.

"I warn you, Valkyrie," Marj snapped, her eyes still not leaving me. "You interfere one more time and you'll be sorry."

"Leave him alone." My stomach churned, my hatred toward her threatening to overwhelm me. "I don't need to prove anything to you."

"How little you know, you silly girl. You should have joined us weeks ago when I asked you." She smiled, and it was the coldest, meanest smile I'd ever seen. "You'd be more powerful and better equipped to deal with this now. Take it. You'll need it."

Torin growled. I looked over my shoulder, silently warning him to stay back.

"Don't look at him. He cannot help you make this choice. He's merely a Valkyrie, someone beneath you and unworthy of your attention. You were born to be a Norn, Lorraine, and Eirik is your first charge. You can control his destiny now. If you need our help…" Her voice trailed off, and she angled her heard, something flashing in her eyes. Fear perhaps. The same cold, stifling sensation I'd felt last night at Cliff House crawled up my chest.

A loud crash came from the front of the store, followed by someone yelling, "That's what you get for cutting the line."

"I did not, you son of a b—"

A thump and then a scream split the air. More voices rose, thuds and screams echoing around the store. Torin and I looked at each other.

"Eirik," we said at the same time and started toward the front of the store.

"We have to get him out of here before things get worse," Torin said.

Frantically, we searched each aisle we passed. The wave of violence hadn't reached the back of the store, but not for long. "Where did you leave him?

"In the Jeep. I knocked him out. He's a lot stronger than I thought."

"Of course he is stronger," Marj said from behind us. "He's the spawn of darkness, bringing out the most vile traits in others. Wives will turn against husbands, children against their parents. Then the violence will spread to neighbors. Before you know it, the whole town will be reduced to chaos. Town to town, state to state, country to country…"

Will she ever shut up? The gruesome picture she painted played in my head. No wonder they were scared of Eirik. Everywhere we passed, people pounded or screamed at each other. Someone crashed into a shelf and sent books flying across our path.

"You don't need to tell me what movie to pick," a woman yelled to our right.

"I'm not watching a stupid chick-flick just to please you," a man retorted.

"You're such a jerk." She slapped him, and he retaliated. I winced.

"Let's split up," I said. "We'll find him faster."

"No." Torin blocked my path. "Stay by me. He might infect you, or worse, hurt you if you approach him."

"Look at me, Torin. I'm not affected like the others. That must mean he can't. Besides, he's more likely to listen to me than anyone."

"Take this." Marj thrust the wrapped artavus into my hand. "You're going to need it if everything else fails."

"I told you, I don't—"

"Over here!" Catie yelled from the end of an aisle and waved frantically. Jeannette appeared beside her. They both looked scared.

I tried to push the weapon into Marj's hand, but she was gone. She reappeared by her friends. Then, like cowards, they disappeared. I stared at the dagger like it was a snake.

"I can't..." I whispered.

"You won't need to." Torin took the dagger from my hand and put it somewhere inside his coat.

"No." I tugged at his arm. "We must throw it away. Destroy it."

"I will. You never have to see it again. Now let's go stop this madness."

My insides shriveled and grew cold. "I'm a Norn. No matter what I say or do, I'm one of them."

"No, you're not. You saved Eirik's life before, and you will do it again. Not as a Norn or even an Immortal, but as you, Lorraine Cooper. You don't need anyone's help or a stupid special artavus."

I ended the pity-fest and nodded. Torin was right. I could do this. "Thank you."

He threw me a grin that was part amused, part annoyed. "For what? Stating the obvious? Move your sweet ass and stop him, because I'll have no problem using my artavus if he doesn't stop."

"You wouldn't dare." I tried to glare at him as we sprinted to where we last saw the Norns.

"Try me. I don't have time for his bipolar, deity, psycho crap."

We ducked flying CDs, DVDs, and books people were hurling at each other. "How can you be so nice one second and a total jerk the next?" I said through clenched teeth.

"Practice, Freckles. It's all part of what makes me irresistible."

We turned a corner and almost bumped into Eirik. He stood in the middle of the chaos, his eyes glazed and a smile of pure delight curling his lips.

Torin backed up. "Talk calmly to him while I come from the other side."

"Don't hurt him," I whispered.

"I won't, unless he does something stupid."

I glared at him, but he was already moving around a rack. I focused on Eirik. "Eirik?"

He glanced at me with unfocussed eyes.

"It's Raine."

"Raine," he repeated, tilting his head to the side as he studied me. His eyes glowed briefly.

I extended my hand toward him. "Yes, Raine. Come with me, Eirik. Let's go home."

"Home," he repeated, then his head whipped to the other side as though he'd sensed Torin's presence. His eyes narrowed. "Valkyrie," he snarled and lunged for Torin.

The force of his attack threw them across the aisle and into a shelf. The shelf dragged across the tiled floor, wobbled, and tipped over, starting a domino effect. Shelves toppled over, trapping people underneath them, but the close proximity of the shelves saved them from being completely flattened. Around us, the people punching each other didn't slow down.

"Snap out of it, damn it," Torin yelled. He had Eirik pinned to the floor face down with his arm twisted upwards in a weird arm-lock. They both had runes on their faces and hands. Maybe I could reach Eirik while Torin held him immobile. I ran to their side.

"No, Raine. Stay back," Torin warned.

Ignoring him, I dropped to my knees and peered at Eirik's face. "Eirik? Can you hear me? It's Raine. Please, listen to my voice. Look at me." Our gazes connected, but there was no recognition in his. "I know you're in there, Eirik. Listen to my voice. Come back to me. Please."

Once again, his eyes glowed, and I was sure he recognized me. Then they glazed over again. He heaved, almost pushing Torin off him and swung with his free hand. I tried to scramble out of the way, but I was too late. His arm connected with my side and sent me flying across the floor.

I wrapped my arms around my head, leaving my side at the mercy of the impact I knew was coming. My ribs connected with the edge of a shelf, and pain radiated through my body. A cry filled the air, and a roar echoed it. The next second, someone plucked me from the floor.

I opened my eyes and stared into Torin's burning eyes. "Did you hit your head again?"

"No. Eirik…"

"Screw him," he snarled. "I told you I won't put up with his bullshit. He hurt you."

"He didn't know what he was doing. Put me do—"

A loud squeak split the air, cutting me off, the sound mingling with the screams and the thumps, which were now fever pitch. Then the shelf I'd hit tipped over and knocked the one behind it. They both went down, merchandize flying every which way. The store looked like it had been bit by a tornado. I turned to find Eirik, but Torin pulled one of his runes-enhanced moves. One second, I was searching the wreckage; the next, he was carrying me through a portal on the glass window.

"No, we can't leave Eirik. He's still affecting people." I tried to wiggle out of Torin's arms, but his hold tightened, putting pressure on my bruised ribs. I smothered a cry. He cursed.

"I hurt you." He stopped, his eyes searching my face.

"No," I fibbed. "I told you to put me down back there."

"And I told you not to get too close to him." Carefully, he lowered me to the ground and touched my arm. "Your arm is bleeding. How are your ribs?"

"I can handle a few bruises, Torin. Eirik needs us."

"I've already taken care of him." He pushed back the sleeve of my jacket, a white artavus in his hand. "Now it's your turn. How come you never listen to me?"

I tried to yank my arm free from his grip, but the sudden movement sent a spasm of pain across my chest. I ground my teeth. "What do you mean you've 'taken care of him'? If you hurt him, I'll scalp you."

He chuckled. "You'll have to catch me first. If you haven't noticed, I'm a lot faster than you, novice."

"Not for long." I tensed and braced myself for the sting. As soon as the blade touched my skin, I felt the heat. It was as though energy shot from the artavus and into my skin. He etched the runes so fast the sting was barely there. The runes, pink and puffy, darkened and coiled, leaving my skin inked. Then the edges started to glow.

"Look at that." He studied his work. "Beautiful, aren't they?"

"You have no modesty whatsoever." They did look beautiful, the glow intensifying before fading away along with the pain on my arm and side. My gaze connected with Torin's. His eyes grew intense.

"I've runed you with my blade," he said.

Just like the first time. "Yes, you have. Is that something special?" Then I remembered why were in the parking lot. "Eirik."

Torin looked beyond my shoulders, the light in his eyes dimming. "There he is."

I whipped around. Eirik was coming toward us. He staggered a little like a drunk, and his expression looked like he'd killed someone. I started toward him.

"Does he know how lucky he is to have your love and selfless devotion?" I heard Torin say behind me. I stopped and stared at Torin with wide eyes, shocked by his words. He sounded sad.

"Raine," Eirik called.

My heart squeezed. Both men needed me, but for different reasons. Torin needed my love, which he had, even if he didn't know it. Eirik was in trouble and desperately needed my help. Not sure who needed me more, I wavered. A prickly feeling of being watched washed over me. I turned my head and found them, the three Norns. Anger slammed through me. Cowards.

"I'm so sorry, Raine," Eirik said, his voice filled with remorse. "I didn't mean to hit you."

"I know. You were, uh, in a trance. How did you snap out of it?"

He rubbed his jaw, glanced at Torin, and shrugged. "I heard you cry out. I don't know what's happening to me. That's the second blackout in twenty-four hours. Did you see the mess back there?" He pointed at the video store.

I glanced toward the store, and my gaze connected with the Norns again. I turned, taking the necessary steps that brought me to Torin's side. Reaching up, I cupped his face and kissed him.

"I love you, Torin St. James. But if you ever doubt my feelings or compare them with what I feel for anyone else, you'd better be as fast as you bragged because when I catch up with you, you'll be very sorry." While he stared at me like I'd sprouted a second head, I pulled the dagger from his inner pocket, turned, and marched to where the Norns stood. People poured out of the store, some apologizing, others voicing their shock at what they'd done, but I didn't let them slow me down. For once, the fear of the Norns was no longer there.

Marching straight to Marj, I stopped in front of her and looked into her eyes. "Stay away from me, my friends, and my family. You had your chance to protect Eirik and failed. Despite all your powers, there's one thing you are incapable of feeling and giving, and that is love. I have plenty of it. For him. For Torin. For anyone I wish to love. Eirik is now under my protection, and he'll be just fine without your help or your stupid artavus." I pushed the dagger into Marj's hand, turned, and marched back toward Torin and Eirik.

"You gave her the blade?" I heard Catie ask, but I didn't look back. I hoped our paths never crossed again.

"Can I talk to them now?" Eirik's gaze was on the Norns.

"You don't want to deal with them. They're nothing but trouble. I'll tell you everything you need to know."

16. HEARTBREAK

Torin settled behind the wheel, a frown on his face. He'd had that expression since I came back from talking to the Norns.

"Where to?" he asked.

"The movie theater," Eirik said from the backseat.

Eirik rarely let anyone touch his car, yet the way he'd handed Torin the keys told me he was still confused after turning evil. I winced, hating that I just thought of the word "evil" and Eirik in the same sentence.

I turned in the front passenger seat to study him. "Are you sure? I thought you wanted to talk."

"We will, but I want to take care of something afterwards. We don't have to watch the movie."

I had a feeling that the "something" was Cora. I glanced at Torin. "I guess we're going to the movies."

Instead of starting the engine, Torin said, "Excuse me." He stepped out of the Jeep, came around to my side and opened the door. "Come with me."

Excitement zipped through me. I'd taken the first bold step and confessed my feelings, and he was about to tell me his. When we were a fair distance from the Jeep, he stopped and studied me with a frown. "Are you sure about telling him the truth now? Out here? He could shift and start what happened in there," he indicated The Hub with a nod, "all over again."

I sighed. He was right. Eirik might take the information hard and get pissed. "What do you suggest I do?"

"Convince him to wait until we get back to my place."

"He might not want to wait."

"You can convince him to wait, Freckles. You are the only person he listens to."

I sighed. "Fine. I'll try, but if he insists, I'm telling him. I hate what's happening to him, and I hate keeping things from him."

I waited for Torin to bring up what I'd told him, pull me into his arms and tell me he loved me, too. Seconds ticked by. He stared at me intently and rubbed his nape. "Okay, that's fine enough for me," he said and took my arm. "Come on."

I dug my feet in. "You got me out of the car to talk about Eirik?"

Torin glanced down at me and frowned. "Yes. It would have been rude to discuss him in the car while he's sitting in the backseat."

Disappointment rolled through me. What had I expected? That he'd be so thrilled to hear that I loved him and tell me he loved me, too? Gah, I was such an idiot.

Back in the car, he made sure I was seated before he slid behind the steering wheel. He threw me quick glances, but I stared straight ahead, pretending not to notice. It hurt that he couldn't even acknowledge what I'd told him. A pat on the back and "you just think you love me, Freckles," or "it's just a girlish crush" would have been preferable. At least then I would have had something to be angry about instead of this hollow emptiness expanding inside me.

Tears rushed to my eyes, and I stared out the window and blinked hard, until I had my emotions under control. He said something, but I didn't catch it. When he reached for my hand, I turned and reached inside my pocket to get out my cell phone. His hand hovered in the air before gripping the steering wheel tightly.

For the rest of the drive, I checked my text messages. All of them were from Cora. The first ones asked where we were. By the sixth text, she was pissed off that I'd ditched her and taken off with Torin. Even though I knew she would have her cell phone off while the movie played, I answered her texts. I was surprised when she texted me back. I grimaced. She was never going to forgive me.

Torin pulled up outside the movie theater, and I jumped out of the car before he could come around and open my door. By the time he reached my side, I'd opened the back door.

"We'll catch up with you later," I said, sliding beside Eirik.

Torin frowned, his eyes volleying between me and Eirik. "Freckles..."

"Just give us a second."

Torin didn't look happy, but he threw Eirik the keys and walked toward the movie theater. I watched him go, my heart aching with regret and yearning. I really shouldn't have told him I loved him. He wasn't ready. Maybe he'd never be. From the way things were going, he'd never recover his memories either, which only made one thing glaringly obvious. He would never be mine again.

My eyes filled up, and I blinked hard, trying to stop the tears again. I didn't succeed.

"What is it, Raine?" Eirik asked.

I shook my head. "It's nothing."

"You're crying."

"I'm not." I sniffled and wiped my cheeks.

He reached up and turned on the lights on the roof of the Jeep. His jaws clenched as he studied me. "What did he do?"

"Who?"

"Who do you think? Torin!" he snapped.

"Nothing. He did nothing." And said nothing. I pressed my fingers against the inner corners of my eyes to stop the tears, but they kept flowing. "It's all this crap with Norns that's getting to me. I wish I never met them. I wish…" No, I could never wish I never met Torin or learned the truth about Valkyries. I squinted and focused on Eirik. I imagined myself in his shoes, waking up every night scared out of my mind without knowing why, blacking out and seeing chaos that didn't make sense. I'd go mad. On top of that, he hated lies. I refused to keep secrets from him, too, but at the same time I hated what I was about to do to him.

"What did the Norns tell you? Was it about me?"

I nodded. The stricken look that crossed his face had me pushing aside my own personal problems. His problems were worse than mine. I had to be strong for him.

I gave Eirik a sheepish smile. "I'm sorry I turned on the waterworks."

"No, don't apologize." He reached out and wiped wetness from my chin. "Just give it to me."

Now that it was time to tell him the truth, I didn't know where to start. I chewed on my lip and mentally went through possible openings. How did you tell someone you loved something inside him was evil? I refused to believe he was evil. Whatever was making him affect people and induce rage in them was beyond his control.

"Just tell me," he urged. "I can handle it."

"You were responsible for the players going ballistic at Cliff House and the people at The Hub turning on each other." My tongue tripped in my haste to say everything and get it over with. "Whatever emotion you feel, you infect people around you."

Eirik sat up, his amber eyes narrowed. "How? Why?"

Exhaling, I explained the things Marj had said, from his background to why we were raised together. I searched his face to see his reaction, but his expression was unreadable. "I'm supposed to protect you, except I'm doing a crappy job of it—"

"No, they had no business making you responsible for me." He shook his head. "I feel ridiculous saying this, but you're Mortal, Raine, not a Norn." He leaned back against the seat and rotated his neck.

"They insist I'm supposed to be a Norn and you are my first charge."

He snorted. "Stupid crones."

I studied him under the Jeep's green interior lights. "Why are you taking this so calmly? There's something inside you, Eirik. Something—"

"Evil," he finished, and I winced.

"Dark," I corrected. "Everyone has a dark side, but we all find a way to deal with it. You will learn to deal with yours."

He shrugged. "I guess so. I kind of suspected I had a Hulk lurking inside me the last few months. It was driving me nuts. Now that I know the truth, I'll be fine. I can deal with it." He glanced at me and flashed a boyish grin. "All I need to do is be happy. This is the ticket to getting whatever I want." Chuckling, he hugged me, then leaned back, his hand still gripping mine. "Thanks for being honest, Raine."

He was taking this much better than I'd thought. "What about Cora?"

"Yeah, Cora." He peered outside at the movie theater. "What time does the movie end?"

I checked at my watch. "Forty minutes-ish. It started an hour ago, and Cora texted me that it was about an hour-forty-five long."

"I guess there's no point in watching it now, but we can hang out with Torin until they come out."

The thought of hanging out with Torin just didn't appeal to me now. I needed time to lick my wounds. Come up with an excuse for what I'd said. I could take it back, but I refused to. I loved Torin and denying it was like denying myself air. "Do you mind dropping me at home?"

His brow furrowed. "Torin is in there waiting for you."

I smiled. "Yeah, well, I'm not in the mood to be social right now. Dealing with Norns tends to suck all my energy," I fibbed.

"Do you want to tell Torin we're leaving?"

I was taking the coward's way out, but I didn't care. "No. He won't mind. I plan to see him tomorrow."

Eirik appeared undecided. Then he nodded. "Okay."

We moved to the front of the Jeep, and I reclined my seat, closed my eyes, and went over the scene outside The Hub. I tried to remember what I'd said word for word, the look on Torin's face. He'd looked surprised. Surprise was good, wasn't it? It meant I had blindsided him. Maybe he needed time to process what I'd said. Or maybe I was just making excuses for him.

"Hey."

I glanced at Eirik. I realized the Jeep was no longer moving and sat up. We were parked in my driveway. "Thanks for the ride. See you tomorrow, or later."

He pointed behind me, and I turned. Torin. He must have used a portal to get here this fast. He crossed our yard, his eyes flashing, stride purposeful. This wasn't good.

"Do you want me to stay?" Eirik asked. I heard the smile in his voice.

"No. I'll be fine." I watched him back out of the driveway and take off, then focused my attention on Torin. "What are you doing here?"

"Looking for you. You ran from me."

"No, I didn't," I said with a touch of attitude. "Eirik brought me home in his Jeep."

Torin moved closer, his gaze unwavering from my face. "Why?"

I shoved my hands in the pockets of my jacket and shrugged. "I'm tired. It's been a long day."

"I would have brought you home."

I sighed. "What do you want, Torin?"

"The truth."

He moved closer until I could feel the heat from his body. His scent teased my senses, and the urge to cry washed over me.

"Did you mean it?" he asked softly.

I swallowed. "Did I mean what?"

"Please, don't play games right now, Freckles. You said you loved me." He blew out air and rubbed his forehead. "Did you mean it?"

My first instinct was to lie. Protect myself. Save face. But then I noticed the tension on his face, his fists clenching and unclenching as though he was bracing himself for bad news, and I knew I couldn't run from the truth.

"Yes, I meant it."

He searched my face. "Then say it again."

"I love you, Torin St. James."

He exhaled, hauled me into his arms, and buried his face in my hair. He was shaking. I wrapped my arms around him, and for a moment, we just rocked.

"Don't ever stop loving me," he whispered.

"Never," I vowed.

He lifted his head and studied my face under the security light. "You are mine now, Raine Cooper."

It wasn't exactly a declaration of love, but I had to be content with it for now. "And you are mine, Torin St. James."

He chuckled, lowered his head, and kissed me. It wasn't a passionate kiss. It was sweet. A whisper of reverence. A vow to cherish. Tears rushed to my eyes. When he lifted his head, he wiped the tears on my cheeks and gave me a sheepish smile. "I'm sorry I always make you cry."

"These are happy tears."

He tucked hair away from face, his touch so gentle. "When I didn't find you in the parking lot, I thought I'd lost you. I never ever want to feel like that again."

"And I never want to feel the way you made me feel outside The Hub. You acted like my feelings meant nothing to you."

He pressed his forehead against mine. "They meant... mean everything to me, but I didn't want to say anything because there's a reason I came back here, Freckles."

I s. "I thought you were here to reap souls of football players, and Kayville was going to be your base for a couple of years."

"It is, and we are here for some of the players, but more important than that, I owe someone a favor. I thought I shouldn't commit to anyone, especially you, until I fulfilled it." He searched my face, his gaze searing. "But I realized I wasn't being fair to you and to us. I can't lose you. I need you. I want you. You are all I think about every second I'm awake." A tiny smile curled his lips. "You even invade my dreams."

If that wasn't a declaration of love, I didn't know what was. I grinned.

"It's not funny," he said, but the corners of his lips twitched.

"So what is this favor you owe a friend?

He smiled and shook his head. "Sorry, I can't discuss it."

"You refused to tell me a lot of things before, too, and look where that got us."

He touched my nose. "Nice try. You can't guilt me into telling you something I've sworn to keep a secret." His focus shifted, and I followed his gaze. Our kitchen lights had come on. Dad must have heard Eirik's Jeep.

"I better go in."

Torin's arms tightened around me, telling me he didn't want to let me go yet. "I'm heading back to the theater to make sure Eirik doesn't do something stupid. Can I come up later, hold you until you fall asleep?"

I grinned, loving the idea. "Only if you promise to tell me who you owe a favor to."

"I can't, but I'm happy this is our new base because I found you. Again."

That shut me up. For now. We kissed, and then he escorted me to the front door, waiting until I unlocked the door and went inside.

***

I peered into the kitchen, but I didn't see anyone. Weird. Whoever had turned on the kitchen light was gone. I went to switch off the light and saw Dad's legs sticking out from behind the counter. What was he doing on the floor? Probably fixing something. He was always fixing something at odd hours.

"Dad?"

His legs didn't move. Panic rolled through me. I couldn't explain how fast I moved, but one second I was in the doorway separating the living room from the kitchen, and the next I was staring down at him.

"Mom!" I screamed and dropped beside his still body. His face was ashen. "MOM!"

Mom entered the kitchen, runes on her body visible through her white lingerie. "Why are you screaming—?"

"It's Dad."

Her eyes widened, and she practically flew across the kitchen and knelt beside me. She reached under his head and felt around. Dad moaned.

"He'll be okay," she said calmly. "He has a bump, but it's not life-threatening."

"He's unconscious, Mom. That's not good." My hands shook as I reached for the phone. "I'm calling for an ambulance."

"No. Runes can take care of him faster." Despite her calmness, she glanced up at me, and I saw the worry in her eyes. She was scared. "Get whoever is at home next door."

Torin. I started toward the door, but he stepped out of the mirror as I crossed the living room. Tears of relief rushed to my eyes. "How…?"

"I told you I always know when you need me. What's wrong?"

I pointed toward the kitchen, "Dad… unconscious on the floor."

He followed me back to the kitchen. He exchanged a look I couldn't describe with Mom and, without saying a word, knelt down beside Dad, an artavus already in his hand. I winced as he etched runes on Dad's arm then studied his face for signs of movement. Life. Anything. He didn't open his eyes, but his color improved.

"Why isn't he waking up?" I asked, my voice rising.

"He will," Mom said, coming to stand by my side. "Give them room."

Runes appeared on Torin's face and arms. Then he placed one arm under Dad's knees and the other under his arms and lifted him like he weighed nothing. Dad might have been on the scrawny side since his return, but he was as tall as Torin.

"Is he going to be okay?" I whispered.

Mom nodded. "Yes. He must have slipped on the kitchen floor. I always tell him not to walk around the kitchen in his dress socks. They don't have traction."

We followed Torin upstairs and into my parents' bedroom. Watching him gently put Dad on the bed reminded me that he'd rescued my father. Mom covered Dad and brushed the lock of wavy hair from his face, her movements gentle.

"Thank you." Mom glanced at Torin. "He'll be okay in the morning?"

Why was she asking Torin?

"And well-rested," he said, "but he needs to take it easy."

"I'll make sure he does. Thank you." Mom smiled at me, yet I couldn't shake the feeling that she was more worried about Dad than she let on. "Goodnight, sweetheart. We'll talk in the morning."

"Night." I kissed her cheek, then walked to Dad's side and studied his face. Leaning down, I pressed my lips to his forehead. "Night, Daddy."

I sagged against the wall after closing their bedroom door, reaction setting in. Torin pulled me into his arms and just held me.

"You okay?" Torin asked.

"No." I wrapped my arms around his waist. Slowly, we walked toward my bedroom. "We almost lost him before, and the thought of losing him again… I don't know what I'd do if anything happened to him."

Torin dropped a kiss on my forehead. "You'd go on because you're resilient."

I leaned back and frowned. "What kind of a response is that? You're supposed to tell me 'nothing will happen to him' or something along those lines. He's the glue that holds my family together. We barely made it—"

Torin pressed his finger to my lips. "Easy, Freckles." He pushed open my bedroom door and closed it behind us. "You are wrong. You are the glue that holds your family together. I see it in your father's eyes and your mother's smile when they look at you."

"You really think so?"

"I know so. Now stop stressing about your father. I'll back as soon as I speak to Eirik." He dropped a kiss on my lips and walked toward my mirror, runes appearing on his arms and face. The mirror dissolved into a portal, until I could see a row of urinals. He winked and stepped through it.

As soon as the portal closed behind him, I went to the bathroom to wash the makeup off my face and brush my teeth. I searched my closet for the right PJs, a two-piece silk and lace lingerie Cora had guilted me into buying. It had been gathering dust in the back of my closet. I put it on, studied my reflection, and grinned. Nice. I crawled under the blankets and waited.

Seconds became minutes, then an hour.

I almost gave up on him coming back when a gentle whoosh of warm air filled the room and the portal appeared. Torin stepped into my room, and his eyes found me. For a moment, time stood still, the smile disappearing from his lips. I wondered what he was thinking. Maybe we were having the same thoughts. I wanted to rip the clothes off his gorgeous body and do really, really naughty things to him. He'd changed into gray sweat pants and a white tank shirt that showed his muscular arms. Seriously, he could wear a sack and still look sexy.

"How's Eirik?" I asked, sitting up.

Torin's eyes widened. He shook his head. "He's fine, but there's no way I'm getting into your bed while you're wearing that."

"What?" I pouted. "What's wrong with it?"

"Where do you keep your real pajamas?" he asked.

I gawked. "Are you kidding me? These *are* real."

"Those are screaming things I shouldn't be thinking about right now," he growled, entering my walk-in closet. He studied the shelves of clothes.

I had achieved my goal. I knelt on the bed and waited for him to turn around. "So what's stopping you?"

"I don't hold back when I make love, Freckles, and I'll make sure you don't, so this is neither the place nor time to make you mine."

Images flashed through my head, and I grinned. I couldn't wait to be his.

"You know, it's bad enough I can't think straight whenever you wear those ridiculously tight jeans, which should be outlawed. And don't let me get started on your tops." He glanced over his shoulder and narrowed his eyes. "Wipe that smile off your face, and tell me where you put your ugliest pajamas."

I giggled. Not thinking straight? Oh, I was going to love being his girlfriend. He hadn't seen anything yet. "I don't own ugly pajamas, but if you prefer boring ones, I'll get something."

"No, you stay put. In fact, get under the bloody covers and pull them to your chin."

"You're a whiner," I said.

"And you are a tease and shameless and..." He studied me. "Tempting. Maybe this isn't such a good idea."

"Yes, it is." The last thing I wanted was for him to leave. I slid under the covers and pulled them to my chin, then gave him a toothy smile. "The pajamas are on the middle left shelf."

He rolled his eyes then dug through my clothes and pulled out two-piece, flannel, red pajamas with white and black reindeers. Not those ones. They were beyond ugly. I usually lounged in them on Sundays during winter. I doubted even Eirik had ever seen me wear them.

Torin held them against his chest and grinned. "Cute."

"Ugly and they're too warm."

"So we'll sleep on top of the covers." Still grinning, he handed the PJs to me and gave me his back. I was tempted to change right there just to tease him, but he did have a point. We couldn't do anything with my parents down the hallway. Mom, if she was still awake, probably knew he was in my room. I flung aside the covers and got out of bed.

"Whiny," I muttered and whacked him on his butt with the PJs as I passed him.

"Witch."

"Jackass."

"Cute ass," he added. I looked over my shoulder and caught him grinning. I forgave him. Anyone who thought my wide butt was cute had me.

I was smiling by the time I closed the bathroom door. The smile disappeared as soon as I changed and looked into the mirror. Argh, the pajamas did absolutely nothing for me. The top swallowed me, making my chest look pitiful. The faded red color was f-ugly, but the bottoms were worse. The reindeers watched me with a mocking gleam in their beady eyes.

Feeling like a troll, I opened the door and shot Torin a mean look. He lounged on my bed with his arms crossed behind his head, and looked amazingly gorgeous and sexy. On principle alone, I should have insisted he changed his tank top. The problem was I loved all that bare skin at my disposal.

He grinned. "You look adorable."

"Shut up." I crawled beside him, lay on my stomach, and studied him. I couldn't believe he was once again mine. "No, I take that back. Tell me more."

He chuckled, stroked my hair, and studied my face as though memorizing it. "You're going to be impossible to love."

"But I'm adorable. You said so."

He kissed me, and I felt the smile on his lips. Soon, I was lost in him. His scent became the air I breathed, his taste the nectar on my lips, and his muscles musical instruments to my caresses. Kissing him was like eating a forbidden delicacy, and I never wanted to stop.

My senses leaped as they recognized his touch. When he nibbled my neck, I tilted my head and gave him better access. A burning fever rolled through me, making the stupid PJs he'd forced on me feel like an oven. As though he knew we were reaching a point when we'd have to take everything up a notch, he lifted his head and studied me with burning eyes, blue flames leaping in their core. He reached over, turned off the bedside lamp, flopped on his back, and cradled me against his chest.

"Go to sleep, Freckles."

"But—"

"No buts. I want you with every breath I take. Don't ever doubt that. But I'm not going to have you while your dad is—" He exhaled. "Your *parents* are sleeping across the hallway."

"Then let's go to your place," I whispered, looping my arms around his neck.

He grinned. "Once I fulfill the favor I owe and you still want me, I'm all yours."

Still want him? What a weird thing to say. A terrible feeling washed over me. Mom once told me if you were meant to die, you couldn't escape death. I reached over Torin and turned on the light. He squinted against the sudden glare while I studied his expression.

"The favor doesn't involve reaping the souls of my friends, does it? You know, Cora, Eirik, and the people I 'saved' during the last meet?"

"No-oo."

"Good, because I'd never forgive you if you were here to reap their souls and didn't tell me."

"I know." He turned off the lamp once again and pressed a kiss to my forehead, cradling me close. "Now go to sleep."

I couldn't help thinking that his favor had something to do with me. It might explain what Andris had meant by Torin was still sacrificing so much for me while I was clueless. Maybe I'll ask Andris.

17. WATERFALLS

I woke up, turned, and reached for Torin, but the other side of the bed was empty. His scent lingered on the pillow and sheets. I burrowed where he'd slept and smiled like an idiot. Torin St. James loved me. He might not have said it, but deep inside I knew that he did.

Stepping away from the bed, I rushed to the window and pulled up the slats. He was seated on his window seat as though waiting for me, a mug in his hand.

"Good morning," I said.

He beckoned me with a finger.

Shaking my head, I indicated my pajamas. I refused to walk across our lawns in my uglies.

He put his mug down and disappeared from sight. In seconds, he walked through the portal and into my bedroom, runes still on his skin. I flew into his arms for a morning kiss. He tasted amazing, coffee mixed with mint and his unique taste, which I loved. The extra zing came from the runes, and I wondered if my senses would be hyped too when I had runes.

"This is how you say good morning," he whispered.

I loved it. "I could get used to this."

"You'd better."

He kissed me again, longer, deeper. When he eased off, he studied my face. "Do you want to do something fun today?"

"Depends. Will you be there?"

He chuckled. "Yes. Remember the waterfalls you said we visited?"

I nodded. "Multnomah Falls."

"Let's go there today."

It might trigger some of his memories. To be honest, I'd already given up on him remembering anything. It didn't matter anymore. We were creating new memories. "Okay."

He dropped a kiss on my lips. "Hmm, someone is cooking bacon and pancakes."

"Blueberry pancakes, Dad's specialty." He must be feeling better to be up and about. "Do you want some?"

He laughed. "No, I'm good."

"Come on. Sundays are breakfast-in-bed for my parents. Dad brings a tray upstairs, and the two of them disappear in their bedroom for hours while I eat downstairs. Alone." I pouted.

He pinched my nose. "Cute, but no. You and I will share many breakfasts together, and I'll cook them just for you. Now go spend time with your father. Your mother is still asleep."

"How do you know? Never mind. Heightened Valkyrie senses." I watched him walk back through the portal. He was still wearing the gray sweatpants and white tank top from last night. Even in wrinkled clothes, he managed to look good. I waited until he reached his room and turned before asking, "When are we leaving?"

"In a couple of hours. Dress warmly. I don't want you to catch a cold."

After the portal closed, I left my room and bounded downstairs. Dad stood in front of the stove flipping pancakes. After the scare of last night, I was happy to see him looking so well-rested. He saw me, smiled, and lowered the volume of the TV.

"Morning, pumpkin. Ready for my special blue-berry pancakes and extra crispy bacon?"

"Absolutely." I gave him a hug and stepped back. "How are you feeling?"

He gave me a sharp glance. "Fine. Why do you ask?"

I didn't know whether to bring up last night or not, so I went with, "You ran far and it's been a while, and then you made dinner."

Dad chuckled. "You think a few miles and whipping up a few dishes would tire me? There's still energy left in these old bones."

"You're not old," I protested, remembering how he'd looked lying on the floor. Like a rag doll.

"Want to count the gray hair you put on my head?"

"I'm a model daughter," I said and grinned when he laughed. "Can I help with anything?"

"Pour me another cup of coffee then start on your mother's tea."

"Is she still sleeping?"

"Like a baby."

I replenished his coffee, poured myself some, and added vanilla creamer to mine. He'd already set the tray for two, and a single rose lay in the middle. It was sweet the way he doted on Mom. I glanced out the window, wondering what Torin was doing. If Dad noticed the way I kept glancing out the kitchen window, he didn't say it.

The weather map popped up on the TV screen. There was a fifty-percent chance of rain, but I didn't care. I couldn't wait to go to Multnomah Falls with Torin. Hopefully, we'd take the Harley. Rod. The name was perfect for the powerful machine.

"Take the tray upstairs," he said when he was done.

He usually took it upstairs himself. "Aren't you coming?"

"Right behind you, sweetheart."

I carried the tray upstairs, propped it against my stomach, and knocked on their bedroom door, but there was no answer. Careful not to make too much noise and wake up Mom, I turned the doorknob, pushed the door open, and peered inside. She was still out. I placed the tray on their bedside table, tiptoed back to the door, and carefully closed the door behind me.

Voices drifted from downstairs. I recognized Torin's voice. He must have decided to join me, or came to cancel our date. I hurried to the kitchen. As though he sensed my presence, Torin looked up and smiled. His hair was wet, and he'd changed. I still wore my ugly pajamas. Life just wasn't fair.

"Hey," I said, my eyes volleying between him and Dad. "What are you doing here?"

"Don't be rude, sweetheart," Dad said. "Torin came to ask if he could take you out for the day."

That was bold and noble, but I could tell Dad wasn't too thrilled. "Oh."

"Well, I better go and wake up your mother before her tea gets cold." He smiled, but his eyes looked troubled. He patted my shoulder as he walked past. I turned to watch him walk away. For some reason, he looked like he'd aged in the last few minutes. Was dating a Valkyrie such a terrible thing, especially one as courteous as Torin? He had done the right thing. The noblest thing. Guys didn't ask fathers if they could date their daughters. Not in this century anyway. On the other hand, Torin came from another time and hadn't forgotten his noble upbringing.

"You came to ask my dad to date me?" I asked.

Torin studied me intently as though thinking over what to say. Then he shrugged, a sheepish expression softening his chiseled face. "Would that be so terrible?"

I laughed and took his arm. "No. It's perfect. What did he say?"

"You are his little princess and if I hurt you, he'll hunt me down like a rabid dog and decapitate me."

I giggled. "My father is not that blood thirsty."

Torin chuckled. "No, he's not. He looked me straight in the eyes and said, 'No man, Valkyrie, or deity will ever be good enough for my little warrior, so treat her with the respect she deserves, young man, or I'll be the soul that refuses to be reaped.'"

That sounded like something my father would say. "He knows about left-behind souls?"

Torin shuddered. "He knows I can't stand them and was taunting me."

"I'm sure he was just shocked by your gallantry." I tugged at his arm and added in an exaggerated British accent, "Welcome, Sir Torin St. James. Your breakfast waits."

"Your accent is atrocious," he said, trying hard not to laugh.

Breakfast was fun and took longer than my usual five minutes. I hated to see him leave, but the thought of spending the next several hours with him had me racing upstairs to shower and change. I dressed warmly in a three-quarter-sleeve top, long pants, and knee-length boots. I grabbed a pair of gloves and hurried upstairs. I couldn't wait to learn how to create portals so I could just slip into his room in a matter of seconds.

Outside, the skies were overcast, but it hadn't started to rain yet. Mrs. Rutledge was doing something on her porch. For once she didn't cross herself or run back into her house as though I was Hel's spawn. She even smiled and nodded. I gave her a tiny smile. She must have decided I wasn't evil anymore.

I headed next door, aware she was still watching me. The garage door was open. Were we taking the SUV? I hoped not. Torin appeared from the other side of the SUV where he kept his Harley, a helmet under his arm. My helmet. I recognized the red lightning bolt on the side.

"This is—"

"Mine," I said. "You remembered?"

A spasm of an emotion I couldn't define crossed his face. "No. I guessed." He came to stand in front of me and carefully slipped the helmet on my head. The first time he'd done it, I'd been nervous about riding with him. Nervous, but excited.

"What's funny?" he asked.

"Just remembering the first time we rode on your Harley." His eyes grew stormy as he tucked my hair under the helmet. This time, I recognized the regret in his sapphire eyes. Any reminder of the past bugged him. "Never mind."

He tilted my chin, rubbed his thumb across my lips, ruining a perfectly applied lip gloss then kissed me. It was a total invasion of my senses and though I welcomed it and gave as good as I got, I knew something was wrong. When he lifted his head, he was frowning.

"It doesn't matter that you don't remember, Torin," I said.

Blue eyes studied me. "It does to me. I feel like I'm competing with myself. My other self."

"But—"

"I know it sounds insane, but the memories the Norns took are part of our shared experience, Freckles." His eyes flashed with determination. "I want them back. All of them."

They meant that much to him? I reached up, pushed the lock of hair from his forehead, and caressed his face, my eyes smarting. "Okay. Then we'll do everything we can to get them back."

His eyes narrowed "Are you crying again?"

"No, I'm not." I straddled the bike and sat. "So Andris decided to give Rod back?"

He chuckled. "I told you he was testing me. He can be an ass, but he's not bad. He knows Rod and I are inseparable." He sat, took my arms, and wrapped them around his waist. "Hold on tight."

"Do you know where we're going?"

"Andris showed me the map on his laptop. It's all in here." He tapped his head.

I rested my cheek against his back. He cranked the engine and pulled out of the garage. I thought I saw Dad at our kitchen window, but I could have been mistaken. Mrs. Rutledge was still outside. She waved.

Like before, Torin went at a regular speed until we hit I-5 and headed north. Runes appeared all over his body, and he picked up speed until the scenery became blurry. Twenty minutes later, he slowed down near the sign to Multnomah Falls, the tallest waterfalls in Oregon, and exited the highway.

He parked, but before we could start toward the falls, he murmured, "The water falls over two cliffs and into a wishing pond at the bottom of the second drop."

"Yes." *Please, let him remember.* I tugged his arm. "Come on."

He looked around as we retraced the route we'd taken the first time we came to the falls. The leaves had completely changed color now that fall was in full swing. We took the paved trail to the bridge. At the guardrail, he wrapped his arms around my waist, pulling me closer, and we soaked in the view. Then we went to throw coins in the wishing pond.

He grabbed my wrist when I was about to toss a coin. "You only make one wish or you dilute the first one. I don't know where I heard that, but it's profound."

I leaned sideways and glanced at him over my shoulder. He was remembering. "My dad said it, and I told you when we first came here."

"It's weird how I remember that, calling you Freckles, and that you told me your name was Raine with a silent E, yet I still don't remember when you said them."

Feeling his frustration, I wrapped my arms around his waist as we walked back to the lodge. I wish there was something I could do to make him remember everything. We took the stairs to the second floor. The restaurant wasn't packed, so we found a nice window table with a panoramic view of the falls.

"We serve Sunday brunch until two o'clock," the waitress said, handing us the menu.

Their menu was extensive. Instead of egg-based dishes, Torin went to the kitchen to talk to the chef. He convinced them to serve us food from their regular lunch menu—prime rib with roasted potatoes and asparagus for him and a chicken potpie for me. I was impressed.

We took our time eating, then moved to a couch near the fireplace and just got lost in our little world. Later, we went downstairs to the gift shop. I made the mistake of telling Torin I loved stuffed penguins because he insisted on getting me a stuffed one and a hand-blown glass one with gorgeous colors made by Glass Eye Studios. When I touched a gorgeous paperweight with the falls, he bought it, too, and another. The description said the ash used to make the glass came from the 1980 eruption of Mt. St. Helens in Washington.

It started to rain, giving us a reason to stay a little longer. Between the cozy lounge and bar area on the second floor and the snack bar, espresso cart, and gift shop downstairs, we had enough to keep us busy. There was even a U.S. Forest Service interpretive center. It was no Columbia Gorge Interpretive Center Museum, which was only half an hour's drive from the falls, but it was worth a walk through. Torin loved history, and it showed when he lingered and read footnotes on the displays.

We didn't leave until closing time at six.

***

At home, Torin walked me to the door. Mom opened it before he could leave.

"Hey, you two," she said. "Where did you disappear to?"

"Multnomah Falls. We would have been home hours ago, but we couldn't ride the bike in the rain," I added when Dad peered at us from behind her. I knew that look on his face. He'd been worried.

"You came home safely, and that's what counts." Mom stepped aside and opened the door wide. "Are you coming in, Torin?"

"No, Mrs. Cooper. I need to check on the others." He touched my hand. "Later," he mouthed then turned and strolled back toward the driveway.

"That was a whole day excursion," Mom said, closing the door behind me. I wasn't sure whether it was a criticism or rhetorical statement.

"You didn't want me home to help with anything, did you?"

"No, sweetheart. But next time you decide to disappear for the whole day, call home."

"But Torin told Dad where we were going and you just said we came safely…"

"It doesn't matter what Torin said, and I was being polite. You always call home to let us know you are okay if you're going to be gone the whole day."

I grimaced. "Okay." I started up the stairs.

"Not so fast," Dad said. "Have you eaten? I cooked lasagna, and it's still warm."

"Torin and I ate at the lodge, Dad."

He and Mom exchanged a glance that set off alarm bells in my head. When he disappeared in the den and left me with Mom, I knew for sure something was up. I could see laundry hampers from where I stood. She usually folded the laundry and kept him company while he watched a game on the television.

"Is everything okay?"

"Mrs. Rutledge said she saw you talking to yourself last night. Is there something you want to tell me?"

Nosey hag. I hated her, but not as much as I hated the three Norns. They must have been invisible, which meant I'd looked like a complete nutcase talking to myself. No wonder Mrs. Rutledge had smiled at me. She probably felt sorry for me.

"Well?" Mom asked.

Sighing, I debated how to handle this. If I told her the Norns had come to the house, Mom would go ballistic. Besides, I couldn't tell her what they said without checking with Eirik first. "Cora rang the doorbell, then she went back to get something from her car. Mrs. Rutledge must have seen me while I was waiting for Cora. Why is she always poking her nose in people's business anyway?"

Mom gave me a censuring glance. "She's lonely. Be careful when dealing with her. She's convinced you are crazy. She even gave me a card of a shrink, a friend of her husband's."

"I hate her." I started upstairs.

"Lorraine Cooper. She's an old woman."

"That's no excuse. Her husband is old too, but he's nice. Goodnight, Mom." I leaned over the stair rail and yelled, "Night, Dad."

"It's barely after six, a bit early to be going to bed," Mom said.

"I have homework packets. I'm this close," I indicated with my finger and thumb, "to getting done."

Upstairs, I glanced out the window. Lights were on in Torin's bedroom. A warm breeze drifted across my room, and I turned just as he entered. One look at his expression and I knew something was wrong.

"What is it?" I asked, searching his face.

"I have to join the others at Chula Vista Olympic Training Center in California. There was a fire in one of the buildings, and several of the trainees and their instructors died." He pressed a kiss to my forehead. "I'll see you later, depending on how many souls we have to reap."

"You cover California, too?" I asked, following him to the portal.

"Just Pacific Northwest for now, but the Valkyries in California need our help." He turned, grinned, and winked. "I'll be back."

For the rest of the evening, I kept checking their house to see if they were back, but the house stayed in darkness. It wasn't until I was in bed that I realized I hadn't heard from Cora or Eirik. I sent them text messages.

"I'm out of town. See you tomorrow," Cora texted back.

Eirik didn't return my texts.

18. FIRST RUNES

I was up early the next morning and took my time getting ready before heading downstairs. My parents weren't up. I chewed on cornflake cereal and studied Torin's place. There was no movement from the house. No sound of the Harley. Were they still in California? Valhalla? Sighing, I grabbed my backpack and headed outside to my car.

It was strange arriving at school and not seeing Eirik and Cora waiting for me in the parking lot. I hoped they made up and were making out somewhere. Torin's Harley was missing from its usual place. That felt strange, too. A few students waved to me, and I waved back. I guess being the girlfriend of the QB erased my Wicked Witch of the West past.

"Raine, wait up," Drew called out before I reached the school entrance, and I turned. He was with his sidekick Keith.

"Where's St. James?" Keith asked.

"He missed the barbecue at Coach Higgins' house."

"He had to take care of some, uh, family business."

Keith placed an arm around my shoulders. "Since you missed our game in Portland, are you attending the kickoff?"

"In two weeks," Drew added.

"Who are we playing?" I asked, trying to show some enthusiasm.

"The Crusaders," Drew said. "The best part is…" He glanced at Keith, and they both grinned. "It's a home game. We just found out."

Jesuit High at our stadium? That was huge. The Crusaders was one of the best teams in the state. They'd advanced to the Final Four several times and won state a few times. We had no chance of beating them. Once again, I faked interest. "That's great."

"Will you be with the pep band?" Keith said.

I didn't need the extra credit. "No. I'll be cheering you guys from the bleachers."

"Great! St. James will deliver if you're there," Drew added.

Yeah, like girlfriends determined who won games. But being the QB's girlfriend had its perks. The boys walked me to my locker. Along the way, a few of their friends joined us. They all wanted to know why Torin had missed the barbecue. I couldn't tell them he'd spent Sunday with me.

"You'll have to ask him," I said then groaned when I saw my locker. More graffiti. Now I had bewitched the new QB. Someone seriously had issues with me.

"Hey," Drew yelled, waving to the students walking or standing along the locker area. "Whoever is doing this shit to Raine had better stop or deal with me." He jabbed his thumb against his chest.

"Me, too," Keith added.

"And me," several jocks said at the same time.

"You mess with St. James' girl, you mess with the entire team," one of them added.

Cora arrived while they were still swearing to dismember the vandals. She made a face. "Their loyalty reminds me of the swim team's before…" Her cheeks grew pink. "Well, before the accident. When are you coming back?"

"I don't know."

"You really should. We need you." She shoved her books in her locker, selected what she needed, and added, "I gotta run. See you at lunch."

I stared after her. The way she'd ignored Drew and Keith was so unlike her. Usually, she'd flirt outrageously. I ditched the jocks and headed upstairs, but Torin wasn't in class and neither was Lavania. That must have been one hell of a fire.

Eirik appeared in the hallway surrounded by several girls from the swim team. I waved for him to come over. He placed one arm around Emma Wheeler and the other around Darby Shaw, and completely ignored me. What was he doing? First Cora acted weird, now Eirik. Getting annoyed, I walked to where they stood.

"Hey, Raine," Emma said.

"When are you coming back to the team?" Darby asked.

"I don't know." I tried to catch Eirik's eye, but he refused to make eye contact.

"We heard about you and the new QB. How did you manage that?" Emma asked.

I glared at her. "What do you think, Emma? I bewitched him. Eirik, we need to talk." Ignoring the girls' protests, I pulled him away. "What are you doing?"

"What do you mean?"

"I haven't heard from you since Saturday. Are you ignoring me?"

"No, I'm surrounding myself with love." He waved to the girls. "The more the better. See you later."

I grabbed his arm and whispered, "I know why you're doing this, Eirik."

He shook his head. "No, you don't."

"Don't believe everything the Norns said. They're manipulating us."

"The Norns didn't hurt you, Raine," he said through clenched teeth. "I did."

I waited for some students to pass then said, "Torin healed me."

"It doesn't matter. This is how I make sure it never happens again."

"By not returning my calls and texts?"

"No, by staying away from you and anyone I care about." He jerked his arm away from my hand. "Leave me alone." A few students walked past and stared. They'd probably heard him.

"That's stupid," I called after him.

"Yeah, whatever." He went back to the girls, who'd watched our exchange and were now busy whispering. By lunchtime, I'd bet they'd have an explanation for the incident.

Shaking my head, I went to class before the second bell rang. Torin's chair was still empty, as was Lavania's. They weren't there in the second period or during lunch. Eirik, once again, was surrounded by swim girls. When Cora slid across from me, I cocked my brow.

"What?" she asked.

"Are you seeing that?" I nodded toward Eirik. He was still in line.

She glanced over at him and shrugged. "He seems happy."

"So you're okay with him hanging out with other girls?"

"It's his choice. As for you," she pointed her fork at me, "if you ever ditch me again like you did on Saturday, I will officially disown you."

I made a face. "Sorry about that. So what happened on Saturday? I thought Eirik came back to the movie theater to see you."

She grinned. "More like to humiliate Jaden. It was epic."

"What did he do?"

Her eyes lit up. "He waited until we left the theater, walked up to Jaden, and told him if he ever treated me with disrespect again, he would break both his legs." She laughed. "Jaden laughed in his face and started to walk away. Then Eirik grabbed him by his collar and slammed him against his car. I thought the car would have a huge dent."

Jaden was a few inches shorter than Eirik, but he was wider and buff. I would have loved to see him humiliated. From Cora's voice, she'd enjoyed it.

"Eirik held him against the car with one hand, Raine. One freaking hand and Jaden couldn't break free. I don't know how he did it, but he was amazing."

"Did you two talk at all?"

The light disappeared from her eyes. "No. He drove away. I came back with Andris and Ingrid."

I frowned. "So you two haven't spoken since?"

Cora shrugged. "No. So what did you do yesterday?"

How could she give up on Eirik so easily? "Torin and I went to Multnomah Falls."

She wrinkled her nose. "Boring."

I grinned. "It's not the place, smarty pants, but the person you're with. What did you do?"

"We went to visit my mother's friends in Salem." She crossed her eyes. "All they talked about was organic this and organic that. Even their daughter, who's my age, just yapped about composts and cow manure... Disgusting." She shuddered then looked up, and her lips tightened.

Eirik sat across from us at a different table with the four girls. Cora's eyes kept straying to them even after Drew and Keith joined us. Eirik completely ignored us. I wanted to march to their table and kick him. I felt so bad for Cora.

***

Torin's garage door was open when I entered our cul-de-sac. They were back! Grinning, I parked and debated whether to stop by their place first. Even as the thought crossed my mind, their front door opened and Andris stepped out. I waved.

"Wait up," he called and partially jogged across their lawn.

"How did it go?"

"How did *what* go?"

"Reaping," I whispered.

He shrugged. "Same as usual. 'But I can't be dead,'" he said in a falsetto voice. "'You most definitely are dead, but you're lucky because I'm taking you to Fólkvangr, where you'll live in the lap of luxury for thousands of years until the big battle at the end of the world,'" he added in his normal voice. "'Can I say goodbye to my parents?'" he added again in a high-pitch. "'Uh, they can't see you, stupid. You're dead,'" he finished, reverting into his regular voice again. He shook his head. "Idiots."

I tried hard not to laugh. Despite his annoying disregard for life, his narration had been funny. "Don't call people names," I said, starting for the front entrance.

He followed me. "They're not people. They're souls, ghosts. Do you have time to hang out?"

Hang out? Okay. "Depends. Where's Torin?"

"Practice, and Lavania won't be here until five. She helped, too, and is still in Valhalla."

"Okay. Come inside." I unlocked the door and stepped aside for him to enter.

"Thank you." He paused before entering. "Did I mention you look rather fetching in your outfit?"

I snorted. "Fetching?"

"Gorgeous?"

I made a face. "You don't have to compliment me, Andris. I've already agreed to hang out with you." I closed the door, putting down my oboe and backpack at the foot of the stairs. Andris looked toward the living room.

"Can I get something to drink?" he asked.

"Sure." I waved toward the wet bar.

He retrieved a glass from above the sink and poured a generous amount of one of my father's alcoholic drinks. "Want some?" he asked, holding up the drink.

"There's soda in the fridge behind you."

He removed one, even got me a glass. I usually just drank from the can. He came around the counter and sat on a stool, then took a long sip of his drink. "So, how was school?"

"Really? You came to my house to discuss school?"

"It's an icebreaker." He drank another mouthful, and I realized he was nervous. Weird.

"School was fine. How many souls did you guys reap in the training place?"

"Twenty, thirty, I didn't keep count."

"Do you know how many football players are going to die?"

"Nope. Don't particularly care either." He chugged his drink.

"Is that why you're not nice to them?"

"It is a lot easier to tell someone you don't like or care about that they're dead, so I try not to get too close. Torin, on the other hand, likes to be nice. It's part of his... thing."

Did that mean Torin had no problem telling people he liked they were dead? I opened the lid off the can, chugged my soda, and waited for Andris to tell me the real reason he was at my house. He still hesitated, draining his drink and pouring more. Maybe I should put him at ease by focusing on something else.

"Do you remember when you thought Torin and I weren't together anymore and you said he was sacrificing so much for me and I had no clue?"

Andris frowned. "I said that?"

I nodded. "Yes. What did you mean?"

He rolled his eyes. "Nothing. You know me, always hoping to get a reaction."

I didn't believe him. "Torin owes someone a favor."

"He does? I'm sure it's not that important or I would have heard about it." He leaned forward. "Now back to me and my question. You promised to tell me about Maliina."

No wonder he was a mess. My interaction with his ex-mate was the reason she'd turned evil. "What do you want to know?"

"Everything."

"Do you remember our first meeting at the park during the Ultimate Frisbee game?"

He winced. "Yeah. I'm sorry I made her jealous. I should never have flirted with you."

I studied him. Was he blaming himself for what she did? "You didn't tell her to attack me, Andris. She chose to react the way she did."

"Did she ever draw runes on you?"

I shook my head. "No."

He put his empty glass on the counter, got up, and paced. "That doesn't make sense. She must have. Maybe you didn't notice. The only way Valkyries turn evil is when they draw evil runes on Mortals."

My mind raced as I tried to remember everything that had happened between me and Maliina. "At the dance club, she thought I had gone outside to meet you and was quite angry. She drew runes on herself."

He stopped. "I checked her rune book and didn't see any evil runes."

I had no idea what drawing runes on her had to do with her book, but I let it pass. Then I remembered the incident at the pool. "She runed Cora one night after we'd gone swimming."

Andris snapped his fingers. "That was it. Did Cora act strange afterwards?"

"Yeah. She almost landed us in a ditch on our way home."

"Have you noticed anything different about her now?"

I shook my head. "No."

"I wonder if that's the reason Lavania doesn't like her."

I snorted. "Lavania doesn't like her because of Eirik. She thinks Cora is not good enough to date him."

"That's crap. A deity can consort with anyone he likes. Mortals, Valkyries, A, Elven, other deities." He chuckled. "He could even date giantesses. Something about Cora bothers her."

I didn't like their attitude toward her. "Yeah, whatever. If the bad runes Maliina etched on Cora are making her give evil vibes, blame Maliina, not Cora."

Andris frowned. "What was she thinking? By marking a Mortal with bad runes, Maliina sealed her doom. She'll never find her way back."

He sounded so sad. He must still be in love with her, which was so heartbreaking. I touched his arm. "Hey. Maybe she will. You never know. "

He shook his head. "No, she won't. Thanks for telling me."

I walked him to the door then went upstairs to start on my homework. At the back of my mind, I kept thinking about Andris.

***

"Today we'll start on runes," Lavania said hours later. Once again, we were seated on the floor in their living room. On the table were the leather belt with the artavo and two books made out of brown leather with runes on the cover and gold clasps. One was thicker and older.

"Can I ask one question before we start?" I asked.

"Sure." Lavania poured water into her glass.

"You said you'd tell me more about the difference between Immortals and Valkyries."

"Once we etch basic runes on your skin, you can engage them to give you special abilities associated with them. Then we'll move to bind runes, which are combinations of several runes. They are more powerful and specific. Bind runes for speed, healing broken bones, protection against car accidents, opening portals, visual acuity so when you move at an accelerated speed you can still see things like a regular person. When you have these abilities, you'll be officially an Immortal. However, not all Immortals become Valkyries."

"Why?"

"Like I told you before, you have to convince souls to leave with you to become a Valkyrie. Some Immortals don't have it in them."

I remembered the souls at the cemetery and shuddered. "Is that so terrible to want to be an Immortal?"

"No. Remember I told you about *Völur*?"

I nodded.

"*Völur* are Immortals, but they are so rare we haven't had one in several millennia. We'll discuss them in detail later. Right now, we'll focus on the other Immortals. They become servants, age faster than Valkyries and gods, and miss out on some of the cool things Valkyries can do."

Yeah, escorting souls. Yippee. "Servants?"

"Someone has to take care of the gods. Eirik's guardians, Johan and Sari, are Immortals. When Valkyries fall, like your mother, they become Immortals. Still want to be just an Immortal?"

I made a face. "For now."

"Then let's turn you into one." She passed me one of the books, opened the leather belt, and gave me an artavus. She opened the second book. Single runes were sketched neatly in rows. The pages were thin, like animal skin on drums. "Practice drawing the runes, starting with the first line. I'll tell you what they mean as you sketch them."

"I sketch with an artavus?"

She grinned. "Try it."

Expecting it to rip or burn, I placed the tip of the blade on the page and sketched my first rune. Instead of cuts or burns, I had a nice black rune. Hmm, interesting. For an hour, all I did was sketch one rune after another. Those associated with the major gods—Odin, Frigga, Freya, Thor, Tiw… Then we moved to the virtues—courage, wealth, health, victory, family, destiny, joy…

We took a break while she made us tea, then we went back to the living room. As soon as I sat and opened my book, I noticed the empty pages. "What happened? I had four pages of runes, and now they're blank."

Lavania grinned. "That's because you're only practicing."

"What do you mean? They self-erase?"

"In a way. When you use the artavus to sketch runes in these books, they disappear after a few minutes. Just like when we sketch on mirrors and walls to create portals."

"But Torin's book has runes on its pages."

"So will yours, once you start etching them on your skin. You see, whenever you use your artavus to etch a rune on your skin, the rune appears here." She tapped on my book. "Over the years, you'll have more and more runes. Think of it as a passport to your immortality. Take the *stillo* and sketch Freya's rune on your arm."

I stared at her. Was she kidding? "Now?"

"Yes."

I shot her a dubious glance. "It's going to hurt."

"Of course, it's going to hurt. You have to suck it up, dear." She stood. "I'm going to make more tea."

I stared at the blade, then my arm, and shuddered. This was so not happening. The door opened, and Torin walked in. He summed up the scene in a glance and smirked. "First rune?"

"No smartass remarks," I warned.

His grin broadened.

I made a face. "Was your first one painful?"

"Very."

"Thanks a bunch for making me feel better."

Chuckling, he closed the door, dropped his gym bag, and walked to where I sat. I highly doubted he noticed Lavania in the kitchen. He sunk his fingers into my hair, gripped the back of my head, and kissed me, taking his time. The artavus fell from my hand. I threw my arms around his neck to hold him in place. He made such a good snack.

He broke the contact and whispered, "You will be fine."

Would I? His eyes said he believed in me. I swallowed. "How do you know?"

"Because you never let fear or anyone stop you from going after what you want. Can you let me go now?" I did, reluctantly. He kissed me again, stood, and grabbed his bag.

Determination coursing through me, I gripped the artavus. *I can do this... I can do this... I can do this...* I looked up to find Lavania and Torin watching me from the kitchen. I glared. "Do you mind?"

They looked at each other and exchanged a grin. Seconds ticked by, my eyes volleying between the blade and my skin, my imagination on overdrive. I saw the tip touching my skin, runic energy sizzling my skin, pain shooting up my arm...

"She's not going to do it," Lavania whispered, but I heard her.

"Give her time," Torin said.

Lavania sighed. "She's not ready."

"She is," Torin insisted.

I wish they could just shut up. Grinding my teeth, I put the blade on my arm and etched. Tears rushed to my eyes at the pain, but I didn't stop. Blinking hard, I clenched my fist and watched as my skin burned. Then the pain ebbed. The rune darkened, the ends moving and curling under my skin as though they were alive.

Grinning, I lifted up my arm and showed it off. Lavania bowed. Torin just smirked. The rune glowed, growing brighter and brighter. Then it disappeared.

"Now check the book," Lavania said, walking back to the living room.

I opened the book, and sure enough, Goddess Freya's rune was sketched on the first page.

"Come with me." Lavania led me to the mirror at the other end of the room. It was the mirror Andris had brought home the other day. I stared at our reflection. Lavania was still the most beautiful woman I'd ever seen, but I didn't mind anymore. I had Torin and had no reason to be jealous of her.

"Now visualize the rune you just sketched. Fill your mind with its image and don't stop until it appears."

It wasn't hard to visualize the rune. After an hour of sketching, it was etched in my brain. As the image filled my head, the rune appeared on my forehead. It grew darker in intensity, the ends curling under my hair, a feeling of well-being rolling through me. Once again, it glowed.

"Let go of the image," she instructed.

I did, and the rune grew dim and disappeared. I laughed. "That was awesome."

"Happy you think so. Come on." We walked back to the coffee table. I was so proud of my first rune I wanted to make it appear and disappear again. Seeing it in my book gave me a sense of accomplishment.

"Thor's rune is next," Lavania said.

I made a face. "Now?"

"Yes, now, my young priestess. Thor is the protector of all mankind, and we all wear his rune. You did amazingly well and shouldn't stop now." Lavania checked at her watch. "We have time."

My watch said it was almost seven. My lessons ended at seven. Focusing, I studied Thor's rune. It was simple, which meant the pain might not be too much. My eyes swung from Lavania to Torin's face. He cocked his eyebrows, his eyes challenging. I made a face and picked up the artavus. This time, my eyes didn't tear up. I checked my book once the rune disappeared. Two runes, hundreds more to go. Lucky me.

"Now for Odin's," Torin said.

"Are you kidding me?" I protested.

Lavania glanced at Torin. "Odin's? Freya is her protector."

"I want her to have Odin's protection, too."

Lavania shook her head. "Why?"

"The Norns are after her. She will need the wisdom of Odin to guide her."

Lavania's expression grew thoughtful. "Have they come back since last week?"

Torin held my gaze, but he didn't answer. I realized he was waiting for me to decide whether to tell Lavania the truth or not. I couldn't. Eirik had to decide who to tell about his problems.

"No, they haven't, but I know they will," I fibbed and glanced at Torin. He didn't say anything, his expression unreadable.

"Well, as long as they're busy with their other charges, we can complete the first part of your training in peace." She patted my hand and stood. "I'll see you tomorrow at four—"

"She needs to add Odin's rune before she leaves," Torin cut in firmly.

"How many runes did you get on your first day?" I asked, dreading etching more runes.

"Ten? Twelve?" He glanced at Lavania.

"Fourteen, but you were in the middle of a battle and needed to be turned fast."

Torin glanced at me and smirked. "Think you can beat that?"

"Easily," I retorted.

"I don't know." He rubbed his chin. "I think five is a good starting number for you."

"Fourteen. If you haven't noticed, I'm in the middle of a battle with three mean and powerful Norns."

Torin snorted. "I faced legions of scimitar-wielding, turban-wearing Saracens every day and—"

"Children!" Lavania ordered. "Enough! You," she pointed at Torin, "out! No. Not another word. And no more interrupting our lessons." Torin looked like he was about to argue, but she narrowed her eyes and he clammed up. She turned to me. "Raine, you don't have to add another rune if you don't want to."

The look in Torin's eyes said this was important to him. "That's okay." I thought about all the runes I'd studied today. "I'll add Odin's and the one for courage, energy, control, honor, victory, strength, and patience because I'm going to need both to deal with some people." I narrowed my eyes at Torin. He laughed. Even Lavania smiled.

Half an hour later, I was done. It was hard to explain how I felt. Energized. Invincible. Maybe it was all in my head, but I wanted to try making the runes appear and disappear. Could I move at a superhuman speed? Have superhuman strength?

"Ten, wow," Torin said as he walked me home. "I was just kidding you know."

I stopped walking and studied him. "You didn't get fourteen runes on your first time?"

He smirked. "I did, but you didn't have to try to beat my record. After all, I'm not your ordinary run-of-the-mill guy."

His arrogance sometimes made me want to knock him down a peg, but at times it was so cute. Like now. "Show off. So can I run at a supersonic speed?"

"No."

"Have super strength?"

"No."

"Become invisible?" I said.

He hugged me, chuckling softly. "You have basic runes, Freckles. You need bind runes for the extra abilities."

"Then why do I feel so energized?"

"New runes do that to you. Each is like an injection of pure adrenaline. You get a courage rune and you feel like you can walk into a burning building and walk out unharmed. Victory runes make you feel invincible. But not until you add the bind runes will you actually be those things."

"That sucks."

He chuckled and pressed a kiss on my temple, then waved to Mrs. Rutledge, who was on her porch. "Good evening, Mrs. Rutledge."

She flashed a beaming smile that could rival the sun. "Good evening, Torin. I heard about the game in Portland. You think the Trojans will win this year?"

Torin chuckled. "I don't know, but we'll have fun trying."

"That's good." Then her eyes narrowed on me and grew cooler. "How are you doing, my dear?"

"Much better. Thanks for recommending Dr. Saitek."

She smiled with approval. "I was happy to help. We all want you to get better."

"Thank you." We crossed our driveway and started for my front door. "Prune-faced crone," I mumbled.

"Be nice," Torin whispered.

"I hate her. She's so self-righteous and nosey and—"

"Who is Dr. Saitek?"

I unlocked the door, turned, and spied Mrs. Rutledge still watching us from across the street. Then her attention shifted. Cora pulled into our driveway. From my position, I could only see part of her car. Then an unfamiliar SUV pulled up to the curb.

"Dr. Saitek is the shrink she recommended to my parents because she saw me talking to myself on Saturday night," I said absentmindedly, my attention on Cora's car, waiting for her to open the door. She wasn't alone, though I couldn't tell who was with her.

"Why were you talking to yourself?"

"I wasn't. The Norns were invisible when they came here," I added. The corners of his mouth twitched, and his eyes twinkled. "I swear if you laugh, I'm going knock you flat on your ass, runes or no runes."

Cora finally stepped out of the car. Kicker came out of the front passenger seat at the same time. The doors of the SUV opened and Jake, Sondra, and Caleb, the three captains of the swim team I'd met with last week, jumped out.

No freaking way. They were not pulling this crap on me.

19. THE VANDAL

Last year, when one of our best swimmers tried to quit the team, the captains and I had paid him a visit and guilted him into coming back. That guy was Caleb. This was not the day to pressure me into rejoining anything. I was on rune overload and worried about Eirik and his craziness.

"Hey, you two lovebirds," Cora said as Torin turned and stood beside me.

"I'm going to kill you for this," I whispered in her ear when we hugged. Stepping back, I indicated Torin. "Everyone, Torin St. James. Torin, Amanda, Jake, Sondra, and Caleb. They are on the swim team."

"Could we talk?" Sondra asked.

I was tempted to tell them no, but I wanted to make my position clear. "Sure. Come inside."

"I'll see you later." Torin dropped a kiss on my lips. He lifted his head, and I caught the devilish twinkle in the depth of his eyes. How I loved that look on him. Made me want to wrap myself around him and never let go.

"I didn't laugh," he added.

"Did too, but I forgive you this time."

He chuckled then turned and strolled away. The others stepped aside to let him pass, all of them turning to watch him walk away. He looked back, ignored them, and winked at me, the wicked smile I loved still curling his lips. I smiled and opened the door.

Inside the house, the guys grabbed the stools at the wet bar while the girls took the sofa. Cora stayed standing, waiting for my wrath.

"Anyone want a drink?" I asked.

I passed out drinks, then gave Cora a pointed look and jerked my head toward the kitchen. She followed me. We went to the farthest end, where the people in the living room couldn't see or hear us. "You should have warned me."

"They ambushed me."

"Sure, they did. Where? It's after seven, and swim practice ended hours ago."

She sighed. "Okay. I was at Kicker's, who's now a captain, when they stopped by."

"Kicker's? You two have become tight."

"What do you expect? You are became wrapped up in one delicious quarterback and quit the team. And don't you dare give me that evil look. Last year you ambushed Caleb and convinced him to rejoin the team, and now he's here for payback." She grinned maliciously. "Karma is a bitch. Let's go."

Pretending to strangle her, I glared at her retreating back. Sighing, I shoved yesterday's lasagna into the oven and set the temperature to two-fifty to warm it, then followed her into the living room.

"Okay, let's talk," Sondra said. "We want to know if you're coming back to the team."

"*When* you're coming back," Jake corrected.

"Cassie took your spot, but she's not you, Raine," Kicker jumped in.

One by one, they heaped praises on me. Even Cora chipped in. I tuned them out a few times. Sure, I'd missed the camaraderie, hanging out in Doc's office before school, team dinners, and knowing I was part of something cool, but I had no intention of going back.

"I, uh, appreciate the talk and I understand about the team's needs, but I can't come back. I don't even know if I ever will." They started talking at once, but I raised my hand. "Listen, I'm undergoing physical therapy right now and until my doctor gives me a clean bill of health, I can't do sports," I fibbed and hoped no one had seen my run on Saturday. From their expressions, they didn't believe me. I didn't really care. My training with Lavania was my first priority now. "In fact I have another therapy session tomorrow after school."

There were no more protests, and I was so happy to see them leave. Cora came back inside with her laptop. "Are you really seeing a PT or were you just blowing us off?"

I was in the kitchen checking on lasagna. "Yes and no. My head is pretty screwy." I grinned at the joke, but Cora didn't crack a smile. "Seriously, I have a few lose titanium screws up here. Want to touch?"

She made a face. "You have such a weird sense of humor."

"You think I'm joking?"

Her eyes narrowed. "Let me see."

I pushed hair out of the way and bared my scalp. She touched it, felt around the edge. "It feels weird," she said and glanced at me. "Does it still hurt?"

"It feels tight sometimes, but I massage it as often as I can." I pushed my hair back in place. "So can you stay or are you heading to Kicker's place."

She wrinkled her nose. "I can stay. Something smells nice."

"Dad's lasagna. Want some?"

"I already ate." She opened her laptop and rebooted it. "Did you hear what happened at The Hub?"

My stomach dropped. "No, what?"

"People went ballistic and trashed the place. It was on the radio a few hours ago. They had people calling in, and some think it's something in the water making people act crazy. Others insisted the football team is on some new drug since they were at Cliff House when it first happened."

Frowning, I stopped serving myself and approached her. She was responding to comments on her vlog. "What else did they say?"

"They're thinking of testing the players for drugs. Apparently, some of them were at The Hub when the fight broke out."

There was no saying what they might find in Torin's blood. Years of using runes must have done something to his body or blood. "Can they do that? Test students?"

She shrugged. "I don't know. I guess all they need is parental consent, and I don't see parents saying no to a drug test."

The door to the garage opened, and Mom's laughter, mixed with Dad's, reached me. Mom saw me first and waved. Dad had on biker shorts and a shirt, which told me he must have gone biking again. He still looked too sickly in my opinion and shouldn't be pushing himself so hard.

"You warmed dinner. Good. We brought dessert. Hey, Cora," Mom added, putting down a brown paper bag with a Joe's Pastries logo.

"Hey. Are you training for the Octoberfest Biker-thon, Mr. C?"

Dad smiled. "No, sweetheart. I don't think I'm ready for that yet. How are your parents?"

Cora shrugged. "Okay. Busy."

"I should stop by and get some fresh herbs and fruit. Maybe next weekend."

"I'll tell them."

While Dad disappeared upstairs, Mom poured herself a glass of wine and sat at the kitchen table opposite Cora. She studied her. "What are you working on so intently there, hun?"

Cora gave her a tiny smile. "My vlog. I'm responding to comments."

"Why aren't you eating?" Mom asked her.

"I already did." She closed her laptop and glanced at me again, a weird expression crossing her face. "Did you hear about the football players acting violent at The Hub and Cliff House, Mrs. C?"

"There was something about that on the radio. Why?" Mom searched our faces. "Were you two there when it happened?"

"Not really." Time to get out of the kitchen. I took my bowl and motioned to Cora. "Let's go."

"I was there," Cora said, not moving. "It was so weird. One minute everyone was having a good time. The next we were pounding on each other."

"You, too?" Mom asked.

I motioned to Cora again that we should head upstairs. She ignored me and added, "Colleen slapped me for no reason, so I hit her back."

"That's terrible," Mom said. "You should never use physical violence to solve your differences, Cora."

Cora gave her a sheepish smile. "I know. I don't know what happened. I hate fighting, but I just had this uncontrollable rage. I had no idea where it came from."

I loved that Cora was comfortable with my parents and could discuss anything with them, but this was one subject I didn't want to discuss with Mom. I would have to lie, and she would know right away. "We'll be upstairs, Mom."

"Where were you when it happened, Raine?" Mom asked.

"Outside with, uh, Torin."

"The people who called the radio station think the football players are doing drugs," Cora added. "I think that's ridiculous because the cheerleaders and I went after others, too. Even the other rock climbers went crazy."

I was seriously considering super gluing her mouth. I grabbed her arm and pulled. "Maybe the drinks at Cliff House were spiked with a chemical that caused their reaction," I said. "Maybe their supplier also sells to The Hub."

"Spiked with chemicals?" Cora said and guffawed when we reached upstairs. "Not original."

I shrugged. "It's the only sensible explanation. What do you think happened?"

"I have several theories." She showed me her latest vlog entry, which was about the incident at Cliff House. She blamed alien invaders. She had no idea how close to the truth she was.

I half listened to her explain her reasoning as I ate, my attention drifting every so often to the window. I couldn't wait to talk to Torin. I worked on my homework while eating. Cora joined me after she finished with her vlog.

"Have you talked to Eirik today?" I asked after we finished our homework.

"No. He basically ignored me during swim practice. Whatever." She shrugged.

I studied her, impressed by how well she was taking all this. The conversation I'd had earlier with Andris flashed through my head. He was so silly. There was nothing different about Cora. The effects of the evil runes Maliina had etched on her never lasted beyond that night. The next day, she'd been back to her normal snarky self.

***

"Have you noticed anything to suggest Cora was affected by the evil runes Maliina etched on her?" I asked Torin later that night.

"No. I haven't exactly paid her any attention. A certain brunette occupies my waking moments."

Just like that, he pushed my concerns about Cora aside. He took over my mind, my body, and my very soul with bold caresses, nips, and licks. All I could do was sigh and go along for the ride.

The tips of his fingers grazed my skin along the area where my pajama top and bottoms met, and heat surged through me. When he slipped a hand under it to worship my skin, his caresses becoming more intimate, I stopped breathing. It was probably stupid, but who needed oxygen at a time like this. I lived and breathed him. When his lips followed his hands, he introduced me to layers of me I never knew existed. It was overwhelming and more beautiful than anything I'd ever felt.

We were so lost in our world and didn't realize we had company until I heard a loud bump. I froze. Torin didn't.

Once second he was in my arms; the next he was gone. I dove for the bedside lamp, turned, and found him twisting Eirik's arm behind him. Eirik looked terrified, his eyes glazed, sweat pouring down his face.

"Let him go," I said, adjusting my pajama top.

"What's wrong with him?" Torin asked.

"He's sleepwalking." I scooted to the edge of the bed, my eyes not leaving Eirik. I wanted to hug him and make this nightmare stop, but I couldn't. "Don't try to wake him up. He may turn on you."

His expression unchanged and his movements uncoordinated like a zombie's, Eirik bent down and picked up the blanket he'd gotten from my closet but must have dropped when Torin grabbed him. He walked forward, yanked out the pullout bed, and dropped onto it. He pulled the blanket over him, barely covering himself. In seconds, he was snoring.

"Hel's Mist," Torin mumbled.

"Sleepwalking is a symptom of night terror." I tugged the corners of the blanket and made sure he was properly covered. "He comes here when he can't sleep. I think my room is like a safe haven for him or something."

Torin's eyes swung between me and Eirik. "You're not scared of him?"

"No. Usually he's wide-awake. This is the first time I've seen him like this." And I didn't know what to expect. I glanced at Torin. Last night he'd held me until I fell asleep. Tonight I didn't want him to leave. "Could you stay a little longer just in case he wakes up or something?"

"You don't need to ask." He turned off the lights and we crawled back into bed, but I could feel his tension.

"What is it?" I asked.

He was silent for a long time, and I began to worry he wouldn't answer. "I was surprised by the pullout bed. I knew he slept here sometimes, but I just assumed you, uh, slept together."

I turned and faced him. "Slept together as in sharing the same bed or making out?"

"Both."

How could someone capable of making me the happiest girl in the world turn around and say something so hurtful? *You did flirt with him while dating Eirik,* a tiny voice mocked in the back of my head. Maybe flashes of those memories were making him say such stupid things. Maybe I needed to make a few things clear.

Before I could respond, a sudden movement came from behind me, and I whipped around. Eirik had sat up and was making weird noises, like he was screaming with his mouth closed.

"It's okay, Eirik," I whispered. "Go back to sleep. Please. "

He responded to my voice. When he gripped my hand, I realized I'd reached out and touched him. Clinging to my hand, he lay down and stopped making mewling sounds. I continued talking to him, until his breathing grew calm. I tried to ease my hand from his, but his grip tightened.

"Freckles," Torin said softly from behind me.

"I've never been with any guy the way I'm with you," I said. "I dated Eirik months ago, and we only kissed, nothing more. He was my first boyfriend."

"He never touched you like this?" Torin's hand slipped under my pajamas and caressed my back. His touch was light as though I was fragile.

I shuddered and whispered, "No."

He continued up my spine, around my side to my stomach. I caught my breath and released it in spurts, my insides turning into jelly.

"Like this?" he asked.

"No." I tried to remove my hand from Eirik's with little effect. Once again, I was caught between a guy who needed me and one I needed. Yes, I needed Torin with every desperate breath I took. If there was a realm for wickedness, he would be the deity ruling it and I'd be his first consort.

"How about like this?" he whispered as he moved higher up my chest, his caresses reverent, his breath teasing the sensitive area behind my ear. I sighed instead of answering and wondered when he'd realize Eirik had my hand in a death grip.

Torin chuckled. "Was that a yes? Because if he's touched you like this, I will beat the crap out of him right now."

I finally eased my hand from Eirik's. "You hurt him and I'll make you pay."

"As long as you do it this way." He bit my shoulder. I gasped and shuddered. Gently, he turned me so we were facing each other, pinned me down with one leg, and once again took me to that place where thoughts ceased to matter and I stopped caring about anything else but him. I became an instrument and he the maestro.

It was a while when he whispered, "I'm happy you waited for me, Freckles."

I grinned. "Me, too."

***

Eirik was gone in the morning, the pullout bed neatly ticked away. Torin was at his window sipping his coffee when I glanced outside. I wanted to one day wake up in his arms, not have him disappear while I was still asleep. He beckoned me with his finger, then he disappeared from his window. I waited for him to create a portal and then joined him in his bedroom.

I forgave him for deserting me after the morning kiss we exchanged. "Why did you leave?"

"Eirik woke me up. Poor bastard. He had no idea how he came to be in your room."

"I feel so bad for him."

"He felt worse. You want a ride to school?"

I glanced outside. It was drizzling, and from the dark sky, it might be one of those days when it rained nonstop. "Unless you have runes that will stop us from getting wet, I don't think so."

"We'll take the SUV."

I liked the idea of hitching a ride with him. "Okay."

"You can watch me practice after school, too."

"Oh, no. I'm not going to hang around the football field like some groupie." I started to move away, but he snuggled my waist and pulled me into his arms for another kiss. I clung to him. When he eased off, I sighed. "Okay. I'll be there. For an hour, then I have to leave."

He grinned and whispered against my lips, "Why?"

"I have an appointment with my physical therapist at four fifteen."

"Great. We're tapering off at practice, so I can take you." I tried to protest, but he silenced me the best way he knew how, with a kiss. "Do you know what I like to do when the weather is this crappy?"

"Use a kiss to mess with my head then ask rhetorical questions?"

He chuckled. "No, snuggle in bed. Want to ditch school and stay in bed with me?"

He didn't play fair. I'd kill to make out the entire day. I visualized years of reaping souls with him and snuggling in bed, and grinned. Tempting as the idea was now, I couldn't ditch school. "I can't."

"You have no idea what you're missing. Just the two of us at home. The things we could do."

I hated him for teasing me like this. I reluctantly eased from his arms. "You're so mean."

A wicked grin curled his lips, his eyes smoldering. "You haven't seen anything yet."

Shaking my head, I disappeared through the portal, showered, changed, and hurried downstairs. My parents were still asleep. Or so I thought. Mom came downstairs and caught me just as I opened the front door.

"Morning and bye, Mom," I said, yanking the door open.

"Not so fast. We'll be going out to dinner tonight."

"Okay. Have fun."

She gripped the door before I could close it. "Slow down. I'm not done talking. We're *all* going out to dinner."

"What time? My lessons end at seven."

"I know. Lavania said you can leave early and go back after dinner if you'd like. She said you were picking up things fast."

I shrugged, glancing toward the driveway. "She's a fun trainer."

"I should hope so." She reached out and touched my hair. "Another thing—"

"I'm going to be late, Mom."

"No, you're not. Torin will wait for you."

I blinked. How did she know he was driving me to school? "Oh, okay," I said slowly.

"You're only seventeen, so don't rush into anything yet. The two of you will have a lifetime to do as you please, including sex."

I cringed, my face burning. She knew about Torin coming to my room.

"Raine?"

This was beyond awkward. I couldn't meet her gaze. "I get it, Mom. Can I go now?"

"Yes." She smiled and tugged one of my curls. "I like your hair like that."

"Yeah. Bye." I pulled the hood of my jacket to cover my hair. She was still staring after me when I turned the corner into the driveway. She was beyond weird. One second talking about sex, the next my hair.

Torin's garage door was open. He came out to meet me before I reached the driveway, took my backpack, and grabbed my hand.

"Where is everyone?" I asked when I noticed the car was empty.

"The others left early to take care of something at school."

"They used a portal?"

"Yep, which worked perfectly. Andris has an aversion to rain." He cranked the engine and backed out of the garage. "If he had his away, we'd have a permanent base on some beachfront property."

"I wouldn't mind."

"You'd hate it after a while." For the rest of the drive, he talked about the bases they'd used around the world. "You'll love visiting new places."

"You don't miss old friends?"

"I don't have old friends."

That was sad. He reaped everyone he befriended. Poor Drew and Keith.

"You'll have to cut ties with your Mortal friends after a few years and never see them again. Otherwise they'll notice you don't age."

Funny I hadn't thought that far. I'd always assumed that Cora and I would be friends forever. As though he felt my sadness, Torin reached for my hand and pressed a kiss on my knuckles. "Don't worry. You can revisit them in twenty years or so and pretend you are your daughter."

"Is that supposed to make me feel better?"

"I told you being a Valkyrie is a lonely existence."

I would have him. I hoped. "So now you're okay with me becoming a Valkyrie?"

He shook his head. "Nope, but I've come to learn that once you make up your mind no one can bully you into changing it." He parked, but didn't let go of my hand. "What are you doing tonight after your lessons?"

"Going to dinner with my parents, but I could get out of it."

"No, don't. We have team dinner at my coach's house, so this works perfectly." He lifted my backpack from the backseat, and we joined the students running to the school entrance. It was raining hard.

Inside the foyer, girls headed to the restrooms to repair their makeup or their hair. Torin's hair was wet from the downpour, and I couldn't help reaching up and sweeping the wet strands from his forehead. My hoodie saved me from looking like a drowned rat. As we headed toward my locker, I searched for Eirik and Cora among the throng of students.

We turned a corner and almost bumped into Andris and Ingrid.

"Did you do it?" Torin asked.

"Absolutely, and we caught her," Andris said, smirking. "Your problems are over, Raine."

"My problems?" I asked, not liking his grin or the malicious gleam in Ingrid's eyes. I ignored her and focused on Andris.

"We caught the person vandalizing your locker," he said.

"I told you I'd take care of it," Torin said, grinning.

"We helped," Andris added.

"Thanks, guys." I touched Andris' arm as Torin and I hurried toward the lockers. I turned the corner, expecting to see, I don't know, Lavania since she wasn't with Andris and Ingrid. Instead, the only person standing in front of my locker was Cora.

"Told you there was something off about her," Andris said.

"This is a mistake," I said. "She's not the one."

"We used the right bind runes," Andris retorted from behind me. "The runes were supposed to lure someone who hated you to your locker and trap them there. The other students walked right past, but not our busty blondie."

I glared at him. "Then you used the wrong ones because she doesn't hate me. I've known Cora since elementary school, and she doesn't have a hateful bone in her body." He opened his mouth, and I added, "Don't even think about saying another word. Unrune her and whatever you did to trap her." I hurried toward Cora.

Cora looked furious. "I'm so going to kill you, Raine Cooper," she snarled through clenched teeth. "I know you did this with your witchy powers. I haven't been able to move for, like, forever. Release me. Right now," she snarled through clenched teeth.

There were black runes on my locker and on the floor around her feet. They looked nothing like the ones Lavania had shown me. I glanced at Torin, but he was busy studying Cora. If he started believing his crazy friends, I was going to knee him where it hurt the most.

"Raine!" Cora snapped.

"Hug her," Torin whispered.

Cora gave me the look that said she'd flay me alive if I didn't get moving.

"I'm so sorry," I said and hugged her. At the same time, Torin pressed the palm of his hand on my locker. The runes grew faint then disappeared. Cora stepped back and sagged against me. She was shaking.

"How did you do it?' she asked.

I exchanged a glance with Torin and shrugged. "It's hard to explain."

She slapped the back of my arm. "Keep your witchy powers away from me."

"I was trying to catch the person writing on my locker, Cora," I said.

"You freaking caught *me* instead," she snapped. "It wasn't funny."

"Sorry. How long were you trapped?" I asked.

"Forever." She pushed against me and went to open her locker. "I came in early to talk to Doc. He wants me to participate at the meet after all, but if he cuts me..." She threw me another hard glare, grabbed books from her locker, and slapped the door closed. "I will hold you responsible."

I watched her walk away, feeling terrible. I glanced at Torin, who'd been quiet since he'd gotten rid of the runes. Andris and Ingrid were gone. Thank goodness. I couldn't stand their smirking.

"She's not the one," I insisted, sorting my books.

"Of course not." Torin was staring after Cora. "Andris said you suspected the vandal was a Valkyrie, and she's definitely not one of us."

"That's right *and* she doesn't hate me."

20. THE SCARS

Lavania entered the class after the second bell, and Mrs. Bates didn't reprimand her. Funny how she'd become the teacher's favorite. I hated suspecting her, but all this mess with Cora and the trapping runes had me worried. Had she poisoned Andris and Ingrid against Cora? Where had she been this morning?

I didn't see Eirik until lunchtime. Torin and I were on our way to lunch when he came around the corner with two of his new "girlfriends". He said something to them and stopped while they continued toward the cafeteria.

"You guys are not going to lunch?" he asked, but he didn't meet my eyes.

"We are," Torin said, his arm tightening around my shoulders. "Just not here."

"Oh." Eirik glanced at me. The lost puppy expression on his face made my heart ache. "Sorry about last night," he said.

"Don't be." I slipped out of Torin's arm, crossed the space between me and Eirik, and hugged him. At first he stiffened; then he relaxed. His arms came around me and squeezed. I leaned back and studied his face. "Come to the house later tonight. I have lessons then dinner with my parents. We should be home by eight. Eight thirty at the latest."

He started to shake his head.

"Don't do that. Be there or… Just be there." I stepped back then remembered yesterday. "And that crap you told me yesterday wasn't cool. You don't push those who love you away, Eirik. It hurts."

He grabbed his chest and grimaced. "Ouch. Now I have guilt."

"Shut up. Be there tonight or I'll come for you." I pointed at him and added, playfully, "You don't want me to do that."

"Now I'm scared."

I made a face. He could be such a goofball. I'd missed that. "Oh, I tried texting Cora, but she didn't return my message. If you see her, tell her I'll talk to her later."

"Okay." He glanced at Torin. "Be good, St. James. You hurt her," he glanced at me then back at Torin and grinned, "and she'll rip you a new one."

I rolled my eyes. Torin just laughed. "I can handle her."

I forgave him the arrogant statement because he was charming and attentive during lunch. The waitresses stared, but I was getting used to that reaction from girls and women wherever we went. He was completely oblivious to them, or if he was aware, he ignored them. Either way, I loved it, and I didn't want lunch to end. But like most fun things, we had to dash back to school.

"So where was Lavania this morning?" I asked as we walked back to the school from the parking lot. Torin didn't answer right away, so I bumped him with my shoulder. "She left with the others, right?"

"Yes. You're worried she might have done something to Cora and caused her to get trapped?"

I stopped and studied him. His uncanny way of reading me was amazing. "Yes, I'm worried about Cora. The runes trapped her by mistake, and now she's angry and probably scared of me again. She was after the meet incident, but when I came back she'd gotten over it. And yes, I wonder about Lavania. She doesn't like Cora or that Eirik likes her."

"I know. I told her you were a good judge of character and wouldn't be friends with an evil person."

I made a face. "Thank you, I think."

"It was a compliment."

I pouted. "Except for the evil part."

Chuckling, he pressed his arms on the wall and trapped me with his body. He moved closer, bringing with him heat and temptation. We had a few minutes to kill before the bell went off. "You know you're quite amazing."

I slipped my arms around his waist, lifted my chin and gave him a playful smile. "I know."

"Shameless, too."

I wrinkled my nose. "I don't think so."

"Beautiful, loyal, and stubborn?"

"Those I like."

We got lost in our little world for a while as he became the master of my senses. Kissing him was like hurtling down a roller coaster at a supersonic speed, thrilling with unexpected jolts to my senses, elevated heartbeat, and danger thrown in because he was so unpredictable.

"School is a place for learning, not foreplay, you two." Cora's voice penetrated the sensual haze Torin had created.

I felt Torin smile against my lips. I didn't want to stop kissing him. Reluctantly, I let him go and glanced at Cora. She grinned and fanned herself.

"The temp in the entire school just shot up a few notches. You do know there's a make out closet a few feet away." She pointed at the closed door.

"I couldn't wait," Torin said.

Cora laughed. "You're bad, but in a good way." She glanced at me and added, "I'll stop by your place this evening."

"Sure." Thank goodness she was no longer pissed at me. If I could make Eirik's problem go away, my life would be perfect.

***

After school, I walked with Torin to the field for practice. Andris and his friend Roger joined me, though they spent part of the time criticizing Ingrid and the cheerleaders' jumps and kicks. When Torin was detained, Andris and Roger dropped me home early. I had an appointment with my physical therapist that couldn't wait. Luckily, the guy didn't bring up the infamous swim meet, but I left the office with a list of what to do and what not to do.

"I think you should be very cautious around your Mortal friend, Raine," Lavania said as soon as I arrived at Torin's house. "She hates you."

She couldn't even bring herself to call Cora by her name. "No, she doesn't. I know her, Lavania. We've been friends for years. And her name is Cora."

"There's something off—"

"Please. Can we, uh, just focus on my lessons?"

Two hours later, Lavania angled her head and said, "She's here."

I went to the window, lifted the corner of the curtain, and glanced outside just as Cora pulled into my driveway. She jumped out of the car. I let the curtain fall and turned. "How did you know?"

Lavania shrugged. "I just do. I told you her essence is a bit off."

I sighed, anger building, but I got a grip on it. "I'll go talk to her."

"No, she'll realize you're not home and leave." As though on cue, my cell phone vibrated. I looked at it then Lavania. "Tell her that you're busy," she added.

I picked up my phone from the table and read Cora's message. "Where are you? Your car is here, but your house is in total darkness."

I debated whether to lie about my whereabouts or come clean.

"This Mortal is only complicating your life, Raine."

"Coming," I texted back, then glanced at my unhappy trainer. "I'll be gone for just a minute."

Lavania sighed. "Fine. Be careful what you tell her," she warned. "And don't stay for too long. We still have an hour of work."

Argh, she was seriously beginning to irritate me. Cora saw me as I crossed the lawn and got out of her car. "Hey. Did I interrupt you and your gorgeous QB?"

"No. Torin is still at practice. I'm really sorry about the trap near my locker."

She shrugged. "I forgive you, but if you put your mojo on me again, I will publicly disown you on my vlog and unfriend you on every social website."

We hugged.

"Coming inside?" I asked.

"Nah, I gotta run." She glanced at Torin's. "So, what were you doing over there?"

"I'm tutoring Lavania. She's been having problems at school, and I offered to help," I lied, my cheeks warming.

Cora made a face. "Hard to imagine Ms. Perfect having any problems at anything. Anyway, when are you going to be done?"

"Six thirty, then I have dinner with my parents. Today has been such a horrible day."

"Why don't we have a sleepover on, uh, Friday? Next week. We have a meet next Saturday. We can have *Supernatural* marathon and ogle the Winchester Boys."

I grimaced. With Eirik sleepwalking into my room in the middle of the night, I wouldn't dare have her spend the night at my place. "Round one of state championship starts next week on Friday, and I promised Torin I'd be there."

"Ah, the dutiful girlfriend." There was a pinch of envy in her voice. "I heard you've been going to watch him practice."

I bristled at the censure in her voice. When she'd dated a ball player, I'd teased her about attending his practice sessions, yet I was doing it, too.

"I went today for an hour," I said defensively. "How did you know?"

"Everything you and Torin do is news."

I made a face. "We could hangout on Saturday evening. Have a late night with the guys."

"Yeah, Eirik would rather slobber over a bunch of airheads than hang out with me. Can't we just hang out the two of us?"

I loved falling asleep in Torin's arms. "I guess so."

Her eyes narrowed, and I could tell she was hurt. "Forget it."

"It's not that I don't want to hang out. I do, but Torin sneaks into my room every night and holds me until I fall asleep."

Cora's jaw dropped. "That's so romantic. Gah, now I'm neon green with envy. Oh, I want to hear everything." Then her eyes widened. "Have you done *it*? Do you worry about getting busted by your parents?"

I laughed. "Yes, but he's so worth it. And no, we haven't done it, nosey."

"What are you waiting for? If he were mine, I would have jumped his bones weeks ago. Okay, fine. You're off the hook on sleepovers, but we're hanging out tomorrow." She glanced at Torin's house. "Are you tutoring *her* tomorrow, too?"

I grimaced. "Until seven."

She made a face again. "I hope she's paying you well."

Becoming an Immortal was priceless. "So we're on for tomorrow after seven. We can have dinner. You know, order pizza or something."

"Or eat out. We have to go shopping for Halloween outfits."

I really didn't want to go shopping. I'd planned to ask Torin if he wanted to go trick-or-treating with us, but I hadn't gotten around to it. Cora, Eirik, and I often went together.

"There are a few people throwing Halloween parties on Saturday," she said. "We could checkout one or two."

"Drew already invited us to one."

She grinned. "Let's talk tomorrow." She opened the door and paused before entering her car. "Have you seen Eirik?"

"I saw him before Torin and I left for lunch. Why?"

"He left the pool early. He had some weird red marks crisscrossing his back. Someone noticed them and asked him about them. He looked, I don't know, scared and couldn't wait to get out of there. He didn't even tell Doc he was leaving." She shook her head. "Totally weird. Anywho, see you tomorrow at school at, uh, lunchtime?"

I shook my head, still mulling over what she'd told me. "Torin hates school lunch."

She rolled her eyes. "Of course he does. Later then."

As I walked back to Torin's, images of Eirik's back flashed in my head. Until he'd turned ten, Eirik had horrible bumpy marks on his back. They looked like strawberry marks you saw on newborn babies, except his had run from his shoulders to his waist.

I couldn't concentrate, and Lavania didn't bother to hide her disappointment. "Your association with this Mortal—"

"Cora. Her name is Cora," I said.

"Your association with *Cora* is affecting your concentration. You need to cut her off."

"She's my friend, Lavania," I protested.

"Then choose what's more important. Your friendship with her or your training. You can't have both." She got up. It was only six. "We're done for today." She picked up my runes book and hers and thrust them at me, her disapproval obvious. "Take these and practice the runes on the next two pages at home. You can also take home your artavo. Do not let her see them."

I just stopped short of rolling my eyes. She was being unfair and dictatorial.

***

I was still pissed when my parents came home, but as soon as I saw my dad, my anger disappeared. He looked pale and appeared frailer than yesterday.

I hugged him, stepped back, and studied his face. "You okay, Daddy?"

"Yes, pumpkin. Just a slight headache."

"Then why are we going out?"

"We're not," Mom said from behind us, and I whipped around. She'd just entered the house from the garage. In her arm was a brown paper bag with a familiar logo. "Your dad and I are tired, so we thought why not have takeout from our favorite Cantonese restaurant. Come on." She pushed the bag into my arms and slipped her arm around Dad's waist. The two walked to the kitchen.

I followed, not liking the way they walked. It almost seemed like she was supporting his weight. Maybe seeing him on the floor a few nights ago was making me imagine things.

I kept an eye on him as I retrieved three plates from the cupboard and placed them on the breakfast nook table. Mom removed boxes of food from the bag while Dad plopped on a chair, leaned back against the ladder-back, and closed his eyes.

"Do you need headache meds, Dad?" I asked, worried about him. He smiled. "Could you?"

I went to the hallway closet by the downstairs bathroom, lifted the First-Aid kit from where Mom kept it on the top shelf, and found ibuprofen. Approaching the kitchen with two tablets, I angled my head to catch my parents' conversation, but they were talking in low voices.

"Not yet, please," Mom said.

"It's almost four weeks," Dad answered.

"Which is too soon," Mom murmured. "Give us one more week." They kissed.

The conversation didn't make sense, but then again, they always finished each other's sentences which made it impossible to understand what they were discussing half the time. I stomped my feet to draw their attention with little effect.

"Do you two need to be alone?" I teased when they continued to kiss. "Because I can grab my food and disappear upstairs."

Dad lifted his head and smiled. There was more color on his cheeks. "Sit down." He glanced down at Mom and added, "Where do you think she gets her insolence from?"

"Me," Mom said and chuckled. "I need it to counteract your stubbornness and impatience."

Dad laughed. "You, my love, know that I don't have a stubborn bone in my body. I have the patience of a saint."

I sat, loving their exchange. Mom's eyes were bright, and Dad looked much better.

"Saint?" She glanced at me. "Let me tell you the story of the day we went to the hospital for the first ultrasound when I carried you."

"No, no, not that day," Dad said, shaking his head.

Listening to their anecdotes, hearing their laughter and seeing their love pushed aside the concerns I'd had about Dad. He sounded normal and was even planning on running the next morning. Even when the conversation moved to my physical therapy, I steered it back to them. They were still talking when I left them an hour later.

Upstairs, I went to the window, but Torin's room was in total darkness, even though lights were on downstairs. I finished my homework, including several oboe tunes, and was working on the book report for AP English when a warm draft filled the room and the mirror dissolved into a portal.

Eirik peered into my room. "Can I come in or are you going to throw something at me?"

Laughing, I stood. We hugged, and then I slugged him in the gut. He doubled over. "What was that for?"

"For acting like a douche."

He grinned. "I was trying to be heroic."

"Then I like you better unheroic. Have you eaten?"

He flopped on my bed and stretched. "Yep. Mom made something." He grimaced. "What did you have for dinner, so I can salivate with envy?"

"We didn't go out. Mom brought food from San Tung."

"I love San Tung."

I angled my head. "They're still downstairs. You want to see if there is any left... Wait up." He was already heading for the door. I grabbed his shirt, forcing him to stop. "Do me a favor. See if you notice anything different about my dad."

"What do you mean?"

"I found him unconscious on the floor on Saturday, and he hasn't been the same since."

"What happened?"

"I don't know. Mom said he slipped. He was wearing silk socks, and there's no traction on the kitchen floor." I rolled my eyes. "He had a bump, but Torin healed him. After my head injury, I don't take any head injury lightly, even a bump."

"Have you talked to your mom about it?"

"She's the one who came up with the traction explanation, which is totally lame. I wish I knew what they were hiding. It's been almost a month, and Dad hasn't fully recovered from his illness in Cost Rica, even though he's gone back to biking and running."

"What did Torin have to say?"

I shrugged. "We haven't discussed it."

Eirik studied me pensively as though thinking over what I'd just told him. "Okay. I'll see what I can find out."

Downstairs, my parents looked up when we entered the kitchen. They didn't look surprised, which told me Mom had known the second Eirik entered my room. Dad didn't ask Eirik how he'd entered our house without ringing the doorbell either, which meant he knew about the mirror portal in my room. Mom waved Eirik to a chair and piled food onto a plate.

Conversation focused on the local 5K and 10K races Dad intended to participate in, a marathon he was hoping to run in spring, and upcoming swim meets. Typical conversation around my house. Dad religiously watched professional and collegiate sports, especially football and basketball. He rarely showed interest in high school until now. Maybe having Torin as the QB had something to do with it or Eirik's enthusiastic recap of last weekend's game.

"You should come to the playoffs, Mr. C.," he said. "We are hosting."

Dad looked at Mom, and she nodded, not masking her excitement. Seriously, the football gene must have skipped me or something.

"Are you going, Raine?" Eirik asked. I wanted to kick him. I wasn't going to be myself with my parents sitting beside me. Besides, I planned to go with him, Andris, and Roger.

"Yeah, with Cora and a bunch of girls," I fibbed incase my parents expected me to go with them.

"Oh, you won't sit with us?" Mom asked and faked a pout.

"No-oo." I stood and started clearing the table.

"Why not? Are you embarrassed to be seen with us in public?" Mom asked, but I heard the laughter in her voice.

"Absolutely. It's social suicide." I glared at Eirik, but he just smirked. "Don't you have a swim meet on Saturday, Eirik? We should all go and cheer for him, Mom." My parents always attended our meets; his only went sometimes.

"What a wonderful idea." Mom touched Dad's arm. "Do you have to bike in the morning?"

"I can bike in the evening."

"I'll invite Sari and Johan," Mom added.

Eirik's eyes narrowed, promising retribution. "When are you coming back to the team, Raine? I heard the captains planned to talk to you about it."

Seriously, an unmarked grave in our backyard was too good for him. I walked to his side, picked up the remaining plates, kicked his shin, and smirked when he winced and bit his lip to stop from crying out.

"They already did," I said, turning and catching Dad's scowl. I wasn't sure whether he'd seen the kick or if my response was the cause. "I told them I can't until my doctor gives me the green light. He hasn't."

Dad exchanged a glance with Mom.

"Your dad and I don't think you should go back to swimming until you can control your runes."

Relieved, I nodded. As an Immortal, I could engage my runes and move faster than most humans. Of course, I would never cheat, but I didn't have to worry about my parents pressuring me to join the team. They used to take such pride in my accomplishments.

I hurried back to the sink, aware that Eirik had gotten up to help me clear the table. I knew he was after revenge, so I shuffled away, ripped sheets of paper towel, and went to wipe the table.

"Goodnight, Dad... Mom." I raced for the stairs.

***

I was checking to see if Torin was back when Eirik entered the room.

"I can't believe you kicked me in front of your parents," he griped, planting his sneakered foot on my gold and brown duvet and lifting the leg of his pants. "It's swelling."

His foot was fine. "I didn't kick you that hard. Besides, I'm wearing sandals, you baby. Quit putting dirt on my covers. So what's your verdict on Dad? Did he seem sickly to you?"

"He seemed fine." Eirik walked to the other side of the bed, pulled out the pullout bed, stole half my pillows, and plopped on it. "I mean, he's still thin, but he seemed okay. Where's Torin tonight?" he asked.

I glanced out the window one last time and dropped on my bed. I scooted to the edge of the bed, so I could see Eirik's face while we talked. "The players had dinner at the coach's tonight."

"So you two already sleep together?"

"He stays until I fall asleep then goes home."

"I mean, you know, before you fall asleep. Do you have sex?"

My cheeks warmed. I couldn't believe he just came right out and asked me. "That's none of your business."

He grinned. "So you haven't. But he's buttering you up with gifts." He picked up the delicate hand-blown glass of a rainbow twirling around a clear arched piece. One base was the northern hemisphere of earth and the other a land with tall buildings grouped together on top of a stone mountain. Torin had surprised me with the piece after our trip to the waterfalls, and I loved it.

"Be careful with that." I took it from Eirik's hand and put it back. "And he doesn't need to butter me up."

"You know what that is?"

"Bifrost, the rainbow bridge connecting Asgard to Earth."

"No, I mean it is a signature piece. Mom collects them, so I know they cost thousands of dollars. He's definitely buying his way into your pants."

"Shut up." I hit him with a pillow. He yanked it from my hands and placed it behind his neck.

"How are your lessons with the Valkyrie?"

Grateful for the change in topic, I didn't reprimand him for calling Lavania *the Valkyrie*. "Great. I have runes now. Watch this."

I visualized Goddess Freya's rune and a tingle started on my forehead, the feeling of well-being coursing through me. I didn't have to look in the mirror to know I had Freya's rune on my forehead. I added Odin's on my right cheek, Thor's on my left, and Tiw's, the god of justice, on my chest.

Eirik sat up, his eyes wide.

"What do you think?" I asked.

"Beautiful." He reached up and touched my forehead. "They make you look, I don't know, unworldly."

"I have more." I focused on the runes of virtues. The beautiful etches spread on my arms like roots of a giant tree.

"That's a lot," Eirik said with awe.

"I etched them the last two days. I still have to add coded ones." He gave me a blank stare. "Bind runes. You know two or more single runes combined to form a new one? Never mind," I added when he still wore a clueless expression. "They're gorgeous, powerful, and tailor-made for specific purposes. Lavania is really good. You should train with her, too."

A thoughtful expression settled on his face as though he was thinking about it. He shook his head and plopped back on his pillows. "Nah."

I let the runes fade. "Why don't you like her?"

"She was rude to Cora the first day we met."

"Are you sure? Cora told me she was nice."

"Cora was just being polite. Lavania was dismissive when she talked to her and did it with that condescending smile. What else have you learned?"

"History of Immortals, Valkyries, the gods, and, of course, Norns." By the time I finished explaining he wore a preoccupied expression. "I showed you mine, so now show me yours." I sat up and stared at him expectantly.

He grinned and hooked his thumb under the waistband of his jeans. "Really?"

"You're disgusting. I meant runes."

He laughed. "Promise you won't be jealous?"

I rolled my eyes. "Quit procrastinating."

They appeared first on his face. He had Odin's on his forehead like Torin, Goddess Frigg, Odin's wife, or should I say his grandmother, on his right cheek. The one on his left cheek was unfamiliar. "Whose is that?"

"I don't know. My father's, I think," he mumbled, his cheeks acquiring a pink tint. Then like he'd opened a floodgate, runes inked his arms. There were so many of them. I recognized some, but majority were new to me. Some were visible on his collar, which meant he had more.

"Remove your shirt," I said.

He threw me an incredulous look. "I'm not removing my shirt."

"I've seen you shirtless countless times, bonehead."

"Yeah, that was before you made out with Mr. Perfect Body next door," he retorted.

I giggled. "I'll tell him you're crushing on him... No, I'll tell Andris." I wiggled my brow. "He's bisexual."

Eirik sat up. "No way."

"Yes way. He's dating some guy right now. Roger. Really pretty. Wears diamond studs." I gawked when Eirik pulled off his shirt. "Whoa, that's a lot of runes. Did you etch all of them?"

He shook his head. "No. They just appeared, and every day I get more."

"What did your parents say about them?"

"Nothing. I mean, I haven't shown them. Do you think deities pass runes through their blood to their children?"

"That's possible."

"I guess mine came from my father and my mother, whoever she is or was." He reached for his shirt, which had dropped on the floor, and I saw his back.

My eyes widened, and it wasn't because of the runes. The scars he'd had as a child were back, just like Cora had said. They were even uglier than I remembered. Something else registered. I recognized virtues runes on his body, but they were upside down or faced the opposite direction. I checked the ones on his face and arms again. Even Odin's was opposite. I should have noticed that right away. What did that mean?

"Well?" he asked.

"Your runes are drawn wrong. They're, like, facing the opposite direction."

Eirik stood and walked to the mirror. I followed, visualizing my runes. By the time I stood beside him, runes coiled on my skin. We compared the familiar ones.

"Why are mine different?" he asked, but he didn't seem concerned.

I studied the ones on his back. "I don't know. When did they start appearing?"

"Right after the meet when the swimmers died."

"And the scars?"

"Friday night."

Friday night was the first time he shifted into his other, evil form. I winced, hating that I always referred to his Hulk persona as evil. I loved Hulk. He was my third favorite superhero after Thor and Ironman. As I watched, the runes disappeared and so did the scars, leaving his back flushed. Were the runes and the scars connected? He pulled on his T-shirt and started for the bed, but I caught his arm.

"What?" he asked.

"I think we should talk to Lavania about your runes and scars."

21. POISONED

Eirik yanked his arm from my hand and gave a brief laugh. "Hel no!"

"Eirik, you have weird runes. That can't be good. If you won't talk to your parents—"

"I'm not discussing my problems with that Valkyrie," he snapped.

"Just because she doesn't like Cora?"

"She treated Cora like she was nothing. Someone beneath her."

I closed my eyes. I loved Cora, too, but he was being stubborn over nothing. "Then ask her to apologize or something." He made a face, walked back to the pullout bed, and sat. Seriously, he could be a real pain sometimes. "Why the double standards? You're not nice to Cora most of the time, hurt her every time you surround yourself with other simpletons, yet you refused to forgive Lavania."

"That's different." He scrubbed his face and glared at me. "I'm protecting Cora from me. My other self. Once all this blows over, I plan to ask her out." His cheeks grew pink. "Lavania thinks Cora is not good enough for me. Who does she think she is?"

"A powerful Valkyrie with amazing knowledge of runes." I closed my eyes and exhaled. She also needed to control her mouth. Being a senior Valkyrie didn't give her the right to say whatever she pleased. "Let me talk to her. I won't mention your name or—"

"No." He jumped up, runes appearing on his body. "This is my problem, Raine. I'll deal with it."

"We're in this together. The Norns asked *me* to protect you."

He bowed. "Then I release you from your obligations." He walked toward me, smirking. "You have a new life as an Immortal. Enjoy it."

"You know I can't do that when you have this thing hanging over your head."

"Over *my* head, not yours."

"Semantics. You and I—"

"Don't!" The mirror dissolved into a portal. Instead of the warmth I often felt whenever Torin created a portal, a frigid draft shot across the room. I shivered. "Don't talk to anyone about the scars or my runes. And FYI, I'm not attending the swim meet on Saturday. Seeing Cora screws with my head."

"Then talk to her. Explain why—"

"No!"

"Oh, you're so annoying." I was seriously contemplating kicking his deity behind. "And don't you dare interrupt me mid-sentence or I swear... I love you, Eirik, but your stubbornness drives me nuts. You are family, and family sticks together through thick and—"

"Family?" He turned and faced me, eyes narrowed. "Just because you throw that word around doesn't make us a family, Raine. Let's be honest here. You are a Cooper. I'm not. You have two loving parents who'd do anything for you. Mine couldn't care less what happened to me, so they dumped me here. Hell, I'm not even human. So yeah, stay out of my business. This monkey on my back and upside down runes are things I inherited from my parents. This is my problem. *My family* problem, so stay out of it." His eyes became unfocused the way they did whenever he shifted. The same demented, evil smile curling his lips, he turned and stepped through the portal.

Hurt rained down on me. I stood there and stared at him. The portal opened into his bedroom, which was huge enough to sleep the entire swim team. He'd been part of my family his whole life. I never cared that he was loaded and pampered and impossible when he didn't get his way. He was like the brother I never had. An annoying brother. How dare he disown me? I didn't care whether his Hulk persona came out to play. I was going to slap him into Asgard.

I started forward, intent on following him. He whipped around and stared at me with a hard expression. I froze. Then something registered. The glaze that had covered his amber eyes was gone. Could he control the shift? I know I hadn't imagined it.

"Eirik?" The portal started to seal from his side, the swirling gray mass filling the short hallway, a chilling draft of air sweeping past me. "Eirik!" I gripped the frame of the mirror and stared helplessly as the gateway closed. The last thing I saw was his smile. It had grown sad. Frustrated, I wanted to scream. I needed to learn how to create portals. No, I needed...

Torin. Where was he?

The portal opened again with a warm breeze, and Torin walked into my room. "What is it? What happened?"

"Eirik..." My throat burned, making speech difficult. Torin wrapped his arms around me, and I buried my face in his neck.

"You're shaking. What did he do?" He looped his arm under my knees, effortlessly lifting me up. He reached the bed and sat me on his lap. "Deity or not, I'm going to make him sorry he hurt you."

I shook my head, tears racing down my face. I couldn't believe I was crying, but no matter how hard I tried to stop, I couldn't. There was a knock at the door. It opened and closed, but when I looked over, there was no one there.

I wiped my cheeks. "Who—"

"Your mother." Torin wiped the wetness from my cheeks, his eyes probing. "What happened?"

"I hate Eirik," I ground out.

"No, you don't."

"Yes, I do." I scrambled off his lap and paced. He got comfortable, piling pillows behind him on the headboard and crossing his arms.

I started talking and didn't stop until I finished with, "I know I should be happy he can control the shift, but all I can think about right now is the things he said. When this is over, I'm going to make him so sorry he won't forget for millennia. I don't need this from him now." Tears rushed to my eyes again, and I blinked hard to stop them. "Dad looks like he has some debilitating disease. You healed him after that fall, but he looks worse instead of better. And to top it all, Lavania told me to choose between my training and Cora. What kind of crap is that? I thought she was nice and sweet, and she's morphed into this imperial high priestess trainer from Hel's Mist. I need—"

"Me." Torin patted the bed. "Come here."

"No. I need to think, come up with a plan. There must be a way to ask her about the runes without arousing her suspicions and—"

"Freckles!"

I paused and stared at Torin. "What?"

"It hurts to see you cry like this."

"I'm not crying. I'm pissed and angry and really, really pissed." I wiped my cheeks.

"Okay. It hurts me to see you 'pissed and angry and really, really pissed'. Come here and make *me* feel better."

He was silly, but I was glad he was here. I crawled on the bed beside him, curled up on his side, and wrapped my arms around him. The tears continued to flow until I was spent. I wanted to pull the covers over my head and never, ever come out of my room again.

"First of all, I healed the bump on your father's head, so the fall didn't hurt him," Torin said softly as though discussing something mundane like the weather. "Second, Lavania had no business giving you an ultimatum. She's my maker and I respect her, but she's your trainer, not your keeper. She should not dictate to you how long you and Cora can be friends. You'll only have about five years together. Ten at the most before she realizes you're not aging. No one should take that from you."

I lifted my head to study his face. "Are you trying to cheer me up or make me more miserable?"

"I want you to be realistic." He kissed me and added, "And last, you have me. I might have lost my runes book, but I know enough to explain the meanings of what you saw. All you have to do is draw… Where are you going?"

"I have your book." I went to the drawer, yanked it open, and reached in the back. "I meant to give it back to you after we talked last Friday, but with the things happening, I completely forgot."

He took the book and flipped it open. "No, that's okay. Let's see if the runes you saw on Eirik are here." He pulled me back on his lap. "Runes that are upside down or reversed like you said you saw usually have opposite meaning to regular runes. Instead of courage, the rune infuses trickery… generous becomes greedy… nice becomes—"

"Mean, I get it. It might explain the creepy grin he wears after he shifts, like he's enjoying people hurting each other." I shuddered. I wanted the old Eirik back.

Torin nodded. "With some runes you cannot tell when they're reversed by just looking at them. Still, they work in opposition to the rune's true power, like Tiw's. His rune represents justice, honesty, and faith. The reverse is cowardice, immorality, and deceit."

"Thor's was there, too."

"Thor's stands for protection and defense," he explained. "The reverse is betrayal, torment, and lies."

I stared at him with wide eyes. When he'd said he knew runes, he hadn't been bragging. As for Eirik, I could just imagine what the runes were doing to him. His reaction this evening wasn't typical. He was stubborn, but never cruel. Evil runes had changed him. Whatever anger I felt toward him slowly disappeared.

Torin and I focused on single runes at first. Bind runes were complicated because they were a combination of two or more runes and harder to memorize. Still we tried, using Lavania's book, which was thicker than Torin's.

A knock at the door and Mom poked her head inside my room. Torin jumped to his feet. "Is everything okay?"

"Yes, Mom."

She still hovered near the doorway, one hand gripping the knob, her eyes searching my face. "Where's Eirik?"

"He and I had a big blow up, but I plan on talking to him once he calms down." *And is not under the influence of evil runes.*

Mom stepped into the room and walked to the bed, her gaze going to the two runes books. "Is there anything I can do to help?"

I was tempted to confide in her. She always had answers for everything, but I couldn't go against Eirik's wishes. Besides, there wasn't much she could do. She was still not allowed to share her knowledge. "No, we have this covered."

"Okay, try to keep it low. Your father is asleep, and I don't want him disturbed."

I looked at my watch. It was barely nine, a little too early for him to be sleeping. "Is he okay?"

Mom smiled. "Of course. He plans to run in the morning, so he decided to go to sleep early. Don't stay up late, you two." She dropped a kiss on my forehead and squeezed Torin's shoulder as she passed him. At the door, she paused. "Is Eirik still having night terrors?"

I sighed. She was never going to leave. "Yes."

"Was he here last night?"

I nodded. I was no longer surprised by her knowledge of everything that went on inside my bedroom when she was at home. "He was sleepwalking last night and came through the portal. He pulled out the bed and fell asleep right away."

"Hmm, interesting. He loves you and knows he can trust you. That's why he gravitates to you when he's scared."

She was laying it on thick. "Mom, I promise he and I will talk. The fight wasn't serious."

She still looked doubtful. "Okay. Goodnight, sweetheart. Torin, make sure you leave at a reasonable time tonight. Tomorrow is a school day." She closed the door softly behind her, and I blew out a breath.

"Nothing ever escapes her," I mumbled, my face warming.

Torin flashed a wicked grin. "She was a Norn-in-training when she fell, so her senses are more acute than your average Valkyrie's," Torin said. He sat on the edge of the bed and gently stroked my hair and my shoulder, his grin widening. "Does it bother you that she knows you can't keep your hands off me?"

I rolled my eyes. "It's the other way round."

"I'm not ashamed of wanting you."

"I'm not either." I caught his hand. "Stop distracting me. We need to find a way to help Eirik."

Torin sighed melodramatically. "He's going to owe me big. Okay, I know three people who can give you some answers."

I stiffened. The Norns. "Don't say their names. After our last meeting, I never want to see them again."

"Then talk to the one you said was nicer."

I sat up and scooted to the edge of my bed. "No. I can't deal with her either tonight."

"It doesn't have to be tonight."

"Or tomorrow. Or ever," I ground out.

"At least think about it." Torin came and stood between my legs, cupped my face, and tilted it. He studied me, his smile becoming gentle, making my insides melt. I couldn't refuse him anything when he smiled at me like that or looked at me like I was the most precious person in his life.

"Fine," I gave in grudgingly.

"Think of it this way. You're doing this for Eirik, not for you."

"He's *not* on my favorite people's list right now."

Torin chuckled, leaned down, and rubbed his lips against mine. "You're adorable when you pout."

I loved it when he spoke against my lips. His warm breath made my lips tingle. We exchanged a breath before we kissed. "I don't pout."

"Yes, you do. I gotta go. I promised to take care of something for Lavania before she goes to bed."

"Are you coming back?"

"Of course." He ran a finger along my lower lip then touched my nose. "I love making you happy before you fall asleep."

I loved it, too. Anticipation coursed through me, my imagination kicking in.

"And listening to you snore afterwards," he added.

"I don't snore." I meant to push his head, but his hair was so soft and inviting. I forked my fingers through it and pushed back the locks falling over his forehead. He turned his head, planted a kiss on my arm, leaned lower, and claimed my lips in a long, hot kiss. Then he was gone, striding across the room. Runes appeared on his skin, and the mirror dissolved into a doorway. He paused, looked back, and smiled. I missed him already.

"Come back soon or I'll be asleep," I warned.

"Then I'll wake you up," he vowed and disappeared.

***

Torin didn't need to wake me. I was wide-awake. As usual, I fell asleep surrounded by his warmth and scent, and I woke up in the morning feeling refreshed. The pullout bed was still out, exactly how Eirik had left it. He hadn't wandered into my bedroom, which meant he'd slept through the night.

Dressed, hair styled, and makeup done, I bounded down the stairs, almost bumping into Dad at the bottom. He was already dressed in his running pants and shirt.

"Careful," he warned. "You still race down the stairs with little regard for yourself or anyone else."

"Morning, Dad." I planted a kiss on his cheek and slipped under his arm. "Don't want to be late for school."

"I made oatmeal if you want some."

I made a face. No matter how often he tried to get me into the habit of eating oatmeal, I still hated the stuff. "No, thanks. Still hate it and will continue to hate it until I die."

"When you reach my age, you'll change your mind." He started upstairs.

"Don't hold your breath." I noticed his empty running water bottles on the counter. I put frozen waffles in the toaster and started filling up the bottles. I was eating when he returned downstairs.

"Thanks, pumpkin," he said when he noticed the filled bottles.

"How far are you going today?"

"I don't know. Depends on how I'm feeling." He added electrolyte gels and protein bars in the pouches on the belt. I had worried about him for nothing. He looked ready to conquer miles this morning.

"I think someone is waiting for you," he said, glancing at the window.

I followed his gaze and grinned. Torin was staring at our house. He was giving me a ride to school again. I kissed Dad, grabbed my backpack, and hurried outside. Aware that Dad was probably watching us, I turned just before I reached Torin and waved.

"Your dad?" Torin asked.

"Yeah." I slipped into the front passenger seat then turned. Andris and Ingrid were having a heated discussion in the backseat, but once again, Lavania was missing.

Andris looked up and winked. "Are you going to watch the guys practice?"

"Yeah. You?"

He grabbed her pom-poms and waved them. "I'd hate to miss out on Ingrid's toe touch jumps." He imitated cheer moves. "Give me a K... Give me a V..."

"Shut up." Ingrid slapped his arm and tried to wrestle the pom-poms from his hands.

They continued bickering while I scooted closer to Torin as he left the cul-de-sac. "Where's Lavania?"

"She left early to check on something at school."

"Please, tell me this is not about Cora again."

Torin shook his head. "I don't know. She didn't explain."

"It is," Andris said from the back.

I turned. "Why is she convinced Cora hates me enough to vandalize my locker? Besides, Officer Randolph tried to catch the person and couldn't."

"You still think one of us is behind it?" Ingrid asked. She tended to act like I didn't exist. Even when I went to their house for lessons, she'd cut through the living room, where we often worked, nod at Lavania, and completely ignore me. "We're not that petty," she added.

I shrugged. "I don't know what to think."

"Randolph is incompetent. Do you know how many guys bring weed to school? He probably lied to save his ass," Andris added.

Funny that hadn't crossed my mind. Eliminating the Valkyries meant Cora could be guilty. I found that hard to believe. "How do you know about weed?"

"It's my duty to find corrupt young minds and enable them," Andris said. "Do you know how many high schools and colleges we've attended? And how boring they are?"

"You really smoke weed with students? That is so..." I shook my head.

"Shameless is the word you're looking for," Ingrid said.

Andris smirked. "I know. Makes life interesting."

"You really shouldn't," Ingrid added, talking in low tones.

"Why not. I'm here to collect souls, not save them."

Listening to them, I realized Ingrid might not be so bad after all.

At school, Torin parked across from the building. The first person I saw was Eirik. Once again, he was with a group of girls. If he saw us, he didn't show it.

"Do you want me to talk to him?" Torin asked.

"No. He'll come around." I tensed as we approached the lockers. I turned the corner, expecting to see Cora trapped by runes, but she wasn't there. I sighed with relief. There were fresh runes on the floor and the lockers.

"Lavania added different runes," I said.

Torin sighed. "I noticed. You shouldn't take what she and Andris say about Cora seriously. Listen to your gut."

Unfortunately, my gut was making me second-guess myself. I'd known Cora most of my life. She didn't have a hateful bone in her body. There was no way she could be deliberately screwing with my head by vandalizing my locker. On the other hand, she'd been so scared of me after that horrific meet when our teammates had died. Yet when I'd come back from the cruise, she'd completely changed. In fact, she'd gotten a kick out of the fact that I had known about the swimmers' imminent deaths. That didn't mean she hated me or that she was evil. It just meant she was fickle.

***

The next day, I wondered if maybe Cora had a problem with me. She didn't make it to my house as she'd promised. Something came up, her text said. Crappiest excuse ever, but I didn't mind. I ended up shopping with Torin. He got a Dracula costume with a purple waistcoat, which matched my purple and black Dracula bride gown. We were being corny, but I didn't care. Torin looked amazingly hot in his costume.

On Saturday, Cora bombarded me with text messages during the meet. They weren't doing so well, and every message made me feel guilty for quitting the team. The texts stopped when the meet ended.

I had told Torin we might be going to a party and he seemed okay with it, but I might as well not have bothered. I didn't hear from Cora again. I left her countless messages, which she didn't return. Pissed off, I sent her a long, nasty text and ended up trick-or-treating with Torin, Andris, Roger, Ingrid, and two of her cheerleader friends. Then we stopped by Drew's house.

I didn't see Eirik, though I knew how much he liked Halloween. I was tempted to text him a few times, but I had to remind myself he was the one who'd cut me off. Still, that didn't stop me from missing him and Cora. We'd celebrated Halloween together since junior high and often pigged out on candies afterwards. If Torin noticed how quiet I was, he didn't show it. He focused on making our time together memorable.

"I'm so sorry about Halloween," Cora told me Monday morning, hugging me tight. "Please say you forgive me. We totally bombed. I mean, we were fifth out of seven teams. Fifth! Even the Mustangs beat us. It was total humiliation."

I tried not to wince even though she was being melodramatic. "I can imagine. And the guys?"

"They came in third. They could have won if Eirik had been there. At least that's what they said. You want to hang out later in the week? Dinner will be on me since I missed our shopping and Halloween."

"Sure." But I wasn't holding my breath. I knew she'd blow me off again. I had no idea what was happening to her. "Text me."

The week rolled by. No one drew more graffiti on our lockers, which was a relief. I saw Cora between classes, sometimes in the mornings. She always acted the same—enthusiastic and funny—yet I felt a distance between us since trapping her with runes.

Eirik kept his distance during the day but sleepwalked right into my room practically every night and tucked the pullout bed back every morning. Sometimes runes covered him and a cold wave of frosty air followed him, but at times, he came in with a warm breeze. Either way, it didn't bother me. It *did* bother Torin, who insisted on spending the night to keep an eye on him.

My training grew intense. We moved from single to bind runes. It took me two days to decode a few bind runes—break them down into basic runes. Lavania refused to allow me to etch them on my skin until I did. I became better and earned a few. I could move faster. Not as fast as Torin, but faster than your average human. I could also engage my runes and fade—become invisible.

Dad continued to train, though he still looked emaciated. He and Mom kept disappearing through the portal to have private dinners at some fancy restaurant they'd visited before I was born. They'd come back in high moods. I didn't mind. I got to spend more time with Torin, eat fancy takeout from places I couldn't pronounce, and got plenty of souvenirs.

The excitement about the playoffs had started on Monday even though the game was on Friday. By Wednesday, the halls and classrooms were decorated with flags and school colors.

Torin and I turned the corner, and a sudden chill washed over me. I stopped and looked around. Behind us, Catie stood at the end of the hallway. Alone. Where were the other two Norns?

"What is it?" Torin asked.

"Don't you see her?"

Torin followed my gaze and frowned. "Who?"

Catie was still there, which meant she was invisible. "The nicest of the crones. I'll go see what she wants." Torin shook his head, a frown crossing his face. "It's okay. I'll be careful."

He followed me anyway.

Catie turned and walked away. I ran to catch up and saw her disappear inside one of the girls' restrooms. The door opened, and a bunch of girls hurried out. I turned and grinned at Torin. "You can't come inside."

"I'm not leaving you alone with her," he said.

"Torin." I pushed my books into his hands. "Stop treating me like I'm fragile. I have runes now. Besides, you always know when I need you."

His eyes narrowed. "I'll stay right here."

Shaking my head, I pushed opened the door and disappeared inside. Catie wasn't alone. All three of them were there.

"Nice move, Catie." I turned to leave and reached for the door.

"He's getting worse," Catie said.

I paused, remembering the runes. Argh, I hated depending on these three for anything, but I needed help with Eirik. Slowly, I turned. "Yes. The scars are back, too."

They looked at each other and scowled.

"You do know about the scars he had when he was a child, don't you?" I asked.

"Of course, we do," Jeannette said sharply. "What color and shape are they?"

"Pink. Puffy." I felt their sigh of relief. Someone tried to open the door and my eyes flew to it, but it didn't open. The Norns must have changed the person's mind for her. "What does their color have to do with anything?"

"They're supposed to harden and become scaly as his dark side takes over," Jeannette explained.

"She doesn't need to know that," Marj cut in and glared at Jeannette. "All she needs to know is their presence means the boy is close to reaching the point of no return."

I ignored Marj. As usual, her voice alone irritated me. "How can scars he had as a child reappear?" I asked.

"They're not scars," Catie said. "They're a disfigurement he inherited from his mother."

Marj glared at Catie. "Another fact the girl doesn't need to know."

I shook my head. "Are you saying that Eirik has some kind of disfigurement that appears when his evil side takes over?"

Catie and Jeannette glanced at Marj first before they nodded. "You are not dealing with a Mortal, Lorraine," Catie said. "Therefore the laws of what you call science don't apply to him."

Okay, this was way out there. "So the runes have something to do with his disfigurement?"

"What runes?" Marj asked.

I wanted to ignore her, but something in her voice forced me to say, "The ones on his body. They are reversed." They moved closer, forcing me to take a step back. "I wasn't supposed to see them?"

"He's not supposed to have runes!" Marj snapped.

"Catie was right," Jeannette said triumphantly.

Catie nodded.

Marj sighed. "So it appears. I was too blinded by what he was becoming I couldn't see the obvious."

"Hey," I said, drawing their attention back to me. "Catie was right about what? And what do you mean he's not supposed to have runes? They've made him stronger, and he's used them to create portals."

"The boy is a god, Lorraine," Marj snapped and glared at me as though I'd crossed the stupidity line with my comments. "He doesn't need runes to create portals and acquire powers. They are within him.

Like a child learning to walk, then run, these ability will come naturally to him when he comes of age."

A sinking feeling gripped my stomach. "But he showed me his runes last week, and they appear when he has night terrors."

They looked at each other again, silently communicating.

"Did he say how he got them?" Jeannette asked.

"He doesn't know. They appeared after the Valkyries reaped the souls of the swimmers at the meet." They looked at each other again. I really hated it when they did that. "What are you not telling me now?"

"Someone has been drawing runes on Eirik," Catie said. "He's not turning evil by himself, Lorraine. Someone is forcing him to turn."

"Poisoning him with evil runes," Jeannette added.

Marj leaned closer. "And that's something you should have known had you joined us like you were supposed to months ago."

I swallowed, finding it hard to ignore her again. Only someone who knew runes could be doing this. His parents? Or one of the Valkyries?

"Find whoever is doing this and stop them before it is too late," Catie said. She extended her hand toward Marj, who pulled out the sheathed artavus she'd tried to give me before from under her jacket. She offered it to me.

I stared at the weapon with revulsion. "I told you I will not hurt Eirik."

"You need it for whoever is poisoning Eirik," Catie explained. She took the dagger from Marj.

"If I stop this person, will Eirik become better? Is his condition reversible?"

The Norns exchanged another glance.

"I'm afraid not," Marj said. "If he survives this—"

"He *will* survive," I cut off Marj.

"You didn't let me finish," she said, eyes narrowed. "If he survives, he must learn to control that side of him."

"The effects of runes cannot be removed once they are in your body," Jeannette added. "How many runes did you see on him?"

"A lot."

Jeannette glanced at the others. "He's a lot stronger than we thought."

"Do whatever you can to find the person responsible and stop them before you lose Eirik forever," Catie added.

My mind raced with possibilities. His parents could be the ones doing this. They had the means and the motive. They'd wanted to go home months ago, but he'd forced them to stay. Or maybe they'd resented living here all these years. They sure acted like it. To catch them in the act, I had to watch Eirik all the time. Even at night. There was only one solution—get him away from his house, enlist Torin's help, and take turns watching him.

I took the sheathed dagger, glanced at my watch, and groaned. First period was halfway over. "I can't carry this around school."

"Then put it away," Catie said. A portal appeared where the mirror and the sink had been. Through it, I could see inside my bedroom.

"Hide it where no one can find it," Jeannette added. "Not even your Valkyrie boyfriend."

My eyes wide, I glanced at Catie to confirm her words.

She nodded. "She's right, Lorraine. Whoever is poisoning Eirik could be a Valkyrie. You cannot trust anyone. Not even Torin."

22. EIRIK

Torin was still outside, glowing runes covering his visible skin. He looked like some ancient warrior god. How much had he heard? Blue eyes sharpened. "What did she say?"

"More like what *they* said. The other two were waiting inside."

Concern flickered in his eyes. "What did they want?"

"The usual." I glanced up and down the empty hallway. "Let's discuss it later. We're not just going to get a tardy. Mrs. Bates will send both of us to the office for missing half her class."

"Forget about math. This is more important. What did they say?"

I needed time to process what the Norns had said before talking to him. "Could you get rid of the runes, please? If anyone sees us, they'll think I'm talking to myself. Again."

He grinned and offered me his hand. "Then let's go somewhere and talk."

"I'm not ditching school. Can't you just rune Mrs. Bates, so she doesn't see us or remember we haven't been in class?"

"Nope." He stopped right there in the middle of the hallway and crossed his arms.

I groaned. "You know this your-way-or-the-highway attitude won't work with me."

He smirked. "You'll get a tardy without me."

"Argh, you're so…" I growled, turned, and marched to the door.

I got a tardy and a warning—one more and it was Saturday class for me. Torin was already in the back of the class, smirking. I imagined several medieval tortures specifically modified for him.

Once again, Lavania was in class. She frowned when I walked in. Could she be the one? She hated Cora, and Eirik never liked her from their first meeting. Plus, she'd wanted to work with him and he'd rejected her. Maybe "work" meant something else. Maybe having refused her, she'd decided to teach Eirik a lesson.

Nah. I couldn't see the Valkyrie I'd come to admire and respect sneaking into Eirik's room to etch runes on him. Then there was Torin.

Our eyes connected. He winked, a smirk tugging his beautiful lips. I glared. Despite the fact that he made me want to use him for target practice, I knew he wouldn't do anything to hurt me. Hurting Eirik would do that. I'd give him a chance to tell me the truth about the favor he owed a friend before I grouped him with everyone else.

"Ready to tell me what they said now?" he asked as we walked to our next class.

"They couldn't feel Eirik's essence and knew he was getting worse."

"And the runes?"

"They're accelerating his transformation. The scars are part of it, too. As he embraces his dark side, the scars will harden and become scaly."

Torin's eyebrows shot up. "Scaly?"

"They are part of a disfigurement he inherited from his mother." I wondered if she was a mermaid. "You don't happen to know scaly beings in," I waited for some students to pass us before whispering, "Asgard?"

"No, but I've heard of some that can shift into serpents and animals." I didn't know if he was serious or not, but he became very quiet. After history, I didn't see him until lunchtime.

He was by the door with Drew and Keith, the jocks hanging on his words. Students passed and turned to smile or say something. Torin seemed so at ease, like he was a normal student. Why did he insist on keeping secrets from me? Maybe after centuries of getting close to people so he could reap their souls, lying came easily to him.

He pulled me closer when I joined them, the sexy grin I loved curling his lips.

"Later, guys," he told his friends. Outside, instead of going to a restaurant, he headed east and away from the town square.

"Where are we going?" I asked.

"Home. I want to do something special for you."

"Something special" often involved decadent and mind-numbing things that could shock the pants off every girl, and guy, around my age. Having a boyfriend with centuries of experience under his belt had its perks. My imagination went into overdrive.

"Special?"

He chuckled. "You have a one-track mind, Freckles."

He sounded pleased with himself. My face warmed. I hated that he could read me so well. "And whose fault is that?"

"I'm not taking all the blame. Your enthusiasm matches mine." He put his arms around my shoulders and pulled me closer. "I do have other favorite pastimes, you know."

"I hope it involves food because I'm starving."

He laughed and was still laughing when we pulled up outside his place. Inside the house, he directed me to a stool, offered me a can of soda, and disappeared behind the fridge door. "Are you allergic to any vegetables?"

"No, but I hate mushrooms."

He peeked at me from behind the fridge door. "How can you possibly hate mushrooms?"

"They taste funny." I made a face.

Laughing, he came back to the counter with bags of frozen vegetables, including fresh shiitake mushrooms, and arranged them on the table. "You see this? It cures ulcers, high and low blood pressure, liver problems…" Still listing mushrooms' healing powers, he dived in the fridge and came back with cooked pasta.

"It doesn't matter what you say, mushrooms are disgusting. Uncooked they taste like… cardboard. Cooked, they are slimy."

"I'll make you change your mind." He got a cutting board and knife.

I watched in awe as chopped up vegetables. Then he slowed down before he started cooking. I joined him. I had no idea what spices he added. It didn't matter. He was poetry in motion, and the food smelled so good. Too bad I had no appetite and my insides churned with nervous tension.

Usually, I liked being alone with him, when nothing else mattered but us. Today I felt like a fraud. A traitor. Who in their right mind would suspect the guy she loved of doing something so evil? Part of me wanted to give him a pass, which was the right thing to do when you loved and trusted someone. No, loving him messed with my reasoning. I should at least get mad at him for keeping a secret from me. Unfortunately, all he had to do was smile and I forgave him for everything. Gah, I was so whipped.

"You're not eating?" he asked.

I tried to eat, but every time I swallowed, my throat closed and my stomach threatened to rebel. I pushed a piece of shrimp around the plate like a puck on an ice rink, guilt tugging at my conscience.

"You don't like my cooking?" he asked, his eyes volleying between my face and the food.

The flutter in my stomach grew. "No, that's not it. I'm worried, uh—"

"About Eirik," he finished, putting his fork down.

That too, but at the moment I was more worried about him and how he would react to what I was about to ask him. Taking a coward's way out, I forked a piece of shrimp, placed it in my mouth, and chewed without tasting it. "This is really good."

He rolled his eyes. "Now she humors me."

"It really is."

"You just ate a piece of mushroom."

I reached for the paper towel to spit it out, but the way his eyes lit up told me he'd been teasing. "You're a jerk."

"Love you, too." He went back to his food as though he hadn't just told me he loved him. He'd never told me he loved me, not even before he lost his memories. Should I ask him if he'd meant it, or should I focus on what the Norns had told me about Eirik?

Thinking about the Norns only made things worse. My mind kept going in circles. Torin got a second helping, while I struggled through half of mine. When he was done, he sat back, sipped his drink, and studied me with a questioning expression. I squirmed. I hated it when he stared at me as though he could read my mind.

"Okay, Freckles. Out with it."

I bristled. "Out with what?"

"Whatever is on your mind," he said.

"I got a tardy today because you refused to help me," I said and pouted.

"You can move fast, fade, and sketch forgetful runes. You don't need my help anymore."

"I've barely learned those things, Torin. I can't practice on a teacher."

"Why not?"

"Because… because she's my teacher and I could do something wrong, and I didn't carry my artavus."

He sighed. "Don't worry about Mrs. Bates. I already took care of her memories. In the meantime, talk to Lavania about carrying an artavus. You need two, one for your skin and another for portals." He looked at his watch and leaned forward. "We don't have much time. Tell me what's really bothering you."

I took a deep breath and steeled myself. "You said, uh, that you came back because you owed a friend a favor."

His eyes narrowed. "Yes."

"What's the favor?"

He shook his head. "I can't talk about it."

"Does it have anything to do with Eirik?"

Torin frowned. "Eirik? Of course not."

I studied his face. He seemed genuinely surprised, which meant he wasn't the one hurting Eirik. Still... "Why can't you just tell me what it is?"

"Don't do this." He got up. "I gave my word, and I can't break it."

"Not even for me?"

He rubbed his eyes. "You should never ask me to break a promise, Freckles. I wouldn't be the guy I am if I did that."

Dang it! He was right. I looked down at my hands, my face warming.

"I don't know what happened between this morning and lunchtime, but I have a feeling the Norns have something to do with it. I'm here if you need to talk or—"

I gave an unladylike snort. "So it's okay for me to share things with you while you keep secrets? You know I hate double standards. They suck."

He sighed. "I know, and I'm sorry, but I can't explain anything now."

I got up, feeling tired and a little weepy. "You said the same thing months ago, Torin, and we almost lost each other."

"I will never let that happen again." He got up and gripped my arms. "Never."

"You don't know that. As long as you continue to keep your secrets, anything is possible." I turned and started for the door.

"Freckles, wait!"

I wanted to ignore him. My heart dueled with my mind. My heart won. No matter how much he hurt or disappointed me, my heart would always belong to him. I stopped and turned. He closed the gap between us, blue flames leaping in the depth of his eyes.

"You mean everything to me." He reached up and tucked a lock of my hair behind my ear, his eyes fierce. "I'm not going to lose you over this."

I searched his face and saw the truth in his eyes. I should have known loving a Valkyrie wasn't going to be easy. Yet I couldn't have him any other way. I covered his hand and pressed it against my cheek. "Of course you're not going to lose me. I just don't understand."

"The favor is personal. You'll understand once you learn the truth. Will you give me a few days, please? A week at the most. Please. For us."

How could I refuse such a plea? I reached up and touched his lips. His beautiful sculpted lips. He could make me agree to anything when he turned on the charm. "Okay."

He grinned. "Will you tell me everything the Norns said?"

I laughed. "You're charming, Torin St. James, but not *that* charming. You keep your secrets, and I'll keep mine. I'll take my car back to school." I turned and opened the door.

"Why?"

"You have football, and I have errands to run after school."

"My practice will only last an hour. We're tapering down."

"I need to stop by the store to see my parents then pay a certain deity a visit. Alone," I added when his eyes narrowed with disapproval.

"Are you sure that's a good idea?"

"I can handle Eirik." Torin followed me outside, still protesting, and watched me walk to my house. He was still standing on his porch, looking annoyed, when I drove past. I smiled and blew him a kiss.

***

If morning had been stressful, the afternoon was torturous. Teachers taught, but I didn't hear a word they said. I kept going over what I planned to say to Eirik. He wasn't returning my texts. When I tried to catch him between classes, he was always surrounded by his groupies. I never thought of Eirik as a chick-magnet, or an annoying, pig-headed douche. He was now both. I refused to compete for his attention.

I stopped by the store after school. Jared looked surprised to see me. "What's up, kiddo?"

"Nothing. Thought I'd stop by and check on them." I nodded toward the office.

He checked his watch. "They should be back from lunch any minute now."

"Lunch? Where did they go? The North Pole?"

He chuckled. "Home. I always close up when they have their late lunches."

Lunches? So they weren't just sneaking off to have private dinners. Their dinners were really extended lunches. The thought of my parents sneaking off to make out the entire afternoon and into evening was… weird. Once again, a note on the fridge door said they'd be late coming home.

Next stop was Eirik's house. Most homes in his neighborhood were gated. At least his gate was open. I tensed as I parked beside his Jeep. He couldn't avoid me now, unless he'd brought home the girls I'd seen him with.

His mother answered the door with a smile. That was a first. I guessed training to be an Immortal made me someone worth smiling at now.

"What a nice surprise, Lorraine," she said, giving me a hug.

That was new, too. Surprised, I stood stiffly until she let me go and stepped back.

"You haven't visited us since you started your training."

And way before that. I avoided coming here like the plague even though they had the perfect home, complete with an indoor swimming pool. They were cold and unwelcoming.

"Yeah, Lavania is keeping me busy, and then there's school. Is Eirik home?" Of course he was home, but her enthusiastic welcome was spooky and making me nervous. When nervous, I tended to babble.

"He's in his room. So how's your training?" she asked, closing the door behind us and walking me across their grand two-story foyer with its winding staircase and marble floor.

"Good." Her husband appeared in the arched doorway leading to the living room and smiled when he saw me. He wasn't as tall as his wife, but he had a presence and cold, steel-gray eyes that never missed a thing. While I could tolerate the wife in small doses, he often gave me the willies. "Hi, Mr. Seville."

"Johan, please," he said.

Okay, now I knew someone had replaced Eirik's parents with their doppelgangers, or aliens. Stupid conclusion. They *were* aliens from another realm. Or they could be trying to hide something, like poisoning Eirik.

"So have you started learning runes yet?" Eirik's mother asked.

Was she going to follow me all the way to Eirik's bedroom? I could feel her husband's eyes on us. "Last week. I'm on bind runes."

"Already?"

"Lavania said they're so complex and hard to master she wants me to learn them along with single runes."

"I can see how that can be helpful. Well," she stopped and indicated Eirik's door, "here we are. It's been nice talking with you, dear. You should visit us more often."

Yeah, right. "I will, Mrs. Seville."

"Please, call me Sari."

I gave her a tiny smile and waited until she walked away before knocking on Eirik's door. I could hear muted sounds. I knocked louder, opened the door, and peeked inside. He was on top of his bed fast asleep, but a game was paused on the TV screen.

I entered his bedroom and closed the door behind me. His bedroom was huge. One side had a flat screen TV, a couch, several gaming chairs, and every gaming console on the market. On the other side was a table with cameras and lenses. The corkboard, which took up quite a bit of wall space, had pictures and swim medals pinned on it. Most of the pictures were of me and nature. There were some of Cora, taken when she wasn't looking at him.

I moved closer to the bed and studied Eirik. He looked so innocent. Sweet. Nothing like the mean person who'd hurled those damning words at me. I nudged his knee. He mumbled something and rolled over.

"Come on, Eirik." I yanked at his toes. He jerked his feet away. "We'll see how you like this." I marched to his bathroom, which was huge and done in blue marble, grabbed a paper cup, and got some water. Just enough to knock him into consciousness.

"If you pour that on me, you'll be sorry," Erik warned as I approached his bed. He was still curled up, his eyes closed, intent on ignoring me.

I raised the cup and tilted it, drenching his face, shirt, and hair. He swore and jumped off the bed. "What's wrong with you?"

"That's for the hurtful things you told me yesterday, you douche bag."

He shook the water from his head, and his amber eyes narrowed. "You're such a b—"

"Say it! I dare you!" I yelled back.

"Bitch!" Evil runes appeared on his skin.

"And you have shit for brains." He started around the bed and, for the first time, uncertainty flickered through me. Okay, maybe I had gone too far. I backed up. "Eirik?"

"Did you think you'd come into my room, pull that stupid stunt and get away with it?"

"You wouldn't dare hurt me."

"Really?" His eyes glazed over.

Fear rolled though me like a dam had broken. "TORIN!"

Eirik kept coming, the evil smirk I hated twisting his lips. "He's not around to rescue you."

"This is ridiculous, Eirik. I've splashed you before and you never acted like... like..." I gulped. More evil runes appeared on his arms. I reached for the door just as the portal appeared on his mirror and Torin walked in.

Eirik stopped. Unfortunately, he was between us, so I couldn't go to Torin.

"What's going on?" Torin glanced at me. "Are you okay?"

I started to nod then shook my head. Andris, Ingrid, and Lavania followed him into the room. The door opened behind me, and Eirik's mother asked, "What's going on here?"

"What have you done?" Lavania asked. She was staring at Eirik in horror.

Eirik glared at her. "I didn't hurt her. I just wanted to scare her, so she'd leave."

"I'm not talking about Raine." Lavania walked past Ingrid and Andris who were staring at Eirik with morbid fascination. Torin was beside me, though I couldn't remember seeing him move. "The runes. Where did they come from?"

Eirik looked at his arms, his runes starting to fade. The ones on his face were still dark. He shrugged. "I don't know."

"What do you mean you don't know?" his father bellowed from behind me.

"Did you sketch them?" Lavania asked, throwing Eirik's father a censuring look.

Eirik made a face. "You think I put these on me? Of course not."

Lavania's eyes narrowed on Eirik's parents. "You! You dared to do this to him? Who do you work for?"

"We would never do this to him," Eirik's mother snapped, her eyes volleying between Lavania and Eirik. Torin and I stepped aside to let her and her husband walk farther into the room.

"How dare you accuse us of this… this atrocity?" Eirik's father roared. "We've been dutiful to the boy."

Everyone turned to stare at Eirik. I didn't. I searched the others' faces. They all looked horrified, yet one of them was responsible for Eirik's runes. Which one? Lavania's reaction had seemed genuine, but was it real? The shock on the faces of the others all indicated they knew the runes were evil.

"Eirik?" his mother asked softly.

He shrugged. "They just appeared."

"Runes don't just appear, young man," his father snapped. "You're *not* even supposed to have them. Worse, they are reversed, the worst—"

"STOP IT!" Lavania's voice cut through the room. "You don't talk to him with such disrespect."

"We are his parents, Valkyrie," Eirik's father retorted.

"You are his *guardians*. Immortals, subject to Immortal laws."

Laughter came from the other side of the room, and everyone turned. Eirik was seated on the arm of his couch, legs apart and hands on his knees, ambers eyes twinkling. What was funny? Was his evil side taking over again?

He shook his head. "This is all very entertaining, but I think you should all leave now. You too, Mom and Dad." He glanced at me and frowned. "Raine can stay."

"Don't you understand?" Lavania said, moving closer to Eirik. "You're not supposed to have runes."

"So I have weird runes, big deal. I have an evil side that releases something that causes people to go crazy, too. Now that's a discussion we could all sink our teeth into. Except I'm not in the mood, so out."

No one moved.

"Evil side?" Eirik's mother whispered.

"What are you talking about, son?" his father added.

"What evil side?" Lavania added.

Eirik looked at me as though surprised I hadn't told them. I shook my head. He sighed, stood, and walked to his mother. He gripped her hands and peered into her eyes. "Mom, I'm fine. I'm dealing with the changes—"

"You're not supposed to change, Eirik," his mother said. "Your powers have always been there. All you need is someone to help you channel them." She glanced at her husband, who hurried forward to join them. "Johan and I are not qualified to do it."

"I am," Lavania said.

"You can't work with him until we get our orders," Eirik's mother said.

"Orders from who?" Lavania asked.

"The Norns," Eirik's father said.

The Norns? I exchanged a look with Torin and tucked away that information for later.

"What evil side are you talking about?" Andris asked.

"What does having upside down runes mean?" Ingrid asked at the same time.

My eyes stayed on Eirik. As the others threw questions at him and the noise level rose, a cornered look entered his eyes. He was close to losing it again.

"Excuse me," I called out. No one stopped talking. I moved away from Torin to where Eirik stood. "HEY!" I yelled, waving my arms to get their attention. "I think you should all do as Eirik asked and leave."

Silence followed, then everyone started talking at once. His parents insisted they still wanted to talk to him. Lavania didn't bother to hide her annoyance with them. I could tell she thought they were epic failures. Andris and Ingrid were busy hounding Torin for answers. He smirked and ignored them, arms crossed, his gaze on me for some reason.

"Eirik will talk to you when he's ready. Right now, he needs space." No one moved. I glanced at Eirik, hoping he would support me, but he was glaring into space. "Eirik!"

He looked at me then the others. "Do as she says. Not now, Mom," he added when his mother appeared ready to argue. "Please."

She nodded and led the way out of the room. For the first time, I saw something I had never seen in her eyes before—love. She kept glancing back, and I could have sworn her eyes were bright with unshed tears. The Valkyries surprised me by following them instead of leaving through the portal. Torin didn't move.

"I'll be fine," I reassured him.

He gaze swung to Eirik then back to me.

"I'll call you if I need you."

He nodded then said, "Eirik."

"I wasn't going hurt her. Maybe throw her into the pool to teach her a lesson." He waited until Torin left then glanced at me and added, "Upside down runes. Evil half. I'm screwed, aren't I?"

"No, you're not. I talked to the Norns this morning, and they explained everything." That got his attention. "Someone is doing this to you, Eirik."

He scowled. "What do you mean?"

I talked, starting with his scars. Halfway through, he stood and started pacing. "So one of them is doing this to me?"

I nodded. "But I've eliminated Torin from the possible suspects."

"Why?"

"Because I asked him. Torin can be annoying about some things, but he is honest. Even when he keeps secrets from me, he'll tell me he is and why. Like right now. He's keeping something from me, but it has nothing to do with you."

Eirik made a face. "The Raine I used to know would never let a guy get away with a secret?"

I was different now. "I sort of understood. I mean, sometimes circumstances make it impossible to share things. I didn't tell him what the Norns said this morning either, because I figured it wasn't up to me. I assumed you'd decide who to tell after you and I talked."

Eirik studied me intently then nodded. "Thank you."

"We need to figure out who is doing this to you." I reached for his hands and gripped them. "How are you learning the runes? You also said you'd used an artavus to open a portal to my house. Who gave it to you?"

He looked at our locked hands, his cheeks growing pink. Weird response.

"Eirik?"

"I'm an idiot." He pulled his hands from mine and walked to the bathroom to splash water on his face.

I followed him. "Don't say that. Did your parents give you the artavus?"

He gave a brief laugh. "First of all, I don't know even know what the hell an artavus is. I saw Dad open a portal a few weeks ago with a knife-like thing, and I later asked him about it. He called it a stillo."

"A stillo is a kind of artavus," I explained. "So your dad—"

"Didn't give me his, uh, artavus. If you're thinking my parents did this to me, forget it. They didn't. They couldn't. I haven't been studying runes, Raine. I just said that to get out of working with Lavania, who's probably doing this to me."

I still believed she couldn't do this to Eirik. Even her reaction when she'd seen the reversed runes had seemed genuine. "I don't know if Lavania is guilty or not. She's really nice. Strict, but nice. How did you create a portal if you don't sketch runes?"

He rubbed his eyes and sighed. "I didn't need the runes. I was standing in front of my mirror thinking about you. Remember, I'd just learned you and Torin were, uh, had been seeing each other while we were dating. I was pissed and was going over what I planned to say to you when the portal to your place appeared." A tiny derisive smile crossed his lips. "I freaked out. I didn't know what to do, or even how to close it. Then I overheard your conversation with Lavania. You were discussing me. If you recall, I wasn't wearing shoes. Once the portal closed, I had no idea how to open it again, so I pretended I'd forgotten my stillo. Since then, I just focus on a mental picture of you if I want a portal to appear in whichever room you are in, and it does. When I focus on my bedroom, it leads me here."

"I barely started on runes for creating portals, but wow, they were right about your powers. They work differently from runic ones."

Eirik shrugged, but his expression was pensive as though his mind was elsewhere. He started for the door. "I'm going to find out who did this to me."

I followed him. "How?"

"I'm going to ask them." He stopped by the door, turned, and closed the distance between us. He pulled me into his arms and held me tight. He was shaking. I wrapped my arms around him and held him tight, tears rushing to my eyes.

"Thank you, Raine."

"You don't need to thank me."

"You're always there for me, and I acted like a total douche to you. I'm sorry for yesterday." He leaned back and sighed when he saw my tears. "I couldn't think of a way to protect you, except sever the tie between us."

I smacked him on the chest. "You could never do that. Try it again and I won't be this nice. I will whoop your ass."

"You could try."

"Deity or Hulk, I'd fight dirty and win." The corner of his mouth twitched, but the smile didn't appear. I missed his sunny smile. "However, you must make amends this time, make it up to me."

"Anything."

"I want the latest iPad, 32 gigs, and the entire Supernatural series on my iTunes, so I can drool over the Winchester boys wherever and whenever."

He chuckled, stepped back, and opened the door. "I'm amazed you can joke at a time like this."

"Who said I was joking?" I hurried to catch up with him. "You called me a bitch."

He laughed. "You're going to milk this."

"To the bone." I didn't really need an iPad or Supernatural to ogle Sam and Dean, the two main characters. Torin was hotter than both guys combined, and I didn't have to fantasize about him either. He was mine. Still, I'd made Eirik laugh.

"Okay, an iPad and Supernatural it is." Eirik grabbed my hand. "Now shut up, and let's find the traitor."

23. SECRETS

"Not so fast." I grabbed his shirt. "We need a plan."

"I have a plan. You tell them what the Norns said, and I watch their expressions to see who looks guilty."

He sucked at reading people. Otherwise he would have known I was into Torin while he and I were still dating. I dug my heels in and forced him to stop.

"I think I should tell them about the Norns and what they said about your Hulk side, but we shouldn't mention that someone is poisoning you. This way, the person doing it will think he or she is getting away with it, become comfortable, and try it again. Remember the Norns said a few more and you'd join the dark side."

Eirik shuddered. "I've seen the aftermath of my dark side, and it isn't pretty. If we eliminate Torin, Lavania, and my parents, that leaves Andris and Ingrid."

His parents were still on my list. Could Andris have done this? A few weeks ago he'd been ticked off that I was back with Eirik. But could he have hurt Eirik? That would be taking brotherly love too far. I just couldn't see him doing it.

"Andris does things when he's bored, but he'd brag about it without showing an ounce of remorse. He has a twisted sense of right and wrong."

"Ingrid?"

"She blames me for what happened to her sister, but hurting you to get to me, I don't know."

He shook his head. "That leaves us with no one, Raine. You're like Cora. You refuse to see the evil in people. I'm telling you, one of them is guilty."

I still believed his parents had the means and the motive. Maybe not his mother. From what I saw earlier, she might actually love Eirik. His father, on the other hand, was hard to read.

"Well?" Eirik asked.

"I'm going with my gut feeling, but I could be wrong. The only person I'd bet my life on is Torin." Eirik rolled his eyes. "Don't do that. Lavania, Andris, and Ingrid believe that Cora was the one vandalizing my locker."

"What?"

"Ridiculous. Right? They used hate runes around my locker and trapped her. They said she hated me."

"That's stupid. Her locker is by yours, and you two are tight."

"Thank you. Torin didn't jump on their stupid bandwagon. He told me to go with my gut instinct. He's the only one who believed me when I said Cora couldn't hate me or wouldn't do anything to hurt me."

Eirik nodded. "Damn right."

I smiled. "That's why I know he couldn't hurt you."

"So now what?"

"We go with my plan, and you sleep at my place until we catch the person doing this to you."

"No way. I'm not going to run from this bastard. Let's go."

Raised voices reached us as we approached the foyer. I recognized Lavania's and the deep one that belonged to Eirik's father. Eirik and I looked at each other and broke into a run. They stopped as soon as we entered the living room, but tension hung heavily like a wet blanket.

His mother came toward us. "Eirik, you must tell us everything that's been going on."

"Raine will." He put his arm around her and escorted her back to her seat.

Six pairs of eyes stared at me. Exhaling, I started. "The Norns came to see me at school the Monday after the cruise and asked me to watch over Eirik. They said he was in danger and I should protect him."

"Danger?" Eirik's mother said and gripped her husband's hand, her eyes going to Eirik as though to silently ask him why, but Eirik was busy watching Ingrid and Andris.

"Why didn't you tell me or your mother?" Lavania asked.

"Because I didn't believe them. They'd manipulated me before, and I was sure they were up to their old tricks again. I had no idea what Eirik was, so I focused on that."

"Is that why you wanted to know about him?" Lavania asked.

I nodded.

"You should have told us what the Norns said, Raine. You are a child, hardly the right person to assume such a responsibility," Lavania added.

"The Norns said I'm meant to be a Norn and Eirik was my first responsibility."

Lavania gave a short bark of laughter. "And you believed them? You are novice with untapped potential, but watching over a deity?"

"Don't do that," Torin said in a hard voice, his eyes frosty as he stared at Lavania. "You have no idea what Raine's been through at the hands of those Norns, so don't belittle what she's done or talk to her like she doesn't know what she's talking about. Let her speak. Please."

Silence filled the room. If I wasn't in love with him, I would have fallen for him hard right there and then. Blowing out a breath, I explained the incident at Cliff House and The Hub, learning about Eirik's split personality, and the latest meeting with the Norns. "The Norns said the runes on his body are unlocking his second personality. They don't know where the runes came from either."

Most of the questions that followed were directed at Eirik. His parents stayed quiet as though waiting for everyone to leave before questioning him. Lavania, Andris, and Ingrid did most of the asking while Torin just sat there. He stared at me with half a smile and a bemused expression as though he was seeing me for the first time. A few times, when our eyes met, I cocked my brow in question. His grin just broadened as though he as enjoying a private joke. It was hardly the right attitude to have when Eirik was being grilled like an escaped felon.

I sighed with relief when it was time to go.

"Text me," I told Eirik.

He nodded and slouched lower in his chair. It was time for him to face his parents. Alone. From his father's narrowed eyes, I didn't envy Eirik. We went through a portal into Torin's living room.

"We won't have lessons until I come back, Raine," Lavania said briskly as soon as the portal closed. "Work on decoding and sketching more bind runes while I'm gone. Torin, you're coming with me." She turned and touched Andris' arm. "Tell the coach Torin will not be around for the game on Friday."

Andris nodded. Torin's only response was the tightening of his lips. Weren't they going to protest? Say anything? He couldn't leave. I needed him.

Lavania started for the stairs. "We leave in five minutes, Torin."

"He can't. We need him. He's the quarterback," I protested, shamelessly using football as an excuse. I didn't want him to go.

Lavania, who'd reached the base of the stairs, gripped the handrail and turned. "Excuse me?"

"Torin can't miss the game. The team is depending on him." I glanced behind me and caught Andris' eye roll. Torin shook his head in warning while Ingrid scowled harder. "We can't win without him."

Lavania stepped away from the stairs and walked to me. "My dear, naïve protégé. We are here... They," she nodded at Torin, Andris, and Ingrid, "are here on Valkyrie business. Playing football, swimming, or even cheerleading," her glance touched Ingrid, "is a means to an end. Torin knows that. They all know that. Valkyrie business comes first."

"Why does he have to go now? Did people die somewhere? Another accident?"

Lavania exhaled, and I could tell she was trying really hard to be patient. "Raine, something is wrong with Eirik. You have known for weeks and didn't say anything. We just found out. Of course we have to tell his grandparents what's happening. It is time he went home."

"What? Eirik can't leave." I looked at Torin, but he didn't say anything. Was this the secret he'd been keeping? I whipped around to face Lavania. "Why are you doing this?"

"Doing what?"

"Taking Torin and refusing to let him play on Friday, threatening to take Eirik from me."

"Sweetie." Lavania shook her head, her eyes filled with pity. "This is not about you. The game means nothing to us, unless the Norns told you something about it that we don't know about. Did they?" She searched my face.

I shook my head. "No."

"Then it is inconsequential. As for Eirik, he's not yours to keep. He never was, despite what the Norns told you. Living here was for his safety, but the darkness we all feared still found him. No one knew he had it inside him." Lavania reached out and rubbed my upper arms then gripped them and peered at me. "Eirik needs to be with his own kind. He needs to be surrounded by his family."

My throat closed. "He has a family here. We..." Tear sprung to my eyes. I blinked hard and lifted my chin to stop them from falling. "We are his family. We've always been there for him, while they haven't. His guardians can go back if they like, and Eirik can stay with us. My parents won't mind. Mom loves him, and Dad treats him like a son."

"Your dad..." She sighed, patted my arms, and stepped back. "Eirik *will* be going home soon, Raine. He doesn't belong here."

No. I shook my head, my throat tight.

Lavania started upstairs, paused, and turned. "Oh, I almost forgot. I know that there's something you're not telling us. I hope it has nothing to do with him."

I blinked.

She sighed. "Why do you kids think you can hide things from me? I'm old enough to know when someone lies or keeps secrets from me." Her gaze shifted, and I followed it to Torin. She knew his secret? "If anything happens to Eirik because you're keeping something from me, you will feel the wrath of the gods."

I swallowed, panic slamming through me.

"Don't talk to her like that," Torin said, coming to stand beside me, one hand resting on my waist and the other on my arm. I sunk against him, seeking his support. "You're scaring her."

"Good." Lavania's eyes flashed. "She keeps forgetting Eirik is a deity, someone that must be protected at all costs." Her eyes narrowed on me. "What are you not telling us?"

I wanted to tell her the truth, but something held me back. What if she was the one hurting Eirik and this was a ploy to make me confess? Indecision ate at me. My stomach churned, and the feeling of impending doom coursed through me. Torin's arms tightened.

"Eirik and I told you everything."

She shook her head. "Fine. Keep your secret. Come along, Torin." She continued upstairs.

I could only stare at her. Torin turned me around to face him. I studied his face, memorizing his beautiful features—the sculptured cheekbones, the beautiful lips, the sapphire eyes burning with love even though he'd never said he loved me. I swallowed, but my mouth tasted like sandpaper. My heart pounded, threatening to burst. "Will you come back?"

"Yes."

"When?"

"I don't know. Getting an audience with the gods takes time." He cupped my face. "But I will come back, Freckles."

He wouldn't lie to me. Still… "What do I tell Drew and Keith if they ask me where you are?"

He made a face. "Don't worry about them or the game. Like Lavania said, they are not really important. Take care of Eirik." He glanced to his right, where Andris and Ingrid were talking in low voices. "Andris! Once again, I am entrusting you with the most precious person in my life. Do not let anything happen to her again."

Andris smirked and bowed, but his eyes said he took his orders seriously. "I'll guard her with my life, sleep in her room if—"

"No," Torin and I said at the same time.

Andris chuckled. Then he took Ingrid's arm, and the two disappeared somewhere in the living room. Then what Torin had said registered. "Again?"

"My memories are coming back." He grinned. "They started when you yelled my name earlier in Eirik's bedroom. I felt your fear. I remember the night you landed in the hospital, Freckles. I felt your fear that night, too."

That was the night we kissed for the first time and he told me how he felt about me. "Everything?"

"Not yet, but the memories are coming back fast." He ran his knuckles along my jaw and touched my lips, eyes smoldering. "I remember our first kiss, the way you felt in my arms, the fear of almost losing you. I never want to feel like that again."

"Me either." Yet I was feeling it now, and I couldn't explain why.

"I remember the first time I saw you. You opened your door and looked at me with—"

"Awe," I said, laughing, surprised I could with everything that was going on.

Torin chuckled and touched my nose. "Disappointment. You took my breath even as you called me rude and condescending. Minutes later, you looked at me like you couldn't wait to rip my—"

I blocked his mouth, fighting a blush.

"Torin!" Lavania called from upstairs.

He removed my hand, cupped my face, and looked into my eyes, the smile leaving his face. "You mean everything to me, Freckles. Nothing matters without you in my life." His eyes darkened, his gaze darting across my face as though memorizing my features. "I'll be back. Not for the game. Not for the souls. For you. I'm coming back to claim you as mine, Raine Cooper."

He lowered his head. I met him halfway, threw my arms around his neck, and hung on tight as we kissed. There was something different about his kiss. It was as though he'd been holding back before. The dam broke this time. With his lips, he gave me a glimpse of the world he planned to give me. The barriers between our souls disappeared as mine melded with his. Two halves of a whole coming together and completing each other. I thought I heard Lavania call, but nothing could penetrate the sensual haze we'd created.

"Now, Torin." Lavania sounded closer.

We moved apart, both of us breathing hard. "I love you," I whispered.

"With all my heart," he finished.

"Oh, for goddess's sakes," Lavania snapped. "Catch up when you two are done."

We both looked up as she floated away. She'd changed into one of her floor-sweeping gowns. "She's angry with me."

"No, she's worried about Eirik and maybe a little jealous that he trusts you and not her." He brushed his lips against mine. "I don't want to leave you, Freckles." We kissed again, deeper, longer. I didn't want him to go either, but I knew he had to.

Before he could lift his head, I whispered, "The Norns said someone is sketching the runes on Eirik and forcing him to turn evil. That's what I left out." I leaned back and checked his reaction.

Panic flashed in his eyes. He glanced upstairs where Lavania had disappeared behind me as though searching for Andris. He cursed softly under his breath. "This is bad. Trust Andris. Talk to him. And please, don't try anything until I come back."

I nodded. Another lingering kiss and he was gone, moving fast, glowing runes on his body. My eyes followed him up the stairs, my heart already missing him. I blew out a breath and nipped my lower lip to stop it from trembling. The foreboding feeling intensified. He was coming back. Why then did I feel like I'd never see him again?

"He'll be back," Andris said, looping an arm around my shoulder. "Torin is one of the few Valkyries I know who keeps his word. Sanctimonious-arrogant-and-a-general-pain-in-my-ass-but-very-dependable is his middle name."

He'd better come back. I couldn't imagine life without him. "That's a bit mouthy for a name."

"It suits him though. So, what do you want to do? Hang out, order dinner, and—"

"I'm going home."

"Oh, come on." He gripped my shoulders and peered at me. "I understand about wanting to cry alone and hug the pillow with his scent, but that will only make you more miserable. You need to stay busy."

"Hug the pillow with his scent?" I asked, trying hard not to laugh, tears still threatening to flow. "You're so romantic for such a cynic."

He smirked. "I know. My level of complexities impresses even me. But seriously, are you going to give me a hard time about watching over you?"

"No, Andris. You're in charge, and I'll respect that. I'm going home to study bind runes, and Cora is coming to visit me at seven. Please, no snarky comments about her," I added when he made a face. "She's my friend, and you guys must accept it. She will also keep me busy, so I won't worry about things." Or miss Torin. I removed Andris' hands from my shoulders. "I promise to tell you if I'm going anywhere."

His eyes narrowed. "Really? Why are you being so nice and agreeable?"

"Because Torin said to trust you." I started for the door, but Andris pointed at the portal.

"House rule number one: you come through a portal, you leave through a portal."

***

Darkness crept in while I worked on bind runes. Tried to and failed was more like it. Wind whistled and rattled the glass windows. A storm was coming, and it suited my mood. I couldn't concentrate and kept checking Torin's window even though I knew he wasn't back. Eirik also hadn't returned my call. I still wanted him to sleep at my place. Having him with me would ease my worries. Focusing on him would keep me from thinking about Torin.

I removed the dagger the Norns had given me, pulled it from its sheath, and studied it. It was all black and had runic markings on it. The handle had four ridges that made it easy to grip. I ran a finger along the blade, touched the tip, and winced. Blood pooled on the pad of my finger where I'd nipped it. The blob slowly grew smaller as my body took it back. The cut sealed, leaving behind no trace that I had cut myself.

I was an Immortal, yet I'd never been so unhappy and alone.

Putting the dagger away, I grabbed my cell phone and checked for messages. No response from Eirik. I sat on my window seat and texted him again. I was contemplating my next move when Cora pulled up. She saw me and waved. Hopefully, her incessant chatter would to take my mind off things.

I raced downstairs.

"Brrr, it's freaking cold tonight," Cora said, entering the house, her laptop clutched on her chest, backpack on her shoulder. She pushed the door with her foot, dropped her backpack, and hugged me. "Ooh, you're so warm and toasty. "

Her hands and the laptop were freezing cold against my skin. "And you are a human icicle." I tried to push her hand away when she tried to slip it under my shirt. She always did that. "Eek! Cut that out!" I ran toward the kitchen to get away from her.

"I need a hot drink before I can function," she said, following me.

"What do you want? Coffee, hot chocolate, or apple cider?"

"Yuck. You know I can't stand apple cider." She put her laptop on the counter and blew on her hands. "Or apple pie, apple dumplings, apple cheesecake, apple cream meringue, apple cake, apple Bavarian tort, apple cobbler…"

I tried not to laugh. I tended to forget her family grew organic apples, and her mother baked and sold her apple desserts to the local stores. They had so many varieties of apples I always looked forward to picking some when I visited.

"Coffee is fine," Cora added when she finished her tirade against everything apple. "Do you have time to help me with a math problem?"

I laughed. Her math problem usually meant more than one. "Sure. I have homework too, and I already ordered pizza."

"Toppings?"

"Bacon and pineapple."

"Side?"

"Cinnamon sticks."

"Yummy. This is like old times. Gah, I wish I'd worn gloves." She sat on her hands, and I laughed. She did that whenever she was cold, but I doubted it worked. It probably cut blood to her hands.

"What happened to your car?" she asked.

I stared at her blankly then remembered I had driven to Eirik's house, but came back through a portal. "It broke down outside Eirik's, but I was hoping he'd fix it," I fibbed and turned to get a can of coffee and two mugs from the cupboards before she could notice my red face. "Instant coffee okay?"

"Anything but the cider. So you and Eirik are back to being friends again?" she asked.

There was a trace of jealousy in her voice. "Nah," I fibbed again. "Mom asked me to drop off something at their house. I tried texting him, but he's not returning my messages." While I heated the water in the microwave, I removed vanilla creamer from the fridge. "So what have you been up to?"

She shrugged and opened her laptop. "The usual. School, swimming, vlogging. So Eirik will drop off your car?"

"I hope so." I glanced at her and caught her frown. "Is that going to be a problem?"

"Nope." She typed something on her laptop. "I just want to, you know, mentally prepare myself, seeing how I ceased to exist in his world."

"That's not true."

She shrugged. "It's okay. He doesn't matter either."

Liar, I wanted to say. We took our drinks upstairs, and Cora noticed the blown-glass ornaments right away. "Gorgeous. Where did you find them?"

"Multnomah Falls. Torin bought them."

She studied one ornament after another, then lifted one of the paperweight ones. Inside it was the waterfalls captured in its fall splendor. It would always remind me of our first time there. But my favorite was the Bifrost Bridge. Cora found it and studied it curiously. She put it down without commenting. She probably didn't know what it was.

I managed to steer Cora's attention to homework. Seated at the window, she kept staring outside, probably anticipating Eirik's arrival. No matter what she'd said, she was still into him. I pretended not to notice even though my eyes strayed to Torin's window, too. We were two peas in a pod, both of us waiting for the men we loved, yet we couldn't admit it to each other. How pathetic was that?

"Pizza is here," she said before the doorbell rang. "My treat."

"No, it's okay."

"I've been a sucky friend, so let me do this." She pushed a twenty-dollar bill into my hand.

I gave the delivery guy an extra large tip because it was raining hard and the poor guy was drenched. Back upstairs, I found Cora studying my cell phone. Maybe I shouldn't have mentioned Eirik.

"Did Eirik text?" I asked.

"No, just admiring this." She turned the phone and showed me a picture of Torin. I'd taken it at the waterfalls. "He really is beautiful."

He was, and he was mine. "I know."

She threw my phone on my bed, walked to the table, and selected two slices of pizza before returning to the window seat. "Is he going to join us?"

"No." I put my homework away and rescued hers. "He thought we should have a girls-only night."

"Oh, how sweet. But he'll be here later, right?" She wiggled her brows.

The urge to cry rolled through me. He'd barely left, and I already missed him. Missed making out with him. Laughing. Fighting. Later tonight, I'd miss listening to his heartbeat as I fell asleep.

"Raine?"

"Yes. I'll see him tonight." In my dreams.

"He's, like, the best boyfriend ever." Cora sighed melodramatically and took a bite of her pizza. Swallowing, she added, "After the Portland game, I did a piece on him on my vlog, and the responses... phew. The comments were X-rated. Better chain him to your side, girl. There're girls out there who can't wait for you to slip up."

I laughed. "They wouldn't stand a chance."

"So confident, aren't you?"

"I know how he feels about me." He hadn't said he loved me, but he'd finished my sentence. At least it had sounded that way. I got two slices of pizza and sat on the bed. We ate and conversed, but Cora always brought the conversation back to Torin.

"Is he excited about the game?"

I didn't care about the game. I just wanted him back.

"Yeah, he is," I fibbed.

"Have you seen what they've planned for the pep rally on Friday? It's huge."

I was busy chewing, so I shook my head.

She rolled her eyes. "You've been wrapped up in your little world. It's on the website. I'll show you." She opened her laptop and typed with one hand. "Drew said some of the players, the cheerleaders, and the Kayvees will do a mob flash dance. They even asked other students to join them."

I glared. "Thanks for spoiling the surprise."

She wrinkled her nose. "You're welcome. It's not like you'd be paying attention anyway. I know for sure Torin is not doing it, but we're hoping he'll volunteer for the kissing booths."

My drink went down the wrong way, and I coughed. "What?"

"Hey, don't give me that look. When I said 'we' I meant my vlog followers. See?" She turned her laptop and showed me another entry.

The title of her entry was Kissing Booths and Hot Guys. I read the first page of comments and rolled my eyes. Even guys wanted to know which jocks would be at the booths. Now I was happy Torin wouldn't be around.

My cell phone dinged. I read the text and sighed with relief. "Eirik's on his way. He can finish the pizza."

Cora jumped up and disappeared into the bathroom. The doorbell rang, and I headed downstairs. It was almost eight, but my parents were still not back. I didn't know whether to start worrying. I opened the door and blinked. Andris, Ingrid, and Roger stood on my porch, not Eirik.

"Hey. What's, uh, going on?" I asked.

"Just checking on you guys," Andris said. "Can we come in?"

"Sure." I stepped back. Cora came downstairs, hair fluffed, lip-gloss applied. Andris saw her and groaned. "Behave," I warned him from the corner of my mouth then added louder, "Cora, you know Andris and Ingrid, and this is Roger, Andris' friend."

The way Cora eased into conversation with the Valkyries you'd never guess she didn't like them. We were crowded around the wet bar, talking and laughing, when Eirik arrived. He heard the voices coming from my living room and frowned.

He dropped my car key in my hand. "I was planning on using your mirror to get home."

"You still can. Come inside." I grabbed his arm and tugged, but he didn't budge.

He shook his head. "I'll head to Torin's."

"No one is there. Torin and Lavania are gone, and the others are here. Come and hang out with us for just a few minutes. Please."

"Hey, what's keeping you guys?" Cora called out, and the effect on Eirik was instant.

He grinned. "You didn't say she was here. Let's go."

"Whipped," I whispered as he followed me.

"Shut up!"

For an hour, we just hung out like normal teenagers. Eirik and Cora even went back to their playful teasing and flirting. When she left at nine, she was smiling.

"Where are your parents?" Andris asked before they left.

"Out, but they should be back any minute now."

"I don't like leaving you alone," Andris said.

I made a face. "I'm seventeen, Andris, not five. Besides, he's going to hang around until they return." I indicated Eirik with a nod. He was in the kitchen wolfing down the rest of the pizza.

Andris hesitated, but he gave me another lecture on not going anywhere without telling him. I closed the door and marched to the kitchen to call my parents. They weren't picking up. Now I was really worried. I texted them, and we went upstairs.

***

It was another hour before sounds came from downstairs.

"They're back." I ran downstairs. "Where have you been? I called and texted you guys for like…" Dad looked dead tired, and Mom's eyes were red as though she'd been crying. "Mom? What's wrong?"

She smiled, but her lips trembled. "Come here."

We hugged. But when Dad joined us, I knew something was wrong. "You guys are scaring me. What's going on?"

"Sit down, pumpkin," Dad said, his arm going around my shoulder. Mom took my hand. Together, they led me to the couch.

Turning my head left and right, I studied their faces. The foreboding feeling I'd had earlier returned. "What's going on? Is it about Torin? Did something happen to him?"

"No, honey," Mom said. "This is not about Torin. It's, uh, about your father." Her voice shook.

"What about Dad?" I studied his face, his pallor, which seemed to have gotten worse. "You're ill, aren't you?"

He nodded. "At the beginning of last summer, my doctors diagnosed me with stage IV tumors in my brain."

No. My mind screamed what I couldn't articulate. My eyes clung to him, my chest squeezing.

"They ran tests and confirmed that the tumors are too deep and too advanced," Dad continued. "They couldn't operate, and chemotherapy would have been useless."

"Why didn't you tell me?" I cried.

"Your mother and I decided to wait until we exhausted our options before talking to you. After my diagnosis, I received a call from a specialist in Hawaii, an oncologist who'd developed a radical treatment using a virus. The virus could kill brain cancer cells and not healthy ones. That's why I went to Hawaii last summer. We usually use portals to deliver mirrors, but this time I flew because his people were waiting for me at the airport."

It explained the flight to and from Hawaii. "What did the specialist say?"

"She started me on the treatment. They were supposed to continue every month, but my plane went down. The tumors grew."

I shook my head, tears racing down my face. "No. No, I refused to accept this."

"You must." Dad wiped my cheeks. "During the cruise, I stopped by to see her when we disembarked in Honolulu. Today we confirmed it. The tumor has metastasized, and I am no longer qualified for the treatment."

I shook my head. "No, it can't be true. There must be something we can do." I looked at Mom. She was weeping silently. "We can use runes, can't we, Mom? We'll heal him. Make him Immortal."

Mom shook her head. "Runes heal wounds, not mutated cells. He can't be turned, sweetheart."

"Then we'll use them to keep him alive." I turned to face Dad. "I'm not giving up, Daddy. I'm not losing you again."

He sighed and pulled me into his arms. I didn't know how long I cried before his words penetrated. "You have to let me go, sweetheart. You have to. We've had seventeen years, and we will have a few more weeks... months..."

"No." I pushed his arms. He tried to tighten his grip, but I wouldn't let him. I wiggled out of his arms until he let me go. I jumped up, knocking my knee against the coffee table without feeling the pain. "I won't give up. I won't. I'll find the right runes, the right doctors."

"If I depended on doctors, I'd be pumped full of pain meds and bed-ridden. Runes have eased my pain these past weeks," Dad said.

"I'll create new ones. Torin will help me."

Mom shook her head. "He can't."

"He will!"

She sighed. "Sweetheart, I didn't manage your dad's pain. Torin did, and he knows a lot more about runes than any Valkyrie I know."

Was this the secret he'd been keeping from me? Dad's illness? Was he here to reap his soul, too?

"He brought me back from the brink of death when he found me after the plane crash," Dad said. "He has done enough."

"Then it's my turn." I looked down at my father, his face gaunt, his eyes shimmering with unshed tears. I'd known he was ill. I just hadn't wanted to accept it. "I love you, Daddy. Don't ask me to give up and accept things the way they are because you didn't raise a quitter. I will find a way to make you better."

24. GRIMNIR

Tears racing down my face, I entered my bedroom. Eirik stopped pacing, his eyes red as though he'd been crying. "You heard?"

He nodded. "Yes."

We met in the middle of the room, finding comfort and solace in each other's arms.

"He can't die, Eirik. I won't let him."

"I know." He lifted me up the same way Torin had yesterday and carried me to bed. Part of me wished he were Torin; the other knew he understood what I was going through better. He loved my father, too. He didn't speak again, just held me until I fell asleep. He was still there the next morning and woke me up.

"I don't want to go to school," I mumbled and burrowed deeper under the covers.

"You have to. Staying in bed won't make your dad better. In fact, it will only make him feel guilty for telling you. I think this is why they didn't tell you in the first place. They knew you'd indulge in self-pity and—" He jumped out of the way of my kick.

"I'm not indulging in self-pity. I'm thinking." I *was* feeling sorry for myself. I couldn't lose my father.

"Well, think your way into the shower. You smell, and your hair looks like you haven't washed it in—" He dodged the pillow I'd thrown and disappeared through the portal.

"I hate you, and I don't smell." I forced myself to shower and change. A few minutes later, I left my room. I was about to knock on my parents' door when I heard their voices coming from downstairs.

Dad was cooking breakfast while Mom read the newspaper out loud. The scene was so familiar tears rushed to my eyes. I wanted to be angry with them for keeping this from me, but as long as there was a chance that I could help, I had to focus on that. I had a plan. Well, sort of. I just needed to get out of the house first.

I cleared my throat, and my parents both looked at me. "I'll help with the breakfast."

"No, you will not," Dad retorted. "Cooking, running, and biking are a few things I plan to savor for as long as I possibly can, so sit down."

I opened my mouth to argue, but Mom caught my eye and shook her head. I sat and watched him for any signs of, I don't know, fatigue, eyes-rolling in the back of his head. His fall last weekend made sense now. The cancer probably messed with his balance or something. Why did he run and bike when he could keel over any second and die? It didn't make sense.

If I didn't know the truth, watching my parents discuss and laugh over newspaper articles would have been normal. I couldn't relax, let alone laugh at Dad's teasing. In fact I found their nonchalant attitude irritating. I wasn't sure what I wanted them to do. Walk around with long faces? Fight back?

"You should have told me," I said when there was silence.

"Sweetheart—"

"No, Mom. You've known for months, and it's been weeks since Torin found Dad." The late lunches and dinners made sense. I got angrier. "You've been spending more time together knowing he could be gone any minute, while I…" my voice trembled to a stop. "And last week he wanted to tell me and you asked for one more week. You should have told me!"

"Raine," Mom took my hand, "I wanted you to have time with him without his illness coming between you. Think about all the things you've done. The fun things you did on the cruise, running and biking on Saturdays, your discussions—"

"I don't care," I snapped, tears threatening to fall again. "You should have told me." I jumped from the table and stomped away. I could feel their eyes following me until I left the house. Andris tried to get my attention, but I pretended not to see him. I was in no mood to talk to anyone.

At the parking lot across from school, I sat and stared at the students walking past, dreading getting out of the car. Three weeks ago I'd dreaded leaving my car because of what had happened at the meet. Today I wished I had the power of premonition, so I could know how long Dad was going to live. My eyes welled up with tears.

Torin. How I wished he were here. I texted Eirik then went back to staring at students.

I jumped when my front passenger door opened and Andris slipped into the seat. "Hey, you okay?"

"Yeah." I wiped at my cheeks.

"You're crying."

"So?"

"So you're better than this. I know you miss Torin, but this…" he indicated me with a brief wave of his hand, "weepy, pathetic excuse of an Immortal is not—"

"Andris." I cut him an exasperated look. "Leave. Now. I want to be alone."

"Okay. You don't have to tell me twice. I'll shut up. In fact, pretend I'm not here." He got comfortable in his seat. I wanted to curse him out, scream at him, but then I remembered what Torin had told me. I could trust Andris.

Staring straight ahead, I tried to keep my voice calm as I spoke. "Last night, I found out that my father is dying of brain cancer and no one told me. I'm pissed. And if you ever call me pathetic again, I will slug you."

"I'm sorry."

I turned and studied him. He seemed contrite. "Sorry for what?"

"For your father's illness. For calling you pathetic and clingy. You have to admit you're weepy though."

For once, I didn't find his warped sense of humor funny. I got out of the car and grabbed my backpack. We walked into the building without speaking. I groaned when I saw Drew and a bunch of jocks in the foyer. I didn't want to deal with them or see the excited faces of students. The stupid game wasn't even today, yet everywhere I looked were flags and crimson, black, and gold decorations.

"Where's St. James, Raine?" Drew asked, his gaze bouncing between me and Andris.

"Do we look like his keeper?" Andris asked rudely and steered me past them. For once I appreciated his rudeness. No one bothered us again.

I waited until they couldn't hear me before I turned and smiled at Andris. "Thanks. I couldn't deal with them. Not today. Are you going to give the coach Lavania's message?"

"Yeah. You want to come?"

"No, thanks." He walked me to my locker then disappeared. Cora was talking about tomorrow's game with some girls near the lockers. They were already pumped even though the game was tomorrow. I couldn't care less. Drowning in my own misery, I hardly paid attention to her as she prattled on. She didn't even notice when I slipped away and headed upstairs.

Instead of entering my math classroom, I opened the make-out closet and turned on the lights. It was empty and big enough for four people. I wasn't sure it would work, but I had to try.

"Catie! Marj! Jeannette!"

I waited. No one appeared. I closed my eyes and tried again. *CATIE. MARJ. JEANETTE. GET DOWN HERE NOW.*

I opened my eyes and waited. Nothing happened. Torin had gotten it wrong. I couldn't summon the Norns. The first bell rang as I left the closet. People gave me weird looks as they hurried past. Let them speculate why I'd used the closet. I didn't care.

Math and history classes felt empty without Torin's presence. My father's situation made his absence even more painful, or maybe it was the other way around. I couldn't tell. I was miserable and angry. Third period was over when I saw Eirik waiting for me by the door.

"Where have you been?" I asked.

"I couldn't sleep last night, so I went home and crashed. How are you holding up?"

I shrugged. "I tried to contact the Norns, but they didn't appear."

"What? Why?"

"I want to make a deal with them. I will willingly join them in exchange for my father's life."

He stopped in the middle of the hallway. "No, you can't. What will Torin say?"

My throat thickened. "This is my decision. He'll understand."

"No, he won't. That's equivalent to being a nun, Raine. I'm not letting you do it."

"I wasn't asking for your permission. I wish I hadn't told you." I brushed past him.

"Raine!"

"I expected your support, Eirik. I thought you of all people would understand just how important family is. I guess I was wrong." Students walking past turned to stare. Then I saw the Norns standing at the end of the hallway. I hurried after them.

"Cafeteria is that way," Eirik said.

"I'm not hungry." They were walking away. I ran to catch up.

"RAINE!" Eirik yelled.

I ignored him, turned the corner, and saw the Norns disappear into the band room. Last time, I'd made a deal with them in that same room. I burst through the doors, my breathing harsh. I closed it softly behind me, my eyes swinging from face to face, my heart pounding. The temperature in the room was cooler, but that didn't bother me anymore.

"How dare you summon us?" Marj demanded.

"Easy, Marj." Catie moved closer. "Why did you call us, Lorraine?"

"Did you catch the person poisoning Eirik?" Jeannette asked.

I shook my head. "No, but I will. I want to make a deal. If I'm one of you—"

"A deal?" Marj asked, and I could almost taste her anticipation.

"Haven't you learned something from our past interaction, young Mortal?" Jeannette asked. "We don't make deals. We are Norns. We shape destinies."

"Yet, I keep changing mine," I snapped. "That either means I'm one of you, like you keep claiming, or I'm something else." Uneasiness entered their eyes.

Silence followed, the shock in their eyes telling me I was on to something.

"What am I? What makes me so different? Why do you desperately want me to join you?"

"We saved you and because of that you are now one of us," Marj said, but I knew she was lying. Then something Lavania had said weeks ago flashed through my head.

"I can see you in whatever form when others can't, feel your presence, summon you, but the best part, I can stop you, at least your evil faction, from taking lives."

"You got lucky," Jeannette said in a sneer.

"Then I'll get lucky again. If I'm just one of you, like you claim, I want to be in charge of two destinies. Eirik's and my father's."

"Your father?" Catie asked. "Your father is already dead, Lorraine. We don't deal with the dead."

"He is not dead," I snapped.

"According to the records, your father's soul was reaped months ago and sent to Hel's Hall," Jeannette added.

"Your father is still alive?" Marj's eyes narrowed.

I swallowed, uneasiness creeping through me. Had I made a mistake coming to negotiate with them? "Yes. So what?"

"So someone let him live." Marj moved closer and slowly walked around me. "Someone who was supposed to reap his soul gave him a pass. Now who would do that for you, Lorraine?"

Torin. Oh no. Cold fingers crawled up my spine.

"Who would alter someone's destiny without our say so?"

Dizziness washed over me. Behind me, the door flew opened and Eirik, Andris, and Ingrid walked in. They looked around.

"Are you alone?" Eirik asked.

They couldn't see the Norns. Good. "Yes."

"Phew," Andris said. "We thought you were in here with the Norns making another deal."

Marj and Jeannette wore tiny smiles that screamed they'd won. Catie looked pissed. I wasn't sure whether she was angry with me, her sister crones, or Torin. What had he risked to bring my father back to me? And now, in my grief, I had clearly condemned him. Worse, my father was headed to Hel's Hall for eternity.

"No, I just came for my oboe." I hurried forward and grabbed my oboe case from the shelf.

"I didn't know you were playing in the pep band tomorrow," Andris added as we left the room.

"I'm not. I'm going home early, and I need to practice a piece."

***

I wanted to curl up in bed and cry myself into oblivion, but I couldn't afford it. I didn't have the luxury. I had screwed up, and now Torin was in trouble. There must be a law against not reaping a soul. I spent the afternoon pouring over runes, combining single runes to create new ones. I had to find a rune that could cure my father.

As soon as Andris drove up, I raced downstairs and reached their garage before he closed the door. He was with Roger. Ingrid was missing. "Hi, Roger. Andris, we need to talk."

"Really? Now? I have plans."

"This won't take long." I waited while he opened the door for Roger. Then we went to my house. He made a beeline for the wet bar and poured a drink. "Did you know that Torin was supposed to reap my father's soul?"

His eyes narrowed. "Who told you that?"

"It doesn't matter how I know. My father is dying, and Torin's been helping him manage the pain. The Norns told me he's supposed to have died months ago."

His eyes narrowed. "When did you talk to the Norns?"

"This afternoon in the band room."

His eyes narrowed. "They were—"

"There when you guys arrived, yes. I offered them a deal. Put my father's destiny in my hands and I'd willingly become a Norn."

"Hel's Mist, Raine!"

"I'm not going to let my father die if I can stop it, Andris. What's the point of learning about runes and having abilities when I can't help the people I love?"

Andris sighed. "We are in the business of the dead, sweetheart, while you want to keep your father alive. The two don't mix. As for the deal, it won't work. You can't become a Norn. Torin won't let you."

I knew that. "The Norns mentioned sending my father to Hel's Hall. Dad is an athlete. He runs and bikes. He belongs in Valhalla, not some cold hall in the middle of a mist."

Andris drained his drink. "I think that's Torin's plan."

I cocked my brow. "Plan? What plan?"

"Torin wasn't supposed to reap your father, Raine. When he arrived at the hospital in Costa Rica, your father was dying and a Grimnir was waiting to take his soul. A very ornery and pain-in-the-ass Grimnir named Echo. Torin made a deal with him. I don't know the details, and when we spoke he didn't know either because of his scrambled memories."

"Then how did you find out about it?"

"Echo bragged about it to me, the ass-hat." He grimaced. "You have to meet him to understand why I can't stand him. I told Torin about it when we spoke about you and your lovey-dovey past. According to Echo, Torin brought your father home to give him more time with you and your mother, and more time to prepare. If he'd died at that hospital, he would have gone straight to Hel's Hall. Now..." He grinned.

Everything fell into place. If Dad died running or biking, Torin could take his soul to Valhalla. That had been his plan. That wasn't the case anymore. The Norns knew Dad was alive. Nausea churned my insides.

"They know," I whispered.

"Who?"

"The Norns know my father is alive and that Torin helped him. What's the punishment for a Valkyrie changing a destiny?"

Andris shook his head. "I don't know, but we must tell Torin what's going on as soon as he gets back. Hey," he gripped my shoulders, "it's not bad. You could always say *you* spared your father."

"What are you talking about?"

"You saved the lives of seven swimmers and changed their destiny. The Norns didn't put you on Hel duty. Instead they only want you more."

"They erased Torin's memories."

He scoffed. "Big deal. He got them back. Something about you scares them, Raine. Use that to your advantage. Do what you do best. Stick it to them."

Maybe Andris was onto something. I jumped up and hugged him. "Thank you."

"I could get used to this," he mumbled, squeezing me.

Laughing, I wiggled out of his arms and stepped back. I also reached a decision. As we walked to his house, I told him about the origins of Eirik's runes. "Torin said to trust you. So if I need you, will you be there?"

Andris made a face. "What do you think? You want my cell phone number?"

"You have a cell phone?"

"Of course. I'm not barbaric like some people we know." He recited his phone number and made me repeat it.

Back at home, I texted him and got a snarky response. I texted Eirik next then got busy cooking. Nothing complicated, just chicken stir-fry and rice. The look on Dad's face when they came home was worth it. Dinner that night was a sober affair. Despite everything, I was still angry with Mom for keeping Dad's condition a secret. She'd made him keep the secret from me.

"Do you want to bike on Saturday, Dad?" I asked before heading upstairs.

He and Mom exchanged a glance, and then he nodded. "Sure, pumpkin."

Once again, I felt their stares as I left the kitchen. Upstairs, I got ready for bed, occasionally glancing at Torin's window. I wish he could come back already. I hated going to bed not sure of what was going to happen tomorrow. Would the Norns come looking for me? Would Torin come back before they got to him? I missed him so much.

I was almost asleep when the portal opened and a warm breeze drifted into the room. Torin. I sat up and turned on the bedside lamp. Eirik. Disappointment washed over me.

"Don't mind me," he said.

Good Eirik—warm air. Evil Eirik—cold air. I'd have to remember that. "Where were you? I texted you about dinner."

"I thought you might want to be alone with your parents. You know, to talk."

I snorted. "What's there to talk about? He's dying, and she didn't bother to tell me."

"You're angry with your mother?"

"What do you think?"

"That's not fair."

I pulled the covers over my head instead of answering him.

He yanked the covers down. "Who are you really angry with, Raine? Your father for becoming sick? Your mother for keeping his illness a secret? Torin for leaving when you need him the most? Or you for not noticing that your dad is sick?"

By the time he finished, I was crying again. I couldn't come up with a snarky response or throw a pillow at him. He slid in beside me and, once again, held me while I cried. When I calmed down, I whispered, "All of the above."

"I'm sorry for being brutally honest."

"It's okay." I missed Torin's arms. Eirik's weren't bad. They just weren't Torin's.

I fell into a fitful sleep. Hours later I shivered. Eirik. Had he turned evil again? I moved my arm to find him, but I was alone in bed. I lifted my head to check if he was in the pullout bed and then saw a movement from the corner of my eye. Eirik walked to the pullout bed and bent over. I smiled. He must have decided to move to his bed.

I opened my mouth to tell him goodnight, but the words froze in my throat. When had he changed into a hoodie? No, not a hoodie. A hooded robe, like a grim reaper's. My stomach hollowed out as realization hit me, my heart pounding. This wasn't a grim reaper. It was a Grimnir. And the only reason for a Grimnir to be in my house was to get my father's soul. What was he doing in my room?

Anger slammed through me. Watching the Grimnir bend over Eirik, I carefully reached the bottom drawer where I'd hidden the dagger the Norns had given me. I opened it slowly and reached inside. My hand touched the bottom of the drawer.

The dagger was gone.

Starting to panic, I moved my fingers around, desperately searching for it. The Grimnir must have heard me because he froze. I froze too, heart pounding. Then a glow came from the bed. A familiar glow. The glow of fresh runes. I tried to use the glow to see his face, but because of the hood, I couldn't. I saw the artavus in his hand. Why would a Grimnir etch runes on Eirik?

Instead of continuing to search for the dagger, I reached up and turned on the lights. Light flooded my room. I caught a glimpse of a face and blonde hair under the hood before the Grimnir leaped across the room at a super speed and disappeared through the mirror portal.

No, it couldn't be.

I scrambled from my bed and knelt by Eirik's side. The runes were gone, but his skin was still pink, showing the outline of the runes. As I watched, the pinkness disappeared, too. I stared at the mirror where the Grimnir had disappeared. Grief must be messing with my head because... I covered my mouth with trembling hands, reaction setting in.

There was no way the person poisoning Eirik and impersonating a Grimnir was Cora.

25. WHY CORA?

"I got your texts," Andris said walking toward me. "Ten of them. Where are we going at this ungodly hour?"

It was six thirty. First period didn't start until seven forty. "To Cora's. We'll take my car."

He didn't move. "May I ask why we're going to the home of the girl trying to turn your BFF into a monster?"

"I want to know who she's working with."

"Why? It doesn't make her any less guilty."

"I know. Let's. Just. Go."

He made a face. "Okay, but we'll take the SUV." He grabbed my backpack from the back of my car. I locked my car and followed him across the lawn. My parents were still asleep. Eirik had left early, but I hadn't told him what I'd seen last night. He wouldn't believe me. Cora could do no wrong in his eyes. If, and that was a big if, she was guilty, he'd need proof. I needed proof. I still couldn't believe she was an Immortal. Was she always one or had Maliina done something to her and started the process? Were her parents Immortals, too?

I got in the front passenger seat and realized Ingrid was in the back.

"She knows everything," Andris explained. "You can trust her."

Looking into her eyes, a memory flitted through my head, but it disappeared before I could grasp it. I shook my head, trying to understand.

"Why are you shaking your head? You don't trust me?" Ingrid asked, sounding insulted.

"No, that's not it."

"I am not my sister, Raine," Ingrid said, her voice rising. "I'm not manipulative or mean, and I would never poison Eirik. And to clear the air, I don't blame you for what happened to her. I might have at one time, but I don't anymore. I know what she did to you and Cora, and how she manipulated Andris to turn me into an Immortal."

I sighed. I had enough crap to deal with without this. "I didn't *say* I don't trust you, Ingrid. Okay?" I took a deep breath to calm down. There was no point taking out my frustration on her. I faced forward, more confused than last night. There was something about her and last night that was bugging me. When I glanced at Andris, he just shrugged.

He started the car and left the cul-de-sac. "Okay, start talking. What do you think is going on?"

"I don't know what to think. Cora etched Eirik with new runes and moved like an Immortal, yet the Cora I know would never hurt Eirik. Not willingly anyway. Someone is making her do this."

"Did you tell Eirik what you saw?" Andris asked.

"No way. We can't tell him yet. One, he won't believe us. Two, if he thinks someone is out to hurt Cora, he'll get pissed, and when he's pissed—"

"His dark side takes over," Andris finished.

"The only way to prove she's the one is catch her in the act. Can you sketch runes around my bedroom to trap her in case she comes back?"

"Sure. Although Lavania used powerful bind runes I've never seen before."

"I remember them," Ingrid said. "If you like, I can sketch them."

I turned and smiled. "Thanks, Ingrid. That would helpful."

"So why are we going to Cora's place?" she asked.

"To watch and follow her. I've dealt with Norns before, and this has their names written all over it. They are determined to make me join them. If she's working with them, we'll have the proof we need to confront them." And leverage in case they came after us.

"Would they poison Odin's grandson to get to you?" Andris asked. "That's pretty extreme."

I shook my head. "Like I said, I don't know what's going on. All I know is Cora cannot be doing this on her own. Remember the dagger I told you guys the Norns tried to force me to take?"

"The one meant to kill Eirik when he changes?" Ingrid asked.

"Yes. I took it."

"What? Why?" Andris and Ingrid asked at the same time.

"I did it to stop whoever is poisoning him, not to use it on Eirik. The Norns told me it could kill her. It's missing. My room wasn't ransacked by whoever stole it, which means the person knew exactly where to look. The Norns are the only ones who saw me put it away." Thinking about the crones only pissed me off. Cora must have taken it last night. "They probably never meant for me to use it. I bet it was all part of an elaborate scam to manipulate me into joining them. "

"How?" Ingrid asked.

"For me to help Eirik, I had to accept him as my responsibility. To do that his life had to be in danger."

"You do know this is all just an assumption," Andris said. "You still have to prove it."

"Or we could just trap Cora and force her to confess. We'll have what we need to get rid of the Norns once and for all. I'm just surprised they are willing to turn Eirik into a monster. He will live with those runes forever."

"Who told you that?" Andris asked.

"The Norns. They said Eirik will always have them in him and he must learn to suppress their effect." My gaze swung between Andris and Ingrid. "What if they lied?"

Silence followed as we digested that piece of information. If they'd lied, Eirik would be okay. Please, let Eirik be okay.

I gave Andris directions, until we entered the road leading to Cora's farm. He pulled up under a tree where we had a clear view of the farmhouse and the barn. Cora's car was missing from the front of the house. I was so hoping it would be where Ingrid could etch it with trap runes.

The more I thought about Cora, the angrier I became. The girl I'd known all these years couldn't hurt Eirik or me. Assuming she hadn't always been an Immortal. Was she a willing participant in all this or a helpless pawn? Would she be willing to help me? Surely, our friendship meant something to her.

"Change of plans, drive to the house," I instructed Andris.

"Raine—"

"I'm going to talk to her."

Andris turned and faced me. "What are you going to tell her?"

"I don't know. I'll wing it."

His brow shot up. "Wing it? How? 'Hey, Cora, I know you're an evil Immortal, but since we're BFFs help me stop three of the most powerful beings in the world from ruining my life.' FYI, the Norns want you. The rest of us are expendable as far as they're concerned. They can erase our memories and screw up our destinies without losing sleep as long as they get what they want. And that's you. Think very carefully what you plan to say to their little pawn because they'll know about it."

I swallowed, hating the thought that I might put him and Ingrid in danger. "When we get there, stay in the car, so she doesn't see you."

Andris grimaced. "What? Do I look like a coward to you? Torin left me in charge, so wherever you go, I go."

"Seriously?" I glanced at Ingrid.

"Don't look at me," she said, her lips twitching. "He's an annoying mass of contradictions."

He gunned the engine, drove down the narrow road, and parked in front of the house. The barn door opened before he switched off the engine and Cora's mother stepped outside. As usual, she wore dungarees, galoshes, and a heavy jacket. From the two baskets on her arms, she'd been collection eggs from the chicken coop. I got out of the car and waved.

"Who's that?" Ingrid asked. I hadn't realized she was out of the car until she spoke.

"Stay in the car." But I might as well have been talking to myself. She and Andris were right behind me as I went to meet Cora's mother. "You need help with those?"

"No." Her grip tightened on the baskets. "What are you doing here, Lorraine."

Her voice was cold. She was usually so nice and warm. "I came to pick up Cora. You know, save her the drive to school. We have playoffs today."

"She's not ready to come back to school yet." She eyed Andris and Ingrid coldly. "So you and your friends just get going." She brushed past us.

I exchanged a bewildered look with Andris and Ingrid. "Mrs. Jemison—"

"Lorraine," she snapped and turned. "It's going to take Cora a long time to fully recover, and when she does, she will be home-schooled. I thought I explained it in the text message I sent you on Thursday night when we got home." She shook her head, gray eyes narrowed. "I told James there was no point in telling you Cora was home, but he insisted. He sees the good in people where there is none."

I swallowed, not understanding her animosity or what she was taking about. "I didn't get a text from you, Mrs. Jemison. And Cora and I are friends."

She sighed and tilted her head to the side, her eyes narrowing. "Then where have you been since she was admitted at PMI. I know you had to deal with a lot after you lost your friends during that meet, but so did Cora. She had nightmares about seeing glowing people, you and your mother walking through walls. It's taken her weeks to accept that what she saw was induced by grief—that it was not real." She sighed. "It broke my heart that you never called to ask us how she was doing or whether she was allowed visitors when you used to be so close. In the last couple of weeks, she asked about you every time we went to visit her."

Panic slamming through me, I tried to keep up with the information she was throwing at me. Providence Mental Institute, or PMI, was a psychiatric hospital in Salem. If Cora had been committed, who was impersonating her at school?

"I swear I didn't know Cora was at PMI," I said.

"Really? I find that very hard to believe. I don't understand you kids. You live for the moment and value your social status more than being there for a friend." She sighed. "Please, go to school, Lorraine. Cora needs to be surrounded by her family and those who care about her. I will not have her recovery jeopardized by anyone." She marched past us to the house.

I stared after her, my throat tight. A feeling that we were being watched washed over me, and I glanced up at Cora's bedroom window. I thought I saw a face, but I could have been mistaken. "Let's go."

"What is PMI?" Andris asked as we pulled away.

"Providence Mental Institute. Whoever is pretending to be Cora must be a Norn."

"Norn?" Ingrid asked.

"Yes. They can impersonate people. Catie, Marj, and Jeannette do it all the time. Funny how I can sense them, yet I couldn't sense the fake Cora. Maybe I was emotionally too close to her. She acted just like Cora, her mannerism, her likes, dislikes... everything." I grinned. "But this is great. Cora didn't try to hurt Eirik. All this time it was..." I covered my mouth. "Oh God."

"I was wondering when it would hit her," Ingrid murmured.

"Me too," Andris said.

"I'm the worst friend ever. She was in a mental hospital, and I never visited her. She probably thought I'd abandoned her, that I didn't care." I stared out the window and fought tears. "No wonder her mother was so cold and mean. I let Cora down."

"You're being too hard on yourself," Andris said.

"No, I should have known she wasn't Cora. She was too happy when I came back from the cruise, and she used a curling iron on her hair. Cora would never do that to her hair. She uses rollers and a heating cap. A big fat red flag. She also hates greasy-haired Jaden Granger. Another red flag I ignored. And she would not prefer to hang out with Kicker and her group of friends instead of me. We've always been tight." She'd skipped shopping with me for Halloween when she loved nothing better than to force me to buy inappropriate, skanky costumes. Then there was trick-or-treating, a tradition she, Eirik, and I never missed. And Cora would never deliberately make Eirik jealous. No, she would, because she took no crap from anyone. "I should have known."

***

At school, Andris found a place to park, and we started for the school building.

"So, what are you going to do?" Ingrid asked.

"I'm going to stay glued to fake Cora, but we must set up a trap for her at my place. If she comes near Eirik again…" Then I remembered something. "There will be kissing booths in the gym during the pep rally. Keep an eye on Eirik, Andris. Whenever Cora flirts with guys, he goes ballistic. We don't want a repeat of what happened at Cliff House or The Hub."

"Where's Torin?" someone yelled as soon as we entered the front hall. Like yesterday Andris said something rude in return. I tried to explain.

"Is it true he won't play?" someone asked from my right.

"I got a tweet that he's gone," another one called out from behind us.

"That blows."

"We're so going to lose."

"How can he miss the game?"

The coach must have told the players Torin wouldn't be at the playoff, and bad news spread fast at my school. The worst part was everyone acted like it was my fault. When trying to explain failed to mollify them, I just shrugged. Let them blame me. I didn't care. I had more important things to worry about—a Norn masquerading as my best friend.

Fake Cora was by the lockers with Kicker and a bunch of girls and guys from the swim team. They wore their swim T-shirts and sweatshirts with the slogan 'Our Sweat, Our Blood, Your Tears'. Since I was no longer on the swim team, I'd chosen to wear my 'I See Band People' T-shirt. We also had sweatshirts with 'If Marching Band was any easier it would be called Football', but I doubted anyone was dumb enough to wear one today. In fact, every sports team wore their T-shirts, sweatshirts, or jackets. The students not in sports or clubs wore generic shirts with Kayville High colors. The Kayvees, our cheer squad, pranced around in their miniskirts and got people psyched. The excitement was contagious.

Fake Cora saw me and waved. I pasted a smile on my lips. She ran to give me a hug, playing the part so perfectly if I didn't know the truth, I would never have guessed she was a Norn. I wanted to choke her, gouge her eyes out.

"Is it true about Torin?" she asked.

I made a face, feigning sadness. "Yeah."

"Have you talked to him? Is he going to make it to the game?" she asked. The other students moved closer to hear my response.

"He is," I fibbed. *So he can help me trap your sorry ass,* I added. If I knew trap runes, I would do it myself. I'd never loathed anyone as much as I did this Norn. She even topped Marj on my hate list.

"Let me know as soon as you hear from him, so I can tweet about it." She pulled out her cell phone and starting typing.

If I listened to her for one more second, I was going to scream. I grabbed my books and started for the stairs, then remembered I had to keep an eye on her. "See you at lunch, Cora."

"Sure. If you don't, save me a seat in the gym. I plan to check out which jocks will be in the kissing booths." The other girls giggled.

I hope she caught mono from kissing someone. Upstairs, Eirik was taking pictures of some cheerleaders. He wore his swim team jacket even though he'd quit the team a week ago. Part of me wanted to warn him about Miss Fake. He'd be devastated to learn that Cora had been in a mental hospital and he never visited her.

Classes were ten minutes shorter than usual to create time for the pep rally, so the morning went by quickly. My thoughts kept drifting to Cora and clues I'd missed about her impersonator. Lunchtime came and went. I sat with her and her swim buddies, faked interest in the upcoming game, made more excuses for Torin's absence, and tried not to throw food on her face every time she said something the real Cora would have said. I was so happy to leave the cafeteria.

The last fifty minutes of school, students poured out of classes, some running and others yelling as they headed to the gym. The gym was decorated in gold, crimson, and black. Tables were set for those who wanted their faces, stomachs, or chests painted. Fake Cora and her friends giggled as they joined me.

"We saw the guys in the kissing booths, Raine," Cora said, hugging my arm.

Yeah, bite me. "That's great! How much per kiss?"

"Fifty cents. It's for a good cause, Kayville Humane Society. Are you going to do it?"

I wanted to punch her Cora-like nose and yank out her Cora-like hair. Would she reveal her true self?

"Raine?" she asked when I didn't respond.

"No way." I shuddered at the thought. I had no interest in kissing any guy except Torin. "You?"

"I have my eye on Drew." She glanced to our left where Eirik sat and grinned.

"The cheerleaders plan to have four booths, too," Kicker said from Cora's other side. "Some turd was talking about getting tongue-action from Olivia Dunn."

Olivia Dunn was the same cheerleader who'd asked me to read her future. She was both admired and feared by most guys. "She'll probably bite off his tongue," Fake Cora said.

"Or Jake will beat the poor guy into a pulp," Kicker added. Jake was on the wrestling team. I tuned them out as someone announced that the rally was about to start.

The Kayvees performed several of their dances. Then the five football players and the school mascot followed with a stomp routine that had the crowd laughing and caterwauling. I cheered and clapped along with everyone, but inside my tension mounted. Speeches followed. The flash mob dance was supposed to take place last during the kissing booths fundraiser.

I texted Andris. "Get Eirik out of here after the speeches."

"I've tried already," he texted back.

I wish Torin were here. He'd just knock out Eirik. What was I going to do? The speeches were almost over when inspiration hit me. If Eirik stayed, Cora impersonator had to leave.

I thought about my father, how my life would be without him. Tears filled my eyes. Treasured memories of things we'd done together zipped through my head, each like a stab through my heart. A sob escaped me, my pain no longer a means to manipulate the Norn seated beside me. It was real and gut-wrenching. My father was dying.

I covered my mouth to block the sobs and got up. "Excuse me."

"What's wrong?" Cora asked, standing too.

"I can't... I have to go." I started down the bleachers. People stared and moved out of my way. I reached the floor of the gym just as the coach started winding down his speech. The students were getting restless, and the four football players wearing Crimson kissing booths by the entrance paced nervously.

"Hey," Drew said when he saw me.

I shook my head and kept going.

"Raine, wait up," Cora called out.

"What's wrong with her?" I heard Drew ask.

"I don't know," she answered. "Probably Torin."

"Remember, you owe me a kiss," Drew reminded her, but I didn't hear her response. I was hurrying across the parking lot separating the sports complex from the school building when she grabbed my arm and forced me to stop.

"What is it? You're beginning to scare me."

"My father has a brain tumor and... and... he doesn't have long to live."

She put her arms around me and instinctively, I stiffened. If she noticed she didn't show it. "When did you find out? How come you didn't tell me?"

"I found out two days ago." How could she look and act like the real Cora, yet be so evil?

"Do you want me to drive you home?" she asked.

Yeah, like I'd ever let her in my house again. I wiggled out of her embrace, and her arms fell to her side. "No. You don't need to do that."

Her eyes narrowed. "You know, don't you?"

"Know what?"

"The truth. Who I really am." She laughed. "You have no idea how often I wanted to do this." Her eyes changed and became blue. Her hair lightened as her features shifted as though a sculpture was remolding her skin and bone structure. In seconds, I was staring at Maliina. "Being a Norn has its perks. I can take any form I want, do whatever I want, and wreak havoc and get away with it. Fun, right? This is just the beginning."

"You bitch!" I fisted my hand and raised it, but she grabbed my wrist.

"Watch it. Eirik will not approve of you hurting his precious Cora." Her features changed until she looked like Cora again, complete with gray eyes.

Now I understood why I'd taken one look at Ingrid and a memory had flashed in my head. Cora's eyes were gray. Last night, they'd appeared blue. Maliina and Ingrid had the same color of eyes. "I don't care what Eirik—"

"You should. Here he comes."

I turned to see him, Andris, and Roger walking toward us.

"What's going on?" Eirik asked.

"Her Dad has a brain tumor," Fake Cora said, ignoring the others and focusing on Eirik. "Did you know?"

"Yes." Eirik studied me. "Do you want to go home? I can drive you. The pep rally is over anyway, except for the stupid kissing booths. With that lot back there, any girl dumb enough to kiss them will probably end up with mono."

Andris laughed. He wouldn't be laughing once he knew about Maliina. "I don't want to go home. The game starts soon, and we'll get crappy seats if we leave. Andris, could I talk to you?"

"Oh come on. Not now. I'm so sorry about your dad, Raine." Fake Cora put her arms around me and hissed in my ear, "If you tell him who I am and screw up my plans, I'll make your life a nightmare. Don't worry about seats, guys," she added louder. "Drew made sure we got the front bleachers."

We walked as a group toward the field. A few times I tried to catch Andris' eye, but Maliina made sure I didn't get close to him.

26. NORNS' AGENDA

The crusaders were killing us, but I had zero interest in the game. Being humiliated on our field wasn't something new, but as usual, it didn't dampen the cheerleaders' enthusiasm, the band's tempo, or the students' spirits. If I didn't want to kill a certain Norn, I would have soaked it all in, from the shirtless guys baring their painted pasty chests and bellies to the screamers in the back bleachers.

To my far left, Eirik, Andris, and Roger sat on the other side of Kicker and Maliina's new friends while I was stuck by her side. I'd tried to move away from her, so I could sit by Eirik and Andris, but she'd yanked my arm, almost pulling it from its socket.

I waited until the noise level went down before asking, "Which Norn pretended to be Cora's mother when I went to her house last week?"

She grinned. "That was all me. Brilliant, wasn't I? You texted me that you were coming, so I rushed to the farm and made sure her parents were out of the way. I met you outside as her mother, used a portal, and made it to her room before you got there."

"So you're an evil Norn working with good Norns now?" I asked.

"Norns are Norns, Raine. Yours, theirs, good or bad are just semantics. We all have one purpose."

"Screw people's lives?"

She chuckled with glee. "No, keep the balance. Make sure the circle of life continues. We all can't live forever. The Norns you've dealt with guide Mortals, so you can live your charmed lives while we, their badass counterparts, do what we can to make your lives more, uh, interesting. Life without misfortune and pain is boring." She blew Drew a kiss then glanced toward Eirik to see if he was watching. He wasn't. "Is Andris really dating that boy?"

Scared of what she might do, I ignored her question. "What are you planning, Maliina?"

She laughed. "This is my first job as a Norn, and I'm going to make sure no one ever forgets."

I clenched my fist. "Is Eirik part of your first job? Is he going to die? Is that why you took my dagger?"

"You just left it there in your drawer. Such a powerful weapon." She cupped her mouth and yelled, "Go, Drew! Woo hoo!" Then she continued as though she never stopped, her eyes following the players. "I saw the dagger in your drawer two nights ago while you went to pay for pizza. I knew I had to take it before you did something stupid with it."

"I wasn't going to use it on Eirik," I retorted. "It was meant for you."

She smirked. "Then I'm happy I took it. It is one of the few weapons known to kill Valkyries, Norns, and gods. Very fascinating weapon." She jumped up and cheered with everyone again then sat. "As for Eirik," she added, "don't worry about him. No one is touching him tonight or any other night. He gets a free pass."

I didn't believe her. "What do you want with him then? Why are you always trying to make him jealous?"

She chuckled. "The Hub and Cliff House were nothing but test runs to see if my runes were working. You see, Eirik is the perfect pawn in the game between you and the Norns. Or should I say between you and anyone who wants *you* on their side?"

"Why would anyone want me?"

She studied me. "You can't be this naïve. You must know why Norns are after you."

"Yeah, I can stop them from doing their job," I said.

She laughed. "This is bigger than saving a few Mortals. You can see them, feel them, and probably hear them if you bothered to listen, and it's driving them crazy. Stupid crones."

"You don't seem bothered by it," I retorted.

"That's because I have a plan." She smirked again. "I don't plan to be one of them for long. I'm under the protection of someone much more powerful. That's why you couldn't see through my disguise or feel me. I don't plan to stick around so you can decide my fate either."

I shook my head. "What are you talking about? How am I going to decide your fate?"

"Not just mine, the Norns, the gods, the nine realms. You get to give the first signal that starts it all."

I stared at her, totally confused. "Start what?"

"You don't know anything, do you? Why do you think the Norns are so scared of you? You are a seeress, Raine. A powerful and unusual seeress. They even have a special name for you. You will be able to see the exact moment the battle of the gods begins. Whoever controls you will have an advantage over the others. Will it be the gods, the giants,

Hel's army of murderous misfits, or the Norns? The Norns don't plan to leave things to fate. No, they intend to survive, continue running things when the new world begins, and you are going to help them."

A powerful seeress? I shook my head. "I don't believe anything you say."

"Why would I make such an elaborate story?"

"Because you are an evil liar."

She laughed. "Oh, little, confused Mortal girl. Believe or don't believe. I don't care. The Norns own you. Without their protection, you'll not last a…" The rest of her words were swallowed by screaming students. We almost had a touchdown. The band started a tune. My mind went in circles, panic slamming through me. A powerful seeress who could foretell the day Ragnarok started? Me? No, I refused to believe it. Maliina was trying to manipulate me.

I thought I heard the sound of a Harley, but the music was too loud to tell for sure. I angled my head and listened. I couldn't hear anything, but I knew Torin was back. I felt him. My heart pounding, I started to get up.

Maliina's grip tightened on my arm, and she yelled in my ear, "SIT."

If she thought she'd stop me from going to the man I loved, she had another thing coming. I engaged strength and speed runes. Under my clothes, my skin felt like tiny electric currents skidded across it. I waited until tendrils appeared on the backs of my hands. Maliina didn't realize my intention until I gripped her arm and snapped it just above her wrist.

She smothered a cry. "How did you…?" She saw the runes on my hand. "You're not supposed to have those."

"You're not the only one with secrets, Maliina. And FYI, no one owns me." I jumped up and ran toward the stadium's parking. Behind me, a chant rose.

"Torin! Torin! Torin!"

The band started playing the "Hey Song".

I saw Torin as soon as I passed the bleachers. He was already in full football gear. Tears of relief rushed to my eyes. I ran, laughing and crying at the same time, and threw myself at him. He caught me, lifted me, and turned around, our lips meeting. Sensations coursed through me.

Someone yelled his name. Our lips reluctantly parted ways, and we turned. Several players waved him over.

"Go. I'm happy you're back, but they need you out there."

"I couldn't miss this for anything," he said, grinning, wiping my tears.

"You've already missed over half of it."

"I'm not talking about the game. Us. Our beginning. Be there when I walk off the field, Freckles." He stole another kiss then took off.

Still laughing, I stared after him. Our beginning. I loved that and refused to let Maliina's revelations bother me. I heard a chuckle and whipped around, expecting Maliina. It was Lavania.

"Thank you for bringing him back," I said.

"The game was important to you, and he was determined not to disappoint you. Have you learned anything new while we were gone?"

I wondered where to start. "First, I, uh, I want to apologize for not telling you someone was writing runes on Eirik. We just didn't know who to trust."

Her eyes narrowed in confusion. "What are you talking about?"

Torin hadn't told her? I quickly explained what I'd failed to tell them at Eirik's house and why, then what we'd learned about Cora and Maliina. "You were right not to trust her, and I'm sorry for thinking you hated her because she's human."

Lavania took my arm. "No need to apologize. Mistakes are part of learning, and trust must be earned. I hope you can now trust me with anything."

"I do."

"Good. I'm also going to trust you with information you can never share with anyone." She searched my face. "Eirik will be going home. No, don't shake your head. He'll be back whenever he can, but Asgard will be his home from now on."

I was going to lose Dad and Eirik. It was unfair. I fought tears. "How long do I have?"

"A couple of hours." She nudged me toward the bleachers, where the crowd was screaming. "You see, it's only a matter of time before his mother finds him."

"Who is she?"

She grimaced. "That is another piece of information you can never share with anyone. Torin already knows because he was there when I was given the news." She paused then whispered, "Eirik is Loki's grandson. Hel's son."

Vertigo hit me hard. I stopped walking, bent over at the waist, and lowered my head. This explained everything—his evil side, the scar on his back. Goddess Hel had a face that was half mummified. Her siblings, the other sons and daughters of Loki, preferred their animal forms. Poor Eirik. What a terrible lineage.

Lavania patted my back. "Come on. Pull yourself together. Eirik needs you to be strong."

I wiped my cheeks as I straightened. Lavania studied my face and shook her head. "This will not do." She pulled an artavus from under her dress and sketched something on my cheek then smiled. "There. Much better. Now chin up."

"There's something I need to tell you, too," I said, then just dived in, telling her everything Maliina had told me. Her eyes kept widening as I spoke. When I finished, her grip was like a vice around my hands.

"Oh, you poor child. I should have known this had something to do with Ragnarok. It is the one event the gods fear the most. No wonder Freya sent me to help you." She gripped tightened. "Look at me."

I stared at her helplessly.

"You are not to worry about a thing. The Norns will not win. You have the gods on your side. Remember that."

I nodded, feeling relieved. A little.

"Good. Let's go and deal with this insufferable little Norn."

Maliina was gone when we arrived back at the field.

"Where's Cora?" I asked Kicker.

"She just left." Her eyes didn't leave the players. "I don't know why she'd want to miss this. We only have five minutes to go."

"She's gone," I whispered to Lavania.

She patted my hand. "Don't worry, we'll find her."

Feeling the burden lifted off my shoulders, I pushed thoughts of Maliina aside and focused on cheering for Torin. The crowd rose on its feet and grew eerily quiet, their eyes on the players. The scoreboards showed that we were tied with the Crusaders, and they had the ball. I didn't understand football. All I knew was the scrimmage was closer to their goal. The Crusaders could win. Beat us on our own field. That would be beyond humiliating.

From the scrimmage, Torin stole the ball and took off, running and dodging the Crusader's players, our defense paving the way for him. The whole stadium erupted. My parents were watching the game at home because they'd chosen not to come, but I wished they had. Torin was amazing, and the last play was the most memorable in football history. Well, my pitiful and short football watching history.

When Torin scored the last touchdown, the crowd went wild and there was mass exodus from the bleachers as everyone ran onto the field. I cheated with runes and met Torin before the other players.

"You were awesome," I yelled.

He scooped me into his arms, sweat and all. We were still kissing when his teammates lifted us up and ripped us apart. I reached for Torin's hand as he reached for mine, but the two groups moved apart. I forgot about my problems and Maliina, Dad's condition, and Eirik leaving and laughed, enjoying the moment. I'd tell him about Maliina later.

Then I felt a familiar clawing feeling saturating the air. It was stronger than before. More menacing. The grandson of Loki was coming out to play.

I searched for Eirik just as fights broke out everywhere. Players from our team leaped at the Crusaders, supporters pummeled each other. Even cheerleaders were going at it.

"Torin!" He was already on the ground, running toward me. "Put me down," I yelled to the students carrying me, but they didn't listen.

Torin snatched me from their arms. "Find Cora. Whatever she's doing is causing this. I'll get Eirik out of here."

"It's not Cora. It's Maliina. The real Cora has been under psychiatric care since the meet. I'll explain later." Then I saw Maliina. She was all over Drew, her legs around his waist, hands in his hair, lips locked. Eirik watched them from the bleachers, eyes glazed. Andris and Ingrid were trying to talk to him with little effect. "There he is."

"I see him. I'll get him out of here."

"I'll find Maliina!"

"Engage your runes," Torin ordered as he took off, using the crowd to hide as he became invisible.

Imitating him, I dived into the crowd and engaged my runes at the same time. They flashed in my head in quick succession. Strength. Speed. Protection. Defense. The crowd made it hard to reach Maliina, but when I finally did, I yanked her from Drew's arms. He wore a bewildered expression as she fell backward. I landed on top of her and brought both fists down on her chest. The ground shook around us.

She screamed obscenities and aimed a punch at my chin, almost knocking my teeth out. The force sent me flying backwards into Drew, knocking him and several students down. By the time I stood, Maliina was speeding away.

Someone grabbed my arm and pulled me away from the crowd. I stared into Lavania's eyes, runes all over her face. "Disengage your runes and re-engage them in this order: transformation and regeneration, protection, strength, defense, speed."

In seconds, I was covered with runes. Holy crap! Talk about being zapped by a sudden surge of energy.

"Follow me," she ordered.

I did, scared that everything would be blurry and I'd run into people, but the way my eyes processed images had changed. It was as though time had slowed down and everyone was moving at a slower pace while I moved at normal speed. I could see clearly and dodge people and obstacles. No wonder Torin rode his bike like Hel was chasing him and never hit anything.

***

We stopped in a restroom inside the sports complex. It was the same restroom Ingrid had used the first time I'd seen her use a portal. The mirror dissolved and opened into Eirik's living room. Sounds came from somewhere in the house.

"They are here," Lavania said.

I followed her inside the room. A thud hit the wall and rattled the pictures. Eirik's parents peered at us from behind a door. Lavania indicated for them to stay put as more thuds shook the house.

We followed the source to the foyer, which was like a war zone. The walls and marble floor had cracks and dents like they had been created by a demolition ball. Broken glass and picture frames littered the floor. One wall had several holes, and I could see right through them to the pool deck.

I ducked as a bust of Alexander the Great flew past my head. Eirik and Torin were still fighting, but they weren't the only ones in the room. Marj, Jeannette, and Catie stood on the grand staircase. Watching, doing nothing like always. They never dirtied their hands, the cowards. Maliina stood at the other end of the foyer by the hall mirror. In her hand was the dagger the Norns had given me. From her filthy clothes, she must have been fighting Torin, too.

"Let's go, Eirik," Maliina begged. "He's not worth it."

"He's not going anywhere," I yelled.

Eirik stopped from ripping a slab of plaster off the wall, which I presumed he meant to use as a weapon, and angled his head toward me. His eyes were still glazed, but he responded to my voice. "Raine?"

"I'm here," I said, stepping forward, careful not to trip on the debris.

"She's here with Lavania, Eirik," Maliina said in her best imitation of Cora's voice. "They are working together. Lavania doesn't want us to be together." Eirik turned toward her.

"Keep her talking, I'll get your mother," Lavania whispered from behind me and disappeared.

Why would she want to get my mother involved now?

"That's not true, Eirik," I said. "I want you to be with Cora. The *real* Cora. She was sick, but she's home now. That is not Cora. She's Maliina." I frantically waved Torin over.

"Don't listen to her," Maliina said. "Remember when we kissed after we left Cliff House. You said you were crazy about me, but we couldn't be together. We can be together now. We'll live with your mother. You want to meet your mother, don't you? She wants to meet you too, Eirik."

"My mother?" Eirik asked.

So that was Maliina's plan. Take Eirik to his mother. Hel must be the protector she'd bragged about earlier. I glanced at the Norns. The shock on their faces was comical. They'd been played, too. Bested by one sick trainee they thought was a pawn. Serves them right.

"This is not working," Torin said, having reached my side while I'd been distracted. "Take her out while I take care of him."

"Don't." I focused on Eirik. "Don't listen to her, Eirik. Your mother deserted you. She never visited you for seventeen years. You belong with me and Cora, people who love you." Torin was right. This was getting us nowhere. "We need Cora."

"Good idea. Focus on his feelings for you; it's his Achilles heel," Torin said. Then he disappeared into the living room, presumably to use the mirror portal. Eirik stood in the middle of the foyer looking thoroughly confused.

"Eirik. I'm hurt. Please. Help me." He turned toward me, his eyes glowing. "OUCH. It hurts."

"No, don't listen to her," Maliina screeched, moving away from her position near the mirror. I didn't like the way she gripped the dagger. Would she hurt Eirik despite the fact that she was working for his mother? As Eirik moved toward me, she followed him and raised the dagger.

I dashed across the hall, runes coiling on my skin. I hit her at full speed, but she recovered fast and sent me flying with a kick. My back connected with the wall, pain shooting through my body. I landed on the floor on all fours and barreled into her. She used my weight and momentum against me and whipped me around. I grabbed her arm and didn't let go.

We rolled on the floor until she pinned me. She raised the dagger and brought it down. I gripped her wrist, barely stopping the blade from sinking into my chest. If the dagger could kill gods and Norns, it sure as Hel could cut my life short. Sweat poured down her face, and her eyes narrowed like a demented person. I shook my head to stop the sweat dripping into my eyes.

"You can't defeat me. I have Norn runes," Maliina bragged, panting.

She was stronger, but I was pissed. I planted my legs on the ground and tried to buck her off me. "You were going to kill him, you bitch."

"Just following instructions. Take Eirik home to his mother or finish him—"

Someone plucked her off me and sent her flying. She hit the wall and crumbled on the floor. My eyes connected with Torin's. Once again, he'd saved me from Maliina. He offered me his hand and pulled me into his arms.

"Raine, are you okay?" Eirik asked, drawing my attention. His eyes were clear, and he was carrying Cora, whose her head lolled to the side. Torin must have brought her back while I was fighting with Maliina.

"She's asleep, but I runed her just in case she wakes up," Torin explained.

"Can someone explain to me what's going on?" my father bellowed. He stood by the hall mirror with Mom and Lavania. For a dying man, he had some serious lungs.

"Yes, why are there two of Cora," Eirik added.

Torin went to where Maliina lay like a rag doll, her arms and legs at weird angles. He picked up the dagger and shoved it under his waistband, then leaned over Maliina and sketched runes on her arm with his artavus. Her features changed until she was herself again. Shock crossed Eirik's face.

"Raine, do you want to explain?" Lavania asked.

"Actually, I think they," I waved toward the stairs, where Marj, Catie, and Jeannette stood, "should explain." The bewildered expression on the Valkyries and my father's faces confirmed my suspicions. The Norns were invisible. "Everyone needs to see you."

The three Norns didn't look happy, but they became visible.

"We don't explain ourselves to anyone," Marj said.

"Then I'll explain to you while you failed." I summarized what Maliina had told me and finished with, "Maliina decided she'd rather deliver Eirik to Hel than to you."

The Norns didn't respond, their expressions unreadable. Eirik looked confused while Torin and Eirik's parents, who'd walked into the foyer, stared at me as though seeing me for the first time. The way Mom grinned told me Lavania must have explained about me being a seeress. Why she'd chosen to do so while we were battling Maliina was beyond me.

The silence that followed was spooky. Mom was the first to break it.

"My little girl, a seeress," she said with pride, moving to my side and gripping my hand, her eyes watery as though she was fighting tears. "Not just an ordinary seeress." Then she turned and faced the Norns. "You knew. You three…" She shook her head. "I don't know where to begin. You saw the future and decided to change it. No wonder you marked her when she was born, tried to manipulate her into joining you, and rescued Eirik from Hel. I will personally inform Goddess Freya of what you'd planned and what you put my child through."

"You're not allowed in Valhalla," Jeannette said with a sneer.

"One foot there and you'll be sent straight to Hel's Hall," Marj added.

"She won't, not after the gods learn that her daughter is not just any seeress," Lavania cut in. "She is a *Völva*, one that sees all and hears all."

Mom grinned. "One whose destiny you bitter old hags cannot control and whose actions you cannot punish."

"It's been a while since we had one like her, not since the beginning." Lavania glanced at my mother, and they traded smiles. When Lavania faced the Norns again, she was no longer smiling. "Raine is now under the protection of the gods. You touch her and you will feel their wrath."

The fury in the Norns' eyes was memorable. I couldn't help grinning even though I was still trying to wrap my mind around the fact that I was one of the *Völur*, seers so powerful even the gods consulted them about their future. Lavania had covered them during our study of Asgardians. It was a *Völva* who had told Odin about how the worlds were created, how they would be destroyed during Ragnarok, which gods would die and which ones would survive, and how the new worlds would be repopulated. Norns might control destinies of everyone, including gods, but they didn't control the destiny of *Völur*, which explains why they wanted me.

"Okay, let's finish here," Lavania said, taking charge. "Eirik, take Cora home."

Eirik's arms tightened around Cora. "No."

"Yes," Lavania said firmly. "Cora will be here when you come back. She's not going anywhere." She signaled Torin. "Take Raine home then head to the stadium. Ingrid and Andris need your help."

My stomach dropped. That meant some of the students had died. How many this time?

"Torin can't leave," Marj's voice cut through the two-story foyer. "He has to face the consequences of his actions. He altered his," she pointed at my father, "future when he made a deal with a Grimnir meant to take his soul. No Valkyrie can alter the destiny of a soul without punishment."

My parents' reaction told me something new. They hadn't known what Torin had done. Mom stared at him with gratitude, and Dad... whatever reservations he might have had about Torin, I doubted they still existed.

"I can," I said, and everyone's attention shifted to me. The Norns were clearly shocked. "I'm the one who told Torin to find my father and bring him home. I, not him, altered my father's destiny. So if you want to blame someone, blame me. Not him. If you touch him, mess with his memories again, or even think of sending him away, you will have to deal with me."

Their expressions changed from shock to fury. Their bodies, clothes, and hair changed as they took their true form. Ancient faces wreathed with wrinkles, eyes starting to glow, flimsy gowns floating to the floor—I had unleashed something primal in them. Funny thing was they didn't scare me anymore.

They floated down the stairs and moved toward me. Not sure what they planned to do, I watched them move closer and closer. Torin appeared on my left and Mom on my right. Lavania joined her. Dad, completely out of his depth, watched us from across the room. Even Eirik stopped staring at Cora's face and wached. His parents kept their distance.

"You might be able to see everyone's future, but you cannot see your own, Lorraine," Marj said, her voice echoing eerily in my head. "That will be your demise."

"Most *völur* are Norns. They might not be as powerful as you, but they would have guided you if you'd joined us," Jeannette added.

"Be careful, Raine," Catie added. "You might be under the protection of the gods, but not all the gods are good, as you've learned tonight. So if you ever need our help, or the help of the other *völur*, summon us." The others glared at her, but she didn't back off. "We will make sure you get it."

I nodded and watched them continue toward Maliina's unconscious body, frigid air following them like the tail of a comet. They picked her up and disappeared.

I burrowed against Torin's chest. He smelled of sweat, blood, and dirt, but I didn't care. I was never letting him go. He was my safety net. This world of theirs had just thrown me a curveball, and I wasn't sure what to think anymore. Was I even meant to be a Valkyrie?

"What did they say?" Mom asked.

I glanced at her. "You didn't hear them?"

"No," she said.

Torin shook his head, too. "You nodded, so they must have said something."

Lavania, Eirik, and his parents stared at me expectantly, all waiting to hear my answer. Not wanting to rehash what the three Norns had said, I focused on Catie's offer. "They said if I ever need their help to summon them."

Mom laughed. "They never give up, do they? You will never go to them for help."

"Not while we are around," Lavania added. Even Torin nodded.

I couldn't foresee my future, so they were all I had protecting me against the Norns. And the gods, of course.

"Take Cora home, Eirik," Lavania said. "When you come back, I'll explain to you and your parents a few things. Torin, you know what to do."

I glanced at Mom, who had left my side and was talking softly to Dad, their arms around each other. They didn't need me. I was happy they knew what Torin had done for us. He looked like he'd been hit by a ton of bricks. No, a giant skyscraper of reinforced steel, since I was sure a ton of bricks would lose if it landed on him.

"Come on," I whispered and pulled his arm.

For the first time, I used my artavus to create a portal to my bedroom. Once the portal closed, Torin cupped my face and stared at me with awe, a smile tugging the corners of his lips. The look didn't suit him. I liked him cocky and bold.

"Don't look at me like that," I warned.

"The way you stood up to the Norns..." He grinned.

"Yeah, well, I think everyone is allowed to piss them off at least once in their lifetime."

"You've done it twice."

I shuddered. "And hopefully for the last time."

"They wouldn't mess with you now. You are a *Völva*."

"And you are a Valkyrie, so we're perfectly matched."

"Not even close. You advise gods. I advise souls. You are scary powerful while I—"

"Need to shut up and kiss me."

Laughing, he kissed me, taking his time, showing me that our powers didn't really define us. Our love transcended such things. The intensity of his kiss, the reverence in his touch, and the beating rhythm of his heartbeat proved it.

When he eased off, his eyes were gentle. "I love you, Freckles."

Finally! "With all my heart," I repeated the words he'd spoken to me a few days ago.

We kissed, and then he stepped back. "I've got to go. Wait for me."

"Always." He was going to reap souls then escort them to Valhalla. It might take hours or several days, but I knew he would be back. For me. For us. "I'm not going anywhere."

EPILOGUE

Eirik arrived just as I walked into my bedroom from downstairs several hours later. He was leaving. My throat thickened with sadness, and I had to clear it before speaking. "For someone who's going home to see his family, you look glum."

He flashed a sad smile. "I hate leaving when nothing is settled."

"You mean you and Cora?"

He nodded. "I wish we'd known she was in that hospital. She probably thinks we don't care about her."

"I know, but she'll understand once you explain."

Determination flashed in his eyes. "I plan to tell her everything when I come back. Try to reconnect with her while I'm gone."

"You don't need to ask." My eyes smarted. "Do me a favor, too, and keep an eye on Dad when he comes to Valhalla."

"You don't need to ask either." He smiled, a naughty gleam flashing in his eyes. "Look at us, talking about going to Valhalla like it's a trip to Portland. You are a powerful seeress, and I am the son of an evil goddess." His voice changed, becoming haunted. "Hel's spawn just took on a new meaning."

I crossed the gap between us, and we hugged. "You are Eirik, and I'm Raine. Best friends forever. That's all I care about."

"Me too," he whispered then stepped back. He wiped his hands on his pants, showing his nervousness. "We are leaving in a few minutes."

"They're going to love you up there and never want to let..." My voice shook to a stop.

"Don't. I swear if you cry I'll... I'll only come back to see Cora." His eyes grew bright.

"Try it and you'll feel my wrath. Don't forget I'm a *völva*."

"Yeah, you see the future. Big whoop. I can turn this town into a kill zone." Laughing, we hugged. "Don't lose my pullout bed. I'll need it when I come back."

"Promise."

I'm not going to cry... I'm not going to cry...

He disappeared through the portal, and the tears started. I was at the window seat imagining my life without him and Dad when Torin walked into my room. I still had him. He lifted me up off the window seat, took my place, put me on his lap, and wrapped his arms around me. We sat like that for a very long time. Occasionally, he pressed a kiss on my hair or forehead and wiped away a teardrop.

"How many died tonight?" I whispered.

"Four. One of theirs. Three of ours, one of them a cheerleader."

No wonder Ingrid had joined the squad. "Drew and Keith."

"Drew is fine. He said something knocked him and a bunch of guys down and he twisted his ankle. He hobbled off the field. Leaving saved his life. You didn't happen to have something to do with that, did you?"

"Maliina threw me against him, and since we had runes... Keith didn't make it?"

"No."

So sad and tragic. I sighed.

"I'm so sorry I couldn't tell you about your father's illness. I gave him my word."

"It's okay. Thank you for giving us time to say our goodbyes. I don't know how long he has, but I'm going to make the most of it." I shifted, so I could see his face. "What did you promise the Grimnir for not reaping him?"

"Echo? Nothing. I asked him to look the other away, and he did. He's cool like that."

I searched his face. Grimnir worked for Hel, and she might be coming after me now that Maliina had failed to deliver Eirik. "Don't lie to me about this because I cannot afford to lose you, too. Eirik is gone, and Dad doesn't have long. If you promised him anything, I need to know, Torin."

"I didn't promise him anything, and I'm not going anywhere, Freckles. Ever. You and I have forever to plan. But first, we have to turn you into a Valkyrie." He grinned with anticipation. "*Völur,* if you must know, sit around all day while Immortals wait on them and gods vie for their attention. I want you with me. Here. Always."

I wanted to make a snarky comment because I still found the idea of reaping souls distasteful, but I just smiled. For Torin St. James, I would learn to reap souls, because forever with him sounded perfect.

THE END

BIOGRAPHY

Ednah is the author of The Guardian Legacy series, a YA fantasy series about children of the fallen angels, who fight demons and protect mankind. AWAKENED, the prequel was released in September 2010 with rave reviews. BETRAYED, book one in the series was released by her new publisher Spencer Hill Press in June 2012 and HUNTED, the third installment, will be released April 2013. She's working on the next book in the series, FORGOTTEN.

Ednah also writes Young Adult paranormal romance. RUNES is the first book in her new series. She is presently working on book 3, GRIMNIRS.

Under the pseudonym E. B. Walters, Ednah writes contemporary romance. SLOW BURN, the first contemporary romance with suspense, was released in April 2011. It is the first book in the Fitzgerald family series. Since then she has published four more books in this series. She's presently working on book six.

You can visit her online at **www.ednahwalters.com** or **www.ebwalters.com**,. She's also on **Facebook, twitter, ya-twitter, Google-plus**, and **RomanceBlog, YAblog**.

Made in the USA
Lexington, KY
12 January 2015